Deadly cadenza

In the Control Room of the recording studio in London's Kingsway Hall, all is rapt silence. In the hall above, Konstantin Steigel is conducting the Beethoven Violin Concerto with a comparatively unknown soloist, Sandor Berman. The violinist's brash and cocky ways haven't endeared him to the musicians and recording technicians, nor to Mark Holland, his new agent, but his dazzling playing makes it clear that he is a new virtuoso. Then, as the glittering cadenza heralds the end of the movement, there comes a shattering explosion. Rushing upstairs, Mark Holland is appalled to find the young soloist lying dead, with a bullet hole between his blindly staring eyes.

So begins Paul Myers's second superb thriller set in the world of classical music and musicians. As the police start investigating the apparently motiveless crime, Mark Holland and Penny Scott, the record company's publicity girl, discover some disturbing facts about Berman, and an air of mystery surrounds the background of the young violinist.

Mark, an ex-undercover agent who now promotes and represents musicians, would like to leave the investigation to the police. But he can't. Not only do several angry strangers threaten him over the next 24 hours, claiming to be 'business partners' of Berman's, but Mark's own musical expertise turns out to be vital to the crime's solution.

As Mark's pursuers draw closer, the mounting tension and excitement culminate in a thrilling chase through the echoing stairs and corridors of the Royal Albert Hall.

By the same author

Deadly variations (1985)

Paul Myers
Deadly cadenza

Constable London

First published in Great Britain 1986
by Constable and Company Limited
10 Orange Street London WC2H 7EG
Copyright © 1986 by Paul Myers
Set in Linotron Plantin 11 pt by
Rowland Phototypesetting Limited
Bury St Edmunds, Suffolk
Printed in Great Britain by
St Edmundsbury Press
Bury St Edmunds, Suffolk

British Library CIP data
Myers, Paul
Deadly cadenza
I. Title
823'.914[F]   PR6063.Y4/

ISBN 0 09 466790 X

For Mary, Nicholas and John

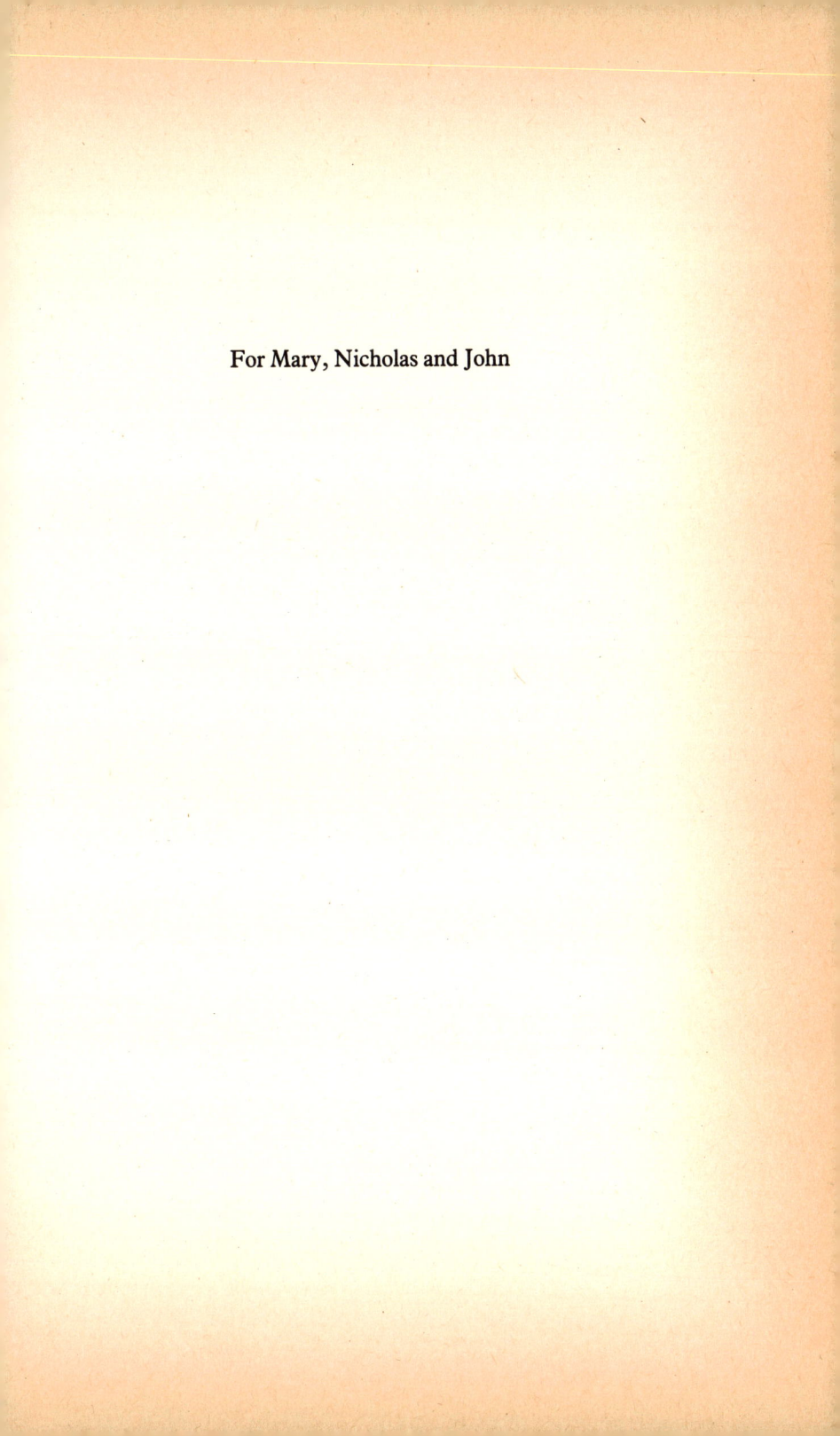

I

The record producer pushed a button marked 'Talkback' on the desk in front of him and leaned towards a small microphone.

'Why don't we try a take? Stand by, please.'

For a moment, there was silence. Then the loudspeakers at the other end of the room erupted with the random cacophony of an orchestra tuning up.

'Christ, why do they always do that?' he asked no one in particular. The elderly engineer at his side did not bother to reply. His hands were moving gently over the complicated controls of the recording console, as though making final, careful checks of each setting. He had supervised more recording sessions than the young producer had eaten hot meals. Any experienced record man knew that, at the start of a session, a call to 'Stand by' for the first take of the day would have the same response. Would he prefer them to play out of tune?

They were sitting in the Control Room of London's Kingsway Hall, a shabby, windowless, utilitarian cell built under the stage. Its spartan furnishings, most of them electronic, and Public Works Department colours did little to suggest the elegance or glamour of the classical-music world. The hall above them was a defrocked Methodist church whose polished wood floor and glass-domed ceiling created the superb acoustics that had sired thousands of memorable recordings. It was filled with musicians in shirt-sleeves and comfortable clothes, seated as though for a concert, while microphones on tall chromium tripods stalked among them like praying mantises in search of food. They had been rehearsing for the past half hour, warming up for the session while the engineers moved microphones, adjusted console settings and balanced their sound.

The producer glanced at his watch uneasily and drummed his fingers on the desk. Three-hour recording sessions were becoming increasingly expensive in London. The engineer sat back, folding his arms, satisfied that each dial was responding accurately. He surveyed the settings on his grey metal console, which dominated the room, its banks of knobs, dials and meters looking as though they could be adapted to pilot Concorde across the Atlantic. Set slightly apart, along the right-hand wall, a further battery of metal cabinets winked green and red lights to indicate the activities of the digital tape machines under the watchful eye of a second engineer.

The noise slowly subsided. The producer continued to wait, his finger poised over the Talkback button. At length, the voice of Konstantin Steigel, the conductor, emerged from the loudspeakers. He sounded slightly irritated.

'Very well, commence please. We are waiting for you!' The control engineer gave the ghost of a smile, the tape engineer pushed several remote-control buttons to start the tape machines and said: 'Rolling.'

The producer sighed and pressed the button. 'Thank you, maestro. This is the Beethoven . . .'

A new voice interrupted. 'Hey, just a minute! You didn't ask me if I was ready. Don't I get to play, too?' It was the soloist, Sandor Berman. Several of the orchestra musicians chuckled audibly. In addition to being a talented young man, Berman fancied himself as a wit.

The producer looked to the engineer for support, but the man stared at the loudspeakers, waiting for the music to begin.

'I'm sorry, Mr Berman. Are you ready, too?' He was beginning to sound edgy.

'Sure. Nice of you to ask!' There was a further chuckle.

The producer kept his voice calm. The young violinist could be suffering from a few nerves of his own. 'Very good. Here we go, then. This is the Beethoven Violin Concerto, First Movement, Take One.' He removed his finger from the button and added: 'Cheeky bugger!' then flicked a switch, and a small red light bulb lit up on the wall above one of the loudspeakers. Complete silence descended upon the room and, almost in a whisper, the timpanist played the opening notes of the concerto.

Seated in a row of chairs placed against the rear wall of the room, behind the producer and engineers, Mark Holland stretched his long legs comfortably and settled back to enjoy the performance. Visitors were not particularly welcome when Magnum Records was in the studio, and the recording team studiously ignored him. Since he was the manager of both the conductor and the soloist, they suffered his presence, especially as he had flown in from his office in Geneva for the young Israeli violinist's recording debut.

Mark did not really enjoy recording sessions. After the first take of the day, the arduous repetitions of the music seemed to diminish its mystical qualities to a craggy search for right notes and clean ensemble playing, but he was eager to hear how the violinist would acquit himself. He had recently agreed to manage the young man, and had only had the opportunity to hear him at two concerts with the Orchestre de la Suisse Romande in Geneva. He had been very impressive, but the demands of a recording session, with its time-watching tensions and technical perfections, created special conditions under which to make music. Mark had worked for some years with Konstantin Steigel, inured to the old maestro's predictable fits of temperament. He was accustomed to the goldfish bowl environment of a recording studio. If nothing else, Konstantin would steer Berman through a thoughtful and well-balanced reading.

From the corner of his eye, he noticed that Penny Scott, the attractive young public relations girl from the record company, had leaned forward, anticipating Berman's first entrance after the long orchestral introduction. Her ash-blonde hair fell across her face, partially obscuring it, and her hands were clasped together over her knees. When they had met at the start of the session, she had claimed to know little about classical music, having newly arrived at Magnum Records from the television world. Apparently, she knew enough about the Beethoven Concerto to recognize Berman's first solo. Beyond Penny was Heidi Steigel, the conductor's cheerful little Austrian wife. She always travelled with him, attending to his every need with the expertise of a well-trained servant. A compact, round-faced woman, whose lively red cheeks contrasted strongly with her vanilla-white hair, her hands were in a constant state of animation. At this moment, she was busily knitting an unidentifiable woollen garment destined for one of her many grandchildren. Mark smiled to himself. She managed to do it without allowing the knitting needles to click. After forty-six years of marriage to a conductor, she was a veteran.

Berman began to play, entering with a hushed, *sotto voce* tone that Mark had not expected. The sound of the violin grew in volume and, as it did so, created a sort of momentum, carrying everything forward. It was breathtaking. For all his off-stage brashness and braggadocio, and a seemingly endless patter of bad puns and old musical jokes, Sandor Berman was a superb violinist, with an unexpected strength and maturity that was not going to be diminished by the claustrophobia of the studio. The instrument sang, rising above the orchestra on wings of sound, and Steigel, clearly caught up with the inspiration of the moment, added delicate nuances of expression. They might have performed the concerto together for many years, displaying a kind of extra-sensory perception of each other's ideas. Mark found himself leaning forward, as though imitating Penny, captivated by the music. At one moment, Penny turned towards him, her eyes shining, and smiled radiantly.

The producer followed the music on his score, marking the pages with unintelligible hieroglyphics. He scarcely spoke to the engineer except to give an occasional commentary: 'Woodwinds coming up – now', 'Cellos a little too much', 'Can you help the solo there?' The engineer remained silent, nodding his head slightly, his hands moving across the control panel to make delicate adjustments that Mark could not detect. At one quiet moment, a chair in the hall creaked audibly, and the engineer muttered: 'Noise!' The producer nodded irritably and made a mark on the page of the score. High fidelity had reached such a point that the unwanted sound would have to be covered by another take.

The orchestra slowed for the climactic solo display at the end of the movement and, as the final *tutti* chord died, Berman launched into the Kreisler cadenza, his violin soaring. The noble opening theme was repeated amid filigree decorations, and Berman played with dazzling, youthful exuberance, balancing Olympian strength with sudden moments of serene calm.

Halfway through the cadenza, the producer said: 'He might as well do this at the end of the session, after we've let the orchestra go.' He reached towards the Talkback button to interrupt the performance, but the engineer put out a restraining hand.

'Not if he's going to play like this. You may not catch another performance like it.'

The producer nodded and sat, head bowed, as Berman danced through feather-light arpeggios and seemingly impossible double-stops. The cadenza came to a close, and the violinist played the theme a final time with a sort of nostalgic peace, as though all the conflicts of the preceding pages had been resolved. Two final chords sounded, and it was over.

There was a long silence. Nobody dared to break the spell. When Konstantin Steigel spoke, his voice was hushed.

'Bravo, young man. Bravo!'

The orchestra began to applaud. It started with a few bows tapped across violins in the traditional manner, then voices called out and players clapped enthusiastically. Recording musicians did not usually react spontaneously in this way, but the players recognised that they had taken part in a fine performance. The cheering continued until Steigel clapped his hands for silence and called the producer.

'What would you like us to do? Do we take the break now?'

'Yes, please. We'll need about half an hour.'

'Very well.'

Penny turned to Mark. 'My God, he's marvellous! I don't think I've ever heard it played like that before.'

Mark nodded silently. The music was still in his ears, like the image of a bright light that remained in his head after he had shut his eyes.

Heidi looked up from her knitting. 'That's a very talented young man, Mark.' The blue Viennese eyes twinkled wickedly. 'Who would have suspected it?'

The peaceful isolation of the Control Room was shattered as

members of the orchestra thumped down the wooden stairs and into the room, talking cheerfully, to range themselves along the back wall for a playback of the take. One of them lit a cigarette, despite a baleful glare from the control engineer. Konstantin Steigel entered slowly, his tall frame stooped, his glasses constantly in danger of falling off the end of his bulbous nose. He was dressed in a shapeless black rollneck sweater, now stained with sweat, and a pair of equally shapeless trousers. His bald head, with a tonsure of silver hair, gleamed wetly. Mark stood up to greet him, but he waved a hand distractedly, calling to Heidi, who was hovering close by.

'My towel! Where is my towel?'

Heidi produced it immediately, and the conductor handed her his glasses and buried his face in it, like a bather emerging from a long swim. As he dried himself, Heidi opened a vacuum flask and poured a cup of steaming black coffee.

From the doorway, Sandor Berman, his eyes sparkling with triumph, said: 'Now that's what I call service.' He eyed Penny admiringly. 'What about it, honey. Are you going to service me?'

Penny's smile froze, and one or two of the orchestra players laughed uneasily. She recovered quickly with a cool nod, and said: 'I'll see if I can find you a coffee. How do you take it?'

Berman grinned again. 'Any way you'd like to give it to me.'

She was wearing a navy blue tee shirt and printed over her left breast was the inscription 'Magnum Records' together with the record company's logo. Berman inspected the lettering and concentrated his attention on the material, through which her nipples were clearly outlined. He made a show of inspecting the words.

'Nice! And what d'you call the other one?'

Penny was no longer smiling. 'I'll see about the coffee.'

'I like it hot and sweet, honey. It suits my personality.'

At that moment, the control engineer silently offered him a mug of coffee, but the violinist shook his head, nodding towards the violin he was clutching.

'Let me put my baby away first.' He glanced at Penny. 'She takes priority over everyone.'

Mark watched him as he walked across the room to the table where he had placed his violin case. He was a stocky young man, broad-shouldered as a prize-fighter, with a shock of frizzy black hair that was now matted with sweat. He had not bothered to shave, and tiny beads of perspiration gleamed on the dark stubble of his chin.

Berman's violin case was rectangular in shape, with a soft cloth covering. He opened the lid to reveal a second violin already fitted into the velvet-lined interior. It had a curiously red mahogany colour, and the wood glowed softly in the light.

The violinist winked at Mark as he placed the second violin into the moulded space in the case. 'This is my other baby: a seventeen-oh-five Strad. That one's all mine.'

'What are you playing?'

'A del Gesù. It was loaned to me by Arnold Silverman in New York. Isn't it a great instrument?'

'Magnificent.'

'It's called "The Meadowlark", dated seventeen thirty-one. As soon as I tried it, I begged Arnie to let me use it.' He grinned. 'If you get me enough recordings, I'll make him an offer for it.'

The producer laughed. 'You'll need an awful lot of those!'

'Right. That's what I'm counting on.'

'Why not play the Strad?'

'I could. It's a fine instrument, but it has a brighter tone. It's right for a big hall. For recordings in a studio, with the mikes right there, nothing beats the mellowness of a del Gesù, especially this one.'

Penny whispered to Mark. 'Is there really that much difference?'

Berman heard her. 'Sure there is, honey, just like a woman. Every great violin makes a sound of its own. It depends how you stroke it.' He turned to the first violist from the orchestra. 'Hey, Richard, if you were lost in a forest and couldn't find your way out, who would you ask for directions: a good violist, a bad violist, or a pink elephant?' He did not wait for a reply. 'You'd ask the bad violist, because the other two are a figment of the imagination!' He laughed loudly at the joke, and several onlookers smiled politely. The violist smiled with cool eyes and said: 'Very droll!' Berman waved a hand. 'I was only kidding.' He turned to Steigel and said: 'Konnie, do you think we could move it ahead when I make that first entrance? It seemed to be dragging.'

The conductor stiffened slightly. Mark remembered that, some years earlier, an ambitious young American record producer had once approached the maestro and said: 'Look, since we've been working together for the past two years, is it all right for me to call you Konstantin?', to which he had replied: 'Most of my close friends call me Mr Steigel!' 'Konnie' was even less likely to endear the young violinist, and the orchestral players watched with interest, anticipating a sizzling reply. None came. Instead, Steigel consulted the score.

'I suppose we could do that, Mr Berman,' with a very slight emphasis on 'Mr', 'In which case I suggest you do not take quite such an exaggerated pause before you play.'

'Sure. I'll make a teensy pause, but no coffee break.'

There were chairs and a table directly in front of the recording console and, coffee cups in hand, the conductor and soloist seated themselves there with the producer, close to the loudspeakers, ready for the tape playback. As though obeying an unwritten rule of protocol, everyone else in the room stayed behind them, grouped around the console and along the back wall. The console engineer hovered nearby, in case his opinion was needed on a technical point. Wearing headphones, the tape engineer was reeling back the tape to the beginning of the movement. As they settled themselves, Penny wandered over to the table where Berman had left his violins. She opened the case to peep inside, and Berman looked up quickly.

'Don't touch that!' His voice was sharp, and she jumped, letting the lid fall again. When he spoke again, Berman's voice was mocking. 'Unless, of course, you love me. Touch my violins and you touch me!'

There was an angry red glow on Penny's cheeks. 'I'm sorry. I was only going to look at them.'

'Listen, honey, those two are worth something like a million and a half dollars. The Strad's about six hundred and fifty thousand on the open market, and the del Gesù would get you no change from eight. They're not toys.'

Penny's eyes blazed. 'I didn't think they were. I wasn't going to touch them . . .'

'Well, just so you know. That's a hell of a lot of money sitting under your pretty fingers.'

One of the players nearby said: 'They must cost you a fortune in insurance.'

Berman shrugged. 'It's one of the liabilities of the job.' He winked at Mark. 'That's why we have managers to demand outrageous fees for us! Anyway, my real insurance lies with Beethoven, Brahms and Mendelssohn . . .' He paused, as though enjoying a private joke, adding: 'In that order.'

Konstantin Steigel had watched the exchange with growing impatience. 'I suggest, Mr Berman, that we concentrate on the Beethoven aspect of your insurance.' He looked at his watch. 'Otherwise, we will not have enough time to finish this movement before the end of the session.'

Berman shrugged. 'Okay, Konnie, you're the boss. Most of my friends call me Sandy, by the way.'

Steigel permitted himself a small smile. 'I am your conductor, Mr Berman, which is not quite the same thing. I am also delighted to be your colleague in this enterprise. Perhaps, when we have listened to this playback, you will decide what you would like to be.'

The record producer nodded his head to the tape engineer, and the room was immediately silent for the playback. The music began again, faithfully reproduced, and Mark found himself once more caught up in its passionate fervour. But under the watchful ears of the conductor and soloist, tiny discrepancies became apparent. Here and there, a woodwind entrance was not quite together, the intonation of the first violins was slightly sharp, a timpani entrance was late. Each time, Konstantin called for the tape to be stopped and replayed, so that they could listen again to the suspect phrase, and the producer scribbled additional notes on his score. It occurred to Mark that recordings demanded much more of the players. Tiny errors passed unnoticed in a concert, and one's musical memory was short. Under the microscopic inspection of a tape playback, the performance was subjected to a heartless critical analysis.

Even so, the quality of the playing was undeniable and, when the movement ended, Steigel sat back in his chair, nodding his approval. 'That's a very good start.' He placed a hand on Berman's shoulder. 'Now we should go out and play a performance!'

The producer looked anxious. 'Do you really want the whole movement again? I would have thought we could cover the places that need re-making and use this as the basic take.'

Berman nodded agreement. 'I'm happy, as long as we cover everything we need. I want to do that cadenza again. There's a couple of notes in there I wouldn't wish on my worst enemy.'

Steigel shook his head. 'No. We are here to make music. You won't achieve that with some patch-cobbler's job. We'll play it again. There is still plenty of time.'

The producer consulted his watch. 'Not much more than an hour and a bit.'

'Exactly. If we do another complete performance, we will still have time for any minor corrections.'

Berman added, 'DV.'

Konstantin's eyebrows raised. 'That's very erudite, young man. *Deo volente*, eh?'

Berman laughed. His Israeli accent became more pronounced. 'No. Don't Vorry!'

'Ah.' Konstantin was tiring of the violinist's humorous repertoire. He turned to the producer. 'We will make another take, and you will tell us if anything else needs to be covered, *ja*?' The producer nodded. 'We do not need to listen again, until after the orchestra has gone. I will trust you to tell us. You have marked all the bad places?'

'I hope so.'

'So do I. Heidi, I need a dry shirt!'

She smiled contentedly. 'Yes, Tino. There is one hanging in the cupboard of that little dressing room at the top of the stairs.'

'Good. How much of the pause is left?'

The producer said: 'They're ready to start now.'

'You should have warned me. We are wasting time!' Steigel got up slowly. It seemed to Mark that he tired easily these days. 'Now, I will change my shirt and think about Beethoven for a minute. It's not just right and wrong notes.' As he passed Mark, he smiled and patted his arm. 'I think it starts well.'

'It's a fine performance, maestro.'

'*Ja*, but it can always be better.'

'It's hard to imagine how.'

'We will see. I hope you will, too.'

'I'm sure I will, but that first take was outstanding. I was very moved.'

'Of course you were. It was Beethoven you were listening to the first time. This time, it will be Berman and Steigel's interpretation of Beethoven that you will hear!' At the door, he turned to Berman, who was taking the del Gesù from its case. 'Don't worry about the opening, young man. I will make it move for you.'

'DV?'

Steigel smiled fleetingly. 'No. *Piu mosso!*'

A few minutes later, calm had returned to the Control Room. The producer and engineers were seated in their appointed places, coffee cups and ashtrays had been removed, and an air of tranquillity was restored. Heidi Steigel was engrossed in her knitting, a quiet smile on her face. Only Penny Scott was missing. Mark settled himself again, awaiting the second take.

The producer made his announcement, the red light flicked on and, in the momentary silence before the timpanist began, there was a low rumbling, steadily increasing. The control engineer, without looking up, said: 'Train.'

One of the only disadvantages of Kingsway Hall was that it lay directly above the Piccadilly line of London's Underground system. In louder sections of the music, the trains passed beneath them unnoticed. In quieter passages, they were painfully evident. The producer said: 'Shit!', glanced nervously in the direction of Heidi Steigel, and pressed the Talkback button. 'I'm sorry, maestro, but I'm afraid we've got a train.'

There was a pause before the conductor replied. 'This was not good in the first take?'

'I suppose so, but I'd rather have a clean start.'

'Very good.' He addressed the orchestra. 'Gentlemen, it seems we are not only at the mercy of Beethoven and Magnum Records, but we must also submit to the irresponsible intrusions of London Transport! We will start again. Please tell me when you are ready.'

'Thank you, maestro. It's gone now. This is the First Movement, Take Three.'

They began again. It was probably better than before but, to Mark's ears, some of the original magic was missing. Perhaps Konstantin had been right. He could have been confusing his reactions to Beethoven's great concerto with the way they had played.

The door of the Control Room had been left slightly ajar and, as he stood to close it, he glanced up the short flight of stairs to see Penny standing in the corridor outside the main hall. Seeing him, she waved and beckoned. Mark nodded and, moving quietly, let himself out of the room, gently closing the door behind him.

She was standing in the doorway of the small dressing room that was available for the artists. 'I had to make a few phone calls.' She smiled. 'And I was dying for a cigarette!'

Mark lit one of his own. 'Me too, now that you've reminded me.'

She led the way into the dressing room. 'We'd better stay in here, if we're going to talk. I think I've had all the criticism I need for one day.' She stared moodily at the frosted-glass window. 'I know he's a super violinist and one of your artists, but your Mr Berman is a first-class little creep!'

'I noticed. I'm sorry about that. Some musicians seem to be the last defenders of male chauvinism.'

'Oh, it's not that. I just didn't know why he had to keep picking on me.'

'He probably didn't mean to. It's nerves, mainly. All that adrenalin in the system needs some sort of an outlet. Take away their instruments, and they're very ordinary people.'

'I know. I saw *Amadeus*.' She inhaled deeply from her cigarette. 'I wish I knew a bit more about music. Why did he have to make such a fuss about his violins? He left that other one sitting in the Control Room all the way through the first take. Anybody could have walked off with it.'

'I doubt it. The engineers and I were sitting there the entire time.'

'I suppose so. He still didn't have to make such a song and dance about it.'

'I think the extra attention was intended to tell you he thought you were attractive, if you really want to know.'

'Thanks a lot!' She softened. 'Are they really worth that much?'

'Easily. They're extremely precious and very rare.'

'I take it "Strad" meant Stradivarius. Even I have heard of that. What's a del Gesù?'

'Another great violin-maker from the beginning of the eighteenth century: Giuseppe Guarnieri, the son of Andrea Guarnieri.'

'I thought that was called a Guarnerius.'

'Same thing.'

'Then where does the "del Gesù" come in?'

'Giuseppe inscribed the letters "IHS" on the label of each instrument: *Iesu hominum Salvator*. That's how you can tell it's one of his violins.'

'I see. What makes those old violins so great?'

'Nobody really knows. Some say it's the wood; others the varnish, or even the glue that holds them together. For some reason, around the end of the seventeenth century and the first forty years of the eighteenth century, the Cremona school of violin-makers created instruments that have never been equalled or even duplicated. A lot of people have tried. You can make perfect copies of them, using the same wood, but they still won't sound the same.'

'And you can really hear the difference?'

'Absolutely. A friend of mine once stood on the stage of the Festival Hall and played three different violins: a Strad, a del Gesù and an excellent modern violin. The difference between them was amazing.'

'No wonder they're so expensive.' She smiled. 'There's

something rather touching about playing a violin that's more than two hundred and fifty years old. Think who could have heard it over all those years!' She changed course suddenly. 'Why do you live in Geneva? I mean, I assume you're English, aren't you?'

'Yes.'

'I suppose I shouldn't go by blond hair and blue eyes. After all, Leslie Howard always portrayed the "typical Englishman", and he turned out to be a Hungarian. Am I being nosy?'

'No. It's a long story. I wanted a change from London.'

'Didn't that mean asking all your artists to change over with you?'

'No, not really. I started my agency over there, after I left London. I wasn't involved with the music world before that.'

'I see. I think I'd like Geneva. One gets so sick of life here, with the bloody miners' strike and the cost of living and God knows what else.'

A shadow crossed Mark's face. 'Yes. It's very peaceful there.'

She eyed him curiously. 'You don't sound very sure of that.'

He shook his head, as though dispelling a memory. 'No, it's really very quiet and uneventful. How about you? What made you change from the glamorous world of television?'

She laughed. 'The oldest reason in the world: a better salary! That and a lot of office politics. Television's no bed of roses, and the glamour's saved for the people on camera. Anyway, as you know, Magnum Records is an American organisation. They always pay better than anyone else. I've only been there two months, and I haven't met any of the big boys from New York yet. They sound like a pretty frightening lot. On the phone, they keep talking about moving "product" and *gestalt*.' She smiled. 'I had to go and look it up in the dictionary after they hung up. It's a good thing they couldn't see me. I'm sure my body language was a disgrace!'

Mark laughed. 'I've met most of them, one time or another.'

'What are they like?'

'All right, mostly. They live in a different world. I don't get the impression they're too involved with the sorts of problems that preoccupy our friends out in the hall. They spend most of their working day thinking about a thing called the bottom line.'

Penny paused by the door, listening to the music filtering through. 'I suppose we ought to get back before our absence is noted. Every time maestro Steigel fixes me with that stare of his, I have the feeling that he's about to subject me to a music quiz.'

'Don't worry. He puts on that fierce expression because he thinks conductors are supposed to behave like petty tyrants. He's actually a very mild man.'

'He could have fooled me. I was watching you during some of the playback. You're fond of him, aren't you?'

'Yes, I am. He helped me a lot when I first started the agency. I also happen to think he's a great artist.'

'And Berman?'

'I don't really know much about him yet. I only took him on recently, and I'm still finding out about him as I go along. One thing is certain: he's an extraordinary violinist.'

Penny sighed. 'I suppose so. That first take was wonderful. I still think he behaves like a shit!'

'He's young, and probably very insecure. It's his first recording, and his stomach's probably tied up in little knots, whatever he says or does.'

Penny took his hand. 'We'd better get back.' Her grip tightened. 'And thanks for talking to me. I was feeling pretty terrible earlier. I'll lead the way.' As they descended the stairs, she giggled. 'That bloody old engineer keeps scowling at me every time he looks in my direction. I don't think he approves either!'

'They never like visitors. They're always afraid we'll start talking or making unnecessary noises in the middle of a take.'

'I know, but in his case, I don't think that he likes women in any situation!' She held his hand until they reached the bottom of the staircase. Then, with a conspiratorial grin, she placed a finger to her lips and edged the Control Room door open with exaggerated caution.

The first movement was near completion, the development section building again to the sustained chord that would precede the cadenza. Penny slid into the chair nearest the door, and

Mark remained standing, eagerly anticipating Berman's display. The young man launched into the cadenza faster than before, with a kind of controlled passion that was even more impressive. Complicated figurations of the main themes were decorated with arabesques that spun glittering musical webs. The sound grew in volume and intensity, then suddenly dropped to a whisper. A delicate series of descending trills heralded the return of the orchestra to play gentle *pizzicati* under the soloist.

The producer turned to the engineer. 'My God, that was incredible!'

There was a sudden explosion, a sharp crack of sound like the snapping of a branch of a tree. The meters on the recording console flickered wildly. Then there was a heavy thud, like a muffled bass drum.

'Jesus Christ!' The producer stood up. 'What the hell was that?'

Within seconds, there was a total confusion of sounds. Members of the orchestra were shouting, a woman screamed, there were scuffling feet and a chair was knocked over with a loud clatter. Somebody was swearing. Mark bounded up the staircase, three steps at a time, and threw open the door into the hall. He had recognised the sound.

The orchestra was crowding round the space occupied by the soloist. Above them, from his position on the podium, Konstantin Steigel was peering down anxiously. Mark gently pushed several players out of his path until he had made his way to the centre of the group. At their feet, Sandor Berman lay flat on his back, his face ashen. Between his blindly staring eyes, there was a small red circle, not more than half an inch in diameter, from which blood had oozed, running in a thin stream across his temple. Mark pushed the nearest spectators back with his outstretched arms, then knelt by the violinist's body. A rifle bullet had passed cleanly through Berman's forehead and out of the back of his head. Because he was lying flat, the extent of the damage was not visible, but there was a dark, viscous stain seeping on to the floorboards surrounding his hair. He was already dead. He had fallen backwards, probably knocked over by the force of the bullet. Cradled in his arms and held tightly against his body, protected from the fall, was the precious del Gesù violin.

2

The police Inspector, who had installed himself in the dressing room, motioned Mark to a lumpy armchair without raising his eyes from his notepad. Despite his obvious youth, he had a weatherbeaten face with coarse, pockmarked skin. He was wearing an army-style raincoat over a shiny, crumpled suit, his tie was at half-mast, and the two top buttons of his shirt were undone. Mark wondered whether television directors were true to life, or whether London policemen now modelled themselves on their video counterparts.

At length, he looked up from his notes. 'Sorry to keep you to the end, but I thought that, as the dead man's manager, you might be able to give us a few more details than the others.' He gave a rueful smile. 'That Mr Steigel' (he pronounced it 'Steegle') 'gave me a bit of an earful for making him wait around with the rest. Seems he lives by a certain fixed routine, and I was keeping him from his lunch! His wife was pretty aggressive."

'She looks after him very carefully. He's in his seventies and he's not as strong as he looks, so she's very protective.'

'I know, but I have to ask questions. Good God, the man was shot before his very eyes. He treated the whole thing like a deliberate plot to disorganise his daily routine!' He shrugged. 'Anyway, neither of them was much help, so I sent them back to the Savoy. He said that if the chauffeur service charged for the extra waiting time, he'd tell the record company to send me the bill!'

'I wouldn't worry about it. Conductors are used to giving orders. They don't like to be kept waiting.'

'I suppose not.' He put his notepad to one side and took out a battered pack of cigarettes, offering one to Mark. As he struck a match, his eyes watched cautiously. 'What do you make of it all, then?'

Mark inhaled. 'I don't really know. It doesn't make any sense at all.'

The Inspector consulted his notes. 'Let's see, you were down in the Control Room when the shot was fired, weren't you? What happened?'

'I can't tell for sure. We heard the shot over the loudspeakers, and then all hell broke loose. I ran up into the hall and found Berman lying in a heap on the floor. Somebody appears to have picked him off with a rifle from the back of the hall.'

'How do you know it was a rifle?' The question was sharp.

Mark looked up. The Inspector was watching him closely. 'From the sound of the shot, the accuracy with which he was hit, and the force of the blow. He must have shot at him from the doorway at the back of the hall, about a hundred feet away, or more. He would have to have been a pretty good marksman to do it with a hand gun.'

'You sound as though you know a bit about guns.'

'A bit.'

'How's that?'

Mark sighed. Records were computerised by police forces everywhere. His name would show up in one of them sooner or later. 'I used to work in – security.'

'What sort of security?'

His smile was forced. 'I believe they liked to call it national security.'

'I see.' He made another note. 'When would that be?'

'Quite a long time ago.' The policeman would still have been at school in those days. 'My department used to be run by a man called Willis, but he would have retired by now. The department didn't like publicity.'

The Inspector paused over his notepad. 'I think I've heard that name mentioned. Rather specialised sort of work, wasn't it?'

'Yes, very specialised. I think your lot used to call it the department of dirty tricks.'

The young man's face broke into a smile. 'DDT? Yes, I've

heard of them.' He seemed to relax slightly. 'Well, perhaps this throws a little light on the whole business, sir.' His tone was respectful.

Mark shook his head. 'Not that I know of. I left that job a long time ago. I wouldn't know what they're up to now, and I wouldn't want to.'

'All right, if you say so. At least it explains how you recognised a rifle shot. I've only had a brief look, but as far as I can tell, you're right. I'll wait for confirmation from the technical boys, but it appears that the shot came from the back of the hall, where those frosted glass doors are. But wouldn't someone have seen him – or her?'

'Not unless they were in the corridor outside.'

'What about the orchestra? There were eighty or ninety people sitting there in the main hall.'

'They were facing in the other direction, towards the stage, concentrating on the music they were recording. The only two people facing in the direction of the door were the conductor and Berman. Steigel would have had his head down, either looking at the music or listening to the soloist, and Berman was playing the cadenza to the first movement of the concerto. He probably had his eyes closed.'

The Inspector looked puzzled for a moment. 'I get the picture, but there's one thing I don't quite follow. As I understand it, the orchestra players were sitting with their backs to the door, facing the conductor, right?'

'Right.'

'Which means that the conductor would have been the only one facing the back door of the hall. I go to the odd concert now and then. I like the classics, as long as they're not too heavy. Now, if it was the way you describe it, wouldn't the soloist have been facing away from the door, like the rest of the orchestra?'

'Not for a recording. When you record a concerto, everyone is in the normal concert seating, except the soloist. He usually stands by the conductor's left shoulder, facing inwards.'

'Why's that?'

'Better contact, so he can see the conductor all the time, and watch the orchestra. He plays into his own microphone, which is very often only opened on his side, so that it picks him up cleanly. If he faced the other way, as he would at a concert, there's always the danger that the full sound of the orchestra would swamp him.'

'I see.' The Inspector smiled charmingly, displaying crooked teeth. 'So what's all this I read in record magazines about natural sound?'

'I think they mean that the end result sounds natural. Few critics go to recording sessions.'

'I suppose not. I couldn't make up my mind who was supposed to be in charge downstairs. I was talking to the older fellow, but the young man with the stop-watch kept insisting he was in charge.'

'He is, basically. He's the producer. The engineers look after the sound.'

'Then what does the producer do?'

'Takes the overall responsibility and supervises the rest, tells the engineers if it sounds right and tells the musicians if they're playing it right.'

'I wouldn't fancy his chances with that Mr Steigel! It sounds like a pretty responsible job for a young man. So the producer's the one who has to keep the critics happy?'

'I think the musicians have to do that. Anyway, producers never win with the press. If they like a recording, they always write that the engineers did a good job. If they don't like it, they usually say it was poorly produced!'

The Inspector grinned. 'Well, it's nice to know there are other jobs where you get left holding the baby. Anyway, that explains why nobody would necessarily have noticed a gunman at the back of the hall. From the way you describe it, there could have been a whole firing-squad lined up! Now, there's just a short hallway between the doors to the hall and the main entrance from the street. I don't imagine whoever did it just walked out into Kingsway, carrying a rifle in broad daylight. It's not the sort of thing you expect to see in a London street, although I'm beginning to wonder. I've got a sergeant out there now, asking a few questions up and down the road.'

'If you want my guess, he was probably carrying a music case;

something like a cello case would be the right size. Kingsway Hall's a very well-known recording site. Anyone working round here will tell you that you'll see musicians walking in and out of it all the time. Suppose a man carrying a cello case walked in? Nobody would give him a second look. He could wait by the glass doors to the hall, make sure nobody's about, open the case, take out the rifle, push open the glass door far enough to allow for the rifle barrel, fire his shot, drop the rifle back in the case and walk out into the street again. The whole thing would take less than a couple of minutes.'

The Inspector watched Mark in silence for a moment. Then he laughed. 'My God, you've got the whole thing worked out so well, you could have planned it yourself.'

'Don't worry, I didn't, but I've had enough time to think about it while you were questioning the others. It would certainly work, the way I've described it, but it's still only guesswork.'

'You've probably got it right, all the same. The real question is: why?'

'I don't know. I wish to God I did.'

The Inspector frowned. 'I was hoping you could help, or at least give us a few leads. You're the man's manager, aren't you?'

'I was, but I only took him on recently. That's one of the reasons I flew in from Switzerland. My office is in Geneva. I wanted to come to the recording session, and I was hoping to spend a little time with him while I was here, finding out a bit more about him and making some future plans.'

'Well, let's start with what we do know about him. He's an American, isn't he?'

'No, he's an Israeli. He lived and studied in America, but he was born in Tel Aviv, and he travelled on an Israeli passport.'

The Inspector made notes. 'That may get us somewhere. Could there be a political motive behind killing him?'

'I wish I knew. I doubt it. He's not well enough known to create that sort of interest. It's no help to you, but I simply don't know enough about Berman. He came to see me in Geneva last month, after a couple of concerts there. We talked for a while, and I agreed to represent him in Europe. We didn't have a lot of time to talk, because he was leaving to give some recitals and concerts in France, so I arranged to meet him this week in London. I already knew about the recording sessions, because Magnum Records had contacted me with a contract for Konstantin Steigel, but I scarcely knew Berman.' He shook his head. 'He was a wonderful violinist. It's a lousy business!'

The Inspector closed his notebook. 'Well, we'll start digging and we'll see what we come up with. I take it you'll be staying on in London for the next few days?'

'Yes. I'm at the Westbury.'

'Very well, sir. I'll be contacting you again. I'll give you a card with my number, in case anything turns up your end.' He paused for a moment. 'What made you move into this line of business, after your old job?'

Mark smiled. 'Believe it or not, I was hoping for a bit of peace and quiet! What happens next?'

'Not a lot, on the surface. We'll start going through our records, to see what we can find, and the rest has to be pieced together. We haven't got very much to start on. Of course, if it was political, we may get a phone call, claiming responsibility. It's happened before.'

'I remember. At one time, the PLO threatened a number of leading Israeli artists. One or two of them had to give concerts in Germany with plainclothes policemen standing on the stage.'

'That must have been very theatrical.'

'Perhaps, but it couldn't have helped their concentration.'

'No, I suppose not. Anyway, thanks for your help.' He paused. 'Would you like me to get in touch with your old department?'

'Not unless you want to. We didn't part on the best of terms.'

'Oh?'

Mark hesitated before speaking. 'Let's just say I wasn't getting any job satisfaction.'

The young man nodded. 'I'd better get out of here and set up shop in the office. It looks as though this one is going to be a long job.'

In the Control Room, Mark found the producer pacing back and forth angrily. Penny sat in a corner, staring into space, her face sombre.

Seeing Mark, the producer glanced at his watch with further irritation. 'Has he finished in there? I need to use the telephone. The office doesn't know what's happened yet.' He seemed to be enjoying the drama.

'He said he was leaving now.' The young man nodded and left. Mark turned to Penny. 'Were the Steigels all right?'

She nodded. 'I think he's tougher than he looks. I expected him to be shattered. I know I was. I've never seen somebody killed like that.' She shivered. Mark sat on the chair beside her, and she smiled bleakly.

'I'm sorry. I don't know why I'm reacting like this, but one minute he was so alive, playing so beautifully, and then . . .' She lapsed into silence.

'It was horrible, and pointless. What a waste.'

'I feel bad about saying unpleasant things about him.'

'There's no reason to feel guilty. He was being obnoxious.'

'I know. All the same, I saw him lying there a few minutes later, and I regretted it. That's all. I must have some sort of guilty conscience.'

'Why are you still here? I thought you would have gone home.'

She looked at him for a moment before speaking. 'I was waiting for you. I thought you might need a lift somewhere, and my car's outside.' She hesitated. 'No, that's not quite true. I hoped I could talk to you for a few minutes. I'm still a bit shaken up. I'm behaving rather childishly.'

'Don't worry about it. It's a shocking thing to witness.'

The producer entered the room. 'I couldn't get through to anyone. They're all out at lunch!' He was obviously disappointed.

'Did you call New York?'

'What? Oh, no, it isn't even nine o'clock there. Nobody will get in for at least another half-hour. I'll go over to the office.' He paused by the table where Sandor Berman's violin case lay. 'What are we going to do about his violins? I put the del Gesù back when you gave it to me. I thought it would be safer to keep them down here. Do you think we should have given them to the police?'

'No, I don't think so.'

He looked nervous. 'I wasn't quite sure what to do about them. You heard him talking about how valuable they are. They're a hell of a responsibility. Do you think you could look after them? I mean, I can take them with me, but I'd hate anything to happen to them.' He lifted the case uncertainly, using both hands.

Mark walked over to him. 'I'll take them, if you like.'

'Thanks. I'd be awfully grateful if you would.'

'Where was he staying?'

Penny spoke. 'He has a flat in George Street. Cumberland Mansions, on the corner of Seymour Place. I picked him up there this morning.'

'I thought he'd be staying at a hotel.'

'No. I think he said he'd bought the flat. He was talking about planning to live in England for the next few years.'

'Did you tell the police Inspector?'

'No, I forgot.' She looked apologetic. 'He didn't ask me, and I didn't think to tell him.'

'It doesn't matter. We can phone it in. Was he alone at the flat?'

'I'm not sure. No, wait a minute, a woman answered when I pressed the buzzer downstairs. She said he'd be down in a minute.'

'Why don't we go there now? We can leave the violins with her.'

The producer looked relieved. 'Good. If you two go there, I'll be at the office. I'll have to start trying New York in about twenty minutes. I don't have their home numbers, so I can only reach them in office hours. God knows what they're going to say!' He looked as though he feared they would hold him responsible.

At that moment, the elderly console engineer appeared in the doorway. His face was angry. 'If you lot have finished in here, I'd like to lock up. The hall's still littered with coppers taking pictures and dusting for fingerprints, but the caretaker can look after them. I want to go home.' He shook his head fiercely. 'It's horrible, this whole bloody business! He had talent, real talent. Why did they have to kill a talented young man like that? It's sickening!'

As they walked up the stairs, Penny turned to Mark. 'I think he's more upset than any of us. He really seems to care.'

Mark nodded. 'Don't let engineers fool you, just because they sit there quietly, carrying out the producer's instructions. Some of them, especially the older ones, know more about music than all the rest put together.'

There was a narrow service lane at the back of the hall, and Penny had parked her car close to the street, blocking the exit for the engineer's car, which was parked farther in, next to the rear door of the building. He glowered at her from his driving seat, waiting impatiently for her to move.

As she took out her keys, Mark said: 'Would you like me to drive?'

She shook her head. 'I know the way, and concentrating on driving will do me good.' She took a deep breath. 'I've got to get a hold of myself.' The engineer sounded the horn of his car, looking over his shoulder, and she shouted angrily: 'All right, for God's sake!'

She backed slowly into the street, manoeuvring the Mini expertly into the traffic, and drove in silence. The road was not very busy. It was a sparkling August day, the bright overhead sunlight cutting deep shadows into the buildings. Office workers in shirt-sleeves sauntered along the pavements from late lunches, tourists strapped to their cameras roamed in search of photogenic quarries, and girls in brightly coloured dresses examined their reflections in the shop windows. There was a light breeze to dispel the heat of the sunshine. After the gloom of the hall, Mark founded himself squinting into the light and put on a pair of dark glasses.

Penny glanced at him. 'Now you look more mysterious than ever.'

He smiled. 'I didn't think I was mysterious at all.'

She drove steadily, her eyes on the road. 'You don't give away very much, do you? I have the feeling you're a good poker player.'

'I doubt it. I've never played.'

'You know what I mean. You're hard to fathom.'

'Not really. I'm probably a still water that runs shallow.'

'I don't think so. Some of the time, when you were listening to the music, your face was very sad.'

'I didn't know I was under observation.'

'You weren't. I just noticed, and I warned you I was inclined to be nosy.' She drove on in silence, taking the car through back streets that Mark did not recognise.

'Perhaps it's as well you are driving. I haven't a clue where you're going.'

Her face relaxed. 'My own route. It avoids the traffic. Always watch the way the London taxis go. They know the short-cuts. Were you able to tell the policeman very much?'

'Virtually nothing. I hardly knew Berman. We were supposed to meet this week to sort things out. What about you?'

She paused at a traffic light to light a cigarette. 'I told him what little I knew. Berman came into the office yesterday for the first time, and I asked him a few questions about his career. It was the usual sort of material. One of my jobs is to prepare artists' biographies, so that I can send out a press kit when his record's released.' Her face darkened. 'That's not going to happen now, is it?'

'No. You probably know more about him than I do. When he was in Geneva, he left me some papers, as well as his current concert itinerary. There were a few other bits and pieces, but nothing very personal, so you could have learned more than I did.'

'I suppose so. He left a whole sheaf of reviews for me to go through. He seems to have spent most of his time in South America thus far.'

'What there's been of it. He was just starting out.'

She glanced sideways, a slightly puzzled expression on her face. 'He's been around quite a while, you know. He wasn't as young as all that.'

'Really? I'd put him at about twenty-three.'

She shook her head. 'Twenty-nine last April, to be exact. I know, because he wanted to know my astrological sign, and said he was an Aries looking for a soulmate born under the right star.'

'And?'

'I told him I didn't believe all that star-sign rubbish. It's an awfully corny come-on, isn't it?' Mark nodded. 'Besides, I'm older than he is – was – and, anyway,' she paused slightly, 'I've always preferred slightly older men.' Mark said nothing, and she continued quickly. 'I suppose the problem is that I'm still feeling guilty about him. He was a marvellous violinist, wasn't he?'

'Yes.'

'Even someone with an untrained ear like mine could tell that, but it didn't make him any nicer. He was so damned arrogant! I tried to be pleasant, but he deliberately misunderstood everything I said and turned it into some sort of heavy-handed double-entendre. If he had been just a pushy kid, I wouldn't have minded so much, but he was old enough to know better.'

'I had no idea he was as old as that. He gave me the impression he had only just finished at the Juilliard School of Music. I knew he had been sponsored by Arnold Silverman in New York. Arnold's an amazing man. Despite his own career, he's helped dozens of young musicians over the past twenty years.'

'I know. Berman told me about him. Silverman brought him over from Tel Aviv, where he had won a violin competition. He took him into his own house, paid for Juilliard, helped him find a violin and started him on his career. But that was quite a long time ago. They still keep in touch, of course, but Berman was making a career of his own, and pretty successfully, from the scrapbooks he showed me.'

'It's strange. I should have heard about him sooner. His name only came up a few times in the past year or more.'

'Well, he seems to have spent most of his time in Brazil and Mexico, with a certain amount of work in California. I thought he had a manager there.'

'Yes, he told me about it. It was one of those little agencies in San Francisco, and the woman who looked after him is about to retire. I asked him to get in touch with her before signing with me. We work so far ahead, and I would have been planning from autumn next year at the earliest and into the following season, so I didn't want to get any crossed wires with her. Anyway, he sent me a cable about a week ago, saying that he'd been in touch with her, and asking me to contact a lawyer here in London who looks after all his personal business.' He looked at the violin case on the back seat. 'I'm beginning to wonder why I said I would look after his violins. I'll talk to the lawyer about them.'

'He must have been doing pretty well to afford a Stradivarius.'

Mark was thoughtful. 'Yes, although it's probably mortgaged to the hilt. Good violins only come along now and then, so you take them when you find them. He's probably put up five years of optimistic concert fees for it. Arnold may have helped him, too.'

Penny steered the car into George Street, accelerating to cross a traffic light before it turned red. Mark looked at the Middle Eastern banks and the fashionable boutiques that had replaced the musty antique and second-hand furniture shops he remembered from the past. He frowned. 'It's very strange. We seem to be talking about two different people. Let's hope we can find a few of the answers at his flat.'

They arrived before a large, austere red-brick Victorian mansion building, recently redecorated, which covered a complete block of streets, with entrances on all four sides. The metal railing surrounding it had been repainted, and the doors were polished to a high gloss. Penny drove to the rear of the building, where it faced a quiet, tree-lined street. Through the open window of the car, he could hear birds singing. A few feet away from the front door, she found an unoccupied parking space.

Lifting the violin case carefully from the back seat, Mark sat for a moment, lost in thought. Penny watched him silently. An elderly woman came out of the front door, shuffling slowly, accompanied by a small mongrel dog. They watched her as she made her way painfully slowly along the pavement. The mongrel seemed to be walking equally stiffly.

'I wonder who we'll find in there.'

'It could be anyone. The woman may still be there, whoever she is. I don't think he had any family of his own.'

"What about his parents?'

'He gave me the impression they were both dead.'

'Did you meet her this morning?'

'No, we just talked over the intercom system. When I pressed the bell, she said he'd come down, and I waited in the street. I don't know who she was.'

'Could be a servant, or some other relative.' Mark opened the car door. 'We'd better find out, and break the news.'

There was a panel of buttons next to the front door. Mark noticed that the nameplate, with 'S. Berman' printed on it, appeared very new. He pressed the button, turning to Penny. 'It looks as though the flat's in his name. I didn't know he was planning to settle here. He didn't mention it in Geneva.'

They waited for a while and, when there was no response, he pressed the button again, allowing his finger to remain there longer. Almost immediately, a voice said: 'Who is it?'

Penny leaned forward. 'It's Penny Scott from Magnum Records again.'

The woman's voice said: 'Oh. Is Sandy with you?' The intercom speaker had a metallic rattle, partly distorting the words.

'No, but can we come up?'

There was a slight hesitation. 'I guess so. It's the second floor on the right as you come out of the elevator.' There was an unmistakably American inflection to her voice.

The door buzzed, and Mark pushed it open. Inside, there was a small foyer, heavily carpeted, leading to five stairs and an old-fashioned lift with a trellised metal door. The walls were panelled with polished mahogany.

Penny nodded approvingly. 'Rather plush! These old buildings have all been tarted up in the past few years. The flats cost a fortune these days – nearly all Arabs!'

'I suppose so.'

As they entered the lift, sliding the gate shut behind them, she added: 'He must have been doing better than you thought.'

'Yes.'

Leaving the lift, they were confronted by a small landing with a door on either side. Apparently, there were only two flats to each floor of the building. Mark rang the doorbell, turning to Penny. 'These old mansion buildings were originally designed for fashionable young bachelors and newly-weds. They occupied the rooms facing the street, and the servants used the ones on the inside of the corridor, looking over the centre building well.'

Penny smiled. 'Those were the days!' She looked nervous.

From behind the door, the woman said: 'Who's there?'

Penny raised her eyebrows at Mark and called out: 'It's Penny Scott. I just spoke to you downstairs.'

'I can hear a man's voice.'

'Yes, it's Mr Holland. He's with me.'

'Who?'

Mark spoke. 'Mark Holland. I'm Sandor Berman's manager. D'you think we could come in, please?'

There was a pause, and they heard the sound of bolts being drawn and a lock turning. The door opened only a small way. Penny leaned into the space and said: 'It's quite all right. There's no need to be nervous. I have some identification on me if you'd like to see it.'

'No, I guess it's all right.' The door opened fully, and Mark was surprised to find an attractive young woman standing in the hallway. She had dark, curly hair, cut quite short, which was tousled and uncombed. She might have been awakened from sleep. She wore no make-up, and there were heavy shadows under her eyes. Her face seemed luminously pale in the tessellated light thrown by a small crystal chandelier. She was wearing a man's shirt, open at the neck, the sleeves rolled up, which hung loosely over dark corduroy trousers.

She stared at them for a moment, then brushed nervously at a lock of hair on her forehead and stood to one side. 'You'd better come in. Where's Sandy?' Her voice was low-pitched, and

Mark could understand why Penny had thought that 'a woman' had answered in the morning. From her appearance, however, he guessed that she was in her mid-twenties. A handkerchief was clutched tightly in her right hand, her knuckles white with the pressure of gripping it.

'Hello. I'm Penny. I think I talked to you this morning. This is Mr Holland – Mark.'

The girl stiffened slightly, backing against the wall as they moved forward. She was slimly built and slightly shorter than Penny. She watched them cautiously. 'You already told me that. Where's Sandy? Why isn't he with you? I need to talk to him. Where is he? I tried to call the record company. Nobody seems to answer the phone. Where's Sandy?' The words came out in sharp, staccato sentences, emphasising her nervous state. When neither of them replied, she spoke again. 'Look, I need to know what's going on! They keep telephoning, asking for Sandy, and every time I tell them I don't know where he is, they – they . . .'

Mark spoke for the first time. 'What do they want?'

She turned in his direction, her eyes unfocused. 'They – well, they sound like – threatening . . .' Her voice trailed away.

'What did they say?'

She looked at him more closely, her eyes coming into focus. They were a very deep blue. She considered his question for a moment, concentrating hard. 'I don't know, exactly. They just sound – sort of menacing, like they're going to threaten something. They didn't really say anything specific, except that he'd better be here when they call back.'

'I see. How many times have they called?'

'I can't remember. Twice, I guess. No, maybe three times.' She clutched the handkerchief with both hands and closed her eyes, her teeth pressed against her lower lip. When Penny put a hand on her arm, she started like a frightened animal, then allowed herself to be guided down the hallway towards the open door of the living room. Penny led her to a chair, but the girl resisted, standing almost defiantly in the centre of the room.

'They're going to call back again in a few minutes. They said they would. Where the hell's Sandy?'

Mark stood in front of her and moved to take her hands, but she flinched, moving back a pace. He kept his voice very even. 'I wonder if you'd mind telling us who you are.'

She looked puzzled. 'Why?'

'Well, simply that Penny and I have introduced ourselves, and we don't know who you are.'

The girl thought about this for a moment, then bowed her head. For a moment, Mark wondered whether she might be high on drugs. Her head still lowered, she said: 'My name's Karen – Karen Ackerman.' She looked up almost defiantly. 'I'm a friend of Sandy's. For Christ's sake, where is he?'

Mark said: 'Why don't you sit down?'

'I don't want to sit down! Where is Sandy? Please!'

Mark took a deep breath. He was conscious that Penny, at his side, was watching him intently. 'I'm afraid something's happened to him.'

She frowned, as if trying to comprehend the words. 'Happened to him? What's happened to him? What's wrong? Where is he? They're going to call again any time. Where is Sandy?'

He told her. She listened, her eyes closed, as he spoke. Then her body started to sway, her hands dropped to her sides, and she began to fall. Mark caught her, his arms around her waist, and lifted her off her feet as she teetered backwards. She was surprisingly light, and he carried her to a sofa under the window, laying her gently along the length of it, with a cushion under her head. He was conscious of a faintly musky perfume.

3

At the door of the living room, Penny said: 'I'd better find some water. There's a kitchen opposite.'

He called after her: 'You might look in the bathroom for a damp face-cloth. And see if you can find something stronger than water.' He knelt by the sofa, watching the girl. Afternoon sunlight slanted across her face and arms, and she lay very still.

Without speaking, Penny handed him a damp face-cloth and walked across the room to a trolley laden with bottles and glasses.

'Brandy or scotch?'

'Brandy.' Mark placed a cloth on the girl's forehead, stroking stray curls aside, and her eyes momentarily flickered under long lashes. She was more beautiful than he had first realised, with high cheekbones and a narrow, finely shaped nose. Her mouth was wide and sensuous. She was deeply suntanned, and there was a soft down on her arms, bleached blonde by long hours in the sun.

At length she stirred, opening her eyes, and Penny handed him a small glass of brandy. Placing his left hand behind the girl's head, he pressed the glass to her lips, so that she could swallow a few drops. She gagged slightly, screwing up her face like an angry child. Her body gave off a warm, earthy smell which blended with her perfume.

'Jesus, the top of my head feels as if it's coming off!'

'Just relax. Don't try to talk for a minute, and don't move around too much.'

She leaned back again, closing her eyes, and seemed to fall asleep. Standing behind him, Penny said: 'Do you think we should call a doctor?'

'No. It's just the shock.'

After a moment or two, Karen slowly opened her eyes and half raised herself on the sofa, resting on an arm. 'I'm all right now. You took me by surprise. What happened? Why?'

Mark sat on the edge of the sofa, looking down at her. She looked very vulnerable. 'I'm sorry we had to tell you this way. We don't know why it happened. We were hoping you might be able to help us.'

'Me? Why would I know anything?' She seemed genuinely surprised.

'Because you're here. Aren't you staying in the flat?'

'Yes.' He waited, but she offered no additional comment. She continued to watch him.

'Neither of us knows very much about Berman – Sandy. We

hoped you could tell us a little more. What happened this morning doesn't make any sense to us.'

She sat up, moving painfully, and leaned forward, pressing the cloth to her face. Mark and Penny exchanged glances, and Penny settled herself into an armchair. Her voice slightly muffled by the cloth, Karen said: 'I don't know anything about him. I don't know anything at all.'

'But aren't you a friend of his?'

'Sort of.'

'How do you mean?'

'We only met a few days ago, in Monte Carlo.'

'I see.'

She pulled the cloth from her face, her eyes hurt. 'No, you don't see! We're just – friends.' She closed her eyes again and buried her face in the cloth.

For a while, there was silence, and Mark was aware of the insistent ticking of a Chippendale clock on the writing desk in the bay window at the other end of the room.

Eventually, Penny spoke. 'We're really not trying to pry, and it's none of our business anyway. Neither Mark nor I know anything about Sandy. We only met him professionally in the last few days, and we hoped you might be able to help. The police are trying to piece together . . .'

Karen looked up sharply. 'The police?' Then she nodded slowly. 'Of course. I hadn't thought about police. What do they have to say?'

Mark placed his hand on her arm, and she looked at it with a sort of curious interest. 'They don't seem to know anything more than we do at the moment. Someone came to the back of the recording studio this morning, shot him, and disappeared back into the street before anyone realised what had happened. I can give you more details later, if you want.' She shook her head silently. 'The police have started to investigate, but they haven't got much to go on, and we're trying to find out whatever we can. You're the first person we've found who might know something about him. I'm sure the Inspector will want to talk to you as soon as you're feeling well enough.'

She stared at the carpet. 'I suppose, but I don't know

anything about him.' Her voice was a monotone. 'I met him four days ago in Monte Carlo. I told you.' Penny and Mark exchanged further glances, and she watched them. She spoke slowly, as though choosing her words carefully. 'He was staying at the same hotel – the Mirabeau – and we got into conversation. He mentioned that he was driving to Paris the next day, so I asked him for a lift.' She looked up at Mark, her eyes large. 'I've been hitching across Europe, bumming rides, trying to see as much as I can, for the past two months. I'm an American . . .'

Mark smiled. 'I'd noticed.'

For a moment, the ghost of a smile played on her lips, and her face relaxed. Colour was returning to her cheeks, and she gently released her arm from Mark's grip to take a cautious sip of brandy. 'I guess it shows. Americans always feel so dumb around Europeans!'

'I simply meant that I noticed your accent. When did you meet?'

'It must have been four evenings ago. I was having a late-night drink in the bar, and he was standing next to me. He said he was driving north the next day around noon, so I asked for the ride. We went from Monte Carlo to Beaune that afternoon, and stayed there overnight.' She looked at Penny pointedly. 'We had separate rooms.'

Penny's expression did not change.

Mark said: 'Look, we're really not concerned with your private life, but you must understand the situation.'

She nodded bowing her head. 'Yes, I do. Oh God! Why would anyone do that? He was such a nice kid.'

Mark was aware that Penny was watching him, hoping to attract his attention. Ignoring her, he said: 'You must have talked to him on the drive. What did you talk about?'

'Not very much, that first day. I was tired. I'd been on the road for three or four days before that, coming from Rome. There didn't seem much point in staying in Monte Carlo, especially at those prices! So, the first day, I asked him if he'd mind if I sacked out in the back of the car, and I slept.' She smiled ruefully. 'It's a great way to see Europe, sleeping in the back of a Mercedes! I remember he played the radio all the time

– some sort of classical music. I was hot and tired and sweaty, and lay there in some kind of stupor, with the sun shining on me and that lousy music blasting out of the front seat.' She shook her head at the memory.

'You don't like that sort of music?'

She shook her head. 'No, I don't. I don't mind it, but I never listen to it, and it kept waking me up all afternoon. Half the time, I didn't know if I was dreaming or awake. I was exhausted.'

'You could have asked him to turn it off.'

She shrugged. 'It was his car. He told me he was some sort of classical musician, so I didn't like to ask him to turn it off. The whole journey is one vague fuzz in my memory.'

Penny spoke. 'What about when you got to Beaune?' Her voice was cool.

She looked up. 'I was feeling a little better by then. We stayed at one of those hotels in the main square, next to the place with the coloured tiles on the roof, and we had dinner somewhere in the square.'

'What did you talk about?'

'Nothing much. I don't remember.' She closed her eyes for a moment. 'We talked about Mexico, mostly. He seems to have spent a lot of time there, and I once had a holiday in Mexico City and spent a few days in the Yucatan. Mostly, we compared places we'd been to. You know: all the normal tourist spots like the pyramids and the Alameda Park and the anthropological museum. I guess everyone visits the same places.' She smiled. 'I remember he talked about Montezuma's Revenge.'

Penny asked: 'What's that?'

'The runs. Anyone who goes to Mexico spends at least two days sitting on the can! You make a great point of not drinking the water, but you forget the lettuce has been washed in it and the ice has been made with it, and you end up the same way!' Her expression changed, and she shrugged helplessly. 'It was like that. I don't remember what we talked about. He told me about concerts and musical people, but most of it was over my head. He kept mentioning names of people I guess he thought I should know, but half the time I didn't know who he was talking about, and I just nodded or smiled. He talked quite a lot about himself, I guess, but it was always about music.'

Mark smiled. 'Most musicians do. It's an occupational hazard. You don't remember any of it?'

'No, not really. I told you, I'm not into that kind of music, and most of it was about places he'd been, or people he'd met. I guess some of it was to impress me, but it didn't really mean anything.' She paused, and her face was sombre. 'But he was sweet. I mean, he was thoughtful, and he had good manners, and he did his best to entertain me. I had the feeling he was kind of shy.'

This time, Mark and Penny exchanged looks of surprise. Penny said: 'I wouldn't have used those words to describe him, whatever he might have been like.'

Karen looked at her. 'Oh, he knew how to look after himself, and he certainly knew his way around. I mean, he spoke French at the hotel and to the waiters, and he was very man-of-the-world, but when we were alone together, he just talked about his musical life and the people he knew. I had the feeling he talked about them to cover up some of his own feelings of inadequacy, as though he was a little scared of talking about things that were important to him. At the end of the evening, he didn't make a pass at me, or anything. I thought he might, but he didn't.' She looked at Penny again. 'I wouldn't have minded if he had. I liked him.' Penny nodded silently, and she continued. 'He wanted to pay for my room, and I wouldn't let him, but he paid for dinner that evening. I tried to buy the gas next morning when we filled up, but he wouldn't let me.'

'What about the next day?'

She seemed fully recovered and, sitting straight, turned to face Mark. Smiling slightly, she brushed a wisp of hair from her forehead. The gesture was graceful, and Mark could not help noticing the gentle curve of her breast as she raised her arm. It was a very feminine movement.

'The next day, we got up quite late, and drove straight through to Paris airport for an evening plane.'

'Did you intend to go straight to London?'

For a moment, she seemed taken by surprise. 'Why do you ask that?'

'You said you were hitching around Europe, and I thought you would have wanted to see Paris. That's all. It's one of the main tourist attractions in Europe.'

A shadow crossed her face momentarily. 'I guess so. Well, the truth was that I was running out of money. Paris is supposed to be very expensive, so I decided to give it a miss and fly on to London. Sandy told me he'd bought an apartment, and invited me to stay there. I figured I could save the money I would have used on hotels, and stay a little longer.'

'Of course.'

For a moment, she was angry. 'Look, there was nothing more to it than that!'

'I'm not suggesting there was. Please don't take offence.'

She laughed unexpectedly. Her teeth were very white and even, like those in a toothpaste commercial. 'I'm sorry, but you sound so – so *British*!' She mimicked him. 'Please don't take offence! I didn't think I would meet people who talked like they do in the movies. I don't mean to be rude.'

Mark returned her smile. 'That's all right. We really do talk this way. Sometimes it needs translating. Do you remember talking to Sandy about anything else?'

Mentioning Berman's name dispersed the lightness again, and her face became sombre. It seemed to Mark that her moods changed rapidly, like those of a person under stress. 'Yes and no. We spent three days together, and we must have talked about a hundred different things. I guess we were just getting to know each other, but I don't remember what we said. Nothing special. We talked about movies we'd seen, and books we'd both read. He didn't really talk very much about himself, like I said, except his musical life. I told him about my home in Cleveland, and the years I spent in college, but he didn't really talk about that part of his life. I even remembered to tell him about going to a summer concert at Blossom Music Center, but I didn't remember what they'd played! He told me he came from Israel, and that he hadn't been there for a long time. His folks were killed during one of those wars in the Sixties, and he lived with an aunt. Then some musician from New York heard him play the violin, and arranged for him to live in the States. He talked quite a lot about that. I guess the man was some kind of classical musician, but I don't remember his name.'

'Arnold Silverman?'

'Yes, that's right! Should I have heard of him?'

Mark smiled at Penny. 'Not if you're not "into" classical music.' Penny smiled back.

'Which means I should have!'

'He's a very famous violinist.'

'Oh. Well, he talked about how this Arnold had helped his career and started him off, but that was about all. We flew to London two evenings ago, and he gave me keys for the front door and the apartment door, and put me in the spare bedroom.' She gestured with her head towards the front of the flat. Looking at Mark, she added: 'His room is at the back of the apartment, over there.'

'What about yesterday?'

'I hardly saw him all day. I heard him playing his violin in the morning. I guess he was practising. Then he knocked on my door and said he was going out and expected to be gone most of the day. He said he had a meeting at Magnum Records. That's a pretty big company, isn't it?'

'Yes.'

'I mean, I know their records from my own collection. They have a lot of rock stars. I thought it was an American company.'

'It is, but they have a London office.'

'Yes, I know. I was trying to call them this morning, when Sandy didn't show.'

'And last night?'

'Last night?' Suspicion appeared again for a moment. 'Oh, you mean, did I see him? Not for very long. I spent the day sight-seeing, and didn't get in until the evening. Sandy was here when I got back. He said he had a recording, and wanted an early night.' Her face saddened. 'We were supposed to have dinner together tonight. Shit, this is horrible!' For a moment, she looked as though she might cry, but she wiped her face with the cloth and drank the remains of her brandy.

Mark walked over to the window, staring out. The elderly woman and her dog were shuffling down the street in the direction of the front door. 'You don't remember anything else?'

There was a long pause before Karen replied. 'No, I don't think so. I don't know what I'm trying to remember for you. I don't know what you want to know.'

'Neither do we. Maybe something will ring a bell. Did you get the feeling that he was at all troubled by anything? Or that there might be someone he didn't like, or who didn't like him?'

'No. He was very cheerful, all the time, and relaxed. He was fun to be with but, as I said, a little shy under the surface. I had the feeling he was a little strung up this morning. As he was leaving, he said something like "Wish me luck", and he looked a little tense, but nothing more.' Her eyes misted. 'That's the last thing he said to me.' She held the cloth to her face again, hiding it, and her shoulders shook as she sobbed silently. Penny walked over to the sofa and, sitting next to her, put her arms around the girl's shoulders. At first, Karen resisted, but Penny held on gently, until the girl's head fell against her shoulder. After a few minutes, she sat straight, drying her eyes, looking from one to the other.

'I'm sorry. I guess I'm not up to this kind of thing. I never had a situation like this.'

Penny said: 'Don't worry about it. We're all a bit shaken up by it.' Karen took her hands and mouthed the word 'thanks'.

Mark remained by the window. 'When we arrived, you were talking about some telephone calls.'

Karen started. 'God, yes! I'd almost forgotten. Do you think they had anything to do with Sandy's . . .'

'It depends what they said. You seemed upset when we came in.'

'I was. It's just that, when you told me what had happened, it made me forget . . .' Her voice trailed off.

'Can you tell us about them?'

'There's not much to tell. About an hour after Sandy left, there was a phone call. It was some man asking me where Sandy was. I asked his name, but he wouldn't tell me. I told him I didn't exactly know where Sandy was, and that he was making a record. I said he'd be back around lunchtime.'

'And?'

'Well, at first, I thought he would say okay and that he'd call back. I was about to ring off, when he said something like "He'd better be back by lunchtime," in a sort of menacing way. I couldn't believe it. He sounded like someone in an old gangster movie. I thought I hadn't heard him right and said "Excuse me?", and he said it again: "He'd better be back." His voice was frightening!' She shivered. 'I was going to say something more, but the line went dead.'

'What did he sound like?'

'I don't know. It was unreal. He had an English accent, and I must have asked him who he was a couple of times, but he wouldn't say.'

'Did he call back?'

'No, but about two hours later, another man called. I'll swear it wasn't the same man. This one just said: "Where's Berman?" as soon as I answered. I told him the same thing, but he didn't seem to understand me. If he did, he didn't believe me. He just said: "Where's Berman?" again, like that. I started to explain again, in case he hadn't understood the first time, but he cut across me and said: "When you see him, tell him we want him. Do you understand?" I tried to ask some questions, but he just said: "Tell him!" and hung up. He sounded angry, but kind of – threatening.'

'And that's all he said?'

'Yes. He called back again, ten minutes later, and gave me the same routine. "Where's Berman?" He must have said it three or four times. I tried to talk to him, but it was as if he didn't hear me. Then he said: "When he gets back, tell him to stay there. We'll be watching for him," and I asked him if Sandy could call him, but he just said: "Tell him," and hung up. He called again, just before you rang the bell downstairs.'

'What did he say?'

'Nothing. He didn't speak. I said hello and "Who's there?", but he didn't say anything. I'll swear it was the same man.

There was just silence at the other end, and then a little click as the line went dead. I was frightened.'

'Why?'

'I don't know. The way he talked, and the last time, when he didn't say anything – just listened to me asking who was there. When he hung up, I found a directory and called Magnum Records but nobody answered. I could hear the phone ringing and ringing at the other end, but nobody picked up. I was starting to feel scared because I was sure he was going to call again, and I didn't know what to say. Then, when you rang the bell downstairs, I was starting to go out of my mind, because I thought it was him.' She looked at them helplessly. 'I know it doesn't sound so bad when I tell it to you here, but you didn't hear their voices. I was scared!'

Mark walked over to the sofa. 'When you talk to the police Inspector, tell him about the calls. They could be connected with this morning. I think you should talk to the man we saw, as soon as you feel up to it.' He reached into his pocket. 'He left me a number.'

Karen looked unhappy. 'Do I have to talk to the police?'

Penny said: 'Yes, you must. You may be able to help.'

'But I don't know anything.' She was almost petulant.

'It would be better to let them decide that. Is there any reason not to talk to them?'

The girl hesitated, looking from one to the other. 'It's just that people – jump to conclusions. It wasn't like that. I mean, I don't do that kind of thing. Sandy was a friend. He treated me very well. I don't like to come across as some kind of pick-up.'

Penny was about to reply, but Mark interrupted her. 'I wouldn't worry about it. The police aren't interested in your private life, but you might say something, without realising it, that helps them find out why anyone would want to have killed him.'

'I guess so.' She was not convinced.

'At least tell them what you know. Did Sandy say anything very much about this flat?' Mark looked around the room. It was furnished comfortably and with a quiet luxury that he had not expected to find. The sofa and armchairs were covered in an old-fashioned silk brocade, and the walls were papered with an elegant Regency candy-stripe. There was a Hepplewhite writing-table in the bay window and a handsome Sheraton bureau against one of the walls. They looked like originals or, at the least, very good reproductions. There were a number of Picasso lithographs and a small oil painting that looked like a Chagall. The carpet had a thick pile. It was a stylish room, displaying the good taste of a bygone era, but an unlikely setting for the young Israeli violinist who had owned it. Perhaps he had hired a decorator. Even then, the place seemed unfinished, uninhabited, like an expensive hotel suite.

Karen's voice cut across his thoughts. 'He said he bought the apartment a few months ago. That's all he told me. He said he was waiting for the rest of his things to be shipped from New York. There's a whole lot of records and books.' Mark nodded. The shelves built into the walls were empty, and there were no books anywhere. That was why it reminded him of a hotel room. She continued: 'I suppose you can look at the rest of the apartment, if you want to. There's a big safe in the hall closet.'

'Really?'

'Sure.' She stood, shakily. 'I'll show you.' She led the way to the hall, where there were several doors facing the centre of the building. Opening one of them, she revealed a deep cupboard, about eight feet long, which had been fitted with coat racks and shelves. At the end, facing them, was a large Chubb safe with a combination lock on the door. Mark and Penny peered at it from the doorway. Behind them, Karen said: 'I noticed it when I hung up my coat. It looks big for an apartment this size. What would he keep in it?'

Penny said: 'The violins?'

'I suppose he might have.' She glanced down the hallway to the front door, where Mark had left the violin case.

'Did you notice where he put his violins?'

Karen looked uncertain. 'I think he may have put them in there. He told me they were very valuable. He said one of them was called Jesus, or something like that.'

'Something.' Mark smiled. 'Do you know if the safe is open at the moment?'

'No.'

'Let's try. We brought the violins back from the session.' He tried the handle of the safe door, but it would not move. 'No go. We'll have to find someone who knows the combination.'

Karen put a hand on his arm. 'If those violins are as valuable as he said, I don't think you should leave them. I mean, I don't know where to put them, and I don't like the idea of just leaving them lying around. Those men who called, they sounded – I don't know – kind of dangerous. If they come to the apartment, I don't want the violins here.' She hesitated.

Penny and Mark looked at each other. At length, Mark said: 'Perhaps I'd better keep them with me. I can put them in the hotel safe until we sort out Berman's affairs.'

'I wish you would.'

'What about you?'

'Me?' She looked puzzled.

'What are you going to do?'

'Oh.' She thought about it. 'I guess I'll go home.'

'The police will need to talk to you before you do.'

'I'll call them.'

'What do you want to do until you leave? Would you prefer to stay at a hotel?' She shook her head silently. 'It might be a better idea, after what's happened, and you won't get any more phone calls.' She shook her head again, her face stubborn. 'Don't you think it would be more sensible?'

'I'll be all right here.'

Penny moved to her side. 'Are you sure?'

'Yes. It was a shock, but I'm fine – truly.' She suddenly smiled and her face relaxed. Her beauty was quite startling. 'Look, don't worry about me. I'm okay – really. In a while, I'll take a walk and get a little fresh air, and I'll call the police as soon as I get back.' Her recovery was surprising. Turning to Mark, she added: 'And thank you, both of you. You've been kind. I appreciate it.' She might have been a small child at the end of a party. 'If the phone rings, I won't answer it if I don't want to.'

Mark watched her carefully. She could still be reacting to the shock of Berman's death. 'I'll write down my hotel number, in case you want to call. If you like, I'll call a little later, to make sure. I'm staying at the Westbury Hotel.'

She favoured him with a warm smile. Her eyes seemed very large. 'Thank you. I'd like that.' She stood in the hallway, waiting for them to leave.

Taking the violin case, Mark and Penny let themselves out of the flat. As he turned at the door, Karen was still standing in the centre of the hall, where they had left her. She smiled in his direction, but did not move.

Mark closed the door. 'I'm not sure we should leave her.'

Penny was thoughtful. 'She seemed to make a lightning recovery.'

'That's the point. She may still be in shock.'

'I suppose so. What do you want to do?'

'I'll call back later, to see how she's feeling.' He stood on the landing, uncertain. The American girl had looked very vulnerable, standing alone in the hallway.

There was a thickly carpeted staircase winding round the lift shaft, and Penny started down. 'Let's walk. I hate those old lifts. When they rattle and creak like that, I'm always afraid of getting stuck half-way.'

Mark followed her. 'Most of them used to be hydraulically operated in the old days, with all sorts of watery noises. Every time you pushed a button to go down, it was like flushing the elevator.' She laughed, but her face remained serious, and they walked in silence to the car.

At the door of the hotel, Penny said: 'I'll leave you here and go on to the office. God knows what sort of hell is breaking loose there. Don't forget that we promised to go and see the Steigels later. Would you like me to pick you up?'

'I can always catch a cab. I must call my office in Geneva.' He frowned. 'I suppose I'd better call New York, too.'

'It's on my way.' She consulted her watch. 'Why don't I pick you up at five?'

'Any time will do. I probably need about an hour.'

'I'll make it five o'clock exactly.' She clicked her tongue. 'I must stop doing that.'

'What?'

'I'm a compulsive appointment-maker. I arrange to call people at a fixed time on a certain day, and half the time I know I'm not going to do it, even while I'm saying it. It's some sort of desire to appear super-efficient, I suppose.' She looked at him for a moment. 'Or to make myself indispensable. I end up by infuriating everyone.'

Mark smiled. 'I'm not even irritated. I'll wait in the foyer, by the front door, from five onwards. That way, it will save you having to park.'

'You're a thoughtful man, Mr Holland.'

He closed the door and leaned through the window. 'Thank you for helping with Karen. I don't think I would have managed without you being there.'

'Any time you need me.' She put the car into gear, lightly revving the engine. Her gaze was steady. 'And anyway, I saw you first.' Before he could reply, she accelerated away, charging into a gap in the traffic and racing through the lights. He stood for a moment, watching the Mini as it cut between slower-moving cars with inches to spare and disappeared in the direction of Berkeley Square.

'Ah, Mr Holland.' The concierge greeted him imperiously, fixing him with a stare that suggested he was late for their appointment. He produced several message slips with such alacrity that he might have been holding them behind his back. 'Your Geneva office called twice, and there are several calls from a Mr Bradshaw.'

'Thank you.' He placed the violin case on the concierge's desk. 'I wonder if I can have these violins put away in the hotel safe. They're very valuable.'

'Of course, sir.' The concierge put the messages down and lifted the case in both hands, holding it before him like a dinner platter. The Westbury Hotel was a favourite with musicians, and he knew the routine.

'Do you need me to sign some sort of document?'

'Oh no, sir. We know you well enough. I'll have a receipt

ready for you when you pass the next time. Don't you worry about it.' He gestured with his head. 'Don't forget your message slips.'

Mark opened the Geneva messages. The first advised him that there was nothing to report except that a Mr Bradshaw in London had been trying to contact him. The second message was to say that the office was now closed, with the answering machine turned on, because Rudi was on his way to a concert in Zurich. It also reminded him to try to contact Mr Bradshaw. Mark frowned. He had hired Rudi because there was too much work to handle alone. The young man's Swiss efficiency should have been reassuring, but he found it irritatingly correct. In the mornings, he had the sinking feeling that Rudi was about to stand and click his heels when he walked into the office. Six months later, he still jerked his head forward with military crispness to acknowledge a request.

He paused, remembering the stillness of Sandor Berman's body, the sightless eyes and the thin ribbon of blood disfiguring his face. It had been as though there were a wall of silence separating him and the dead boy from the noise and confusion of the musicians and technicians in the hall. He had returned, for the moment, to a familiar milieu. But then, he had worked for so long in a profession where death was an everyday event, no matter how ugly or unacceptable, that it no longer shocked him. And he had killed men himself – Willis used to call it 'reducing the opposition' – quickly and efficiently, without hesitation or conscience. His only qualms had been about being discovered or identified. Anonymity was essential in such operations. What had Penny called him? A good poker player. He wondered whether his reactions to the morning's events had been convincing, whether the musicians and engineers, the police, Penny and the American girl, had detected a lack of response to the brutality and senseless destruction. Perhaps he had really felt the emotions he had shown at the time. He no longer knew.

In the lift, he looked at the three messages telling him that Mr Bradshaw had called. They were received at twelve-thirty, two-fifteen and three o'clock. Each time, Mr Bradshaw had left no return number. He had called Switzerland, too, probably to find him. It appeared to be urgent, unless Bradshaw was some sort of musician. In the music world, everything was urgent.

When he reached his room, Mark took out the new file that Rudi had prepared for Berman. The young man had recently bought a stencil set for the office, and had painstakingly printed 'Berman, S. (Violin)' in red ink on the cover. As he opened the file, Mark was confronted by an eight-by-ten black and white photograph of Sandor, smiling confidently, his violin held across his chest in the approved publicity-shot style. Highlights glistened in the irises of his eyes, his hair was brushed neatly, his white tie perfectly in place. Mark looked at the picture. In his mind, he saw the lifeless eyes, the scarlet hole between the brows, and the ribbon of blood running across his temple. He turned the photograph over.

The next page was headed 'Itinerary 1984–85' and was handwritten in Berman's untidy scrawl. Mark remembered watching him fill in the details in the Geneva office. His eye ran down the list of concerts and recitals. Berman had started the season in Mexico, with the period from the middle of September to the first week in October blocked in. He had not bothered to write in the details. The second block of dates, from mid-October to the end of November, was marked 'South America'. At the time, Berman had said: 'You can tell where I played from the reviews I kept. I save the bad ones as well as the good ones!' From 7 to 18 December, there were details of concerts and recitals on the West Coast of America, ranging from San Diego to Portland, with additional appearances in Canada. He had spent Christmas and New Year in New York, starting again in mid-January with a recital tour in the mid-West: mainly college towns and second-class dates. None of the major cities in the American concert circuit appeared, with the exception of Minneapolis. The tour had taken him into the third week of February, after which there was a blank period marked 'Holiday – mainly London'. It was an unusual hiatus in a concert schedule, in the middle of the season, and Mark wondered whether Berman had taken this time off to settle the purchase of his London flat. Karen had said it had been 'a few months ago'. He thought about her for a moment, wondering whether she had taken her walk. He pictured her, still standing in the hallway, unable to move, waiting for the telephone to ring again.

In March, Berman had given a series of concerts in Scandinavia: a recital in Malmö, two concerto performances in Bergen, a radio broadcast in Oslo and further dates in Sweden and Denmark. His American manager in San Francisco had a Swedish name – something like Petersen or Gustavson, he couldn't remember which. It was probably among the rest of the papers in the file. Perhaps she had good Scandinavian connections. Mark read on, tracing his journey on an imaginary map with each new date. At the bottom of the page, he could see the concerts with L'Orchestre de la Suisse Romande, followed by the French tour. The last entries on the page were Toulouse, Monaco and London.

At that moment, the phone rang. It seemed loud in the silence of the hotel room. He set the file aside and lifted the receiver.

'Am I speaking to Mr Holland – Mr Mark Holland?' The voice was light, almost like a woman's, with a marked sibilance.

'Yes, I'm Mark Holland.'

'Ah, I'm so glad to have found you at last, Mr Holland. My name is Bradshaw – Lewis Bradshaw. You're a very difficult man to trace. I've been trying to reach you all day.'

'So I understand. If you had left a return number, I could have called you back a little sooner.'

There was a slight pause at the other end. 'I don't think that would have been appropriate.' He stretched the final word out, as though savouring it. 'It concerns a mutual colleague of ours, Mr Holland: Sandor Berman.'

Mark hesitated momentarily. Perhaps Bradshaw had information. 'What about him?'

'Well, I'm most anxious to speak to him. We are, in a manner of speaking, business partners in a certain enterprise. I have been trying to reach him at home, but he doesn't appear to be there.'

'I see.' Once again, Mark saw Karen standing in the flat, and remembered the fear in her eyes. 'Did you talk to anyone there?'

There was another pause. 'Yes, a young woman told me he was out making a recording but, if I may be frank, Mr Holland, I was not entirely convinced that she was telling the truth.'

'Really? What made you think that?'

There was a slight chuckle at the end of the line. 'Mr Holland, I'm sure we are both men of the world, so there seems little point in beating about the bush in a matter of some importance. The young woman's replies seemed to me to be somewhat evasive. To be honest, I had the feeling that Sandor, for reasons that I don't understand, might have been standing there in the flat, listening while she talked to me.' Bradshaw spoke with a slight drawl, which he used for emphasis. The sound was unpleasant.

Mark felt his irritation increase. Keeping his voice matter-of-fact, he said: 'I think you were mistaken, Mr Bradshaw. Sandor Berman was at a recording session this morning.'

There was another long pause and, for a moment, Mark wondered whether Bradshaw was still there. At length, he returned. 'It is very important that Sandor contacts me as soon as possible. He knows where I can be reached. As I said earlier, we are involved in a business partnership, and I have been waiting to hear from him for the past twenty-four hours.' His voice hardened. 'What are you going to do about it?'

A thought occurred to Mark. 'Why are you calling me, Mr Bradshaw?' The news of his representing Berman was known to a very small group of people.

The man sounded slightly surprised. 'Sandor told me you were his business manager. He gave me your Geneva number, and said you would be looking after *all* aspects of his business dealings in Europe from now on.'

'That's partly true, but he also has a lawyer here in London to look after his financial affairs. I was about to . . .'

'Oh come, come, Mr Holland!' He sounded impatient. 'I hardly think this is a matter for lawyers!'

'I'm sorry, but I'm not with you. My responsibilities concerning Berman are strictly confined to his musical career.'

'But he said you would be looking after all his – interests. I spoke to him a few days ago, in the South of France. He told me to call you in Geneva if I needed anything.'

'I think you may have misunderstood him. I'm simply his musical manager, and . . .'

Bradshaw interrupted angrily. 'Look, I'm sorry to have to be short with you, but that's not the impression Sandor gave me. I don't know exactly what the pair of you are up to, but Berman should have been in touch with me twenty-four hours ago.'

'I don't know what you're talking about. He never mentioned your name to me.'

'Rubbish! Just what are you up to?'

'I'm not up to anything. Do you want to tell me what this is about?'

'As if you didn't know!' The accent had slipped slightly, and the drawl had disappeared. 'If Berman doesn't call me, and soon, the pair of you could find yourselves in serious trouble!'

'What sort of trouble?'

'Very serious.'

Mark took a breath. 'I don't think Sandor will find himself in any more serious trouble, Mr Bradshaw. He died this morning.'

'What the bloody hell are you talking about?'

Mark kept his voice calm. 'He was killed this morning, during the recording session. Somebody shot him.'

There was a long silence. The voice at the other end of the line was almost a whisper. 'I don't believe you.'

'I wouldn't lie about a thing like that, Mr Bradshaw. You'll be able to check for yourself. It will probably be in the late edition of the evening papers, and I imagine it may be on the radio and television news as well.' His voice softened. 'Now, would you like to tell me what you wanted to discuss with him?'

There was a click as the line went dead.

4

When the telephone rang a few moments later, Mark expected to hear Bradshaw's voice again, but the slight hiss of white sound and a sputtering of static indicated that it was an overseas call.

'Mr Holland?' She pronounced it 'Hullind'.

'Yes.'

'Hold the line for Mr Laufer, please.'

Gregory Laufer was the Vice President of Classical Operations at Magnum Records in New York, a dapper man in his mid-forties with a vulpine face and carefully manicured fingernails, more than a little anxious to claw his way up the executive ladder of the company. He wore Gucci shoes, his custom-made shirts were ostentatiously loud, and he affected a predilection for fine wines and *haute cuisine* by the logical process of ordering the most expensive items on a menu. His lack of any real musical knowledge was the subject of numerous anecdotes in the music world, but Mark assumed that he had been hired for his street-wise business acumen. He suspected that Laufer spent his leisure hours reading do-it-yourself primers entitled *The Psychology of Executive Decision-Making* or *Towards More Creative Memo-Writing*. However, being Vice President of the label's Classical department fulfilled Laufer's aspirations to 'class', his favourite catchword, although his most quoted maxims were: 'Dress British, think Yiddish' and 'I'll cry all the way to the bank'.

After a few more seconds of crackle, Vice President Laufer announced himself. 'Hi! I just heard the news.' His voice was rich with emotion. 'It's a tragic loss, not only to music in general, but also to a good friend. This is a sad time for us all.'

'Yes. Did you know Berman well?'

'Well, not exactly.' He sounded slightly sheepish. 'Arnold

Silverman insisted I sign him. You know what a great sponsor of young talent Arnold is.'

'Of course.'

'As a matter of fact, he refused to re-sign his own contract unless I agreed to take the kid on. I'm told Sandor was a fine young man. I didn't actually get the chance to hear him myself, but I know he must have been a great young artist.'

'Yes. He was very talented.'

'How is Maestro Steigel taking it? He must have been horrified. Please remember me fondly to him.'

The last time Greg Laufer had met Konstantin had been during an expense-account Grand Tour of Europe, when he had invited himself to the Steigels' apartment in Zurich. Mark remembered watching him slouch in Heidi's favourite armchair, resting his shoes on a polished coffee-table. At one point, when the Steigels were out of the room, he had taken a handful of *Mozartkugeln* and slipped them surreptitiously into his pocket. After his departure, pockets bulging, Konstantin had dubbed him 'Hail fellow well avoided', and begged Mark henceforth to undertake all Magnum Records negotiations on his behalf.

'The maestro's bearing up very well, thanks. It was an unpleasant shock, but he went back to the hotel to rest. I'll pass on your condolences.'

'Thank you. Listen, I understand Berman was shot right in the middle of the recording, with the tapes running. How the hell could a thing like that happen?'

Mark described the situation briefly, recounting the events as he had done for the police Inspector, including his own theory as to how the assassin had managed it. When he finished, Laufer whistled in amazement. 'Jesus, it's more like a movie than a recording session. Do you mean to say it's all there on the tape?'

'Yes. They were recording the second full take of the movement. He had just finished the cadenza.'

There was a long pause. When he spoke again, Laufer's voice was excited. 'Listen, I've got a fantastic idea. Why don't we issue that tape, just as it happened? It would be a historic document!'

'Gunshot and all?'

'Why not? I mean, this is the first time such a thing has ever been recorded in a studio as it actually happened. Think of that video of Harry Ruby shooting Lee Harvey Oswald in Dallas. That was dynamite!'

'It wasn't quite the same thing. This was a young musician being brutally murdered by an unknown assassin.'

'I think a lot of people would like to share in the experience. It's an important moment in musical history – a document!' Laufer had raised his voice, as he always did when he knew he was on shaky ground.

'No.' Mark's voice was firm but quiet.

'Jesus, Mark, Sandor would have wanted it!'

'I doubt that very much, and if he had known of such a possibility, I'm sure he would never have walked into any studio.'

After a pause, Laufer spoke softly. 'You can't really stop us. We own the tape.'

'I believe, if you look at the contract, there's a clause stating that the artist has final approval of the master tape.'

'Yeah, but he's not there to disapprove it, is he?'

'The same clause is in Steigel's contract. You may remember that he insisted on it after you released his Bruckner Third with three bars missing.'

'Oh. I guess you're right. Do you think you could persuade him to agree?'

'I doubt it very much.'

'Listen, it will sell a lot of records. He's on royalties, isn't he?'

'Yes, but I don't think he would want to earn them that way.'

'Well, will you at least ask him? I'd really show my appreciation.'

'If you want.' For a moment, Mark had the hysterical thought that Laufer was about to offer him a bribe. 'Showing your appreciation' was something you offered New York doormen and janitors when they undertook private errands. 'I'll ask him, but I very much doubt whether he'll agree.'

'I'm counting on you.' Laufer had already made him a fellow conspirator. There was another pause. 'Listen, what are we going to do tomorrow?'

'Tomorrow?' Mark wondered whether a funeral had already been arranged.

'Sure. Tomorrow and the other days. We still have three sessions booked.'

Mark closed his eyes, shaking his head in resignation. Come what may, Laufer was determined to be a successful executive. 'I'm sure the musicians will agree to a postponement. I don't think there's anything in the current union agreement to cover this kind of situation. It doesn't come under Act of God, but I suppose you could call it indisposition or unexpected illness!'

Sarcasm was lost on Laufer. 'I wasn't concerned with that, but we've paid for the hall for the next few days, and the engineers, and installing the equipment. Can't we record something else with the time we have left?' Berman and his 'historic tape' had been set aside.

'Yes, I suppose you could. The musicians are all booked.'

'What could Steigel do?'

'He's been rehearsing the Beethoven *Eroica* this week for a Promenade Concert the day after tomorrow. That uses roughly the same forces as the Violin Concerto, give or take a few.'

'Do you think he could complete it in three sessions?'

'Yes. They'll have already rehearsed it together.'

'Okay, let's go for it.'

'I'll ask him if he will. I haven't spoken to him since this morning. We're supposed to meet later on.'

'He'll do it. What conductor's going to turn down the chance of a Beethoven symphony? Listen, I'm not guaranteeing we'll do any of the others, just because we do one.'

Mark sighed. If he didn't necessarily know a great deal about music, Greg Laufer knew about musicians. 'All right, I'll ask him to record the *Eroica* and call back with a confirmation.'

'Great! We already have the signed contract. I can change the details of the repertoire.'

'And the royalty.'

'What do you mean?' His voice slid from boyish enthusiasm to aggressive suspicion.

'The Violin Concerto involved sharing the royalty with Berman. The symphony doesn't.'

Laufer thought about this for a moment. 'But he agreed to the royalty we offered.'

'No, Greg. I agreed that he would share it with Berman. You may remember that I represent both of them.'

'Okay, we can up him a couple of points to seven per cent.'

'Ten. That's what you were prepared to pay for the Violin Concerto.'

'Yeah, but that was because it was a young talent like Berman.'

'Whom you didn't know!'

Another pause. 'Gee, Mark, it seems terrible to hear you haggle over the royalty, and Berman's not yet in his grave, poor kid!'

'I know, Greg. It takes my mind off that historic tape of him being gunned down.'

Laufer suddenly laughed. 'I guess you've got me over a barrel. Okay, he can have the full ten. I'm not really losing anything, am I? I'll change the contract and send it back for Steigel to initial where the changes are. Are you sure he can make it in time? The *Eroica*'s a long piece.'

'Yes, I'm sure.'

'Then why the hell did we book four sessions for the Violin Concerto, for Christ's sake?'

'I don't know. Your department made the booking. Incidentally, can Arnold Silverman be reached? I'd like to talk to him about Berman. None of us knows very much about him.'

'Arnie's in China, on a goodwill mission. You won't reach him till next week. I'll tell him to call when he gets back. Listen, I'll wait to hear from you about that other tape. I'm not giving up without a fight. See what you can do. Listen, I've got to run. I'm late for a meeting. Good talking to you, and stay well. G'bye.' Laufer was always on his way to a meeting or at a meeting. Decisions had to be made by committees. In that way, if anything went wrong, no individual executive could be found guilty, particularly Gregory Laufer.

Mark returned to Sandor Berman's file and continued reading. The itinerary for the 1985–86 season was scattered with a number of engagements, but he did not bother to read them carefully, and leafed through a handful of sheets on which newspaper clippings in various languages had been pasted. He was searching for a printed publicity 'flier', of the type that most artists had prepared from time to time, that would offer a few details of Berman's past life and career. Surprisingly, none had been included. It was almost as though the violinist had not wanted to reveal very much of his past. At the back of the file, there was a page of stationery from his Geneva office, on which a number of contact names and addresses had been typed. There was the address of Kirsten Petersen in San Francisco, with phone and telex numbers. He wondered whether to call her, but it was still too early in the day for the eight-hour California time change. He found Berman's New York address and phone number, and under 'London' he had given Scutter and Partners in Wimpole Street 'for all financial arrangements', but no details of the flat in George Street.

Mark had known Eric Scutter for some years. He was employed by the very rich and successful. He acted as legal adviser to a number of well-known musicians and had made a speciality of creating tax havens in various corners of Europe: anything from an apartment and 'official residence' in Monte Carlo to a complicated *anstalt* in Lichtenstein and other countries offering freedom from revenue collectors in major European countries. He was an unattractive, obsequious little man with a wet handshake and a hangdog expression, who wore shabby suits and looked as though he should be wearing a green eye-shade. Mark had met him backstage in concert halls in London, Paris and Geneva, looking slightly ill at ease and skulking among the well-wishers and hangers-on as though he were there by mistake. He was also rumoured to be one of the richest lawyers in London, with private apartments in Miami Beach and Los Angeles, and an eight-berth cabin cruiser anchored in Cannes harbour. Sandor Berman hardly seemed to be in the right income bracket to be seeking his advice. Mark dialled Scutter's office and made an appointment with his secretary for ten o'clock the following morning. He avoided talking to the lawyer in person. The evening news would explain his presence.

There were still a few minutes to kill before Penny would return, and he sat and leafed again through the file, reading some of the reviews. Most of them were in Spanish. It was as though he was trying to find some key to the morning's events hidden among the material the violinist had left behind. The air was becoming oppressively heavy, with increasing humidity, suggesting the approach of a thunderstorm. His clothes felt sticky.

His mind returned again to Karen and, for a moment, he thought he detected a faint trace of her perfume still clinging to his jacket. She had been so light when he had carried her to the sofa, but there was a sensuousness to the curve of her body. He glanced at the telephone, wondering whether he should call her, but decided that it was too soon.

The Mini was parked outside the hotel, wedged cheekily between a Rolls-Royce and a Mercedes 600. Penny watched him from the driving seat as he walked towards her. She had changed into a pale blue cotton dress that seemed to complement her blonde hair.

'For once in my life, I was on time. Thank God for summer traffic. I think it's going to rain.'

'I see you had time to change, too.'

'Oh, I always keep a spare in the office.' She glanced at him. 'Do you like it?'

'Yes.'

'Good. I didn't think maestro Steigel approved of tee shirts and baggy trousers, so I made myself more respectable. Did the great Mr Laufer reach you?'

'He most certainly did.'

'Sorry about that. I told him where you could be reached. Is he as awful as he sounds? I've spoken to him on the phone half a dozen times, but I've never met him. What's he like?'

'High-powered, or so he sees himself, slightly neurotic, paranoid and very ambitious.'

'Sounds charming.'

'Not very. American corporate life breeds them with trained responses. He expressed great concern over Sandor Berman and even greater concern over the other three recording sessions you still have booked.'

'Good God, I hadn't even thought about them.' She drove along Piccadilly, where a group of Japanese tourists were photographing each other outside Fortnum and Mason. 'Anything new on Berman?'

'Not really. I was reading his file, but there's nothing very revealing in it. I've arranged to see his lawyer in the morning. Maybe he can help. Have you ever come across a man called Bradshaw, by the way – Lewis Bradshaw?'

'No, I can't say I have, but I'm new to the music world. Who is he?'

'I don't know.' For a reason he could not explain, he decided not to mention his phone conversation. 'He left a message for me at the hotel.'

'It doesn't ring a bell.' There was a flash of distant lightning, and Penny flinched slightly, causing the car to swerve. 'Oh Lord, I don't like that stuff! You know, it's odd, but that American girl seemed to be talking about a completely different person. She called Berman sweet and thought he was shy. Maybe she saw something in him that the rest of us missed, but those are the last words I would have used. Is it just me?'

'No. When he came to see me in Geneva, he was very self-assured and rather aggressive, but I assumed some of it was a cover-up. Musicians are sensitive people. They don't like to admit when they feel insecure.'

'Who does? But you must admit he comes on strong – came on. I keep talking about him as though he were still alive. It's all slightly unreal.'

'Yes. What do you make of Karen?'

She pursed her lips. 'Odd. I can't really make her out. One moment she was in a state of near collapse, and the next, she was completely in control. I suppose her story makes sense, but I find it hard to believe. If I had spent three days in the constant company of another person, I can't imagine myself having so little to say about it. She seems to be making an awful lot of the chastity bit, too. This is 1985.' She seemed to be concentrating very hard on her driving. 'People do get involved without feeling like scarlet women. She's very attractive.'

'I suppose so. I wonder what those phone calls were all about.'

'They could have been less than she made them out to be. Sometimes, in a new place, people sound stranger than they really are. Perhaps the caller didn't understand her American accent, or she couldn't understand him.'

'Perhaps. She was very strung up when we arrived. I'll check with her later, to see how she is.'

Penny stared straight ahead. 'I thought you might.' She drove in silence to the hotel.

Konstantin had changed into an old sports shirt and shapeless slacks. He greeted them with a benign smile, peering over the tops of his glasses. 'Come in, come in. Would you like coffee, or perhaps a drink? Heidi!' She emerged from the bedroom. 'Call the room service, please.' He sank into a heavy armchair. 'Is there any more news from this morning? What a terrible business!' He shook his head.

'The police have taken over. None of us could tell them very much about him. We'll have to wait and see what they come up with.'

'*Ja, ja.*' He sighed. 'He was a very fine musician. It's sad. There was a quality to his playing that I have not heard for a long time.' He turned to Mark. 'Perhaps, some time, you would ask them to make me a cassette of the recording. I would like to listen to it again one day.'

'Of course.' Mark hesitated for a moment. 'I spoke to New York a few minutes ago. They have a rather unusual proposal.' He told them about Greg Laufer's suggestion of releasing the 'historic document'.

Konstantin said nothing, but Heidi was angry. 'They are joking, and in a very bad taste! Surely they can't be serious?'

'Unfortunately, I think they are. I told them I would mention it to you. I also said it was most unlikely that you would even consider such an idea.'

Konstantin nodded. 'You can't give good taste to people who don't have any. No, of course they can't release such a record. Why would they do such a thing?'

Mark shrugged. 'Sales. They're not in the music world; just the selling business.'

Steigel smiled. 'I have no doubt they're planning a major campaign for me at some time in the not so distant future. They probably have the black borders all laid out in the Art department.'

'That won't be for a long time, maestro.'

'Oh, it doesn't bother me, and Heidi will enjoy better royalties.'

Heidi looked hurt. 'Tino, don't tempt providence!'

He smiled. 'Don't worry, my dear. I have no intention of departing before it is absolutely necessary. When I do, and if I'm lucky, I shall tell Brahms how they are savaging his music these days. I must also remember to ask Beethoven about that smudged note in the finale of Opus 109.' He looked up. 'If the good Lord is kind, I hope He waits until the end of the concert. I would hate to think of taking my leave before everything is resolved back into the Tonic.'

Penny said, 'This is a cheerful topic of conversation!'

Steigel beamed at her. 'You mustn't take it too seriously. Musicians are constantly preoccupied with both mortality and immortality. It comes from reading all those reference books with dates in brackets after their names. There's something slightly sinister about the little space on the right-hand side of the dash, waiting to be filled in! Well, Mark, did New York have any repeatable observations to make?'

'They wanted to know whether you would be prepared to continue recording tomorrow. They still have three sessions booked. They asked if you would record an *Eroica* in the remaining time.'

Konstantin shook his head. 'Always dollars and cents: that's how art is measured today.'

'I can tell them no, if you prefer.'

Konstantin walked to the window, looking across the river Thames. There were black clouds rolling in from the west. 'I will do it, but I have some conditions. First, I would like the words "To the memory of Sandor Berman" written in small type – and I mean *small* type – on the back of the jacket. I do not want them to make a meal of it. And I would like the money from the record to be paid to a charity . . .'

'I'm not sure whether they would be prepared to do that.'

He turned from the window. 'No, I don't mean their money. They would make such a tasteless song and dance about it that I would be embarrassed to be associated with it. Make them pay a good royalty, and use that. Choose whatever charity you think would be appropriate. I don't want anything from it.' He turned to Penny, fixing her with a glare. 'And I don't wish this to be repeated outside these four walls, young woman. It is not for public release!'

Penny gazed back at him, unafraid. 'Maestro, if I wasn't slightly scared of you, and Mrs Steigel wasn't watching me, I might just kiss you! You're a nice man.'

His voice was gruff. 'Nonsense. I'm not a nice man. I'm a conductor!' He wagged a finger. 'You stay scared, young woman!' Steigel looked at his watch. 'Now, my dears, if I'm going to record again tomorrow, I'm going to have to throw you out of here in a little while, so you had better order your drinks quickly. Heidi and I will have an early supper, I will read my scores, and go to bed. It has been a very trying day.' He smiled briefly. 'If we record the *Eroica* tomorrow morning, it means I will have the extra rehearsal they wouldn't give me when I asked for it.'

Penny said: 'I'd better call the office straight away. The orchestra will need the parts at the session, and the producer and the engineers will need to be told.' She giggled. 'The producer will probably have kittens when he learns about the last-minute changes! May I use your telephone?'

'Of course. There is one in the bedroom.' He watched her depart. 'That's a nice young woman. She reminds me a little of . . . of . . .' The old conductor was embarrassed.

'Yes, I suppose there is a resemblance.' Mark's voice was calm.

Heidi put a hand on his arm. 'She was such a lovely girl, Mark. Do you miss her so much?'

'No. Not any more.'

'We never had a chance to talk to you. Tino and I were so sorry.' Her voice faltered.

'I knew you were, thank you, but there wasn't anything to be said.' His face bore no expression. They would not understand how she had betrayed him.

Konstantin nodded. 'This one is good. I'm glad she took off her trousers.'

When they left the Steigels, the air had cooled considerably and the sky had darkened. Heavy raindrops were beginning to spatter the pavement, and a sudden roll of thunder reverberated in the short street separating the main entrance of the Savoy from the Strand. Penny took Mark's arm, wincing and closing her eyes. A moment later, lightning cracked overhead, illuminating everything with a brilliant flash of black and white.

She clung to his arm. 'Shall we make a run for it, or wait inside for a few minutes?'

'Let's run.' He was anxious to return to the Westbury. Karen should already be home from her walk.

Dodging scurrying pedestrians and traffic, they ran across the road to Exeter Street, where Penny had found a parking place. Heavy rain swept over them, and they sat listening to the steady beating of the downpour on the metal roof of the car. The windows misted rapidly, enclosing them.

'I won't drive for a minute or two, until the worst of it is over. I've always been terrified of thunderstorms.' The clatter of the raindrops was so loud that she needed to lean close, her mouth almost touching his ear. Her breath felt moist.

'It can't last very long like this. It's too heavy.' He remembered another time and place, with another woman. They had been caught in a storm near the San Bernadino Pass. They had just spent a few secret days together by Lake Maggiore, and the violence of the rain had been such that he had parked his car at the foot of some craggy hills that looked like the miniature landscapes in a Renaissance painting. They had huddled close together in the humid intimacy. It had been the first time he had told her he loved her, and they had sat, holding each other, until long after the storm had passed. It had been such a happy afternoon, hidden away from the outside world. But that was long ago – another lifetime.

There was another loud thunderclap, almost simultaneous with the lightning flash, and Penny gave a sharp intake of breath, her fingers digging into the arm of his jacket. The rain was falling so steadily that sheets of water were flowing across the misty windscreen.

He placed his hand over hers. 'That's probably the worst of it. At least it will cool the air.'

'Yes.' She shivered. 'But I hope it won't take too long to do it!'

Within minutes, the rain reduced in ferocity, and the storm moved on. Penny continued to sit with her head bowed, holding on to his arm. As the tattoo on the roof receded, she straightened, wiping the windscreen with a tiny handkerchief.

'Thank God that's over. I've always been afraid of thunder and lightning. I know there's nothing to be afraid of, and I feel so silly when it's over. It's a little like being sea-sick, isn't it? The moment the water is calm again, you wonder what all the fuss was about.' She started the engine and steered the car into the Strand, heading towards Trafalgar Square. There was only a thin drizzle of light rain, and the tyres hissed comfortably. 'I seem to spend my time thanking you for looking after me.' Mark remained silent. 'I suppose I'm trying to say that it's nice to have you around.'

As they approached the hotel, she said: 'It's still quite early, if you would like something to eat. There are dozens of places round here. Actually, I live only a few minutes away, if you want to take pot luck. I can whip up a mean omelette in a few seconds.' She smiled. 'It's all in the wrists!'

'That sounds lovely, but I think I'd better get back to my room. I've been out of touch with the world for the past twenty-four hours, and I need to make some phone calls. May I, as the Americans say, take a rain-check?'

She spoke softly. 'Of course. You've picked the right weather for it!'

'I really would enjoy it, if you'll invite me another time.'

'Yes.' She stopped the car. 'I think we're all existing on our nerve ends at the moment. It's been quite a day, one way and another.'

Mark unfastened his seat-belt and, after a moment's hesitation, she put her hands on his shoulders and kissed him, leaving her cheek against his face and moving it slightly. Her skin was warm and delicately perfumed.

'Thank you.' He felt her face move as she smiled. 'There I go again!'

'There's nothing to thank me for, and I'm glad you were there.' He opened the door, and the contact between them was broken. 'Anyway, I'll see you in the morning. I'll find you at the session when I've finished with Berman's lawyer. Try to get a good night's rest.'

'Yes, of course.' She paused before letting him go. 'It's an open invitation, Mark.'

There were no messages at the front desk. Lewis Bradshaw had not called back. Mark stopped at the news-stand to read the headlines of the evening papers. One late edition had a small column on the front page, headed 'Violinist Shot', but he did not bother to read all the details. There would be the evening news on both television channels. If there were any new developments, they would be more up to date. When he reached the door of his room, he could hear the telephone ringing inside.

'Hello.'

'Mr Holland? Mark, is that you?' It was Karen. He recognised her voice immediately. She sounded strange.

'Yes.'

There was a long pause. She seemed to be having difficulty in speaking, and he could hear her catch her breath several times before she spoke again. 'Please, can you come . . . I'm . . .'

'What is it?'

'The apartment . . . I'm . . . someone was here, while I was out. They've . . . they've . . . everything's turned upside down . . . They broke in, and I . . .'

'They? Who were they?'

She seemed to be crying. 'I was just coming in . . . They were waiting . . . No, I guess they didn't expect me . . . They threw me on the floor . . .'

'Are you all right? Did they hurt you?'

'No, I'm not hurt . . . I just fell, and they ran . . . But I'm scared! They ran out and down the stairs. It was dark . . . I couldn't see . . .' Her voice broke.

'I'll come over now. Have you called the police?'

'No. I couldn't find your number. I didn't know how to call. Then I remembered Westbury, and I . . . Oh, help me!'

Mark spoke slowly, hoping to reassure her. 'Karen, I'm going to call the police now, before I leave. Lock the door, and wait for me. Don't open it for anyone else. Just wait. I'll press the downstairs buzzer twice, so you'll know it's me. Can you hang on until I get there?'

'Yes.' It was a whisper.

'I should be there in ten minutes.'

'Please hurry. I'm scared!' She sounded like a frightened child.

'As soon as I've called the police. I'll find a taxi downstairs. I won't be more than a few minutes, I promise. Can you manage until then?'

She had already hung up.

5

The taxi seemed to be trundling up Park Street at a snail's pace, reaching each traffic light as it turned red and stopping with an infuriatingly smug acknowledgement of the law. Cars double-parked on the road forced the traffic to move in single file. With mounting impatience, Mark leaned forward to the sliding glass panel that had been left ajar.

'Can't we go any faster? I'm in a desperate hurry!'

The driver leaned back without turning his head. He was an elderly man. 'I can't go any faster, guv'nor. It's always like this when there's been a drop of rain.' They edged past another double-parked car and moved into a free lane, overtaking several vehicles. 'Look at that! If they didn't leave their bloody cars stuck in the middle of the road, there'd be room for the rest of us to move. There's too many bloody foreigners round here, and not enough bloody police. I'd tow away the lot of 'em!'

'Yes. Make it as fast as you can. It really is urgent.'

'All right, all right, but I can't go any faster than I am. Park Lane's at a standstill on the other side, and they keep jumping the lights up at the end in Oxford Street.' He shook his head with disgust. 'Bloody foreigners!'

Mark settled back uneasily in his seat, lighting a cigarette. The last of the rain had gone, and the air had cleared. Through gaps in the cross streets, he could see the sun setting over Hyde Park, casting a red glow on the roofs of the buildings. The sky above was now a deep indigo. He pulled down the window to disperse the cigarette smoke, and a cool breeze blew in his face.

In his mind, he pictured Karen, seated on the sofa of the living room, the telephone pressed to her ear, waiting for him to answer. The fear in her voice had affected him. What was happening? And how had she become involved with Sandor Berman in that oddly inappropriate flat? She too seemed out of place amid all those elegant, old-world furnishings that were brand new and, at the same time, anachronistic. They were too formal for her casual clothes and bare feet. His brain seemed to be leap-frogging from one idea to another, as if to discipline himself against the frustration of the slow-moving taxi. The flat and its furnishings must have cost a small fortune. In the old days, when you went to auctions in country houses outside the immediate vicinity of London, there had been a treasure-trove of antiques available for a few pounds, as long as the more astute local dealers were not part of a bidding ring. He had accompanied his parents on such outings. But that was long ago, fifteen or twenty years – almost before Berman was born – and before the Americans and the Dutch and the Germans had ransacked the country. The setting simply did not match the Israeli's personality. He threw the cigarette out of the window and looked at his watch. A quarter of an hour had passed, and the taxi had only reached the traffic lights in Oxford Street. A bus was blocking their path, waiting to turn, and the lights changed again. He had promised to be there sooner. Almost unconsciously, he lit another cigarette.

If the decor of the flat did not suit Berman's character, did he really know what the young man's true personality had been like? He cast his mind back to their meeting in Geneva. Berman had been aggressive in a cheerful way: cocky, self-assured, full of himself, slightly arrogant. They had talked for less than an hour and his impression had been that the violinist was determined and ambitious, confident of his musical ability, but seeking Mark's advice on the best way to 'break into' Europe. Even so, his office was not so influential that it could provide an easy *entrée* to the major European orchestras: Berlin, Vienna, Amsterdam or London. He had asked Berman why he had chosen his particular agency, but the young man had swept the question aside, explaining that his financial affairs – what financial affairs? – would bring him to Switzerland quite frequently. Having a manager in Geneva would kill two birds with one stone. Berman confessed quite openly that he had approached one or two of the most powerful English and German agents without success. Even a letter from Arnold Silverman had failed to persuade them. He had been charmingly self-deprecatory, asking for Mark's professional advice and guidance. With a frown, he realised he had been subtly lured by the Israeli's flattery. Despite his years as a manager, he was still taken in by an artist whose performances with the Suisse Romande had been so impressive. In the old days, working for Willis, he had believed in nothing except survival. That was why he had left.

His mind returned to Karen, and he looked at his watch again. Twenty minutes, and they were at last gathering speed as the cab entered Portman Square. The next traffic light was

George Street. He felt an aching desire to hold and protect her. She had been so frightened and alone that morning, with a fragile, touching beauty. There was a defenceless quality that stirred a deep emotion he had not known for a long time. And yet, as Penny had said, she had recovered surprisingly quickly, almost sending them away from the flat. Karen had described a totally different Berman to them: shy, insecure, sweet. What had she seen in him, or was it simply the differences in their ages? She couldn't be more than twenty-five to thirty, nearly half his own age. He had found her naïvety refreshing, her ignorance of the music world charming. Penny's opinion was cooler, but she came from the blasé world of television, with its surface gloss of sophistication and its jaundiced view of innocence. Why not a 'chastity bit', even in 1985?

The taxi reached the traffic lights in Seymour Place, and he leaned forward again. 'It's round the corner, on the other side of the building.'

'Right-o, guv. It didn't take long, once we got past Oxford Street. They should never have closed it off like that.'

'I thought the taxis and buses preferred to have it to themselves.'

'It doesn't make any difference in the long run, with all the other traffic having to find its way round. What they ought to do is ban all private cars from the centre of town – especially foreigners!'

Mark jumped out of the cab, leaving too much as a tip, ran to the door, and pressed the downstairs button twice. He waited to hear her voice on the intercom, but the lock buzzed almost immediately, allowing him into the foyer. She must have been waiting by the door, or watching from the window. He ran up the stairs, two at a time, and arrived breathless at the second floor. The door of the flat was open.

Karen was standing in the shadowy hall, her hand at her face. She was dressed as before, except that she was wearing open sandals. He noticed a red mark, little more than a flush, on her right cheek, when she withdrew her hand. She did not move when he entered the flat, closing and bolting the door, but when he turned to face her, she ran into his arms, her face pressed against his chest, her own arms locked around his waist. He had not expected it, and held her tightly.

It seemed a very long time before she spoke. Her voice was low. 'Thank God you're here.' The pressure of her arms increased. 'Oh Christ, it was awful!'

The hallway was dark. When he had entered, the light from the landing had shone on her, but it had been shut off when he closed the door. He leaned his head down, so that his face brushed against her hair. 'It's all right. Tell me what happened.'

She sighed deeply, keeping her head against his chest. 'It was all over so quickly. Jesus, I didn't know what was happening to me.' She lapsed into silence again.

He waited, conscious of her body pressed against his. Her perfume seemed very pervasive. 'Can you talk about it?'

She nodded without letting go. There were long pauses between sentences. 'I waited for a while, after you'd gone. I was feeling a little dizzy. I guess I was more shocked than I realised at the time. I had another drink, but it didn't help. I thought I was going to throw up, so I lay down for a while. I must have fallen asleep. Anyway, when I woke up, my head was aching, and I washed my face and drank a whole lot of water.' She seemed to be reliving her actions, step by step, and he did not interrupt. 'The apartment was kind of hot and sticky. I guess they don't have air-conditioning here, do they? I thought I'd take a walk to clear my head. I must have walked a long time. I went into the big park – is that Hyde Park? – and I walked to the lake with the people in row-boats. There was a hot dog stand, and I bought one, but it tasted horrible – all mushy – and I threw it away. I guess I thought I was hungry.' She paused for a while, as though collecting her thoughts. 'I heard thunder in the distance, and it started to get cold, so I headed back. I walked fast, to beat the rain. It made me feel better. It got so dark, all of a sudden.'

She stopped, and Mark turned her body slightly, so that she could walk towards the living room. She seemed to resist, and they remained standing together, side by side. He put his arm around her shoulder, and she clung again to him. The sun had set, and the hall was almost totally dark, with only a glimmer of light from the open doorway of the living room. Mark guessed that it came from a street-lamp outside.

'What happened next?'

The pressure of her arms increased again. Her face was pressed against him, muffling her words. 'It was starting to rain as I came down the street, so I ran the last few yards. I was feeling better, and my head had cleared. I came up in the elevator, and the landing outside the apartment was dark. I guess they hadn't bothered to turn on the lights inside, and the storm made everything darker than usual.' She paused. 'I went to put my key in the door, and it just – opened. I remember I thought it was strange. I was sure I had pulled it shut when I left. You don't have to lock it. I pushed the door open and walked in, and . . . and . . .' She trembled.

'Tell me.'

'There were two of them. Two men. They were standing, just inside the hall. It was dark, and I couldn't really see them. Then there was a flash of lightning, and I saw them standing there, looking at me. Oh God, I was so scared! I started to say something, and one of them grabbed a hold of me and threw me down on the floor. I thought I was going to faint. I think I wanted to. Then I wanted to call out, or something, but my voice wouldn't work. I just lay there, with my eyes shut, waiting for them to hit me. There was a big crash of thunder, and I felt a rush of cold wind and a slight thump as the front door closed. I didn't know if they were still there, so I just lay with my eyes shut, waiting. I don't know how long I was like that. I remember putting my arms over my head, to protect myself, but nothing happened.' She lapsed into silence again. Her voice became calmer. 'After a while, I realised they must have gone, but I went on lying there, with the lightning flashing, and the thunder . . . I thought I was going mad!'

Mark nodded, but it was now so dark that she could only have sensed the movement. He said: 'What did you do?'

'After a while, I got up. I went to the bathroom and ran cold water on my face. I didn't turn on the light. I was still too scared. Then I walked into the living room and saw what they had done. There was a flash of lightning as I walked in, and I could see it all, like a kind of nightmare. I think I must have backed out of the room, afraid to look, and I felt the wall behind me, and sat down, kind of hunched up, waiting for the storm to stop. I don't know how long I was like that.' She trembled violently with the memory, and Mark placed his arms firmly around her, holding her tightly. She pressed herself against him.

'Go on talking. It sometimes helps to get it all said.' He was again conscious of the contours of her body.

'When the rain stopped, it got lighter, and I went into the kitchen. There was more light in there, from the doorway on to the little terrace out back. I sat in a chair for a few minutes, trying to get my head straight, and then I thought of you. You're the only person I know in London; you and that girl. When you were here this morning, you said you would give me a number to call, but you didn't.'

'No, I forgot.'

'But I remembered you'd said Westbury. There's a wall phone in the kitchen, so I dialled the operator. I kept dialling "o", but nothing happened. I thought I was going crazy! Then I remembered it was different here, and dialled "One-o-o", and tried to talk to the operator. He must have thought I was out of my mind, but he was very good about it. I was babbling! He told me how to dial "Enquiries", and they gave me your number.' She paused again. Her voice was soft. 'I was so grateful when you answered.' She was silent, clinging to him.

At length, Mark said: 'The two men who were here; would you recognise either of them again?'

He felt her shudder. 'No, I don't think so. I'd never seen them before, and it was such a shock – like a bad dream. I expected the hall to be empty, and when the lightning flashed and I saw them, I was paralysed. All I saw were two faces, very white in the flash. I don't know why I couldn't scream. My throat just dried up on me. One of them was bigger than the other, but that's all I remember. The bigger one grabbed me and threw me over.'

'Were you hurt?'

'No, just shocked and scared. I think my face hit the floor. It feels bruised. Oh God, it was terrifying!' She buried her face against him, cutting off further conversation.

After a long time, she relaxed. They remained standing in the darkness of the hallway, silent, their arms encircling each other. Occasionally, the headlights of a passing car threw long, sinuous shadows through the open doorway of the living room. A heavy lorry, turning the corner of the street, changed gears with a metallic grinding. Slowly, she reduced the pressure of her arms until she let them fall to her sides, and moved a step back. She said nothing, but Mark could sense her drawing away from him, as though embarrassed by the sudden intimacy of the preceding minutes.

When she spoke, her voice was low. 'You'd better have a look at what they've done.'

'Yes. Where's the light switch?'

'There's one at either end of the hall, by the door.'

He moved cautiously in the dark, feeling his way along the wall towards the master bedroom until he found a switch. The sudden light from the chandeliers seemed painfully bright. Karen was standing where he had left her, her arms still at her sides, her face down, her eyes closed. She did not move as he walked past her to the door of the living room and switched on the lights.

The room had been ransacked. Drawers had been pulled from the writing table and the desk, their contents thrown across the floor, and the armchairs had been turned over. The sofa had been dragged towards the centre of the room and tipped on its back. The two rectangular cushions that had formed seats had been removed, their covering slashed. At first sight, it looked like spiteful vandalism.

Karen stood in the doorway. 'Oh my God! What have they done? Why?'

It was the same in both bedrooms. The bedclothes had been strewn on the floor, mattresses up-ended, and the contents of the cupboards lay in heaps across the carpet. There was a long gash, made by a sharp knife, the length of each box-spring. Karen followed him from room to room, watching from each doorway, as if afraid to enter. Mark walked among the debris, trying to avoid the clothing and papers scattered around his feet.

His eyes met hers. 'We should try not to touch anything, for the moment, until the police arrive. I'm surprised they've taken so long to get here.'

She frowned, shaking her head slowly, and walking into the hall. At the door of the kitchen, she said: 'They didn't touch this room.'

'Perhaps they heard you coming in before they got to it.'

'I suppose. I guess it's as well Sandy hadn't installed all his things from New York. There wasn't that much for them to damage.'

'Yes.' Mark paused by the door of the bathroom, switching on the light. It, too, had been torn apart, the contents of a mirrored cabinet scattered across the tiled floor. They had even taken off the lid of the lavatory cistern. The cupboard containing the safe revealed more chaos. Shoes and coats had been swept from their storage places, lying in a heap by the door. Whoever they were, they appeared to have made a thorough search. But for what?

When Karen rejoined him, he asked: 'Can you see if anything is missing?'

'I don't know. I can't tell. I don't remember what was here.'

'Leave it for the moment. The police should be here any time.'

'Can we sit in the kitchen? I'm still feeling shaky, and there doesn't seem to be any place else.'

'Of course. Would you like a drink?' She shook her head, grimacing. 'How about coffee?'

'Okay. I can do that. It's only Instant.'

At that moment, a buzzer by the front door sounded. It startled her. 'That's the downstairs bell.'

'It's probably the police.'

She trembled visibly. 'You answer it.'

What was it Mark Twain had said about policemen getting younger all the time? The two men who entered were both in their middle to late twenties and, like the Inspector he had met that morning – God, was it as recent as that? – were dressed in the approved television uniforms: shabby raincoats, the belts tied in knots at the waist, ties loosened at the neck. Only their hair had the suggestion of regulation neatness. He wondered whether they would refer to the intruders as 'villains' or, worse still, 'chummy'. They identified themselves, but he did not catch their names; only that they came from Robbery Division.

One seemed to be the senior of the two. He had dark hair, and Mark noticed a small scar high on his cheekbone. He wondered inconsequentially whether it was an honourable wound from a past encounter with 'chummy'.

'I'm glad you're here. The place is a mess.'

'You're lucky we are. We were on our way off duty when the call came in.' He had a West Country accent. Looking into the living room, he nodded his head at the wreckage, his expression impersonal. 'Are you the owner of the premises?'

'No, I'm a – colleague of the owner.' To describe himself as a friend seemed inappropriate. 'My name is Mark Holland.'

The policeman did not seem to notice. 'I see. And the young lady?'

'She's a friend of the owner, staying here. She's on holiday from America. Her name is Miss Ackerman – Karen Ackerman.'

The second policeman said: 'Can I use your phone? I'd like to check in.'

'Help yourself.' The man departed towards the kitchen.

The first man was making notes. 'Are you staying here too?'

'No, I'm at the Westbury Hotel. I live in Geneva.'

'Right.' He scribbled again. 'Where is the owner, then?'

'He's dead.' The man's eyebrows rose. 'He died this morning. Somebody shot him. He was the violinist Sandor Berman.'

'Oh yes?' He became more interested. 'I noticed the name on the plate downstairs. I saw something about that business in the evening papers. Shot over at Kingsway Hall, wasn't he?' Mark nodded. 'That's quite a coincidence.'

'You don't think this is connected with it?'

'I don't know.' He gave Mark a sharp look. 'Do you?'

'I'm not sure. I don't really know, either, but it could be.'

The man shrugged. 'It's unlikely. There are forty or fifty break-ins a day in the West End, especially these old buildings. You'd be amazed how easy it is to open a front door with a bit of plastic card, and nobody ever thinks it's going to be their place that's going to get done over. I looked at the lock as we came in. It's useless against any kind of professional.' He surveyed the living room, hands on hips. 'They've made a right old shambles of this lot. What's missing?'

'We don't know. It's going to be hard to tell. Neither of us knew the place very well – nor Berman, for that matter.' He followed the man across the room. 'Don't you think it's possible that there's a connection with his death?'

'I can't say, on the face of it. Looks like a normal break-in to me. Anyway, we're Robbery Division, so we don't have any special information. Any idea who's in charge on this morning's job?' Mark reached into a pocket and handed him the Inspector's card. He copied the name into his notes before handing it back. 'I'll give him a call later on. I don't think I know him. Were you there when it happened?'

'At Kingsway Hall? Yes. I was his manager.'

'And the young lady?'

'No. She was here.'

'I see.' He looked through the doorway towards the kitchen, where Karen was making coffee, and lowered his voice. 'What's the young lady's relationship to the owner,' he consulted his notes, 'Mr Berman?'

'She's just a friend. They met a few days ago in France, and he offered to put her up while she was in London.'

'Oh.' He glanced at Karen, and turned back to Mark with an appreciative smile. 'Very nice!'

Mark kept his voice even. 'I think they were what the newspapers call "just good friends", but you'd have to ask her about that.' The man's assumption irritated him.

The policeman nodded. 'Well, maybe she can help. Now, what makes you think there's a connection with this morning?' His voice had hardened.

'From the look of the place. They appear to have been searching for something.'

'Not really. They usually empty everything out as quickly as possible, so they can spot any valuables without wasting time.'

'Then why slash the cushions? You'll find they've done the same to the beds.'

'Money. You'd be surprised where people hide their cash. If they're pros, they know where to look. They're on to all the tricks.' He glanced around the room. 'Fancy sort of place, isn't it? You can see it's worth a few bob. They could have been watching it for some time.' He looked at Mark. 'You don't seem very convinced.'

'I'm not.'

'Why?'

'I'm not sure. I have the feeling the rooms have been thoroughly searched. Nothing appears to be missing, and I still find it hard to believe they would cut their way through cushions and beds so systematically.'

'I told you. That's the first place . . .'

'The other reason is that there's a large safe installed in the cupboard in the hall. With something like that in the flat, why bother to hide anything in the mattresses?'

The second policeman had rejoined them. 'Maybe they didn't know about the safe when they started working the place over.' He had a London accent. 'The natural way would be to go through the rooms. They'd come to the cupboard last.'

Mark nodded. 'I hadn't thought of that, but they even took the lid off the loo in the bathroom. That's a funny place to look for valuables, isn't it?'

The policemen exchanged glances, but made no comment. West Country said: 'The main thing to check is what's missing.' Karen had entered the room carrying a tray with four mugs of coffee. 'Did you have any jewellery with you, Miss? They usually go after anything small that fits into a pocket or a bag. Some of them will walk out of the building, cool as a cucumber, carrying everything in a plastic carrier-bag.'

Karen stood still, looking from one to the other. 'I don't have anything valuable.'

The policemen helped themselves to coffee and sugar, while Mark again looked round the living room. The Picasso prints were hanging at odd angles, as if they had been moved aside in case they concealed anything. There was a blank space on the wall above the Sheraton bureau.

'Just a minute. There was a picture over the desk when I was here this morning. I remember looking at it.'

The policeman ploughed his way through the flotsam and searched around the floor under papers. 'There's nothing down here.' He stood, examining the wall over the desk. 'There was a picture there at some time. The hanger's still there. Would you recognise it if you saw it?'

'I doubt it. It was a small oil painting. I remember noticing it because it looked like Chagall.'

'I see.' He made a note. 'Would that be valuable?'

'Yes. Not a fortune, but a fair amount, if it was genuine.'

'Now we're getting somewhere. About what size would the painting be?'

'I can't remember. It had a narrow frame, quite ornate. I'd say the overall size was about eighteen by twelve. I can't be sure. I only glanced at it briefly. Do you remember it, Karen?' She shook her head.

The policeman seemed pleased. 'What was it a picture of?'

Mark closed his eyes. 'I couldn't describe it in detail. I think it was a man sitting by a camp fire at night, playing a violin. He was dressed in a sort of mauve and red coat.'

'Would you know it if you saw it again?'

'Not necessarily. It was a typical Chagall. He must have painted dozens like it. I still don't know if it was an original. It certainly looked like one, but I'm not an expert.'

The policeman was writing. 'Is that "C-h-a-g-a-l"?'

'Two "l"s.'

'Right.' He closed his note-book. 'Well, I think you've got your answer. There may be other things missing, but we can start with this. If you don't mind, I'd prefer that you left the rooms as they are. You can move the soft materials back, if you want, but we'll send fingerprint people over in the morning, in case they can come up with anything. I doubt if they will. It looks like a professional job. Now,' he looked at Karen, 'will you be staying on at the flat for the moment?'

She glanced quickly in Mark's direction. 'Yes.'

'Good. We can have somebody over about ten o'clock, if you'll let him in. If you think of anything else that's missing, just write it down. We'll need to make a list.' He turned to Mark. 'I think you said you'd be at the Westbury. How long will you be staying there?'

'I don't know. Several more days.'

'Then we can reach you there. I'll call my colleague about this morning, but I wouldn't worry too much about it, if I were you. It looks like an unhappy coincidence.'

'Perhaps. Karen – Miss Ackerman – actually saw the two men who were here.'

'Did she?' The policeman regarded her with new interest. 'What happened?'

Karen repeated her story, less hesitantly than before. From time to time, she glanced in Mark's direction, as though seeking his confirmation. The presence of the three men reassured her, and she spoke rapidly and in a low voice.

When she had finished, the policeman said: 'Are you sure you wouldn't recognise them if you saw them again?'

'I don't think so. It was all so quick, and there was just the one flash of lightning. I was too frightened.'

'All right.' He put the note-book in his raincoat pocket. 'We'll probably come back to you. You never know, once the shock's worn off, you may remember things you can't think of at the moment. I'll give you a call tomorrow, when you've had a chance to rest.'

'Yes.' Her voice was barely audible.

The second man said: 'You had a lucky escape, Miss. Some of these villains,' Mark winced inwardly, 'can be pretty violent. We'll call again, in case you remember something.' He looked at both of them. 'When you've had a chance to clear up and look around, you may notice something else missing.'

The two men walked to the door. The senior man said: 'You'll be hearing from us.' He paused, slightly embarrassed. 'I'm sorry about your friend.'

When they had gone, Mark turned to Karen. 'I don't think you should stay on here.'

'I'll be all right.'

'Don't you think it would be more sensible to move to a hotel, after what's happened?' She shook her head, and walked into the kitchen. Mark followed her. 'Why not?'

Karen sat suddenly in one of the chairs, as though exhausted. Her voice was near to tears. 'I don't have any money. Sandy was going to lend me some, to keep me going until I called my parents.'

'Oh.'

She looked at him. 'I couldn't phone them until tomorrow. They're away at the moment, on vacation. Sandy said he'd cover me until they got home. I was going to ask them to send it through American Express . . .' Her eyes misted.

'That's no problem. I can help you if . . .'

'No.'

'Why not?'

'Because. I'm staying here. There's no need. I have enough to keep going – honest! I don't want to borrow from you.'

'If it's only for a few days . . .'

'No.' Her voice was sharp.

'You shouldn't stay here. Not after this.'

'I'll be all right.' She gave a rueful smile. 'What else can happen?'

'I'm not sure. I'm still not convinced about the break-in.'

She sighed. 'They took the painting. Those policemen seem convinced.'

'What about the phone calls?'

'Oh.' Fear returned to her eyes. 'I hadn't thought about them.'

He stood by the chair, placing a hand on her shoulder. It felt very warm. 'Don't you think you'd be better off away from here?' She shook her head silently, moving her shoulders as if to free herself of his touch. 'Did you call the Inspector?' Again, a silent head-shake.

'I was going to call him when I came back. I'll call him in the morning. Not tonight. I'm very tired.'

'All right.' He came to a decision. 'I'll stay too.' She started to protest, but his voice cut across hers. 'You can't stay here alone, and if you're not prepared to move to a hotel, I'm going to stay too. We can decide what to do in the morning.'

'But there's no need . . .'

'Maybe, but I'd feel happier to be around, in case that damned phone starts ringing again.' With an air of resignation, she nodded, seeming to sink further into the chair. She looked exhausted. 'There are two bedrooms, so I'll sleep in the spare one, next to the front door, and you can have the master bedroom at the end of the hall.' He hesitated. 'If it worries you to be in there, we can make up a bed on the sofa in the living room.'

'No.' Her voice was a monotone. 'I don't care. I'm too tired to care.'

'All right. Drink your coffee, and we'll tidy the place up. Try not to touch anything that might hold a fingerprint. If you'll sleep at the far end, we don't have to bother with the living room tonight. Would you like something to eat?' She shook her head. 'Let's see how you feel later.'

It took them more than half an hour to restore some sort of order to the bedrooms, remaking the beds and returning clothes to closets. They left the polished wood drawers of the bedside tables and the large chest in the master bedroom lying where they had found them, their contents scattered about the carpet. The activity helped to revive Karen's spirits, and she moved briskly between the rooms, also taking time to replace clothes in the hall cupboard.

Standing by the doorway, watching her, Mark said: 'I wish we knew what he kept in that safe. It could contain a lot of answers.'

She continued to hang clothes. 'I wouldn't know. I don't really remember seeing him use it.'

He walked into the kitchen and foraged in the refrigerator and among the shelves. 'What about some food now? There seems to be plenty here. Would you like something light, like an omelette?' For a moment, he thought of Penny.

Karen joined him. 'No. Maybe a piece of toast. There are some packets of instant soup. How about you?'

'Sounds good. I haven't eaten all day.'

'I'll do it.' She busied herself, working in silence. The effort of tidying the rooms seemed to have exhausted her again.

They ate without talking, sitting together at the small kitchen table. Mark's efforts to start a conversation were blocked by her monosyllabic replies, and she appeared to have withdrawn again, lost in thought. From time to time, he watched her face. It was cool and immobile.

When they had finished, she removed plates and glasses, stacking them in the sink. 'I'm going to bed. I'll look after these things in the morning.' She turned towards Mark, her eyes still avoiding his. 'Thank you for everything. I don't know what I would have done without you here.'

Mark looked at his watch. 'Damn! I meant to watch the ten o'clock news. There should have been something about Berman.'

Her voice was colourless. 'He didn't have a television. He was going to rent one this week.' She walked to the door. 'I'm very tired.' He heard her enter the bedroom and close the door. He almost expected to hear the sound of a key turning in the lock.

Mark dozed fitfully, lying on top of the bed. The air had become warm and humid again and, even with the window open, the duvet was too heavy. The street outside was surprisingly quiet for central London. An occasional car passed, its tyres hissing on the wet tarmac. He wondered whether it had started to drizzle with rain. The old building creaked quietly, as though settling down for the night. He found an ashtray amid the clutter on the floor, and lit a cigarette. Its red glow momentarily illuminated the close surroundings each time he drew on it, but the smoke tasted bitter, and he stubbed it out again. He was conscious of Karen's perfume on the pillow. It drew his memory back to the earlier part of the evening, when he had stood in the hall, holding her tightly, feeling her breasts pressing against him in the darkness. The events of the day seemed to melt into each other. Karen's face dissolved and became Penny's as she had leaned forward in the car to place her cheek against his, her hands pressing on his shoulders. Was she just being friendly, with a 'show-biz' embrace, or was there really an open invitation to return her affection? Konstantin and Heidi had been right. There was a distinct similarity to Anne-Marie, except that the Swiss girl had been less demonstrative. And less honest. But Anne-Marie was gone, leaving him to the solitude of his memories. He closed his mind against the thoughts. With slight surprise, he realised that the opening theme of the Beethoven Violin Concerto had been running through his head, repeating itself over and over, but it seemed to be coming from a distant place, perhaps cut off by a closed door. Penny had taken his hand in the little dressing room at the back of Kingsway Hall. All her gestures had been intimate, almost from the moment they had met. Show-biz! He shifted position on the unfamiliar bed, turning his face sideways against the pillow and inhaling Karen's perfume. Sandor Berman's voice suddenly mocked him. 'Every great violin makes a sound of its own, just like a woman. It depends how you stroke it. Just like a woman . . .' Slowly, the images faded, and he fell asleep.

He awoke suddenly, strangely alert, lying on his back. The room was dark and, looking towards the window, he could see a filter of yellow light from the street lamp outside. He did not know how long he had been sleeping, but it was still night. He was about to sink back to sleep again, when he heard a noise. It was the creaking of a floorboard, distinct in itself and different from the nocturnal groanings of the building. Perhaps it came from the flat upstairs. He strained his ears and, again, the sound was repeated. It was too close to be from a different flat.

Mark swung his legs off the bed and, after feeling around in the dark, pulled on his shirt and trousers. He moved quickly across the room on tiptoes, irritated when a floorboard beneath his foot moved and complained. He edged the door open, and was surprised to see a thin shaft of light across the hall floor. The front door of the flat was open, letting in light from the landing. He stood for a moment, uncertain. Could the policemen have left the front door ajar when they went out, so that it had blown open in the night? He had not bothered to check it before going to bed. Or Karen, had she for some reason gone out? He looked down the hall towards her room, and saw a faint glimmer of light coming from the cupboard containing the safe.

He walked carefully down the hall, hoping to make no sound. Another board creaked, and the light from the cupboard disappeared. Someone was in there. His eyes were adjusting to the darkness, and he was aware of a faint ray of light coming from the glass fanlight above the living room door. Passing before it, he faced the darkened cupboard, and was about to pull the drawstring that would illuminate it when a sudden, agonising blow to his stomach made him double up in pain. He threw himself sideways, his shoulder hitting the floor, inwardly cursing himself for not turning on the hall chandeliers with the switch by the front door. Whoever was in the cupboard must have seen him silhouetted against the glow from the fanlight and had kicked at him as he moved forward. He sensed rather than saw his assailant move into the hall and, swivelling his body, threw both legs out, knee-high from the ground, with all his strength. He heard a groan of pain as they connected with flesh and bone, and there was a heavy thud as his attacker fell to the floor. He could see a man outlined against the light from the front door and, drawing in his legs, prepared to spring at him. The man rolled sideways with a grunt, and Mark landed on the floor, his body crashing painfully against the man's outstretched leg. The man gave a cry of pain, and chopped down on the back of Mark's neck with the edge of his hand. The blow was fierce, and Mark felt his senses reeling. He put out his arms to grab at the man, and a second heavy blow landed on the back of his head, behind his ear. He hung on grimly, his hands reaching for the man's throat, but a third blow caught him on the temple, and he felt himself slipping into unconsciousness. His fingers raked against sweaty skin, trying to dig his nails into soft flesh, but the man's arm was preparing to swing again. He relaxed one hand, putting it up to protect his head, but there was another crushing blow, which smashed against his fingers. He was vaguely conscious that the man must be holding a cloth-covered cosh of some sort. Darkness enclosed him, and he could feel the body next to his writhing free. His arms would not obey him and, as he rolled clear, the man kicked savagely at his ribs, freeing himself. Through half-closed eyes, he was aware that the man was already on his feet, standing over him.

He shook his head in an effort to regain his senses, and tried to stand. He was vaguely conscious of a swish of air before a hammering pain struck the base of his skull, and everything disappeared in the blackness.

6

He was conscious of a slow hammering in his temples, like an agonised heart-beat, bringing with it waves of needle-sharp pain. His arms and legs felt paralysed, lifeless, and there was a gnawing ache in his side. From a great distance, a voice seemed to be calling his name and, concentrating his efforts, he tried to move his body. Spasms of raw pain convulsed him, and he sank back into the darkness. The voice continued to call, approaching and withdrawing through waves of nausea. He lay very still, breathing shallowly until the throbbing reduced in intensity. The voice returned, more insistently, and his senses slowly focused.

There was brilliant light, painful against his eyelids, and he turned his head sideways, fighting the burning jabs at the base of his skull. He slowly opened his eyes, wincing as the light stabbed at them, and recognised Karen's voice.

'Mark! Please say something! Oh Mark, what happened?'

The nausea receded as his eyes adjusted to the light. He was lying on the floor of the hall, his head and shoulders cradled in Karen's arms. Turning his head painfully slowly, he looked up to see her face, upside-down, close to his. Her eyes were wide, and her body exuded a strong, feral odour. He closed his eyes again for a moment, summoning resources of strength, and felt her fingers stroking his forehead. They were cool and soothing.

'Oh God! I thought you were dead!'

His voice sounded strangely remote. 'I'll be all right in a moment. Let me rest.'

She held him silently, rocking gently, her hands continuing to stroke his face. Her body felt warm against his shoulders. He relaxed completely, forcing himself to float on the brink of consciousness, and the pain slowly diminished in intensity. The throbbing subsided, and he cautiously took deeper breaths. The pain in his ribs slackened to a dull ache. When he opened his eyes again, he could only see the white of the ceiling. Karen had disappeared from view. He shifted his head slightly, to see that she had leaned back on her haunches, her eyes shut. Tears were running down her face, and she was biting against her lip to keep from sobbing. With an effort, he drew in his legs and put out an arm to steady himself. She helped raise his body until he was sitting upright, holding his shoulders until he regained his equilibrium. He leaned forward, resting his arms against his knees.

He said: 'There's brandy in the living room,' and she ran through to find it, her bare feet soundless on the carpet. She held the glass to his lips, and he sipped slowly. The liquid burned for a moment as it spread on his tongue, but he could feel his senses returning. Taking the glass from her, he drank a mouthful. Kneeling at his side, she watched him in silence. After a few minutes, she helped him to his feet, and he walked stiffly to the kitchen, testing the pain with his movements. He sat on one of the hard-backed chairs and drank the rest of the brandy.

Karen wiped her face with a Kleenex. 'Do you want more?' He shook his head. 'What happened?' She sat in the chair opposite, watching him. She was wearing a cotton dressing-gown over a pair of man's pyjamas. From the length of the trousers, which were rolled up around her ankles, Mark guessed that they belonged to Berman.

'We had a visitor.'

'Who?'

'I don't know. I woke up and heard a noise in the hall. The front door was open. Someone was in the cupboard where the safe is.' He smiled, shaking his head. 'I did just about every bloody thing wrong!'

'But who was it?'

'I don't know. I should have turned on the hall lights before anything else. Instead, I tried to surprise him in the dark, and he hit me first. He must have seen me against the light. We struggled on the floor for a minute, but he had a cosh, and got in a couple of hard ones before I could stop him.' He felt his face and forehead gingerly. There was slight swelling on his left temple. 'He must have knocked me cold and run for it.'

'Oh God! Are you badly hurt?'

'I don't think so – just a bit bruised and battered. I think my pride is more damaged than I am. I behaved like an amateur; made every mistake in the book!'

She looked at him curiously. 'Amateur?' She was puzzled.

He hesitated before replying. This was the wrong time to tell her about his past. 'I once took a course in unarmed combat, something like those karate classes you have in the States. If I'd been more alert, I wouldn't have made such stupid mistakes.' He smiled grimly. 'You would have found him lying on the floor.'

She was close to tears. 'You were just lying there.'

'Yes. I don't know how long I was out.'

Her eyes never left his. 'I must have been sleeping deeply. There was some sort of a crash. I remember opening my eyes and wondering if it was part of a dream. Then I heard the front door shut with a loud bang, and got up to see what was happening. I opened the door, and everything was quiet, so I thought it must have been my imagination.' She paused for a moment, as if remembering. 'No, wait! I heard a car starting up. It drove away very quickly. I heard the wheels skidding. I remember thinking that someone was going home very late.' She looked at her watch. 'It's after four. I was just turning round to go back into my room, when I heard you groan. I turned on the light, and you were lying there. You were so still, I thought . . .' Her voice failed.

Mark nodded. 'I could use some more of that brandy.' He started to get up, but she ran to the hall, returning with the bottle. He poured half a glass, drinking it in a single swallow. The liquid revived him.

'How badly are you hurt?'

'Nothing broken. A couple of kicks in the stomach and ribs, and a few cracks on the head. I'll survive.'

'Are you in pain?'

'Not too bad.' He grinned crookedly. 'Only when I laugh!'

'Oh Christ, this is like a nightmare! What do we do now?' She was trembling violently, as though suddenly cold. Mark flexed his limbs, stretching his neck slowly from side to side. He massaged the back of his head. It still hurt, but it was under control. 'I suppose we should call the police.'

She hesitated. 'Must we?'

'Why not?'

'Because it's so late. He's gone, and there's not much they can do right now. Wouldn't it be better to wait until the morning? Maybe it would be better to call a doctor.'

'No, I don't need one. You're probably right. They'd take God knows how long to get here. We might as well try and rest. I could kick myself for not bolting the front door. That was plain stupid of me.'

'How did he get in?'

'You heard the policemen when they were here. You can open that lock with a piece of plastic card. If I'd bolted the bloody door, he wouldn't have managed so easily.'

'But why, Mark? What do they want?'

'The safe. He went straight for it. They must have found it when they were here before. They obviously think there's something worth taking, or they wouldn't have risked coming back. If they knew this was Sandor's flat, they could have been after the violins.'

'Are they worth that much?'

'About a million and a half dollars.' Her eyes widened. 'Even on the black market, they could find buyers for them.'

'Oh God! I never realised. Sandy told me they were valuable, but I had no idea they were worth that much.'

'If that was what they were after. It's only guess-work on my part. It could also have been that they saw the flat and calculated that a safe as big as this one would have to contain something worth taking. They took the risk that you were alone here.' She shivered. 'That's strange.'

'Why?'

'Because, when they were here before, they must have seen Sandor's clothes. How did they know he wouldn't be here?'

'I don't know.'

'Unless they knew he was already dead.' Mark frowned. 'I still think those damned policemen made too much of coincidence.'

Karen's voice was low. 'Maybe it would have been better if I had been here alone. I might have slept through it and never known.'

'On the other hand, you could have walked in on him . . .' She trembled again. 'I'd like to take a quick look at that safe.'

Mark got up slowly. The brandy had revived him and, although he was still stiff and bruised, the throbbing in his head had diminished to a slight ache.

The hall cupboard revealed little. The safe remained unopened, and there was a small bicycle torch, propped against some clothes scattered on the floor. From the direction in which it pointed, the intruder had used it for light. On the floor in front of the safe, there was a doctor's stethoscope.

Mark motioned to Karen not to enter the cupboard. 'There might be some useful fingerprints in there, but I doubt it. It looks as though he was a professional.'

'Why the stethoscope?'

'To listen to the tumblers in the safe. Those Chubbs usually have three settings, and you turn the dial back and forward to the right numbers. If you listen with a stethoscope and turn the dial very slowly, you can hear the tumblers falling into place.'

'How long was he here?'

'Not more than a few minutes, at a guess. I woke up when I heard the floorboards creak, probably as he was going down the hall. I know, because the same board creaked when I was going after him. He must have heard it. Anyway, we'll leave that to the police.' He walked to the front door and bolted it securely. 'At least he won't be back.'

Karen was leaning against the wall. The shadows under her eyes were pronounced. 'Mark, I'm frightened!' He walked quickly towards her, but she raised a hand as if to forbid contact. 'I'm only just realising what would have happened if you hadn't been here.'

'It didn't happen. There's no point in worrying about it.'

'I don't think I can sleep.'

'You will, in a while. Why don't you have a drink? It will settle your nerves.'

'Okay.' She walked into the kitchen and poured herself a large brandy. Making a face, she drank too quickly, choking on it. 'Do you suppose they'll try to get in again?'

'I don't think so. He probably got the surprise of his life to find me here.'

She nodded, but her eyes were frightened. 'They might make another try. This old building has so many bits and pieces stuck to its outside. It must be easy to climb in through a window. You read about second-storey men . . .'

Mark laughed. The sound was strange. 'I think you're letting your imagination get the better of you. People leaping around the outsides of London mansions aren't a very familiar local sight. Go back to bed. You'll be safe.'

She stood still. 'I'm scared!'

Without speaking, Mark walked down the hall to the spare bedroom. He could feel his strength returning. Reaching down, he pulled the bedclothes free, and lifted the mattress off the box-spring. It was surprisingly light, and he carried it to the master bedroom, placing it along the wall next to the door. Karen watched him.

'I'm going to leave the hall lights on, in case anyone has ideas about a return visit. You get back into bed, and I'll sleep here. We'll sort it all out in the morning.' She followed him meekly into the bedroom and he closed the door. The room was suddenly dark. 'Would you like the light on?'

'No.' There was a rustling of bedclothes.

Mark lay down on the mattress, still clothed. His body ached, but his head was clear.

'Mark?'

'Yes?'

'Are you okay there?'

'Yes.'

'Are you in pain?'

'Not really. If he tries to come back, he'll have a better reception than last time.'

'Yes.' A long pause. 'Mark?'

'Yes?'

'Can you sleep?'

'I will, in a while. How about you?'

'Yes, I guess so. And Mark?'

'Yes?'

'Thank you.'

'Don't worry about it. Try and sleep.'

'Yes.' She sounded very young.

She was silent, and he shifted position on the mattress, making himself comfortable. He turned on his right side, to ease the pain in his ribs, and thought: 'Bastard!' He moved slightly. 'I should have remembered to put on my shoes. In the old days, I would have chopped him down with one hand tied behind my back. I handled the whole thing like a bloody amateur! I'm too old for this kind of thing!'

He lay in the darkness, listening to her uneven breathing and wondering whether she would speak again. She had talked like a child afraid of the dark, making conversation for the reassuring sound of another voice. He could detect the faintest trace of her perfume. He waited, and her breathing slowly became more regular, until he was sure that she was sleeping. Nervous exhaustion coupled with a large glass of brandy had finally released her. He wondered hazily whether she would be troubled by nightmares, but as tiredness enfolded him, felt himself gently drifting into a dreamless sleep of his own.

He awoke a little after seven. His eyes opened and he lay motionless, listening to the sounds around him. A milkman was delivering supplies, rattling crates and clinking bottles in the street below. He was talking to someone by the entrance to the building. Mark could hear the distinctive whine of an electric van. Karen had not closed the curtains of the bedroom, and the overcast sky outside was grey and forbidding after the warm sunlight of the previous day. His body felt sore, and he shifted position cautiously, checking his injuries. There was a slight ache in his side, but his head felt clear.

Karen was still asleep, huddled beneath a duvet, her face

barely visible. The coverlet hardly stirred. Moving slowly to avoid awakening her, he slipped out of the room. His legs and arms ached, but the movement helped loosen his muscles, and he padded down the hall to the bathroom. Using a towel, he swept the floor free of the scattered contents of the medicine cabinet, and ran a bath. He filled it to the brim, making it as hot as bearable, before sinking beneath the surface. The heat soothed his body, drawing out the bruises. There was a packet of disposable razors and a can of shaving soap, and he shaved carefully, examining his face in the mirror. There was a small contusion on his left temple, but the skin was not broken. It felt tender, and he ran cold water on a face-cloth, holding it against his forehead. The fingers of his left hand were still sore from the heavy blow they had received the night before.

By eight o'clock, the building was waking up. The lift rattled and complained, the main entrance door opened and closed with a distinctive thud, cars parked at meters along the pavement started with throaty coughs, and there was a steady, low-pitched hum of traffic along Seymour Place. Mark collected the rest of his clothes from the spare bedroom, and dressed. His shirt was crumpled, the trousers creased, but he looked in the mirror and grinned. 'My God, you look as though you've slept in them! Still, you'll be appropriately dressed for your meeting with the debonair Mr Scutter!' Under the circumstances, he felt surprisingly cheerful. He walked to the kitchen and made a cup of bitter instant coffee, pulling a wry face as he tasted it. He longed for his good Swiss espresso machine in the apartment in Geneva. Only the English could put up with such foul-tasting ersatz coffee! The kitchen felt stuffy, and he opened the door to the little balcony overlooking the well in the centre of the building. It was a small landing, about eight feet long, surrounded by a maze of water pipes and brickwork. The Victorians had used such balconies for cold storage, and he noticed that several of the other flats had brightly coloured metal baskets to hold fresh vegetables.

The clock in the living room chimed the half hour, and he made a second cup of coffee and carried it through to the master bedroom. He opened the door slowly, and was surprised to find

Karen sitting up, her back against the headboard of the bed, the duvet tucked around her body like a travelling rug.

She smiled. 'Hi!'

'Hello. I hope I didn't wake you earlier.'

'No, I heard the traffic outside.' She hugged herself. 'It seems to have gotten much colder. How are you feeling?'

'Better. A hot bath took out most of the wrinkles. How about you?' He handed her the cup.

'Fine. I went out cold. I think it was the brandy.' She drank the coffee and sighed contentedly. 'That feels good!'

Mark sat on the edge of the bed. 'Would you like me to run a bath?'

She stretched lazily. 'In a while. I've been lying here, working out the things I have to do, in the right order.' She handed back the empty coffee cup and counted off her plans on the fingers of her hand. It might have been a shopping list. 'First off, I call the two cops from last night. One of them gave me his card while I was making coffee. I'll tell them about the second break-in and wait for the fingerprint man. They said he'd be here around ten. Next, I'll call your Inspector, and tell him whatever I know about Sandy. I hope it helps.' For a moment, a shadow crossed her face. 'Poor Sandy! He was kind. I hope they catch the shit who did it.' Mark nodded, and she continued: 'I'll call my folks in Cleveland. They should have got in late last night. What's the time change between us?'

'Five hours.'

'Right. It was six in France. I'll wait until around one. Are you seeing Sandy's lawyer this morning?'

'I arranged to meet him at ten, but I can put it off if you'd rather have me wait with you until the police arrive.'

'No, it's better that you talk to him. He may be able to help.'

'What about phone calls? Can you handle them if they start again?'

For a moment, she was thoughtful. 'Yes. After last night, I'll manage.' She gave a tight smile. 'After yesterday, I guess I can handle anything.'

'You're taking it very well.'

'No, I'm not. I was scared yesterday, and when you told me about Sandy, everything turned upside down. I think I fell apart, but I'm not a teenage kid. I can look after myself. Jesus, if you live in New York City, having your apartment broken into is an everyday occurrence!'

'Not when you meet the burglars face to face.'

'Even then. I was lucky. If it had been New York, I would probably have gotten myself raped as well.'

Mark was surprised by her coolness. After yesterday, it was unexpected. He suspected that some of it was bravado. He hesitated before speaking. 'I didn't tell you last night, but I spoke to one of the men who called you.'

She was startled, but quickly regained her composure. 'Who is he?'

'I'm not sure. He said his name is Bradshaw – Lewis Bradshaw. He called me at the hotel.'

She was puzzled. 'I never heard that name before. How do you know he was the one that called?'

'He told me he had.'

'Oh.'

'He talked some nonsense about your being evasive. He said he thought Sandor was in the room with you when you spoke to him, and that he wouldn't come to the phone himself. I told him he was wrong, and that you had been alone. I also told him that Sandor was dead.'

'What did he say?'

'At first, he didn't believe me, and when I started to explain, he hung up. I haven't heard from him since. I doubt whether you will.'

'You should have told me sooner.'

'I would have, but the opportunity didn't arise. You were preoccupied with other events.'

She nodded. 'Did he say what he wanted?'

'Not entirely. He said something about being a business associate.'

'Well, Sandy never mentioned his name to me. I think I'd remember someone with a name like Lewis. What next?'

'I hope he'll call back. You were right about him sounding

sinister. He didn't say much, but he insinuated that he could make life uncomfortable for me if I didn't co-operate.'

'Jesus! Why do you want him to call back?'

Mark walked to the bedroom window and looked down at the street. Some children with tennis rackets were hitting a ball against the wall of a church opposite. 'Because I think he may know the answer to what's been going on. He assumed I knew much more about Berman than I do. If he calls, I'm going to play him along, and suggest I know what he's talking about.' An elderly woman had come out of the church, and was chasing the children away. They waited until she had disappeared into the interior of the building, and started again.

After a moment's silence, Karen's voice was anxious. 'Mark, be careful. It could be dangerous.' She gave a sigh of exasperation. 'I don't understand. How could a nice kid like Sandy have got himself mixed up in trouble like this? It doesn't fit. He was so easy-going and relaxed. He really enjoyed himself.'

'Perhaps, but facts are facts. Sandy is dead, Karen. Somebody shot him down in cold blood. Unless there's a maniac loose on the streets of London, he had to be mixed up in something.'

'I guess so. I keep hoping it was a mistake, or a case of mistaken identity, or something . . .' Her voice trailed off. 'I don't know what I think any more.'

He moved back to the bed. 'When you've talked to the police, we have to decide what you're going to do.'

She stared straight ahead. 'Go home, as soon as the money arrives. There's nothing else to do.'

'It may take a day or two for the money to come through. What will you do until it does?'

'I don't know. I'll think about it.'

'Let me help you.'

'No.' She turned towards him. 'You've done enough already. I'll get by.'

'Karen, you can't stay on here. At least let me . . .'

'I told you, I'll think about it. Will you come back later?'

'Yes, of course. I'm seeing the lawyer at ten, after which I want to talk to the Inspector. I'll tell him about the break-in here, and the return visit, and Bradshaw. Make sure you do, too.' She nodded. 'After that, I ought to see Steigel. He's the conductor of the orchestra. I'll call you later in the morning.'

'I'll be here. I don't know how long the fingerprint men will take, but I have no reason to go out.' She made a face. 'It looks damp out there, and cold! I won't phone home until after one. I don't want to worry them. Will you come back this afternoon?'

'Yes, but I'll probably call you before that, to see how you're doing. It may be a while before I finish with everyone.'

'That's fine.' She took his hand. After a moment, she suddenly smiled. 'You know, I think I'm hungry. Would you like some real breakfast?'

'Yes, I think I would.'

'Great!' She jumped out of bed, throwing the dressing gown around her shoulders. 'Breakfast coming up – two over easy!' At the door, she paused to look at him. 'I'm glad you're here, Mark. I really needed you.' Before he could reply, she had disappeared to the kitchen. He smiled, and followed her. Her recuperative powers were impressive, and Mark had the feeling that she was stronger than he had suspected.

Watching her prepare bacon and eggs, he said: 'I'm sorry you didn't see Paris. It's one of my favourite cities.'

'It will be there next time.' She sighed happily. 'I'm hooked on Europe. I liked everything I saw. It's so different. I'm going to find a way to come back; maybe try for a job. Paris certainly looked beautiful from the window of the cab.'

'I thought you drove straight to the airport.' Sandy could have used the *Périphérique* round the outside.

'No, he had to put his car away before he left.'

'It wasn't rented?'

'No. He keeps it in a garage in Paris, and drives it from country to country when he's playing in Europe. It's a big Mercedes, and he told me he saved a lot on air fares. Why?'

'I just wondered. Most musicians can't spare the time. Where did he leave it?'

'I don't know. Some little street near the big station on the north side of the town. He drove me through the centre, so I could at least say I saw the Champs Elysées and the Arc de Triomphe.' She pronounced them as though they were English words. 'How do you like your eggs – up or over?'

When they had eaten, Mark lit a cigarette. 'I'll have to go soon.'

'I know. Call me when you have a chance.'

'Karen, I don't want to bully you, but you're going to have to decide what to do until your money arrives. You shouldn't stay here. I'm not even sure whether you're supposed to. The police might give you a hard time.'

'Why? I was Sandy's guest. He invited me. I even talked to one of the other tenants a couple of days ago, so they know who I am. What's the problem?'

'Simply that Sandy's now the subject of a murder investigation. It makes your presence here questionable. I don't think you should treat it so casually.'

'I'm not.' She was silent for a moment, and Mark felt he had destroyed her cheerful mood. She sat, fiddling with the fork on her empty plate. 'Mark, I guess I should level with you. Everything I've told you has been the way it was, but I left some of it out.' She took a deep breath. 'You see, when I met Sandy, I was just about flat. Everything was more expensive than I'd budgeted, even with the high rate of the dollar. It was a shock. I didn't have a lot when I got here, and I kept myself going by picking up jobs wherever I went. At first, it was easy. There's always something during vacation time. I must have washed dishes and cleaned my way across half of Europe! In Italy, I tried serving at table, but my Italian wasn't good enough, and I got fired the first day! And I met a lot of kids on the road, like me, who helped out; bought me a meal or let me stay over.' She glanced at him nervously. 'It got harder all the time. Anyway, I headed for Monté Carlo because I figured I could find something there. Not only that, it's always been a big American stopover . . .' She was silent for a while, and Mark waited. 'I wasn't staying at the Mirabeau, like I said. I doubt if I could have paid for more than one night. That town crucifies you! I found a cheap room down the other side, near the port. I tried to find work everywhere, but I was too late. The summer season was ending, the Parisians started going home, and all the jobs had gone. I was getting worried.'

'Did you call home?'

'I couldn't. They were away. My folks always take off for the first two weeks of August. They like to drive to the mountains and stay at motels. Some years, my dad rents a cabin by one of the lakes. I didn't know where they were, and all I knew was that they'd be home by last night. So . . .' She took another breath and lapsed into silence.

'So you tried the Mirabeau bar?'

She nodded. 'It's a fancy kind of hotel, with a lot of Americans. The big one opposite the Casino is too much and, anyway, I wasn't dressed for it. I figured I might get lucky and strike up a . . . friendship. I kept telling myself I could maybe find someone from the States who'd loan me a few dollars to keep me going 'til my folks got home, but if necessary,' she paused, concentrating her gaze on the table, 'I was there for anyone looking for a little companionship.'

Mark nodded slowly. 'Like Sandy?'

'Like Sandy. Except that he was the way I described. I didn't think he was going to be. I didn't like him at first. He was sort of loud and pushy. He bought me a drink, and we started talking. You know how it is. It was funny: the more we talked, the quieter he got. When he told me he was driving to Paris next day and I asked him to take me, he was kind of embarrassed. We arranged to meet, I went back to my *pension*, and the rest was like I told you. Well, almost. He did pay for my room in Beaune the first night. I didn't like to say it in front of that girl who was with you,' she looked up, 'but it was a separate room, and he didn't try anything.'

'I believe you. It wouldn't have been so shocking if he had.'

'I know, but I felt you were watching me when I told you about it. I felt like a hooker!'

'I'm sorry.'

'It wasn't your fault. I guess what I'm really trying to say is that I was prepared to be a hooker if I had to. It was just dumb luck that I met Sandy and he turned out to be the way he was.'

She smiled. 'When you talk with your proper British accents, it makes me feel like a slob!'

Mark kept his voice gentle. 'So Sandy looked after you?'

She nodded. 'He paid my air ticket to London, and gave me a little spending money. He was nice, Mark. He looked after me, and he didn't ask for anything back. I guess he was lonely. After he left, yesterday morning, and we were supposed to have dinner, I was planning to . . .' She left the sentence unfinished. She continued almost defensively. 'I didn't have anything else to offer him. Anyway, I liked him, and I think he liked me. We were just beginning to get to know each other.' She shook her head angrily. 'Oh hell! I just thought you ought to know how it really was. True confessions!'

'There's nothing to confess. Sandy sounds like a kind man. I'm sorry I didn't know him better. He was a fine musician, but I must confess I only saw the pushy side of him. He could be charming. With a few reservations, I liked him when we first met in Geneva. You haven't told me anything very terrible.'

'It could have been different.'

'But it wasn't, so there's no reason to be ashamed. I'm sorry I suggested you were treating his death casually.'

'It wasn't that. I just thought you should know how it was between us.' She paused. 'We've been through a lot together in the past few hours. I just wanted you to know. Listen, it's getting late. You should go, if you're going to make your appointment.'

'There's time. Wimpole Street is only a few minutes away in a taxi. Do you have everything you need?'

'Yes, we bought supplies the evening we arrived. There's a whole bunch of little stores on the corner.'

'And money?'

'I have enough. Sandy gave me some. I don't need any.'

'All right. I'll call you later.'

She walked with him to the door, and gave him a quick, nervous hug. 'I'd better take that bath before the fingerprint man gets here. Call me?'

'I will.' She scampered down the hall and into the bathroom. When he opened the main entrance door, he was surprised to find the Mini parked at the kerb, with Penny sitting in it. She greeted him with a quick wave.

'What brings you here?'

'You do, I suppose. I stopped off at the Westbury, looking for you, but they said you were out, so I made a calculated guess that you might be here. I was about to leave.'

'I thought you'd be at the session. It's about to start.'

She frowned. 'I'm on my way there now. It doesn't matter if I'm a few minutes late. I thought you might need a lift.'

Mark hesitated. If she was looking for him, why hadn't she rung the doorbell? On the seat, the *Daily Telegraph* was opened at the back page. The crossword was half completed. Why had she been waiting?

'How's Miss America?' Something in Mark's expression surprised her. 'What's happened? What's going on?'

Mark described the preceding evening, from the moment Karen had telephoned. He described everything carefully, as if each detail was significant, and she listened thoughtfully without interrupting. When he mentioned casually that he had slept in the spare bedroom, her eyebrows raised, and she said: 'How cosy!'

'Not very.' He went on to describe the second break-in and his fight with the intruder.

Her face showed genuine alarm. 'Good God! What did the police say?'

He was slightly embarrassed. 'I haven't told them yet.'

'What? Why ever not?'

'It was very late, and I didn't want to go through the whole thing again, especially as I couldn't even describe the man. Frankly, all I wanted to do was sleep. I'd just been battered about the head and kicked in the ribs, so I bolted the front door, checked the locks and went to bed.' He decided not to mention the mattress in Karen's room.

'Well didn't you call them this morning?'

'Not yet. I haven't been up for long. It's still early.'

She laughed. 'They're open twenty-four hours a day, Mark. It's not an office!'

'Karen's calling them now. She can give them the details.

When I've finished with Scutter – that's Berman's lawyer – I want to talk to the Inspector again. The men we saw last night came from Robbery. They think the break-in was a coincidence. The way they talk, there's one every five minutes!'

'There probably is. I thought you said they'd stolen a painting.'

'They did. It was the little Chagall, or what looked like one, hanging over the Sheraton desk. Did you notice it yesterday?' She shook her head. 'Well, it is missing, but I'm still not convinced. I'll talk to him anyway.'

'You should certainly talk to somebody.' Penny shook her head again. 'You're a strange man!' She started the car.

'I'll sort it all out this morning.'

'I should hope so!' She sounded angry. 'What's this lawyer's address?' He gave her the number in Wimpole Street, and she drove off rapidly making the car jerk forward. The line of her mouth was firmly set, and she offered no further comment.

As they drove along George Street, Penny slowed, her face relaxing. She was about to speak, when a large, dark blue Peugeot drew level with them and, driving on the right-hand side of the road towards oncoming traffic, raced past them with squealing tyres. Penny pulled her car sharply towards the kerb. About thirty yards ahead, cars were waiting for the traffic lights to change. The driver of the Peugeot suddenly dragged his vehicle back to the left-hand lane, braking fiercely, so that the car stopped in their path, almost at right-angles to the pavement. Penny braked a few yards from it.

'Silly bastard! What the hell is he doing?'

The car in front of them did not move. Mark wondered whether the driver had stalled his engine. Beyond it, the lights had changed, and the traffic moved forward. The Peugeot remained stationary. There was a man in the back seat of the car, and Mark had the impression that he was about to open the door. He had a brief glimpse of a dark face. It might have been Middle Eastern, or perhaps heavily sun-tanned. The man was looking in their direction. In the pit of his stomach, Mark felt a sudden nervous tension.

Penny gave an irritated exclamation. 'What on earth does he

think he's playing at?' She started to back, as if to drive round the other car, but it blocked the road. 'Well, if he's going to play silly buggers, we'll give him something to think about!' She changed forward, steering to her left, and bumped the Mini on to the pavement. Mark could see a look of surprise on the face of the Peugeot's driver. Penny had a grim smile. 'That's the advantage of a small car. Up yours, Charley!' Her fingers made a vee sign at the other driver, and she drove along the pavement, passed the French car, and bumped back on to the road again, accelerating through the traffic lights. She made a left turn, followed by a quick right into Blandford Street. Mark turned in his seat and looked through the rear window. The Peugeot had backed and straightened. It was following them rapidly, racing through the lights as they changed to red.

The road ahead was clear on both sides and, as they passed through a second set of lights, Penny slowed to a safer speed. At that moment, the Peugeot appeared alongside, so close that it was in danger of scraping the Mini's wing. Penny hardly glanced in its direction, but her face turned pale. With a determined expression, she changed down to third gear, racing the motor. The engine complained, but the car shot forward, leaving the Peugeot behind. They were travelling over sixty miles an hour, and the junction with Marylebone High Street was racing up to meet them. Penny muttered: 'Hang on!' and, waiting for the last possible moment, stamped on the brakes as they reached the corner. Mark was aware of a figure jumping back to the safety of the pavement, but his concentration was riveted to the flow of taxis and cars along the High Street. The Mini's tyres whined on the tarmac and, as if by magic, a small gap, little wider than the length of her car, appeared between a taxi and a delivery van. Penny spun the steering wheel, the car skidded expertly into the space, facing right, and miraculously missed both vehicles. The driver of the delivery van sounded a tattoo on his horn.

Behind them, the Peugeot was still racing forward, travelling too fast to stop. It was a much heavier machine, and the momentum carried it onward relentlessly as its driver braked too late. There was a loud scream of tyres, followed by a metallic crash, coupled with the sound of shattering glass. Looking round, Mark could see that the French car had hit the front of a lorry and had slewed round in a wide arc, ending against a shop front and slithering into the plate glass window. Glass was scattered across the pavement, and several workmen were running towards the car. The driver and his passenger, apparently unhurt, were stepping out of it.

Penny continued forward, her face pale, making a quick left into a narrow lane and steering past a parked delivery truck.

'Aren't you going to stop?'

'No.'

'Shouldn't you?'

'I don't see why. The crash had nothing to do with us.' She was breathing heavily, her nostrils flared. 'If they can't drive properly, it's their problem.' She relaxed slowly, piloting the Mini through a maze of small back streets. 'Now, what was the number in Wimpole Street?'

He told her again. 'That was pretty fancy driving on your part.'

She shrugged. 'I don't know what the hell they were up to.'

'Neither do I, but they were chasing us.'

'Don't be silly!' Her voice was sharp.

'I'm sure of it. If you hadn't gone round that car on the pavement . . .'

'Oh, come on! You're getting carried away!'

'Why did they make a double turn, after you left them in George Street?'

'I don't know. They were probably going the same way. There's a one-way system. If you ask me, they were trying to put the wind up a woman driver. You'd be surprised how many of them try.'

'If you say so. I'm not so sure.'

She stopped the car in Wimpole Street, outside Scutter's office. Her face was set. 'Will I see you later?'

'Yes. I must go back to the hotel to make a couple of calls, and I need a change of clothes.' He smiled. 'I slept in these.' Penny made no comment, and her face was sombre. 'I'll come down to the hall for the last part of the session.'

Her voice was cold. 'I'll see you then.'

He got out of the car and, as soon as he had closed the door, she drove off quickly.

7

Unlike its owner, Eric Scutter's office was handsomely appointed. The airy, well-proportioned study was heavily carpeted, the length of one wall covered with custom-built mahogany bookcases filled with leather-bound legal volumes. A long antique oak refectory table, displaying books and magazines, occupied a second wall. Above it, there was a large eighteenth-century oil painting of an English landscape. The room was dominated by an enormous desk, its polished surface glowing and empty, behind which the lawyer was lurking uneasily. It was extraordinary to Mark that, even in his own little kingdom, Scutter looked out of place. There was a window behind the desk, overlooking a small, terraced garden, and Mark saw that the sun was finally breaking through the grey clouds that had started the day. A sudden beam of light from it shone in his eyes.

Scutter stood and, as Mark approached, walked round the desk to greet him. He was a small man, and it occurred to Mark that the desk was so wide that Scutter could barely reach over it to shake his hand. He was dressed in a shabby three-piece brown suit, with shiny elbows and a button missing from the waistcoat. A narrow black tie, crumpled from constant use, was burrowing its way under one side of his collar. His skin had a pale, unhealthy colour, and there was a suggestion of sweat on his balding forehead. The lawyer offered him a limp and slightly damp handshake, bobbing his head deferentially, and pointed to two comfortable leather armchairs, separated by a coffee table, at the other end of the room. They were arranged before an artificial fireplace.

The lawyer coughed nervously. 'I thought we might sit over

there and make ourselves comfortable. Will you take a cup of coffee?'

He spoke slowly, apparently choosing his words with care. Mark had the suspicion that he articulated each phrase carefully to maintain his accent, and that if he spoke any faster, vowels and consonants would slip into a more mundane regional pattern.

'Thank you. That's a magnificent desk.'

Scutter glanced at it and looked worried. 'Is it? Oh yes, I suppose it is. It was willed to me by my father. To be perfectly frank, I have always been a little overwhelmed by it.'

They sat down and, as if by remote control, the door opened. A young secretary entered with a tray containing a silver coffee service and two Royal Worcester cups and saucers. Although conservatively dressed in a simple white blouse and dark skirt, she was sensuously beautiful, unexpectedly inappropriate to the stolid opulence of the lawyer's office. As she placed the tray on the table between them, Eric Scutter followed her with adoring eyes. She gave him a sparkling smile, bending low over the table, and he watched her, fascinated. The upper half of her blouse ballooned out, suggesting a paradise of fleshly pleasures.

'Thank you, Bunny.' His voice was vibrant with gratitude.

She walked slowly to the door again, and Scutter continued to watch, as though hypnotised. He stared at the door after she had closed it. Mark vaguely remembered meeting a Mrs Scutter backstage after a concert: a dumpy, middle-aged woman in a floral dress. He wondered whether she ever visited her husband's office in Wimpole Street. Probably not. Scutter poured him a cup of coffee.

'I'm grateful that you were able to meet me at such short notice.'

The coffee-pot poised, Scutter returned to him as if from a reverie. 'Ah yes. I was a little surprised to hear from you quite so soon, but when I heard the tragic news yesterday evening, I realised the reason for your appointment.' He shook his head slowly. 'What a sad and disgraceful business! Mr Berman telephoned me the day before yesterday, telling me to anticipate a visit from you. It's quite horrifying to think that, forty-eight hours later, we should be meeting under these circumstances.' His voice had become sepulchral.

'Quite.'

'From what I gleaned from the news bulletins, I understand that the police investigating the murder have offered no indication as to who might have perpetrated such a vicious crime.'

'That's right. So far, nobody has been able to suggest any kind of motive.'

'Dreadful, quite dreadful!' He lapsed into silence.

Mark nodded and, when sufficient time had passed, asked: 'Did you know him well?'

Scutter placed his fingertips together, and Mark noted that the nails were bitten to the quick. 'Mr Berman first came to see me about a year and a half ago, I would say.' He looked at Mark nervously. 'I will consult my records, if you wish.'

'No, it's not important. I only met him recently myself, so you probably knew him a good deal better than I.'

'I would not say I knew him very well. He came to see me with excellent recommendations.'

'Arnold Silverman?'

'Exactly so. I have worked on behalf of Mr Silverman for many years.' His voice was reverential. 'A wonderful man!'

'Yes, of course.' Everyone said Arnold Silverman was a wonderful man so frequently that Mark was beginning to doubt it. 'I assumed that it was because Silverman recommended him that you agreed to look after Berman's affairs.'

The lawyer looked puzzled. 'I don't think I understand you.'

'Well, Berman was a young man, just beginning to make a career for himself in the music world. I wouldn't have thought there was a great deal you would have needed to do for him.'

'I'm sorry, but I still don't understand what you are saying. Mr Berman's age was of no particular consequence to me.' Scutter's voice had taken on a note of suspicion.

Mark decided to start again. 'Perhaps I haven't expressed myself very well. Mr Scutter, you look after the business or financial affairs of a number of very well-known people.'

'Yes.' There was a slight question mark.

'Including, of course, a number of very distinguished musicians, like Arnold Silverman.'

'Indeed.'

'Well, what I was trying to say was that Sandor Berman was hardly likely to come into that particular – category of people.'

Scutter seemed genuinely surprised. 'Why ever not?'

'Primarily his age, I suppose, but as his manager – although I only took him on very recently – I am aware of the kinds of engagements he had been playing. I'm also aware of his current standing in the musical community. I wouldn't have thought Berman's income would have required your very specialised services.' He would have liked to add: 'In other words, Eric old man, what was a kid like Berman doing, hiring a high-priced tax dodger like you?'

The lawyer was silent for a moment, tapping the ends of his fingers together. A sunbeam from the window caught the side of his face, and it glistened. 'My services are not really so very specialised, Mr Holland, and they are most certainly not predicated upon the age of the client involved. Without betraying any confidences on his part, I can tell you that Mr Berman requested my services for the purpose of looking after his financial affairs in Europe . . .'

'That's my point.' The lawyer was speaking so slowly that Mark found himself growing impatient. 'Sandor Berman gave me a list of his concert engagements this year, and I wouldn't have thought the income from them would have been enough to require your services.' The lawyer looked up sharply. 'I mean, not enough to warrant first-class legal services such as yours.'

'The actual amount of his fees would not be of any consequence to me, Mr Holland.' He paused for a moment. 'Mr Berman never discussed the sources of his income with me.'

'What did you do for him, if it's not stepping beyond the bounds of professional confidence?'

The lawyer walked over to his desk and opened a drawer. He returned to his seat, carrying a manila file which he read briefly. Now and then, he glanced nervously over the top of it in Mark's direction. After a moment, he set it down on the coffee table.

'Mr Berman asked me to establish a private corporation in Lichtenstein, called Anstalt Waldtaube, which would become the sole employer to supply his services to other parties. In other words, Mr Holland, if a company wanted to record Mr Berman, they would make the contract with Waldtaube, which would in turn supply the services of Mr Berman. It's a very normal arrangement for a number of artists, as you know, but it can, under certain circumstances, prove very beneficial for tax purposes.'

'Yes, but it doesn't usually prove very useful unless you're very successful and making many more records than Berman was. Unless he was planning a long way into the future, it hardly seems worth while. Is that all he wanted?'

Scutter frowned. 'No. I would have described that as the tip of the iceberg. Mr Berman established a holding company in Luxembourg, called Interstrad, for the purpose of making a number of investments. He also sought my advice on various financial enterprises that he was considering. He had a bank account in Geneva, among other places, from which he transferred capital from time to time, either for the purpose of purchasing stock in various markets, or for investing in other enterprises.'

'I see.' Mark was thoughtful. 'Did he say where this capital had come from?'

'No, Mr Holland, he did not. Perhaps I should add that I do not think it would have been appropriate for me to ask. He simply advised me that he wished to invest certain amounts, and occasionally asked my opinion.' Scutter produced a scruffy handkerchief and dabbed at his forehead. 'I can assure you that my answers were at all times cautious, based upon the most reliable information available to me. Finally, I suppose I can mention that he owned a number of properties, including a flat which he recently purchased in London. I looked after the deeds of transfer for him.'

'Yes, I knew about the flat. Would you be prepared to tell me what Berman was worth, Mr Scutter?'

The lawyer looked offended. 'No, I would not. As a matter of fact, I doubt whether the final amount will be clear for some time, because we will have to assemble all the necessary information.'

'Does he have any other legal or financial representatives?'

'Not that I am aware of, apart from yourself. Will you have a little more coffee?'

'Thank you.' Mark wondered whether the delectable Bunny would reappear, but there was enough coffee remaining in the coffee-pot. It was excellent – a welcome alternative to the brown powder in Berman's flat. Watching Scutter pour, he wondered whether Karen had called the police yet.

Scutter said: 'I'm sorry that I cannot offer you more detailed information, Mr Holland, but I hope that what I have revealed will be helpful.'

He hadn't revealed anything, but Mark said: 'Thank you. By the way, did Berman leave a will?'

Scutter looked through the file. 'Not with me, Mr Holland.' He was silent for a moment. 'I had not really thought about that. It could prove to be something of a problem.'

'Why is that?'

'As far as I am aware, he was an orphan, with no direct next-of-kin. If he has died intestate, it could involve a considerable search before his estate can be settled.'

'I see.' Another thought occurred. 'By the way, I'm looking after two violins that he was using during his tour. They're in the hotel safe at the moment. I understand that one of them – a Guarnerius – was on loan to him from Arnold Silverman. The other is his own Stradivarius. The pair of them together are worth a considerable amount of money.'

'They are indeed. I looked after the purchase of the Stradivarius for Mr Berman.'

'I will be returning to Switzerland shortly, so I wonder if I can hand the violins over to you. I've no doubt you'll see Silverman at some time in the near future, and the Stradivarius becomes another part of Berman's estate.'

The lawyer nodded. 'I will see that they are put into a safe place. Perhaps you would be good enough to arrange to bring them to this office.'

'Yes. Incidentally, there is a large safe installed in Berman's

London flat. You wouldn't by chance know the combination of the lock, would you?'

'No, I don't think I do.' He consulted the file again, and looked up with a shake of his head.

'I wonder what we should do about it.'

The man shrugged. 'I suppose we will have to contact the makers. Presumably they have a duplicate of the number. I believe there is also a safety deposit in the bank in Geneva, but I am not sure whether anyone is authorised to open it. I have a feeling that it may take a long time to settle everything.' His voice was glum, but he did not look entirely unhappy with the thought.

Mark stood up, and Scutter followed suit. He seemed relieved that the interview was over. As he walked to the door, Mark turned to the lawyer. 'Mr Scutter, I know that you can't give me an exact figure, but how would you describe Berman financially, leaving aside the value of the Stradivarius?'

'Mr Holland, I think I have already explained . . .'

Mark smiled amiably. 'Oh, I know. I'm not asking for professional reasons. Let's just say I'm curious, as a friend of Sandor's.'

Mr Scutter placed a wet hand in Mark's. His smile was forced. 'Well, I don't think I'm revealing very much when I say he was a man of considerable wealth – considerable! His capital was invested wisely, and divided between a number of sensible . . .' He hesitated, feeling that he had already overstepped the bounds of professional etiquette.

Mark smiled again. 'Thank you. I appreciate your confidence. I expect you'll be hearing from the police at some point.'

'The police?' Mr Scutter looked more nervous than usual.

'Yes, as part of their investigations. You may be able to help them.'

Scutter's face was blank. 'I think that would be most unlikely.'

Before he reached it, the door opened inward. The pneumatic Bunny was standing in the hall, waiting to show him out. He had the feeling that she must have been listening at the keyhole. Eric Scutter's eyes flickered between the two of them, torn between desire and professional courtesy. Desire won, but she closed the door pertly. Mark could have sworn that her hips swayed fractionally more than necessary as she led the way to the front door. He looked at the elegant panelled staircase leading to the upper offices.

'What a lovely building. It must have been beautiful when it was a private house.'

She treated him to a dazzling smile. 'Everything Mr Scutter owns is beautiful. You should see his yacht in the South of France.'

'I heard he owned one. Is it nice?'

'Brilliant!'

'Lucky man. How many does it sleep?'

'I don't know.' She giggled. 'I didn't see the others.'

It was still quite early, so Mark decided to walk for a few minutes. His arms and legs felt stiff, and the exercise would help them. Overhead, the clouds were quickly breaking apart in the bright sunlight, and the air was pleasantly cool. There was a vague soreness at the back of his neck, and he sensed rather than felt a headache, like a mild hangover. But his head was clear. He quickened his pace, trying to piece together the scant information the lawyer had given him.

It was clear, from what Scutter had said, that Berman was rich. For that particular tax specialist to describe him as a man of 'considerable wealth', with investments and property holdings, not to mention a Stradivarius worth more than half a million dollars, was enough indication that Berman was worth a great deal more than his career suggested. But how? Even a brief glance at Berman's itineraries showed that he was not in the class of musicians that earned the kind of income that Scutter suggested, and Scutter would know. Some of his other clients earned more than a million dollars a year, and controlled vast empires of investments. By everyday standards, Berman was successful enough for a relatively unknown artist of his age. His concert dates, without details from Latin America, suggested forty to fifty thousand dollars – sixty at the most – but that was before expenses. Travelling, accommodation, agency fees and all the extras of concert life on the road would account for more than half of it.

Had his parents left him a fortune when they died? It seemed unlikely. What little biographical information there was suggested that Arnold Silverman had taken a poor Israeli orphan under his influential wing. And Arnold himself? Again, unlikely. He had a large family of his own, spread around the globe: a son in Israel, trying to set up a television company, a married daughter in Paris, and a second daughter still in college. Arnold would not have settled any large fortune on the young violinist. It was not his way of doing things. He would use his considerable influence in musical circles, together with formidable persuasive powers that could make or break a career. He was a self-made man and proud of it, and would expect Berman to carve out a career of his own. He had helped any number of young musicians similarly. Anyway, hadn't Penny suggested that they had been seeing less of each other in recent years?

For a moment, his thoughts were diverted by Penny. What had she been doing outside the flat? It was obvious that she had been waiting there for some time. Why hadn't she rung the downstairs bell? He was not sure that he liked being spied on by her. Not wanting to disturb 'Miss America' seemed a lame excuse, and why had she been so irritable? The chase down George Street with the Peugeot had been too lightly dismissed. He was convinced that if she had not driven along the pavement when the other car blocked the road, the passenger from the back seat would have come over to them. Why? What did he want? She had been angry when he told her that the other car was chasing them, and had driven off in a huff. Why? Something about the incident did not ring true.

He paused on the corner of Wigmore Street to light a cigarette, wondering whether to hail a taxi. He needed time to think. It seemed to him that he had been too busily occupied with people and events to think clearly. For the past twenty-four hours, he had hardly been alone. An empty taxi was approaching, and the driver caught his eye with a questioning glance, but he stepped away from the kerb, letting it pass. The hotel was only a ten-minute walk away. For a moment, he considered finding a telephone, to call Karen, but decided that it was too soon. On the corner of Cavendish Square, a Spanish bus was disgorging a group of noisy tourists. They were aiming, handbags at the ready, for John Lewis's, and he quickened his step to walk around them.

If Arnold Silverman had not provided the capital, and he was sure he had not, where had it come from? Perhaps Berman had found a rich sponsor of his own. That could be the reason why he had appeared diffident about revealing his past. During those years in California and Mexico, had he found himself a wealthy patron, eager to 'develop' his career? Classical music attracted would-be protectors of either sex. From Miami Beach to Los Angeles and Acapulco, there were those lonely ladies of a certain age, with time and money on their hands, all too eager to support an attractive and ebulliently physical young violinist with talent and charisma, let alone the elderly, soft-spoken businessmen, retired from successful careers, left with little but time and the *Wall Street Journal* to occupy their fantasies. The classical music world had its own 'groupies', and they came in all ages and sexes. Had he perhaps found himself a rich backer amid those outlandish hotels along Collins Avenue or in the canyons above Beverly Hills? It would explain the missing portions in his biography. Berman had known Scutter for a year and a half, perhaps more. With sufficient tax-free working capital and some astute investments, a man like Scutter knew how to create an effective financial network. Perhaps Berman had found himself several sponsors, coasts apart, doubling up the possibilities. It had happened before, and it could also explain a possible cooling-off between himself and Silverman, who was a hard-working musician, constantly touring and performing long after he had earned enough to retire permanently. It was an interesting theory. But Laufer had said that Silverman master-minded the record contract, insisting that Magnum Records sign Berman. It was a typically generous gesture, part altruistic, part bullying. Arnold liked getting his own way when it came to protégés, and one sometimes needed more than talent or good looks to succeed. Bond Street was crowded with window shoppers, drawn out by the sunny weather. Mark dodged between them, constantly changing step to maintain his pace.

The concierge at the hotel reported with disappointment that there were no messages, and Mark went upstairs to telephone the Inspector. The man was not there, but was expected within the hour, so he left a message that he would call back. His room was empty and silent, the unused bed neatly made. Stripping off his stale clothes, he showered, keeping the water prickly hot and slowly adding cold until his bruised flesh tingled. A second shave and a clean shirt left him feeling comfortably relaxed, and he dialled Karen's number.

'Hello?' Her voice was wary.

'How's it going?'

'Oh, hi!' She sounded relieved. 'Everything's fine. The fingerprint men are still here. They've sprayed everything with a sort of silver powder, but they can't find anything. It seems they were wearing gloves.'

'Did you call the Robbery police?'

'Uh-huh. I told them about the man who came back later.'

'What did they say?'

'Not much. They were a little pissed off with you for not calling them.'

'I know. I should have.'

'I told them you didn't see the man's face because it was dark, and that he knocked you out cold. They seemed to think it was funny.'

'Thanks a lot!'

'Well, they said that you should expect to get hurt if you wanted to behave like a hero. I told them it wasn't like that, but I guess they thought it served you right for not calling them.'

'What else did they say?'

'The same as you: that he must have come back to make a try for the safe. Oh yes, they said they were getting in touch with an art expert who would like to talk to you about the painting. They asked if you would call back later to make an appointment.'

'Yes, I will. We can share the humour of the situation together!'

'Oh, don't be mad. I don't think he meant to laugh. He said something about leaving it to professionals.'

Mark was silent, thinking to himself, he's right; I should know, I used to be one, myself. 'I'll call him later.'

'Okay. How are you feeling?'

'Better. The fresh air did me good.' He did not mention finding Penny outside the flat. 'Have you spoken to the Inspector yet?'

'Not yet. I was about to. I only just made it out of the bath when the others arrived. Where are you?'

'At the hotel.'

'Did Sandy's lawyer help?'

'Not very much. From what he told me, it seems that Sandy was a very wealthy young man.'

'I guess so. I wouldn't know. He certainly acted like he was. What did the man say?'

'As little as he could. He was bending over backwards to be discreet.'

'Oh. Did you tell him about the robbery?'

'No. I suppose I should have. I didn't think about it very much at the time. I was on my own fishing expedition.'

She chuckled. 'What did you catch?'

'A couple of old boots and a rusty kettle, as far as I can see. Did Sandy ever talk to you about his money?'

'How do you mean?'

'Did he suggest he had other sources of income, wealthy friends – someone like a patron?'

There was a slight pause while she thought about it. 'No, I don't think so. A couple of times, when he paid for things, he told me not to worry about it, and made some sort of joke about being loaded. The only person he mentioned was that Arnold somebody-or-other, that I should have heard of.'

'I see. It's not important. I just wondered.'

'I told you everything I knew.' She sounded hurt.

'Yes, I know. I hoped I might jog your memory. It wasn't that I didn't believe you.'

'Yes. You sound pretty down.'

'Not really. Perhaps a little disappointed that the lawyer

didn't help.' He looked at his watch. 'I must go. I said I'd be at the recording session.'

'Okay. Call me later?'

'I will. Don't forget the Inspector. He's out at the moment, but they expect him back within the hour. You sound cheerful.'

'Yes, I guess I am.' Her voice grew softer. 'I miss you. I'm getting used to your being here.'

'I miss you, too.' He made light of it. 'We've got to stop meeting like this!'

'I guess so. Will I see you later?'

'Yes. I'll try to call you from the session. If I don't, I'll come round.'

'I'll be here.'

He replaced the receiver, feeling better.

When he reached the lobby, the concierge called to him. The man was holding a telephone, which he replaced.

'Mr Holland, I was just calling your room. There's a gentleman to see you. I'm afraid he wouldn't give me his name.'

He nodded in the direction of a man who was hovering by one of the armchairs in the foyer, as though uncertain whether to stand or sit. He was a large man, as tall as Mark, with a square, rather chunky face that looked youthful against thinning grey hair, cropped close and carefully parted across his forehead. He was wearing oversized rimless glasses. Except for two heavy furrows on either side of his mouth, suggesting disappointment, his face was not heavily lined, making it difficult to tell his age, but Mark judged him to be in his early fifties. The man was wearing a well tailored, navy blue double-breasted blazer and grey slacks, with a white shirt and a striped tie with a vaguely regimental pattern. There was a pink, unnaturally healthy tone to the skin of his face, like that of a man who indulged himself with hot towels at a barber's shop each day, and although he stood very straight, with a suggestion of military bearing, there was a thickness about his waistline, like that of an athlete run to seed.

He had been watching the concierge and, as Mark approached, took a step forward. His face was curiously blank. 'Mr Holland? I am Lewis Bradshaw. We spoke briefly yesterday.' He did not offer to shake hands. His voice, with its sibilant overtones, was instantly recognisable. It did not suit his face or body.

'I remember.' Mark motioned towards two empty armchairs in the foyer, but Bradshaw remained where he was. 'I assume you were able to confirm Sandor Berman's death?'

'Yes. Most unfortunate.' He gave no indication of his feelings, and his grey-blue eyes, slightly magnified by the lenses of his glasses, remained fixed. The blankness of his stare reminded Mark of a blind man. 'I believe I owe you an apology for the slight contretemps between us. I am sure you'll understand that business pressures sometimes get in the way of the normal courtesies. It was very upsetting to learn about Mr Berman. My partners and I were shocked.' His drawl was less pronounced than it had been on the telephone, but whatever shock he had suffered was not apparent.

Mark nodded slightly in acknowledgement. 'What can I do for you, Mr Bradshaw?'

The man made a sound reminiscent of a chuckle, but his facial expression did not change. 'I think I explained that yesterday, when we spoke. As you know, Mr Berman and I were partners in a small business venture. I had been waiting to hear from him for some time. I am not a very patient man, Mr Holland, so you will have to forgive my short temper yesterday.'

Mark forced a smile. The high-pitched, sibilant voice and the fishy stare were repellent. 'That's quite all right. You explained that it was important to speak to Sandor, but there's not much we can do about that now.'

'No.' The eyes continued to stare blindly. 'That's what brings me here. I'll have to deal with you in his place.'

'I'm not sure that I'm qualified to do so. What exactly do you want?'

The blank expression dissolved into a frown. 'Do we need to play guessing games again, Mr Holland? You expressed great ignorance yesterday, but I find it difficult to believe you didn't know what I was talking about. Berman made it perfectly clear to me that he had spoken to you.'

'Well, we discussed a number of matters, Mr Bradshaw, and we only had a short time to cover a lot of ground. I was hoping to go into greater detail during this visit.'

Bradshaw's voice became harder. 'I wouldn't have thought you needed much time, Holland. It wasn't very complicated. As you are aware, Mr Berman was looking after a transaction on my behalf. He was supposed to meet me two days ago, when he arrived in London.'

'Yes, you mentioned that before. Unfortunately, since then, there's . . .'

Bradshaw interrupted. 'Under the circumstances, we expect you to complete the transaction. I would have thought that was self-evident. I hope this isn't going to take a long time to complete. I'm a very busy man and, as I mentioned before, an impatient one. I'm not prepared to wait around.'

Mark hesitated, and decided to try a long shot. 'Is that why you or your colleagues decided to break into Berman's flat yesterday, and help themselves?'

To his surprise, Bradshaw brushed the question aside. 'That's neither here nor there! We're partners in this venture, and I don't expect you to back out of it now.'

'I'm not backing out of anything. I was never part of it. Whatever business dealings you had with Sandor Berman had very little to do with me.'

Bradshaw took a step closer, lowering his voice. His breath was foul-smelling. 'Listen to me, Holland. Don't try to play the innocent bystander. If Berman got himself killed, it's of no consequence to me except in the practical matter of our agreement. If he's gone, I expect you to settle it. I've got too much invested, so I suggest you either complete the transaction – immediately – or return the money.'

'I told you yesterday that I have nothing to do with Berman's financial affairs. He's got a lawyer on Wimpole Street to look after them. I can give you his name and address if you want. I've just been there, but I ought to warn you that it looks as though his money is going to be tied up for months.'

Bradshaw was growing angry. 'I'm not interested in bloody lawyers, Holland, and if you think you're going to cut yourself into this partnership, you're mistaken. It occurred to me that you might try to, but it won't work. Either you deliver what's rightfully mine, or you return my side of the investment – with interest! This isn't a public corporation!'

Mark paused for a moment. He kept his voice even. 'And if I decide to do neither?'

Bradshaw looked surprised. 'I wouldn't even contemplate that, if I were you, unless you want to end up the same way as Berman. This isn't some City take-over game, Holland. Where do you think you are: sitting in some cosy little coffee house off Cannon Street?' Mark said nothing, and Bradshaw looked impatiently at his watch. 'We'll give you another twenty-four hours to think about it.'

'After which?'

Bradshaw paused, his eyes cold. 'When you've had time to think about it, you'll co-operate.' His voice was contemptuous. 'I'm sure you'll agree that it's the gentlemanly thing to do. An agreement is an agreement. You will hear from me again.'

At that moment, Mark heard his name being called. Turning, he saw the concierge, telephone in hand, beckoning to him.

'Mr Holland, there's a call for you.'

With a gesture of irritation, Mark walked over to the desk. 'Can you find out who it is? I'm rather busy at the moment.'

'Yes, sir.' The man spoke into the telephone and listened momentarily. 'It's your office in Geneva, sir.'

'Oh. Would you tell them I'll call back in a few minutes, please.'

'Yes, sir, certainly.'

Mark turned back towards Bradshaw, but the man had gone. He looked among the various guests and visitors sitting in the chairs in the foyer, but there was no sign of him. Puzzled, Mark walked briskly towards the entrance of the hotel, hoping to catch a glimpse of his departing figure, to find himself face-to-face with Penny Scott, who was coming through the front door. It struck him forcibly that, unless it was pure coincidence, she had an uncanny sense of timing. She started to greet him, but the smile froze on her face as he walked quickly past, calling 'Back in a moment,' and stepped into the street outside.

There was no sign of Bradshaw. He walked past parked cars, to look in either direction along the pavement. Nothing. A uniformed doorman glanced at him inquiringly, in case he needed a taxi, but he gave a quick shake of his head and walked back into the hotel.

Penny looked subdued. 'Well, hello goodbye!'

'What? Oh, I'm sorry. Tell me, did you see a man coming out of the hotel? He was quite tall, heavily built, wearing a blazer. He had glasses on.'

'No, I don't think so.'

'Are you sure? I don't see how you could have missed him.'

Her face was anxious. 'I don't remember anyone like that. Who was he?'

'Bradshaw, Lewis Bradshaw.' He watched her face carefully, but she did not react. 'I was just talking to him, when I was called away to the desk. When I turned round, he'd gone. He must have passed you on the way out.'

'I didn't notice him if he did. Did you look in the bar?' She pointed to a doorway on the right of the front entrance. 'He might have gone through there.'

'I doubt it. Never mind.' Why was she here, at the hotel? They had arranged to meet again at Kingsway Hall. Even more important, or so it seemed, why did she walk in so conveniently just as Bradshaw made his exit? He turned to her. 'I hadn't expected to see you until later.'

'I know.' She brought a hand from behind her back. In it, she was holding a single long-stemmed rose. 'It's a peace offering. I'm sorry I was so ratty when I left you. That stupid business with the car threw me. I didn't mean to be so rude. Pax?'

She was charmingly contrite and, despite himself, Mark smiled. 'So you read the Shortbread Eating Primer, too?'

'The shortbread what?'

'Nothing. It was a Latin book my generation read at school. Everyone inked in the same alterations on the jacket.' He took the rose. 'Thank you, but you needn't have bothered. I wasn't that upset.'

'I was. Those bloody hooligans could have caused a dreadful

accident. It was a bad smash. They could have killed someone. My nerves took quite a beating.'

'You're sure that's all there was to it?' She nodded. 'They didn't look like hooligans to me. I caught a glimpse of the man in the back seat.'

'I didn't see him. What was he like?'

'Dark complexion. It was just a glimpse. He might have been an Arab.'

She shrugged. 'That could explain it. Half of them still think they're playing "chicken" on the streets of Dubai. I've no doubt they pulled out a wad of banknotes to pay everyone off before the police arrived. Bloody Arabs! I wish they'd pack up their tents and piss off!' She seemed unreasonably vehement.

'I don't know if he was an Arab or not. All I saw was a face with a dark complexion. I still think they were trying to stop us. I thought the man in the back was going to come over.'

'Maybe they didn't see you sitting next to me. They've been known to try that, too. Charming!'

'And you don't think there was any connection with Berman?'

She seemed surprised. 'No. Do you?'

'I don't know. You may be right. After last night's fun and games, I may be letting my imagination run wild.'

'Speaking of which, I didn't even ask you how you were feeling.'

'Better, thanks – a bit bruised, but nothing serious.'

'I'm glad. What did the lawyer say?'

'As little as he could. It appears that Berman was a young tycoon. From what he hinted, he was worth a lot – more than he could possibly have earned from stroking his precious Stradivarius.'

Penny recognised the reference and pulled a face. 'I had that impression when I saw the flat. I know concert soloists earn a good living, but that place was a palace compared with what the rest of us can afford.'

'He was flying higher than that. Scutter wasn't giving very much away, but he indicated that Sandor had much more where that came from, involving holding companies, investments and other properties.'

'But where could it all have come from?'

'I've been trying to puzzle it out.'

He told her his theories about wealthy sponsors. Penny listened intently, occasionally nodding in agreement. When he had finished, she sighed. 'It certainly adds up. Not a very pretty picture, but apart from our American lady, nobody found him a very pretty man.'

'No. On the other hand, it doesn't explain why somebody would want to murder him.'

'I suppose not. Maybe the sponsor in question had a jealous husband. I must say, I could have throttled him with my own bare hands during the playback . . .' She stopped, closing her eyes. 'Oh God! That's a rotten way to talk!'

'Don't worry. It's amazing how quickly one becomes hardened, without even intending to. How's the session going?'

'Marvellous! They were just taking the long break when I sneaked out. Steigel's amazing, isn't he? He made a sweet little speech to the orchestra, just before the first take, explaining that he had arranged for the record jacket to carry a small dedication to Berman's memory. They played their hearts out for him.' She looked at her watch. 'We ought to get back.'

'I should call the Inspector. He was out when I tried earlier.'

'Why don't you do it from the dressing room? There's a telephone in there.' She was walking towards the door. Glancing around the foyer, she said: 'I see we're surrounded by the Americans.'

'Really? How can you tell?'

'Look at their trousers. No other race would dare to wear such ghastly colours and patterns! Come on.' She seemed anxious to leave, and he followed her to her car, which was parked up against a Bentley, so close that its bumper was touching. The doorman wagged a friendly finger at her. He was becoming accustomed to her intrusions.

Strapping himself in, Mark said: 'Karen's playing hostess to the fingerprint brigade. I called her.'

'That's nice.' She made it deliberately insincere.

'You don't like her very much, do you?'

'I don't know enough about her to like her or not. I thought she was a bit odd. I said so yesterday, but I don't think I dislike her, beyond my normal xenophobia towards Americans in general. I'm going to have to get over that if I'm going to stay at Magnum. I suppose I didn't find her story very convincing. It was a bit too good to be true, with all that rigmarole about separate rooms and Sandy being the perfect little gentleman.'

'It could have been the way she described it.' He was not prepared to tell her about Karen's 'confession'.

'I suppose it could. Anyway, you can judge that better than I.' She grinned at him. 'You've seen *much* more of her than I have!'

Mark did not reply, and she concentrated on driving, racing round vehicles along Piccadilly and up Shaftesbury Avenue, until they were in the maze of back streets behind Seven Dials. She drove smoothly and aggressively, impatient with slower cars, and edging through spaces that barely permitted the width of the Mini. Within minutes, they had reached Kingsway Hall, and she drove, as before, down the narrow service lane at the rear, switching off the engine and coasting to a stop a few feet behind the engineer's car.

Penny leaned over to the back seat of the car, where she had tossed her handbag, and Mark unstrapped himself and stepped out. As he walked towards the rear entrance, he noticed a man, standing half hidden in the doorway. He was wearing a tan raincoat, the collar pulled high around his face, and a soft felt hat. As Mark approached, the man stepped into full view. He was holding a revolver, to which a long black silencer had been attached. It was pointed directly at Mark's heart. The man said nothing, moving forward until they were a few feet apart.

Mark stood deathly still, watching the man's eyes. From behind, he heard the sudden, rasping sound of the Mini's starter. The engine roared briefly, and he saw the man's eyes flicker in its direction. Mark looked round, to see Penny reversing rapidly out of the lane, steering with one hand, her head turned away from them. A moment later, she had disappeared from view.

8

Mark faced the man, thinking: 'The bitch! No wonder she was so anxious to bring me to Kingsway Hall! But why? Who is she working for? What do they want?' He said nothing, keeping his hands at his sides. At least the man had not fired. If it was to be a straight hit, it would be all over by now. The gunman edged forward, still out of reach. The revolver in his hand was very steady. Mark watched him. There was something vaguely familiar about his face. After a moment, he gestured slightly with his gun hand, motioning Mark to return up the lane towards the street.

'What do you want?' Mark kept his voice calm.

The man spoke with a slight accent. 'A car is waiting at the corner of the street. Walk to it.' He sounded as though he might be French, but it was difficult to tell. He gestured again with the gun.

Mark did not move. If the man stepped closer, there was a chance of catching him off-guard. 'You haven't told me what you want, yet.'

'Go to the car. We will talk there.' The man remained at a safe distance, watching him warily, and turned his head briefly, to make sure the alley was deserted. At that moment, Mark recognised his face. He had been in the back of the Peugeot that morning.

Leaning forward on the balls of his feet, Mark tried to smile. He doubted that it was very successful. 'That was quite a chase this morning. You're lucky you weren't killed. What were you trying to do?'

The man hesitated for a moment, uncertain whether to reply. He gestured again with the gun. 'Walk to the car.'

'And if I refuse?'

The man shrugged. 'You will be hurt.'

'Why can't we talk here?' Was that the extent of his threat?

Apparently, somebody wanted him alive, well enough to talk.

'No. In the car. It is waiting. Do as I say and you will not be hurt.'

Mark swung his body, as if to move away. His weight was placed on his left foot, ready to swivel, and be half turned, as if to speak again. His captor, following too close behind, had let his right hand drop to his side. He brought it up again, to urge Mark forward, but was too late. Mark swung round suddenly, chopping down on the man's arm with the edge of his hand. The gun fell from his grip, landing in the centre of the lane with a sharp clatter that echoed in the confined space. He winced with pain, stepping back as Mark's foot followed through, catching the damaged arm just above the wrist. The man recovered fast, moving out of Mark's reach. For a moment, the two men stared at each other. The man's eyes darted to the left, in the direction of the gun. Mark could see him calculating the distance he would have to throw himself to retrieve it. He watched him closely, taking in his features. The man was no Arab. He was dark-skinned, with the leathery complexion of someone who had spent many hours in bright sunlight. He could be from the Mediterranean coast of France or Italy.

Mark moved in quickly, aiming for the throat, but the man side-stepped him, dodging unexpectedly to his right, away from the gun, and swinging his left hand in a vicious backhand chop that struck Mark on the neck. He staggered headlong, and the man darted quickly into the lane and retrieved the gun. Standing above Mark, but keeping a safe distance, he pointed the revolver again. He was breathing heavily.

'Stand up. If you try again, I will shoot.' He circled behind Mark, his left hand clasping his damaged right arm to steady it. 'I am a good shot. You will not die, but you will be hurt. Don't be foolish.'

Mark stood, brushing himself off. He looked at the gunman and shrugged, and the man gave a tiny nod, as if to acknowledge the attempt. His face was expressionless. Mark bowed his head accepting defeat, and walked slowly towards the corner of the street. Pedestrians were walking past the narrow entrance to the lane, unaware of their presence. The pavement was busy.

'The car is waiting. You will get in. Enter the rear door. I am directly behind you.' The man spoke softly, maintaining a safe distance.

Mark nodded, walking slowly. His shoulder was brushing against the wall of the alley. A steady pulse was throbbing in his temple. He emerged from the shadow of the alley into bright sunlight. From the corner of his eye, he was aware of more pedestrians approaching and, before the man could catch up with him, threw himself to the right, close to the wall. If the man was going to shoot him, he would have to do it in the presence of passers-by, or try to force Mark at gunpoint in front of half a dozen witnesses. It was a gamble worth taking.

As he landed full length on the ground, Mark saw a pair of large black shoes and blue-black trousers and, looking upward, recognised the uniform of a London policeman. The policeman stared down at him in surprise. Penny was standing a few feet behind him, her face tense and pale.

The Frenchman ran round the corner. His eyes widened at the sight of the policeman, and he brought the revolver up, ready to fire. Nobody moved, and he ran a few paces to a small mud-spattered car, which was double-parked in the road, its engine running. Keeping the gun pointed at the policeman, the man called to the driver of the car, and dragged the rear door open. Within seconds, he was in the car, which accelerated away with screaming tyres round a corner.

The policeman pulled a walkie-talkie from his shoulder, speaking rapidly into it, and Penny ran forward to Mark, kneeling at his side and placing her arms round his shoulders.

'Thank God! Are you all right?' She saw the expression on his face. 'What is it? What's the matter?'

Mark stood up, his eyes never leaving her face. 'It didn't work.'

Penny backed away. 'Didn't work? What do you mean?' She realised the implication. 'You don't think I had anything to do with it? You're crazy!'

'You disappeared very conveniently!'

'Disappeared?' She gave a quick intake of breath. 'Of course I did! It was the only chance.'

'Really? How did you work that out?'

'The policeman. I noticed him walking this way as I turned into the lane. I watched for a second or two when that man came out of the door. When he didn't shoot you, I thought there was a chance to get help. I would have run, but it was quicker in the car if I could get it out of there. For God's sake! What are you trying to suggest?' She spoke rapidly, her face pale, but two angry red marks were forming on her cheeks. 'I didn't know if I was going to make it out of the lane. I expected a bullet through the back of my head, for Christ's sake!'

'I didn't see a policeman.'

'Well I did! Why the hell did you think I drove out?' She was angry, close to tears. 'I backed out round the corner and grabbed him. It was the only thing I could think of.' She gazed round to where her Mini was parked in the road, blocking the traffic, and swallowed hard, fighting back tears. Cars were sounding their horns impatiently, while they edged past it. After a moment, she regained control. 'I'd better move my bloody car.'

Mark hesitated. 'I'm sorry. I didn't know what to think. One minute you had driven me in there, and the next, the Frenchman was pointing a gun at me.'

'Frenchman?'

'He sounded French. I don't know if he was. The next thing I knew, you were driving away as fast as you could, leaving me with him. What did you expect me to think?'

She nodded slowly. 'I suppose you're right. My only reaction was to run for help. There was nothing else I could do from where I was.' For a moment, her anger returned. 'But how could you think I would . . .' Mark said nothing, and she sighed. 'What did he want?'

'He told me to get in that car that just drove off.'

'Why?'

'I didn't wait to ask. He said they wanted to talk to me.' The pulse in his temple had slowed. 'He wasn't very communicative. I took him on, but he was faster than I expected. If nothing else, it wasted enough time for you to get here. This doesn't seem to be my week for unarmed combat!'

The policeman clipped his radio back on to his shoulder, and turned his attention to them. 'Perhaps you'd like to tell me what's going on.' He fixed Mark with a cold stare.

Mark said: 'I wish I could.' He described the events as they had taken place, and the policeman listened stonily.

When Mark had finished, he said: 'You'll need to come with me to make a full report.'

'Did you get the car's number?'

The policeman shook his head. 'No, they'd carefully plastered mud on the rear number plate. It looks as though they knew what they were doing. If you ask me, they'll drive it to the nearest car wash and clean it up before anyone spots them. They could be anywhere in the next few minutes. I called in, but there's only a chance they'll be seen in time. Do you know who that man was?'

'No, but I saw him this morning.' Mark told him about the car chase.

The policeman eyed Penny severely. 'Why didn't you report this?'

She gestured weakly. 'It didn't seem important at the time. I thought they were just a couple of stupid bastards playing games with me. Well, that's not altogether true. I was a bit shaken up by it, and just wanted to get away. We had already left them behind when they crashed, and there were plenty of witnesses around. I know I should have stopped.' She stole a quick glance in Mark's direction. 'I was upset. I'm sorry.'

The policeman's face was contemptuous. 'You'd better come over to the station and make a report now.' He gestured with his head. 'Your car's blocking the traffic.' Turning to Mark, he said: 'You seem to have had a lucky escape. I'll need a full statement.'

Mark took the Inspector's card from his pocket. 'Can we get in touch with this man? He's investigating yesterday's murder in the hall, and I'm convinced that this and other events are tied in with it.'

The policeman read the card and raised his eyebrows. 'All right. I'll see if he can be contacted.'

'Thanks. Oh, and one more favour: I'm supposed to be picking up the conductor who's recording in the hall this morning. He'll be worried if I don't show up. I'd like to leave a message for him that I'll see him later.'

The policeman looked suspicious. 'Where is he?'

'Inside the hall. They're in the middle of a recording session at this moment. We were on our way to see him.' Penny had retrieved her Mini, driving it back into the lane. 'I'll leave a message with the technical crew backstage.'

'All right. Make it quick.' Mark walked to the rear entrance of the hall. As he entered the back door, he could see the policeman standing next to Penny, talking again into his radio. Penny, still pale, was standing at his side. Their eyes met for a moment, and she looked quickly away.

Mark left the police station an hour later, tired and irritable. The small interview room had been stuffy, smoke-filled and depressing, and he had become increasingly impatient as the policeman had laboriously prepared a handwritten statement. With each repetition of the day's events, there was a loss of any sense of urgency, and the mundane descriptive phrases failed to recapture what had happened. But then, how could a police report, with its impersonal language and less than perfect grammar, portray the moment when he had faced the gunman, wondering whether it might be his last conscious image? When he had signed the final sheet prepared for his signature, the detective in charge, watching his face, had grinned and said: 'I'm afraid it loses something in the translation,' but it had failed to amuse him.

Penny, walking at his side, was subdued. Her report had been a duplication of his own, delivered in a low monotone, and there had been further delays while it was written out for her to sign. As they approached her car, she said: 'Do you still want to see the Steigels? I'm supposed to go there to arrange a photo session for the album cover, but you don't have to come with me if you don't want to. I can tell them you've been held up.' Her smile was wan. 'The pun wasn't intended.'

'No, I'll come with you.' He glanced at his watch, wondering whether to call Karen.

'As you like. Why wasn't the Inspector there?'

'I don't know. He was still out, apparently. For someone investigating a murder, he's making himself remarkably unavailable.' Penny was silent. 'I'm sorry I attacked you earlier. I made the wrong assumption, but you must admit that it looked bad, driving away the way you did.'

'I suppose it must have. It was the only thing I could think of doing, and I was trying not to panic.' She looked at him. 'I was angry that you even thought I could be involved in something like that.'

Mark spoke quietly. 'I didn't know what to think. Everything has been happening very quickly. Besides, we've only just met. We hardly know each other.'

She continued to watch him. 'I suppose you're right. We hardly know each other at all.'

Konstantin Steigel met them at the door of his suite. A napkin was tucked into the collar of his shirt. 'Ah, at last I am to be honoured with a visit from my distinguished manager!' He gave a mock bow, but opened his arms in greeting. 'Come in, my dear, come in. I was looking for you this morning, and wondering whether you had deserted me for good.'

'I'm sorry, maestro. I was held up.' Mark glanced at Penny, and she smiled briefly.

'Never mind. It was not important. We were just finishing our lunch. Can I order something for you?' Steigel was clearly in high spirits, yet to unwind from the nervous tensions of the morning's *Eroica* session. Sitting at a table by the window, Heidi was pouring coffee. Beyond her, Mark could see sunlight sparkling on the Thames. A sightseeing boat, crowded to capacity, was ploughing its way towards the Tower of London.

'Nothing for me, thank you.' Penny also shook her head. 'I was sorry to miss the session. I had been looking forward to it. How did it go?'

'Very well, I think; better than I had expected. You know, my dear, London orchestras may not be the best in the world, but they are excellent in the recording studio. It's strange, but they react to microphones in a manner quite different from most orchestras.'

'They have more practice than the others. The orchestras here make more records than anywhere else in the world, and if the pound keeps sinking, they'll get even more work than before.'

'*Ja, ja,* you could be right. Maybe we should place a few microphones among the players when they give concerts. It might encourage them subconsciously!'

Penny said: 'I thought London had the best orchestras anyway.'

Steigel smiled at her. 'Not if you're going to include Vienna and Berlin, or Chicago and Cleveland. Those are the Rolls-Royce orchestras. Still, London can provide at least an occasional Mercedes or BMW.'

She smiled: 'That depends who's steering it,' and Steigel looked pleased. 'I promise we'll be at the next session. What did you do today?'

'We finished the first movement, and it was not half bad, even if I am saying so myself. You know, it's full of pitfalls, but the tempo is the great problem. Normally, that doesn't worry me, and too much emphasis is placed on tempo, but if you start the *Eroica* too fast, it sounds frantic.' He was rolling his 'r's with Teutonic relish. 'But if you are too slow, it's a disaster, because the funeral march in the second movement will go on for ever. The tempo has to be related. The little space between those first two chords at the very beginning of the first movement will tell you how long it will take, all the way to the end of the second movement.' He lectured them like a benevolent schoolmaster. 'Anyway, very slow in a concert hall is considered noble and majestic, these days. On a record, it's just boring!'

Penny was surprised. 'Really? Do you mean you conduct it differently on records?'

'Of course! Nobody can see you when you make a record, and you have to make a suitable accommodation.' His eyes twinkled. 'There is a current fascination with slowing everything down. I have no intention of emulating some of my elderly colleagues by reducing everything to an Adagio, even if the distinguished members of the press now consider it wonderful!' He chuckled. 'I am convinced that hardening of the arteries is becoming confused with deep musical understanding.' He beamed at Penny. 'Now, my dear, are you sure you won't have something? At least, a cup of coffee? They brought enough for two, and I never drink it after I have been working.'

Penny nodded gratefully, and Heidi filled a cup. 'I have to arrange photographs for the cover, maestro. Can you spare me some time before you leave London?'

'*Ja, ja*, if you insist, but not until after the concert tomorrow. We will make an appointment then. How much time do you need?' Like most musicians, Steigel affected a dislike of being photographed, but Mark had the feeling that he secretly enjoyed it.

'A couple of hours would be helpful.'

'Very well. Do you think they would come here? I will put on my best suit and sit by the window, looking contemplative. That should be entirely appropriate for Beethoven, and I must confess I am a little tired of all those action pictures, slightly out of focus, showing me waving my arms like a lunatic.'

'I'll arrange it. New York usually asks for action shots.'

'Oh, New York!' He looked heavenwards for consolation. 'They either want that or some outrageous pose that looks like an advertisement for a deodorant. The last time they photographed me, a hairy young man, who could have used some of the self-same deodorant, asked me if I would like to lie down on top of a grand piano, in a "relaxed" position, if such a thing is possible. He thought it would make me look "different"!' He scowled at the memory. 'Fortunately, the piano in question was a Baldwin, and I explained that I was a Steinway artist, making it out of the question.' He peered over the tops of his glasses at Mark, a severe expression on his face. 'I received a call from that dreadful man in New York, Mark.'

'Greg Laufer?'

'*Ja*. He wished to express his condolences over the death of Sandor Berman, and wept crocodile tears into the telephone for at least thirty seconds. He also remembered, in the midst of his sorrow, to cross-examine me, making sure that I could finish the symphony in three sessions, with no overtime.'

'I told him you would, especially with the rehearsals for the concert.'

'I know. I said the same thing. Incidentally, I have arranged for your tickets at the Artists' Entrance of the Albert Hall for tomorrow evening.' His eyes narrowed. 'I think the real reason for his call was to persuade me to conduct some of that idiotic new music he sent me.'

'What was that?'

'Ach, some trite pieces from the so-called minimalist school. He asked me what I thought of them, so I told him I considered it to be music by a composer of minimal talent and minimal imagination, designed for audiences of minimal taste and minimal intelligence.' He was clearly pleased with his definition. 'It's a sort of popsy-wopsy music, intended for earnest young men and women who know nothing about music, and tell each other they are listening to "the classics" with a capital "K". At my age, I'm not going to waste my few remaining years with such nonsense.'

'I didn't know he'd sent you anything.'

'Oh yes, my dear. I think he now tells his friends he is a patron of the arts.' He shrugged. 'The melodies are baby simple, and repeated *ad nauseam*, which makes them easy for him to follow. My God, to think I once asked George Szell whether he had ever conducted Weinberger; you know, who composed *Schwanda der Dudelsackpfeifer*?' He sang a few bars from the famous Polka from the opera. 'George fixed me with that fishy stare of his, and said: "No, and I don't conduct Richard Rodgers either!" *Gott!* What would he have said about this rubbish!'

Penny said: 'George Szell was a pretty fierce old buzzard, wasn't he?'

Steigel smiled. 'No, my dear, not really, but he didn't suffer fools or charlatans.' He paused for a moment, as if remembering. 'He was a musician of enormous knowledge and impeccable taste. Nobody fooled him! But he was excellent company, and he loved a good joke. Sometimes, his stories made poor

Heidi blush!' From her corner, Heidi nodded happily. 'Incidentally, Mark, I must tell you a charming story I heard from a man at Oxford University Press.' He settled himself into a chair, his fingertips together, and Mark had the impression that he had rehearsed the story carefully before telling it. 'It seems there was a bar in New York, and a man walks into it with a little dog, and says to the bartender: "I have a talking dog. If he performs for you, will you give us a free drink?" The bartender says: "No! Go away! I don't like performing animals." So the man ignores him, and says to the dog: "What do you put on the top of a house?", and the dog goes: "Rrroof!"' Again, Steigel rolled his 'r's with gusto. 'Then the man says to the dog: "What did Elizabethan gentlemen wear around their necks?", and the dog goes: "Ruff!", but the bartender is still unimpressed. So, then the man says: "And who was the greatest choral composer of the twentieth century?", and the little dog goes: "Orff!"' Steigel shrugged his shoulders, fully into the character of the story. 'Still the bartender was unresponsive, and threw the man out. So, the man is walking along the street, looking disconsolate, and the dog looks up at his master and says: "Do you think I should have said Stravinsky?" Hah!' Steigel slapped his knee with pleasure, and Mark laughed. All musicians loved jokes, especially if they were about music. There was always a new story circulating between the orchestras.

Penny, smiling, said: 'I'll never remember that. I'm terrible at telling stories.'

Steigel wagged a finger happily at her. 'That's because you are not a musician, my dear. It's a matter of good timing, and that is our speciality.'

They talked for another hour, exchanging the perennial gossip of their world: who would take over which orchestra in the endless musical chairs of the concert scene; which young artists were developing as soloists; how would the opera houses survive the next budget cuts. As they talked, Mark felt himself relaxing. It was good to be 'home' again, in the tranquil isolation of musical life, away from the realities of the past twenty-four hours. Penny listened like an attentive schoolgirl, sitting forward in her chair, the palms of her hands flat on the seat, under her thighs. The police and Sandor Berman and Kingsway Hall were temporarily forgotten. Heidi had returned to her knitting, nodding silently and smiling as she listened. She was accustomed to being a good audience.

At length, Steigel looked at his watch and stood, to indicate that their meeting should end. 'I have another long day tomorrow, my dears, with a rehearsal at ten and a concert in the evening. Will I see you in the morning?'

Penny said: 'I'll come to some of the rehearsal, if I may. It means playing truant from the office, but I don't think I've ever been to one.'

Konstantin beamed at her. 'Of course you may. That's where all the work is done. The concert may be the finished product, but we put it all together at the rehearsal. If you want to learn about music, my dear, go to the rehearsals. The concerts are often less interesting.' He turned to Mark. 'Is there any news from the police about yesterday's business?'

'Not at the moment. Their inquiries will probably take some time." Mark looked at Penny, his eyes warning her not to discuss what had been happening. It did not concern Konstantin or Heidi.

Steigel shook his head. 'It is a bad business. He was a very talented young man. I don't know what has happened to our so-called civilised world. It grows madder every day.' He peered closely at Mark. 'You do not look so well yourself.'

Mark shrugged. 'I'm well enough, maestro. I didn't sleep very well last night.'

Heidi walked over to him. 'That is not good, Mark.' She looked knowingly at Penny, and smiled. 'You should forget the past, and settle down with a nice girl.'

'I will, when I can find the time.'

'Don't wait too long. Time disappears before you notice it has gone.'

As they walked to the car, Penny said: 'What did she mean about forgetting the past?'

'Nothing much.' Afternoon sunlight was casting long shadows across the Strand. 'There was someone I was once very fond of. She died.' There was nothing to add.

'I see.'

'Heidi thinks I still brood about it, and spend too much time thinking about her.'

'And do you?'

'No.'

'I'm sorry. I didn't mean to pry.'

'You weren't. It all happened a long time ago. Heidi has a romantic imagination.'

'She's very sweet. They both are.'

'Don't let Konstantin hear you say that. It would destroy all his illusions of himself!'

'I'm not so sure about that. I didn't have the feeling he was always looking at me like Ivan the Terrible. Wasn't Toscanini supposed to have been a lady's man?'

'All the way into his eighties, if the rumours are true.'

'Well, there you are.' She started the car. 'I don't know about you, but I'm starving. I haven't eaten all day.'

'You should have let them order something for you.'

'I know, but I resent London hotel prices. They're out of all proportion.'

'Hotels always are. Let's go somewhere, then.'

'I've got a better idea. I live a few minutes from here, with a refrigerator full of bits and pieces. It's much nicer than being formal about it. Wouldn't you like something?'

'Not really. I had breakfast.' Penny was silent, and he felt slightly guilty. When she had met him, he had said he had only just awoken. He wondered whether Karen was waiting for his call. 'Anyway, I can watch you eat.'

They drove into a sun-filled Trafalgar Square, criss-crossed with light and shadows and filled with tourists and sightseers. Watching the direction of his gaze, Penny said: 'I've never understood the fascination for feeding pigeons. I hate them flapping around my head.' She turned into Whitehall, past camera-bearing Americans and Japanese, photographing the mounted Guards. 'You're lucky, living in Geneva. It must be such a welcome escape from all the tourists. London gets so littered with them, as soon as the sun comes out.' Her voice softened. 'What was she like?'

He could not bring himself to speak her name. When he answered, his voice was impersonal. 'She was just somebody who was very important to me at the time. We worked together for a while.' He was silent again. What more was there to say about her? That they had lived together, and that he had loved her with all his heart, and that she had betrayed him? It was too complicated a story, and he did not wish to relive it. Penny would not understand.

Why did she want to know? From the moment they had met, and she had asked him about Geneva, she seemed unusually interested in his life. Why? Perhaps her story about seeing the policeman outside Kingsway Hall was true after all. She had certainly found one at the right moment, or had that merely been a lucky coincidence: an alibi in case the Frenchman failed? If they had not struggled for a few minutes in the alley, delaying the man, she would have arrived too late.

Penny's voice cut across his thoughts. 'Is that all you can say about her? You said you were very fond of her. What did she look like?'

His voice felt strained. 'Konstantin and Heidi think she was rather like you. She had fair hair and light blue eyes. There is a certain resemblance. I think they approve of you, by the way. Heidi likes to indulge in a little match-making!'

Penny's voice was light. 'I knew there was a reason why I liked them!' She drove through a crowded Westminster Square, past the Houses of Parliament, and continued along the Embankment. The modern skyscrapers on either side of the river seemed incongruous after the gothic arabesques of the older buildings. At Vauxhall Bridge, she turned right, and steered the Mini through a dozen back streets towards Victoria. She parked the car by a quiet row of houses that Mark guessed to be quite near the station. Penny revved the engine and switched off. 'It's not quite as grand as Sandor's place, I'm afraid, but most of the time I don't see very much of it.'

The flat was on the first floor of one of the houses. It was small and light, with a living room and a bedroom, and a tiny kitchen built into what must once have been a cupboard with a window. Two rooms of the house had been well converted into a self-contained unit. The furnishings were modern and comfortable, with green and beige as the dominant colours. Penny led the way, saying: 'Welcome to Chateau Scott. I'm glad I remembered to make the bed before I went out!' She seemed slightly nervous. 'Are you sure you won't have anything?'

'Sure, thanks.' The window looked across the street towards a similar, neat row of houses. She had attached a flower box to the sill, and the scarlet geraniums in it had a vaguely dusty scent. There was a telephone next to the couch, and he called: 'May I use the phone?'

'Help yourself.' She was busy in the kitchen.

He dialled the Inspector's number, and was surprised to be put through almost immediately. The younger man sounded genial.

'You seem to have been having a busy time, Mr Holland.'

'You could say that. I've been giving various people your name and number, so I assume they've been talking to you and keeping you up to date on my progress.'

'They certainly have. I'm sorry I couldn't make it to the station when you were there. I was talking to the American girl at the time.'

'Karen? Was she able to help?' Penny was standing in the doorway, a piece of Ryvita in her hand, watching him.

There was a pause before the Inspector spoke. 'Not a lot. She wasn't very forthcoming.'

'I don't think she knew much about him, from what she told us.' Penny sat in a chair, listening, and Mark felt himself growing self-conscious. 'She hardly knew him any better than we did.'

The Inspector sounded brisk. 'Maybe. I had the feeling she wasn't anxious to tell me everything she knew.'

'Well, she could have been embarrassed. When we saw her yesterday, I think she was rather concerned that we might think she was a kept lady. She was anxious to make it clear that she was just a friend, whatever appearances might have suggested. That could explain her reticence.' He was conscious of Penny's gaze.

'Perhaps.' The Inspector was not committing himself.

'What about the break-in; or rather, both break-ins?'

'The lads from Robbery told me about your theory, but frankly, I think you may be making too much of it. You haven't lived in London for a few years, have you? Unfortunately, break-ins and burglary have become commonplace in London nowadays. It's getting as bad as America. I'm inclined to think it's nothing more than a coincidence. They nicked a picture from the living room and, from what you told them, it was worth quite a bit.'

'I didn't say that. I thought it looked like a Chagall, from a brief glance, and said that if it was, it was valuable. That's not quite the same thing.'

'I know, but the picture's missing nevertheless, isn't it?'

'You didn't think the place looked as though it had been thoroughly searched? Even inside the loo?'

'Yes, but there's nothing unusual about that. You should see the mess some of those jokers make. They must have found the safe just before she came back. That's what tempted them to go for a second shot. A safe like that could contain all sorts of goodies.'

'And you think they'd risk it twice in the same day?'

'Why not? They probably worked it on the basis that lightning never strikes twice. It's a good thing you were there, but I don't understand why you didn't call us immediately.' His manner had cooled.

'I know. I should have, but I was feeling terrible and decided to sleep it off. I was running late in the morning, or I would have called before I left.' Again, he was conscious of Penny watching him. She knew there had been time for breakfast. 'Did they tell you about the car that followed us?'

'Yes.' He paused for a moment. 'How did the other lady – Miss Scott, is it? – come to be there?'

Mark stared at the floor, avoiding Penny's eye. 'Another coincidence.'

'I see. A lot of coincidences, aren't there?'

'So it would seem. I don't think I've mentioned a man called Bradshaw, by the way: Lewis Bradshaw. He came to see me at the hotel.'

'What did he want?'

'I'm not sure. It appears he had some sort of deal going with Berman. He kept calling it a little business transaction, and he seems to think I should know all about it. He wasn't a very attractive character.'

'And do you know what he wanted?'

'No. As a matter of fact, I was fishing around, trying to find out, but he wasn't giving anything away, except for a few thinly veiled threats.' He described the meeting.

There was a long pause before the Inspector spoke again. 'Sorry. I was making a few notes while you were talking. I'll check with Records and see if we can come up with anybody by that name. It looks as though your Mr Berman had a few funny friends and business associates. I wonder what he keeps in that safe of his.'

'We thought it was probably for his violins, but nobody knows the combination. I asked his lawyer about it this morning, but he couldn't help. He's a sort of financial adviser as well and, much against his will, provided some rather surprising information about Berman's financial situation.' Mark outlined his interview with Eric Scutter, adding some of the details of Berman's unexpected wealth. He suggested the possibility of wealthy sponsors.

The Inspector whistled under his breath. 'He's getting to be a very interesting young man, isn't he? I think I'd better pay Mr Scutter a visit.'

Mark smiled. 'Don't expect a welcome mat, but you'll find the office beautifully furnished, especially a secretary called Bunny.' He winked at Penny, but her face was impassive.

'I'll remember. It sounds as though Mr Berman has been a very busy fellow, from what you're saying. I thought most musicians lived with their heads in the clouds, but maybe that's just a romantic Victorian illusion. If I've heard you correctly, there's an unsavoury gentleman called Bradshaw who's hinting at violence, and a Frenchman with a gun who wants to have a little heart-to-heart talk with you. Do you think they're working together on this?'

'They could be, but I'm not quite sure how. I drove straight from seeing one to being met outside the hall by the other. They must have been pretty fast off the mark to be so well co-ordinated.'

'Not necessarily. A phone call takes a few seconds.' He paused. 'How did you get to the hall?'

'Miss Scott drove me there. It was in the report.' His eyes met Penny's. 'I'm calling you from her flat.'

'Ah yes. Now, was she with you when you saw this Mr Bradshaw?'

'No, she arrived just as he left.'

'Oh.' There was another pause. 'What a lot of coincidences for one day. Life's full of surprises, they say.' His cheerfulness sounded false.

'Yes, I suppose so.'

'Well, there's not a lot we can do for the moment, except add a few names to the file. Are you going to be at your hotel this evening?'

Mark hesitated. 'Possibly.'

He was not sure, but he thought the Inspector chuckled softly. 'Or possibly looking after a beautiful American girl whose reputation needs protecting?'

'Yes, something like that.' He avoided looking in Penny's direction.

'All right. I'll know where to call if I need you.' The Inspector hesitated for a moment. 'Look, I know something about your background, but please don't try to be a hero again. That's our line of work you're getting into.'

'I didn't do it on purpose, I can assure you. Anyway, I wasn't very successful at it, was I?'

'No. We're all inclined to get a bit rusty without practice. Next time, just call us, will you?'

'Yes.'

'I'd be grateful if you'd keep an eye on that American girl. There's something about her that doesn't feel right.'

'If you say so.' Mark found himself trying to keep his voice even. 'I would have thought you could have applied that observation elsewhere.'

'Miss Scott, do you mean? I haven't overlooked her, either.

She seems to have an uncanny flair for showing up at the right time. I take it you can't say very much at the moment.'

'No.'

'Well, call me back later if there's anything you want to add.'

'Yes.'

'We'll be in touch. Thanks for your help.' He hung up.

For a long time, there was silence in the room. Mark sat with his head bowed, staring at the patterns in the Axminster carpet. After a while, Penny walked over to the sofa, sitting close to Mark, her knees touching his. She took his hand. 'I suppose I should ask you all the details of that conversation, since I only heard your end of it, but I'm not going to. I'm tired, and I don't want to think about it any more this evening. Being with the Steigels made me forget about it for a while, and I don't want to start all over again. Not yet, anyway. Do you mind?'

Mark smiled at her. 'Not at all. I wish I could stop, too. It's been a hell of a twenty-four hours, one way and another.'

She took both his hands in her own, drawing them towards her body. Her face was very close, and her eyes looked into his. 'In that case, let's just forget it all for the next few hours.' She looked at him in silence. 'Will you stay?'

Mark shook his head slowly. 'I can't, Penny. I promised Karen – and the Inspector, just now – that I'd look in on her, to make sure she's all right.' At the mention of the American girl's name, Penny stiffened slightly, releasing his hands. He watched her face. 'I'll have to go round there.'

Penny moved away from him, walking to the table to light a cigarette. 'Of course.' She inhaled deeply.

Mark stood up. 'I'm sorry. It would be much nicer to forget them all and stay here.'

Penny avoided his eyes. 'It doesn't matter. I ought to catch up with a lot of chores, too. Are you sure I can't offer you anything to eat?' Her voice was impersonal.

'No, thanks.' He looked at his watch. It was later than he thought, and he had promised to call Karen sooner. 'I really ought to be going. I forgot to call my office back when they rang this morning, but they'll have gone home by now. I'll check at the hotel for calls.' Penny remained by the table, apparently lost in thought. She did not look in his direction as he made his way to the door. 'I'll call you later, if I have the chance.'

'Yes. My number's in the book.' Her voice was expressionless.

He said goodbye and made his way downstairs to the street. As he walked in search of a taxi, he had the feeling that she was watching him from the window, but he did not turn round to see.

9

As he entered the cab, Mark was about to ask for the Westbury, then changed his mind and gave the driver Karen's address. He was late, and could always telephone the hotel for any messages. The afternoon had become warm and humid again, hinting at more rain, and he was grateful that the taxi's windows were fully opened, creating a steady breeze.

He lit a cigarette and stared vacantly out of the window. His shoulder muscles were stiff, and there was a bruise on his hip from where he had fallen in the alley. It felt tender. Talking to the Inspector had been irritatingly frustrating. It was as though the man was deliberately blocking each idea, constantly sloughing it off as yet another 'coincidence'. Some of the pieces had to fit together. But which? And what did he mean when he said that Karen was not telling him everything she knew? It seemed a strange observation to make, unless the man simply lacked the imagination to understand her predicament. It must have been difficult enough for her to find herself penniless and isolated in a strange country, knowing nobody and waiting to call her parents for the money to buy a ticket home, and the sinister phone calls, Sandor's death, and then two men breaking into the apartment and attacking her – God knows why she hadn't had a nervous breakdown on the spot! She had survived it all remarkably well. What didn't the Inspector believe? Her story was plausible enough, especially when she had added the parts she left out when Penny was listening. Why should the man think she was hiding anything?

Mark shifted in his seat. He should not have called the Inspector from Penny's flat. Her presence embarrassed him, preventing him from speaking freely, and she appeared to see herself competing with Karen for him. That didn't make much sense. At least the policeman shared some of his doubts about Penny. Perhaps it was his job to doubt everyone. But how was she involved, and why? Was it just his imagination or a misplaced sense of guilt that questioned her unexplained presence outside Karen's flat? Had she really believed the French driver had been indulging in some sort of insane horse-play, and had she really noticed a policeman outside Kingsway Hall? She had found one, but had that been another of the Inspector's endless coincidences? And why, after what he had said to her, had she invited him to stay with her in the flat? Showbiz affection, or had she made another rendezvous with the Frenchman? He stubbed out the cigarette angrily. The images of the past twenty-four hours kept melting into each other, and the more he concentrated on a single one, the more confused they became. What the hell had Sandor Berman got himself into, and how did Bradshaw and the French delegation fit together? Had Scutter been exaggerating about Berman's wealth, or were they all separate elements in a puzzle to which only Berman had the key? He sighed, leaning back against the seat and feeling his shirt sticking to his shoulder-blades. Maybe Penny was right: forget them all for a few hours, make love, have a good night's rest and think about it again in the morning! No, that was impossible.

The taxi ambled up Park Lane amid light traffic, maintaining a steady path while faster cars dodged in and out. In Hyde Park, families were sitting on the grass, enjoying the last of the afternoon's sunlight. Sweaty men kicked footballs at each other, while their children patiently waited for a go. Two lovers, oblivious to sidelong glances of disapproval, were locked in each other's arms, their bodies pressed tightly together. Above them, a cloud of flying ants, caught in a shaft of sunlight, were performing a mating dance like a benediction. There was a restless queue waiting to buy ice creams and cold drinks at a kiosk under the trees, and a little boy on a tricycle, wearing a red sun-hat, was trying to pedal between their legs. Next to Speakers' Corner, a long row of charabancs, plastered with signs in half a dozen languages, patiently awaited their passengers.

When he went to ring the bell, the front door buzzed open immediately, and he looked up to see Karen watching from the window. She must have heard the taxi pull up. He was tempted to run up the stairs to her, but the lift was waiting on the ground floor. Stepping into it, he realised he was suddenly very tired. Leaning against the wooden panelling, he thought: 'I'm getting too old for this life!' In the old days, working for The Department, he could survive a night without sleep – longer, if necessary – living on a diet of adrenalin and cold fear. But life had been simpler then, without endless unanswered questions to deceive his judgement. And he had been ten years younger. His mind did not feel any older, but his body was. The ancient lift clanked to a stop, and he took a deep breath before sliding the metal doors open.

Karen was standing in the open doorway, wearing white denim trousers and a loose-fitting top whose royal blue matched the colour of her eyes. Her bare feet looked very brown against the trousers.

'Hi!' She smiled nervously, and stepped aside to let him in. After a moment's hesitation, she threw her arms around his waist, hugging him tightly, her cheek pressed against his chest. It was almost a repetition of their previous meeting, but she moved back and, putting her arm through his, walked him along the hall. 'I've missed you!'

'I'm sorry I didn't call. There never seemed to be a telephone available at the right time.'

'It doesn't matter, now that you're here. I knew you'd come back as soon as you could make it. I've been busy. Look!' With an air of pride, she threw open the living room door. Everything had been tidied and restored to place. She had turned over the padded seats on the sofa so that the jagged cuts were hidden, and the wood of the desks and tables gleamed. There was a pleasantly strong smell of scented furniture polish.

Mark smiled. 'I'm impressed!'

'I've done the bedrooms, too.' She was like a happy child, displaying her handiwork. 'It took most of the day. Those fingerprint experts made a mess with their silver powder. I had to polish everything twice to get rid of it. Do you want a drink: scotch?' He nodded, and she ran through to the kitchen to fetch ice and water. It was like an intimate ceremony between them, and he drank the whisky too quickly. It made him feel slightly light-headed.

Karen sat on the floor, resting her back against the sofa, watching him. The silence felt very peaceful. 'What sort of a day did you have?'

He shrugged. 'Busy.' For a moment, he was going to tell her about everything, but changed his mind. Maybe Penny was right. Why not forget it all for a few hours, and relax? And make love? Perhaps. She was very young, but beautiful. Her eyes still questioned him, and he said: 'I'll tell you about it in a while. At the moment, I'm enjoying doing nothing. How about you?'

Her gesture took in the room. 'You can see for yourself. Oh, and your detective came to see me, but that can wait, too.' Her face was sombre for a moment, but she moved to his chair to take the empty glass. 'More?' Mark shook his head. She seemed to be filled with nervous energy. 'Hey, can I bum a cigarette from you?'

'Of course. I didn't know you smoked.'

'I don't, most of the time. When I was working my way, I couldn't afford to – they cost a lot here, don't they? – but I didn't really miss them. Now, it's a kind of occasional luxury.' He struck a match, and she cupped her hands over his, her fingers touching him. 'How are you feeling?'

'Hot and tired. It's been a long day.'

'After a short night. Do you still hurt?' Her hand rested on his knee, and she nestled by his chair.

'Not bad; a bit battered and bruised.' He loosened his tie. 'It's getting humid again.' The windows of the living room were open, and he could hear birds singing accompaniment to the steady rumble of traffic.

'Yes.' She laughed. 'I took two baths. Housework makes me sticky. Shall I run a bath for you?' He nodded, and she darted out of the room. A moment later, he could hear water running. Her attentiveness was touching.

When she reappeared, she was holding several neatly folded shirts. 'If you want a change of clothes, I found these in a closet.' She hesitated. 'Unless, of course, you don't like to wear . . .'

'No, I could use a change. I'll borrow one. Choose it for me.' He stood slowly, and walked stiffly to the bathroom.

She called after him: 'I'll leave it outside the door.'

He undressed and stepped into the bath. The water was warm and soothing, and he settled back. Moments later, he fell asleep.

She awoke him half an hour later, tapping on the door. 'Mark, are you all right in there?'

He opened his eyes, disorientated and cold. 'Yes. I must have fallen asleep for a few minutes.'

'I was about to call in the Marines!'

He dressed, feeling refreshed.

Karen was staring into the refrigerator, a frown on her face. 'I'm trying to think of something we can eat without too much cooking. Is London always as hot and humid as this?'

'Seldom. You're experiencing a rare heatwave. That's why they don't bother with air-conditioning here, but don't complain: you're better off in the summer.'

'Why's that?'

'Because in the winter, the English are inclined to heat their windows and leave their rooms cold.' She looked surprised. 'If you look in most houses, you'll find they put the radiators under the windows. The hot air rises, hits the cold surface of the glass, and wastes all its energy.' He smiled. 'That's why I live in Switzerland.'

'Really?'

'No, not really, but English central heating leaves a lot to be desired.'

'Then why do you live in Switzerland?'

He paused, not yet ready to tell her. 'A number of different reasons. I wanted a change of scene, mostly, but London is my real home. It always will be. There are few great cities that can survive change quite so calmly. Every time I come back home, I regret ever having left it. One of these days, I'll come home to stay – when the memories have faded.'

'Are they so bad?' Her voice was soft.

'Perhaps not. The last few years in London left me very dissatisfied, but that could have been the company I was keeping. It's dangerous to dwell too much in the past.' He was silent, conscious that she was watching him. 'How long is it since you've eaten?'

She shrugged. 'We had breakfast. I was busy all day with the cleaning – and my visitors.'

'Yes, we can talk about them later. Come on, let's eat out somewhere. You've been stuck in here all day.'

She hesitated. 'I don't want to cause you extra expense. There's plenty of food . . .'

'Don't be silly.' He put a hand on her arm, and she in turn clasped it for a moment. It was a small gesture, but it pleased him. 'It's probably better outside. These old buildings have thick walls that retain the heat.'

They walked along the Edgware Road, towards Hyde Park. The sun had set, and the air was cooling. Karen stared at the shops and restaurants. 'Is this London's Mid-Eastern district?'

Mark laughed. 'No, London isn't divided into districts like an American town, although you might begin to wonder when you look around here. A few years ago, at the height of the Arab invasion, the Edgware Road did start to look like a souk every evening around six o'clock, but most of them folded their tents a few years ago. What you see is only a souvenir of their presence. This area has changed so much over the years. It used to be a pleasantly run-down district before the developers realised the possibilities.' He pointed to a restaurant displaying indecipherable Arabic lettering. 'That used to be a very popular Chinese restaurant in the old days. It was one of the few places that stayed open until three in the morning, so it became a great gathering place for London's musicians. They're late-night people, and you'd find them all there, classical and pop, after concerts or recording sessions. Most of the town shuts down after eleven o'clock.' He surveyed the smart new boutiques and Indian trading stores. 'Nearly every one of the shops on this street has changed in the past ten years. I don't know it any more. It's funny to be a stranger in one's own home.'

She nodded. 'You should see Cleveland. They flattened most of the downtown area and started again, not that there was anything worth saving!'

'There's always something. I remember when my parents sold their London house and moved to the country. A property developer bought the whole area. I drove down our road one day, and saw a wire fence along the pavement. When I looked, the house had gone. The garden was still there, with the same trees and flower beds that I'd always known, but they had removed the house. There was just a flat rectangle of cement, like a tombstone. It was strange, as though my entire childhood had been erased.'

She gave a shiver. 'That's eerie. Where are we heading?'

'To a restaurant overlooking the Serpentine.'

'What's that?'

'The lake you walked to yesterday. It's in the middle of the park.'

She took his hand. 'But it's getting dark.'

'That doesn't matter. You're quite safe: this is London.'

'If you say so. I guess I'm conditioned to expect danger.' Her hand remained in his.

As they entered the park, walking beneath shadowy plane trees, he said: 'Do you want to tell me about your various visitors today?'

'No, not yet.' She took a deep breath, stretching her arms wide. 'This air feels so good! It's as though I've been breathing recycled oxygen all day in that apartment! Let's talk about other things: anything or nothing. I don't want to think about it for a few hours. Do you mind?'

His hand held hers more tightly. 'It's exactly what I want, too. I'm tired of thinking about Sandor Berman, and musicians and lawyers and Frenchmen and sinister business men and I don't know who the hell else! We'll give them all a rest.'

'I'm glad. Tell me about Switzerland. All I know about is mountains, watches and candy.'

He smiled. 'You've just about covered it if you add banks.'

They ate a leisurely meal in a quiet corner of the restaurant, overlooking the black waters of the artificial lake. Outside their window, on a patch of grass leading down to the water's edge, a family of rabbits rummaged for food, and through the dark silhouettes of trees, the lights of distant buildings twinkled like beacons. There was a dull red glow in the sky, reflecting the city. At first, they talked quietly, and Mark told her about his life in the music world, but as the evening lengthened, neither spoke for long periods, and they relaxed in the intimacy of each other's company. They shared a bottle of St Estèphe, enjoying its slightly smoky flavour, scarcely noticing the food, and Mark felt himself unwinding for the first time in many hours. It was as though he had known her for a long time. When the hovering waiter finally presented the bill, Karen sighed.

'I guess it's time to go back to the real world.' She put out her hand, and Mark held it. 'Thank you. It was a lovely evening.'

'You're making it sound a little final. We can have others.'

She smiled sadly. 'Perhaps, but you know what I mean.'

As they walked across the bridge over the Serpentine, she hugged his arm tightly. A young couple, their arms entwined, their faces touching, sauntered past, momentarily spotlighted by a passing car. Karen said: 'I've been putting off telling you about that Inspector.'

'What did he have to say?'

'Not very much.' She was silent for a long time, walking in step with him. 'I don't think he believed what I told him.'

'Why not?'

'I don't know. I told him exactly what I told you: how I met Sandy and drove to Paris, and on to London. I didn't leave anything out, and he listened politely, but I don't think he believed me. He was very British and formal and all that, but there was something about the way he looked at me.' She held his arm tighter. 'Oh Mark, I'm scared!'

'There's nothing to be afraid of. Policemen are inclined to be formal. Did he say anything to upset you?'

'Not exactly. I guess it's what he didn't say. He asked to see my passport, and said he hoped I wasn't planning to leave the country. I told him I had called home and was waiting for the money, but he said I couldn't leave without clearing myself with him. For a while, I thought he was going to take my passport away.'

'That's ridiculous! I don't think he's allowed to do that.'

'Well, he didn't actually do it. I just thought he was going to. Maybe I'm just overwrought.'

'I'll call him in the morning, and ask him what he's up to.'

'Would he tell you?'

'Probably not, but he has no right to bully you.'

'He didn't; I mean, he didn't say anything I can quote to you. He just treated me very politely and looked at me sort of coldly, and made me feel guilty. I even thought he might arrest me.'

'But you haven't done anything!'

'I know. That's what scares me.' They could see the lights of the Bayswater Road. 'Mark, can we get out of this park, please. I don't like being in the dark!'

When they returned to the flat, Mark sensed her nervousness. It occurred to him that she was wondering whether he would stay and, without the drama of a break-in to draw them together, it altered their relationship. The intimacy of their evening in the restaurant had dispersed. He brushed the thought aside, and said: 'I wish we knew what Sandor kept in that safe. Did the police take away the stethoscope?'

'I guess so. Why?'

They stood in the doorway of the cupboard, and Mark stared at the Chubb. 'I thought we might try to open it ourselves. It's worth a try.'

'What should we do?'

'We could try a few obvious numbers. Have you any idea when his birthday was?'

'Yes. April eleventh. He's an Aries. I know, because we compared signs. I'm a Scorpio. He wanted to know if we were compatible.'

'And were you?' For a moment, he thought of Penny, and frowned.

'I don't know. We didn't know enough about it. He was going to buy a book.'

'What year was he born?'

'Nineteen fifty-six. He was nearly two years older than I am.'

Mark knelt before the safe. 'Now, these safes normally open on a combination of three numbers, and you usually start by turning to the right. Let's try eleven right, then four left, and fifty-six right.' He dialled the knob, stopping carefully on each number on the bevelled dial, then pulled the heavy handle. It remained rigid. 'That's no good.'

Karen knelt at his side. 'You did it the wrong way round. It should have been four, eleven, fifty-six.'

'You're right. If he had lived in America all that time, he would have put the month first.' He worked the dial again, but nothing happened. Mark sat back on his haunches. 'Damn! I wish we had that stethoscope. I suppose I could try putting my ear against the door and turning the dial slowly, in case I can hear the tumblers.' He smiled. 'It always works in films.'

Karen looked disappointed. 'Do you think so? It sounds too easy.' In the confined space, they were very close, their shoulders touching. He was conscious of her perfume. 'I would have thought the insurance company would have expected him to choose something less obvious than his birthdates. Those violins are worth a lot of money, and if he kept them in the safe for safety . . .'

'Wait a minute!' A sudden thought struck Mark. 'At the session yesterday, we were talking about the violins, and Berman said something about his real insurance being with Mendelssohn, Brahms and Beethoven. No, that wasn't what he said.' He closed his eyes, trying to recall the moment. 'He said: "My real insurance lies with Beethoven, Brahms and Mendelssohn," and then he smiled and said: "In that order". I remember wondering at the time what he meant by that remark.'

'I don't understand.'

'He talked about the composers "in that order" as though it

was some kind of private joke he was enjoying. It struck me at the time that he put them out of chronological order, unless he was thinking in terms of importance, or the way he'd learned them, or even the order in which he hoped to record them. It's not very important, but it stuck in my mind.' A new thought occurred. 'Did you notice an American record catalogue among his things when you were cleaning up today?'

'I don't know. What does it look like?'

'It's a small paperback book, about so big,' he illustrated with his hands, 'called the Schwann catalogue. I thought I saw one on the floor by his desk after the burglary.'

'I'll go see.' She left his side and ran into the living room. A moment later, she called: 'It's here!' and returned, handing him the book.

Mark took out a pencil and leafed through the pages. 'The catalogue lists all the recordings available in America, by composer. Musicians are always fascinated by numbers. I suppose it's because they work with them all the time, one way or another. Let's write down some dates. I don't have to look up Beethoven; that's easy. Seventeen-seventy to eighteen-twenty-seven.' He tore the back page from the catalogue, and handed the book to Karen. 'Look up Brahms. They should show his dates at the start of his section.' He felt a sudden excitement.

Karen turned the pages slowly, finding her way. 'You're right. Johannes Brahms, eighteen-thirty-three to eighteen-ninety-seven.'

Mark wrote down the numbers. 'Now try Mendelssohn.'

She consulted the book again. 'Eighteen-oh-nine to eighteen-forty-seven.'

He wrote again. 'That gives us six sets of numbers. We can ignore the centuries, because they're nearly all the same. Let's try the birthdates of Beethoven, Brahms and Mendelssohn,' he grinned at her, 'in that order! That would be seventy, thirty-three and nine.' Karen watched him in silence as he turned the dial. The safe remained shut. 'All right, it could be the years they died. I'll try twenty-seven, ninety-seven and forty-seven. The fact that they all ended with a lucky number seven might have appealed to him!' He was turning the dial as he spoke, fully anticipating some kind of conclusive click from the metal tumblers. Again, the handle of the safe remained immobile.

Mark sat back. 'Shit! I could have sworn we were on the right track. He was so deliberate about Beethoven, Brahms and Mendelssohn in a certain order.' He shook his head. 'He was probably thinking about something completely different.'

Karen nodded, looking through the catalogue. 'I guess so. Anyway, there are hundreds of composers and thousands of pieces in here. I didn't know there were so many. Why would a violinist remember all those dates?'

Mark sat up. 'That's true, but a violinist might just remember the opus numbers.'

She looked puzzled. 'What's that? I've heard of an opus, but what's an opus number?'

He looked at her with a smile. 'It's the way composers' works are catalogued. It's usually a chronological order. Musicians talk about works that way as a sort of shorthand. When a pianist says he's going to play "K" four-six-six, it saves having to say Mozart's Piano Concerto Number Twenty in D Minor. Look up Beethoven's Violin Concerto.'

'Okay.' She read down the column. 'It says Violin Concerto in D Major, Op. 61. Is that it?'

He set the dial. 'Right. Now try Brahms.'

She read again. 'Seventy-seven.'

'Good. And Mendelssohn?'

She studied the book. 'I can't seem to find it. No, here it is. Sixty-four.'

He re-set the dial, and pulled the handle. After a slight pressure, the metal arm moved smoothly, and the heavy door of the safe swung open.

'Jesus!' Karen spoke under her breath.

The safe was almost empty. On a narrow shelf at the back, there was a wad of banknotes, held together with an elastic band. Mark took out the money, ruffling his thumb through the notes as though they were playing cards.

At his side, Karen said: 'Is that worth a lot?'

He shrugged. 'They're English notes: about a thousand pounds, at a guess. It must have been an emergency fund of some sort.' He returned the money to the shelf and reached in again. 'I'm more interested in the book.'

It was an ordinary pocket diary, such as one might find at any stationer's. Many of the pages were empty in the first part of the year, but from March onwards, there were entries against certain dates, written in a clumsy, semi-legible hand. The overhead light in the cupboard was weak, and Mark walked through to the master bedroom, switching on a reading lamp on the bedside table. It cast a strong white light. Karen sat next to him on the bed, peering over his shoulder.

Mark examined the pages. 'There doesn't seem to be very much here, except the names of streets in various towns. I can recognise some of them.' He was disappointed, sensing an anticlimax after the excitement of opening the safe door. 'It's just a diary, listing the places he stayed. Look.' She leaned forward. 'There's the date he came to see me in Geneva. He's written in Quai du Mont Blanc, because he was staying at the Noga Hilton, and he's written the address of my office in the Rue des Marbriers.' He turned a handful of pages. 'Let's look at this week.' He pointed again. 'George Street. I wonder if there's anything at the back, in the space for notes.'

There were a few familiar names and telephone numbers, including the address of Magnum Records in London and Eric Scutter's office on Wimpole Street. However, on the final page, Mark found two columns of entries. On each line, written against a capital letter, were a series of words that he did not understand. He read slowly down the columns, puzzled by words that he knew but that had no particular connection, until he reached the final line. His hand reached for Karen's. 'Look at this!'

A – Buchman	F – Vanzo
B – Cammaerts	I – Cerutti
Ch – Fontaine	Nl – Gout
D – Lehrer	S – Sjoberg
E – Munoz	Gb – Bradshaw

Karen read the columns. 'I don't understand what they

mean. Why does the list go from "A" to "F", and then start skipping around?'

'That threw me for a moment, but he gave himself away with "Ch" and "Gb". I thought it was an alphabetical list, just as you did, but it's a list of countries.' She looked puzzled. 'They're the international identification letters for European cars, which makes "A" Austria, "B" Belgium and so on. "D" is for Germany, and "E" is for Spain. If you look at them that way, the words that follow make more sense. Switzerland is usually a capital "CH", and Britain is capital "GB".'

'What about the words?'

'I was trying to translate them. "Lehrer" is German for teacher, and obviously "Fontaine" is French for fountain. But then I saw Bradshaw at the end. These are all names of people. When you look at the list again, they're all quite common surnames, as long as you identify the right country. It could have taken me hours to work it out, but I've met Mr Bradshaw. So have you, on the phone!' He felt a mounting excitement.

'Then what does it mean?'

'Berman has written out a list of people's names and, presumably, the countries where they live. If Bradshaw is anything to go by, this is a list of all Sandor's business associates in various parts of Europe. He seems to have quite a network of them. Well, musicians spend their lives travelling from one country to another. They've become the nomads of the civilised world. I wonder why he built up so many contacts in so many places.' He was silent for a moment.

'Couldn't they just be people in the music world? He'd have to know them in every country.'

'I suppose they could, but Bradshaw certainly isn't. He scarcely seemed concerned with Sandor's musical life. Either he's the odd man out, or we've found the key to Berman's mysterious financial set-up.'

Karen nodded. 'What are you going to do with it?'

'I'm not sure.' He put the diary in his pocket. 'First, I want to check all the places he's listed on specific dates against the itineraries he wrote out for me in Switzerland. They're in my file at the hotel. There could just be something I've overlooked at first glance. After that, I think the Inspector should have a look at the list of names. He could feed them into his computers and see if they come up with anything. My guess is that Eric Scutter could give him a few answers, after a little persuasion.' He turned to face her, his hands holding her shoulders. 'If we're really lucky, we may even begin to find out who killed Sandor, and why.'

'Oh Mark!' Her eyes were shining, and her arms reached for him.

Quite suddenly, they were kissing. For a moment, her mouth rested against his, soft and unyielding, and then her lips parted and her arms tightened about his neck, returning his embrace passionately. They fell back together across the bed, and she pressed her body into his, straining closer. They remained locked together for a long time, until he drew his face back for a moment, so that he could look into her eyes. They seemed to fill his vision, and he smiled. 'I've wanted to do this all evening.' She did not reply, but closed her eyes and pressed her mouth to his again. His hands reached inside her shirt to find bare flesh, and he felt her shudder and her breath quicken. The tips of his fingers moved gently, touching and exploring, and she held him tightly, responding with tiny cries. For a long moment, he held her in his arms, his palms against her bare shoulder-blades. 'I think we're a little overdressed for this!'

Her lips were against his ear. 'Oh Mark, I wanted you, too. Turn out the light. I'm still shy to undress in front of you.'

He reached over to the light switch, and the door was darkened, with a small shaft of light coming from the hallway. Despite his excitement, he was filled with an overriding sense of peace and, for the first time in many months, he was completely happy.

He awoke from a deep sleep, lying on his back. Karen, still sleeping, was pressed against him, her head resting on his shoulder, her body sprawled across his. He could hear cars in the street below. A thin shaft of bright light came through a parting in the curtains. He turned his head, so that her hair brushed his face. The musky scent was intermingled with the perfume of her body. His left arm felt slightly cramped from where she had laid upon it, and he moved it gently to avoid disturbing her. She sighed, rearranging herself, and he stroked her back with his free right hand, his fingers tracing the line of her spine.

Her lips pressed into the hollow of his neck. 'What time is it?' Her voice was sleepy.

'I don't know.' He crooked his left arm to see his wrist-watch. 'Some time after ten. Did I wake you?' The tips of his fingers caressed her thighs and the swell of flesh below her navel.

She sighed. 'In the best possible way.' Raising her head slightly, she rested it on the pillow, facing him. Her eyes were a darker blue than he remembered. 'Good morning!' She smiled. 'Do we have to get up yet?'

'I don't see why. How did you sleep?'

She stretched luxuriously. 'Wonderfully! I seemed to be floating.' She curled against him, her fingers twining themselves in his hair, her lips against his throat. 'I want to stay like this for ever!'

'You'd soon get bored – and hungry!'

'No I wouldn't. There are some things you don't tire of. I don't want to get up, ever again!'

He lay contentedly, letting his body sink into the mattress. 'Well, if not for ever, at least another half hour.'

'Um.' As though copying his movements, she trailed her fingers across his shoulders and chest. They paused at the scar on his shoulder. 'What's that?' Her finger explored the raised skin.

He opened his eyes, following the line of her fingers. 'That? Just a scar.'

'What happened?' Her index finger circled, as though examining by touch.

'I was – wounded. It was a long time ago.'

'Where?' Her voice was still sleepy.

'In Berlin, near the wall.'

'What were you doing there?'

'Nothing very much. Go back to sleep.'

She raised herself on an elbow, looking down at him. 'No.

Tell me about it.' She looked at the mark on his skin, frowning. 'That's quite a scar. What made it?'

'If you really want to know, an East German bullet.'

'Jesus! How did that happen?'

'I was helping someone over, one night. It went wrong. They turned on searchlights and opened fire. I was hit.' For a moment, he remembered the night and the rain, the shots from the guards as the searchlights came on, and the frantic race across a patch of open land. A stray bullet had thrown him to the ground. 'I told you: it was a long time ago.'

She was silent for a while, her fingers continuing to stroke. 'Are those some of the memories you'd like to erase?' He nodded, his eyes closed. 'Why?'

'I didn't like the sort of world I was living in, or the part I was playing in it.'

'Were you some kind of a spy, or something?' She sounded very naïve.

'Something like that.' He was silent again, while she watched him. 'Anyway, I decided it wasn't going to go on being my world. The rules had all changed.'

'Rules?'

'Perhaps that's the wrong word. Reasons. The reasons changed. We started off with all the right motives: the best of ideological reasons. We had to be right! But as time went by, it was just our side against theirs. Winning was all that mattered. We were no better nor worse than they were, I suppose. Just professionals, in a deadly kind of game.' He opened his eyes. Her face was very close to his. 'So, I quit. That's why I moved to Switzerland and became a manager.'

She nodded, only half understanding. 'Poor Mark!'

'You don't have to feel sorry. I was lucky. I survived.'

'I'm sorry, because I see your face and your eyes, and they tell me the parts you've left out.' She leaned across his body, pressing her lips to the scar, then allowing her tongue to trace a pattern around it. It felt moist and soothing. Her tongue continued to circle on the surface of his chest, slowly moving downwards, and Mark lay back, lost in the sensation. She raised herself, continuing to search and touch. When, at last, the excitement became unbearable, he took her shoulders and lifted her bodily so that she straddled him, and said: 'Welcome aboard!', but by that time, her eyes were closed, her lips slightly parted, and her body had begun to shudder involuntarily. When it was over, they lay damply together and drifted back into sleep.

They awoke an hour later, their faces touching, gently sweating in the heat of the day. Her lips brushed his cheek when she spoke. 'I guess this is the moment when love rears its ugly head.'

His face was sad. 'Don't make fun of love. It's a precious commodity and very rare.'

She watched him. 'I wasn't making fun. It's too soon to say a lot of things, and I'm frightened of saying them wrong. I'm scared of words like love, especially after such a short time, but we've been through so much together in the past day and a half. I guess what I'm trying to say is that I don't want it to be just last night.' She smiled. 'And this morning, if you want to be pedantic about it.'

'Neither do I. There are so many more things for us to do together. We've only just found each other.'

She nodded. 'I wish I'd met you when I first came to Europe. You know so much about everywhere. It would have been so great, seeing everything for the first time with you.'

'There are plenty of places left. When we've finished with London, I'll show them to you. You don't have to go back yet. It's still summer.'

'You mean that?'

'Why not? You could stay on, and we could be together. I was planning to take a holiday after this. We could spend it together.'

She kissed him. 'I'd like that. But not only new places. I'd like to revisit all the ones I saw, and share them with you: places like Rome and Florence – even that lousy Monte Carlo! You could show me Paris and Geneva, and I could take you back to Beaune. I never even got see that old hospital with the coloured roof.' Her eyes shone. 'I'd love to walk again with you through those little winding streets in Carcassonne, and sit in the square . . .'

At that moment, the telephone rang. The bell startled them, sounding relentlessly. Mark said: 'Shall I answer it?' and she shook her head. It continued to ring. 'I suppose I had better.' He lifted the receiver. 'Hello?'

'Mr Holland?' The voice was immediately recognisable. 'This is Lewis Bradshaw. I think I told you that you had twenty-four hours. They are just about up.' His voice had a hard ring.

'What do you want?' Seeing his expression, Karen knelt at his side, pulling the duvet round her body, as though to protect herself.

Bradshaw's voice relaxed into its sibilant drawl. 'I think you know perfectly well what we want. My colleagues and I are waiting outside. If you care to look down into the street, you will see us. Perhaps I should add that I have made contact with Sandor Berman's French partner. He is here with me, and is most anxious to talk to you. We'll give you five minutes to come down and join us. Otherwise,' he paused for a moment, 'we will have to come up and fetch you. We're quite prepared to do so. Now, I don't think you'd want that, would you? The young lady with you might find the experience most – distressing.' His drawl had lengthened. 'By the way, there's no point in telephoning the police or anyone else, for that matter. As soon as this call has finished, your phone will be disconnected, so I suggest you avoid any further unpleasantness.' He made a sound approximating a snigger. 'What is it that fellow says on the television show? "Come on down!" We're waiting.'

10

Mark put the telephone receiver on the bedside table and walked quickly over to the window. Opening the curtains a few inches, he looked down into the street. A builder's van was parked by the front door. The Frenchman, wearing a pair of scruffy overalls, was leaning against it, looking up at the window. Their eyes met for a moment, and the Frenchman gave a small nod of recognition.

From the bed, Karen said: 'Who is it?'

'Bradshaw. He's brought company with him. They're on their way up here.'

'Oh Jesus! What are we going to do?'

Mark moved back to the bed. 'Get dressed, as quickly as you can. I have an idea.' He picked up the telephone. 'Are you still there?'

Bradshaw sounded pleased with himself. 'I assume you were verifying my statement. Did you see him?'

'Yes.' He remembered the name in the diary. 'Is that Monsieur Vanzo?'

The man laughed. 'My my, for somebody who claims he doesn't know what's going on, you have a remarkable knowledge of names! Now, are you on your way down, or do we come up? You'll notice that Mr Vanzo has taken the precaution of impersonating a builder's mate. It makes forcing a door open look so much more authentic, don't you think? There's really no need for us to indulge in this sort of play-acting, Mr Holland. All you have to do is return Mr Vanzo's property, and we'll go our separate ways.'

Mark glanced across at Karen. She was almost dressed. Placing his hand over the telephone speaker, he whispered: 'Take the money out of the safe. The door's still open. And keep your passport with you. Have you got something to carry things in?' She held up a canvas shoulder-bag, and he nodded. 'Put in a change of clothes. You may need them.' Returning to the phone, he said: 'I'll come down in a few minutes, but I'd like to make a deal.'

Bradshaw hesitated before replying. 'I hardly think you're in a position to bargain with us. What do you want?'

'Leave the girl out of this. She's not involved.' Karen started to speak, but he waved a hand at her to remain silent. 'She's just a friend of Berman's. He only met her a few days ago. This has nothing to do with her.'

'Are you sure of that?'

'Of course I'm sure. She was hitch-hiking across Europe, and

Berman offered her somewhere to stay in London. She hardly knew him.'

There was another pause. 'That's very noble of you, Mr Holland. Why don't you just come down yourself, and we won't bother with the girl.'

'No.'

'What do you mean?'

'Let the girl go first, and then I'll come down.'

Bradshaw was irritated. 'There's really no reason to haggle like this. If I give you my word . . .'

'Your word doesn't mean a thing to me, Bradshaw. Let her leave the building and walk away. I'll follow her down when I'm satisfied you've given her enough time to leave. I'll be watching from a window.'

There was another pause. 'Very well. I don't know why you're making such a song and dance about it if she's not involved. We're not interested in what happens to her.'

'Good. She'll be down in a minute or two, when she's finished dressing.'

'Don't let her take too long about it.' The line went dead.

Mark replaced the receiver, still holding it. A few seconds later, he lifted it again and listened. For a moment, there was the normal dialling tone, followed by a slight crack and silence. Bradshaw had kept his word about cutting the line.

Karen was now fully dressed, running a comb through her hair. As Mark pulled on his clothes, she turned to him, her eyes wide with fear. 'What now?'

He was buttoning his shirt, fumbling in his haste. 'You heard what I told him. You're going to walk out of here and away from the building.'

'What about you? What are they going to do to you?'

'With any luck, they're not going to find me. Have you taken the money from the safe?'

'Yes, but it's an awful lot . . .'

'Never mind about that. Sandor's not going to need it any more.' He was tying his shoes. 'Now, when you go out of the front door, I want you to turn left, and walk slowly to the corner of Brown Street. You may see a workman standing next to a builder's van when you come out. Take no notice of him.'

'Who is he?'

He spoke rapidly. 'It doesn't matter. He shouldn't bother you. When you get to the corner, turn left again, and walk to George Street. Do it slowly, even if you have to force yourself. Do you know where I mean?' She nodded. 'After that, I want you to turn left again, and continue to stroll along George Street, away from the Edgware Road.'

'But Mark . . .'

'Just keep walking, and don't look back. They'll leave you alone.'

'But what about you?'

'I'll be near by. I've no intention of meeting Mr Bradshaw or any of his funny friends. Now, as soon as you're away from here, make your way across to Oxford Street. Do you know roughly where it is?' She nodded silently. 'Stay among the crowds. If one of them should decide to follow you, he won't try anything if you're surrounded by people all the time. Oxford Street will be full of tourists and window shoppers, and they can't follow you down it with a car. All right?'

'Yes.'

'After that, take a taxi to one of the airlines, and buy a ticket to Cleveland. It doesn't matter which line, but you'll find TWA in Piccadilly.'

'But I thought we . . .'

'Don't book any particular flight for the moment. Just buy a ticket and tell them you'll confirm the flight later. That's your insurance if anything goes wrong.'

For a moment, she clung to him. 'Mark, I'm not going to leave you!'

'Don't worry. Nothing's going to happen.' He held her for a moment, then gently released her arms.

'Where will I find you?'

He thought for a moment. 'Be sure you don't come back near here. There's a Promenade Concert tonight at the Albert Hall. I'm supposed to go there. Do you think you can find it?' She nodded. 'I don't know if all the seats are booked, but you can always get in among the promenaders. There's usually a queue outside the hall from about six o'clock.' He looked at his watch. It was a few minutes after twelve. 'You'll have to kill the rest of the afternoon, but it will take a while to walk down Oxford Street and find your way over to Piccadilly for the air ticket. If you want to stay out of sight, you can always go to a cinema.'

'But where will you be?'

'I'm not sure, but I'll be in the Albert Hall tonight. I don't know where I'll be sitting – probably in the rows of seats next to the promenade, on the left side of the hall, opposite the violins.' She nodded nervously, following every word. 'I'll be looking out for you.'

'What's the promenade?'

'It's the central floor of the hall. There are no seats there, and people sit or stand for the music. You'll understand when you see it. If it's not too crowded, you can move about from one part to another.'

'How will I find you if you miss me?'

'At the end of the concert, go backstage. It's a little confusing to find your way, because the hall is circular, and it's sometimes difficult to judge how far you have to walk round. Anyway, when you find yourself behind the stage, you'll see two doorways leading downstairs. One of them usually has a sign saying "Orchestra Personnel Only", or something like that. The other often has a man in charge to stop the public from going down. You can use either door. If anyone tries to prevent you, tell them you're with the orchestra. Make up a name and say he's your husband or boyfriend. They'll let you through.'

'Where will you be?'

'I'll be waiting downstairs for you, near the conductor's dressing room. There'll be dozens of people milling around, and anyone will show you where it is.' He held her shoulders for a moment. 'Don't worry; I'll be there.'

'And if you're not?'

'Then I'll be at the Westbury. I can always leave a message for you.'

There was fear in her eyes. 'And if you're not there either?'

His arms held her tightly, his face against hers. 'Take the next plane home. Don't worry about anything the Inspector said. Just go.' She started to speak, but he held her tighter. 'That's only a last resort. I'm going to be at the hall.' He held her at arm's length, and smiled. 'You promised me a holiday!' She was about to speak again, but he looked at his watch. 'You'll have to go now. They won't wait much longer for you to appear. I've stretched the time about as far as I can. Do you think you can remember everything I've told you?'

'Yes.'

'Try to look casual. Just stroll out of the door, and walk slowly. It's important.'

'Why?'

'It gives me more time for what I'm going to do.' They were standing by the front door of the flat. Mark looked at her for a moment, then kissed her. Before she could say anything, he placed his fingertips on her lips and said: 'Don't worry; I'll see you backstage tonight at about nine thirty.' He opened the door, and she slipped out.

He closed the door and bolted it, then went quickly to the kitchen and opened the door on to the balcony at the back. Stepping out, he peered down into the central well of the building. It was empty. Running down the wall to his right was a large drainpipe, recently painted black. It was one of many in a maze of ancient plumbing that criss-crossed the walls of the building. Over the years, there had been alterations and extensions, and successive generations of plumbers had not bothered to remove the original installations.

Mark reached over the iron railings of the balcony to grab the pipe, pulling at it. It seemed to be firmly fixed, and he climbed over the railing and held the pipe with both hands. It was wide and difficult to grip, but he swung himself towards it, his toes searching for a resting place. For a moment, he hung in mid-air, supporting himself with stretched hands on the circular surface, but his right foot found a small niche in the brick wall, allowing his arms a moment's respite. Moving cautiously, he worked his way several feet down the pipe, the toes of his shoes scrabbling against the brickwork in search of a hold. The drainpipe groaned and shifted slightly. Looking up, he could see a rusty clamp easing its way off the wall, and the pipe began to tilt outward, borne down by his weight. His hands started to slip on the painted surface and, as the pipe slowly swung outwards, he clambered down a few more feet, working hand over hand, his feet curled around the section that was hanging dangerously free. There was a tearing scrape of metal and brickwork as the pipe pulled completely away from the wall, but he was now level with the kitchen balcony on the floor below. Holding his breath, he turned slightly and pushed backwards into space. His body swivelled and, as he fell, his hands grabbed at the metal railings of the balcony. His body swung against it, winding him as he thudded against the rails, and his wrists ached as they took the strain of his weight. Pulling with both arms, he swung his legs up until they were resting on the outer ledge of the balcony, and he paused for a moment, panting for breath. Beads of sweat ran into his eyes. He slowly lifted himself level, and stepped over the iron railings. There was no sound from the kitchen beyond the door, and he waited for his pulse to slacken. There were still two floors to negotiate to the yard below, which was at the basement level of the building.

The drainpipe down which he had travelled now hung out at an eccentric angle, offering no further support. He was thankful it had not broken away completely, to land in the yard with a clatter. Leaning over the balcony, he inspected the wall to his left. A series of narrow pipes, about two inches in diameter, were running along the wall, parallel with the ground. They were approximately seven feet apart. Mark judged that, by hanging from the upper pipes, he should be able to reach the lower set with his feet, allowing him to edge his way along the wall to the next vertical drainpipe, about ten feet away. He looked at his watch. Only two minutes had elapsed since Karen had left. Allowing her about a minute to reach the front door of the building, he calculated that he still had another four or five minutes before Bradshaw and Vanzo would become suspicious and enter the building. It was possible that one of them had already entered the downstairs foyer.

Climbing over the railings again, he reached up to take hold of the narrow horizontal pipe. It looked newer than the others, possibly more firmly fixed to the wall, but not designed to hold the weight of a man. For a moment, he closed his eyes, then swung again into space, feeling with his feet for the next line of piping. His toes rested on it and, moving slowly, he inched his way along the face of the wall.

Suddenly, his foot slipped, and he hung, clinging desperately with his fingers, until his feet found the lower pipe again. His sweaty palms started to slide on the upper pipe and, at the moment when he thought he had lost his hold, his shoes regained their foothold. He paused for a moment, leaning against the wall, his cheek brushing against the rough brick surface.

After what seemed an agonisingly slow progress, he reached the drainpipe. Feeling gingerly with one hand, he pulled at the heavy pipe, risking as much of his weight as he dared. Nothing shifted, and he clambered against it, tearing a fingernail as his hands slithered on the shiny painted surface. His body was covered with sweat, and his eyes were blurred and stinging. After resting for a moment, he slowly worked his way downward. The pipe held firm, and he passed the balcony of the ground floor flat with a feeling of relief. Moments later, he was a few feet above the concrete courtyard, and jumped. He looked at his watch again. A little over three minutes had passed. Bradshaw and Vanzo should still be waiting outside.

Standing close to the wall, he took out a handkerchief to wipe his face and hands, and brushed dust from his clothes. Above him, there was no movement on any of the balconies. He could hear distant music. Somebody was playing Radio One in an upper flat, and he recognised the inane chatter of the disc-jockey without being able to identify his words.

Mark ran across the courtyard until he was on the far side, facing Berman's flat. A small wooden tradesmen's entrance, painted yellow, led to the lift shaft and foyer on the other side of the building, opening on to George Street. Mark had gambled that Bradshaw would not expect him to find his way to the opposite side, a street away. With luck, the men might not guess that the two sides were interconnected and, unless Bradshaw was commanding a small task force of 'colleagues', he would not have enough people with him to cover all the entrances to the mansion building.

Keeping an eye on the balcony of Berman's flat, he slipped through the tradesmen's entrance, to find himself in the basement of the building. He climbed the carpeted stairs silently, hesitating as he reached the foyer. It was furnished exactly like the entrance on the other side, with wood panelling and a small table for messages and deliveries. An elderly man, dressed in a grey overall, was polishing the table. He looked like a Head Porter, but it occurred to Mark that the term was a left-over from more luxurious days. In the London of the 1980s, the man was probably the only porter in the building, also serving as Superintendent, janitor and odd-job man.

Seeing Mark, the man nodded politely. ''Morning, sir. Another nice day.'

'I hope so. The summer passes all too quickly.'

'Ah, isn't that true?' The man put down his duster, prepared for a chat. 'Why is it that summers were always better in the good old days?'

Mark nodded gravely, walking to the front door. He half opened it, peering cautiously out. The street seemed to be empty. He was aware that the man was watching him curiously, and turned back. 'I just wanted to make sure it doesn't look like rain. I left my umbrella upstairs.'

'Ah well, the television said it was going to be fine all day again.' There was a finality in his voice, reassured by the omniscient satellites of Breakfast Television, but he added, incongruously: 'Not natural, is it?'

Mark opened the door again, and stepped into the street, glancing in both directions. There was nobody in sight, but two cars were parked along the road to his right, in the direction of Brown Street. The first was a small grey Honda. The second was a red Mini. Penny Scott was sitting at the wheel.

He ran towards the Mini. As he approached, Penny looked up with a smile of surprise, and leaned across the seat to unlock the door.

'Hello! You've popped up from a funny direction!' Her expression changed. 'What on earth are you doing?'

Mark had entered and, instead of sitting down, had pushed the front seat forward and flung himself into the back of the car. He crouched on the cramped space of the floor. Penny started to laugh and was about to speak again, but the look on his face silenced her, and she turned pale. 'What's wrong?'

'I'll tell you in a minute. Face forward, as though you are alone – please!' She turned round, staring through the windscreen. Her eyes flicked up to the rear-view mirror, to meet his.

'What are you doing?'

He did not bother to reply, asking: 'Has Karen walked past you?'

'I don't know. I don't think so.'

He paused for a moment. What the hell was she doing here? That would have to wait, for the moment. 'Are you sure?'

'Almost. I only parked a minute or two ago.'

'That would be long enough. She should be walking along George Street.'

Penny looked through the windscreen again. 'She doesn't appear to be. You can see all the way down the road.' Her eyes moved to the mirror again. 'Here she is, now. She's just come round the corner of the building, behind us.'

Mark huddled lower. 'Is she alone?'

'Yes. Why?'

'Is there anyone near her, walking in the same direction?'

'No, I don't think so.' She looked again. 'No, I'm sure there isn't. There's nobody else.'

'Thank God for that!' It was spoken under his breath.

'She's only a few yards from us. Shall I call her?'

'No! Don't even look at her!' He kept his voice low. 'Just let her walk past. Someone may be watching her.'

'I don't see how. There's nobody else in the street.'

'Please! Just do as I say!'

Penny was silent, looking down. From his position on the floor, Mark could see nothing. After a short interval, Penny said: 'She's just passed us. What do you want to do?'

'Just stay as you are. Don't do anything at all.'

Minutes passed slowly. A ray of sunshine was shining on Mark's back through the rear window, making him sweat again. He shifted position slightly, raising his head far enough to see Penny's face in the mirror. 'Can you still see her?'

'Just about. She's turned right, walking up towards Marble Arch.' She paused. 'She's out of sight, now. What happens next?'

'Wait a little longer.' Another minute passed. 'Can you see anyone behind us?'

Penny looked in the mirror. 'I don't think so. Oh, a man's just walked round the corner. He's standing there, looking in this direction.'

'What is he like?'

'Tall, with fair hair, wearing a blazer. Rather a pale face. I can't see much else. He seems to be just standing there. Do you know him?'

'I think so. He's the elusive Mr Bradshaw.'

'I think he's starting to walk in this direction. What shall I do?'

'Start the car.'

She switched on the engine. For a moment, it fired, then died again. Under her breath, Penny said: 'Damn! I must get this car tuned properly. It overheats in this weather.' The starter turned uneasily, and she looked again in the mirror. 'He's walking this way. He's about ten yards from us.'

Mark closed his eyes, waiting for the car to start. A moment later, the motor caught. Her foot was pushing the accelerator too heavily, and the engine complained loudly.

Mark said: 'Pull out slowly, and drive straight ahead.'

The car started to move. 'Shall I go the same way as Karen?'

'No. Keep going to Baker Street. Take it slowly.'

Penny drove steadily, passing through traffic lights at a stately pace. As they approached, she said: 'Here's Baker Street.'

'Turn right.'

'Where are we supposed to be aiming for?'

He thought quickly. 'Can we go to your flat?'

She made a right turn, driving in silence. After a moment,

Mark sat up in the back seat, taking off his jacket and loosening his tie. They were crossing Oxford Street and heading towards Grosvenor Square. Penny's face was angry. 'We can go to my flat if you want, but I'd like to know what the hell's going on.'

Mark explained what had happened, keeping his description to a minimum. When he told her about climbing down the pipes of the building, she frowned. 'Why didn't you walk down the stairs and across the yard. You could have saved yourself the heroics!' There was an edge to her voice.

'I thought of it, but I didn't want to risk meeting one of them in the foyer. It's easy enough to open the front door.'

'What about Karen?'

'I've arranged to meet her after the concert tonight. She'll be at the hall. She has to stay away from that flat, in case they watch it.'

Penny nodded, and her eyes met his in the rear-view mirror. 'You'd better call the police, as soon as we get in. This cloak and dagger business has gone far enough.'

'Yes, I will.' He asked casually: 'What brought you to George Street?'

She shrugged. 'I called the Westbury from the rehearsal. When they said you were out, I knew where to find you.'

'Why didn't you come up?'

'I was about to.' She sounded irritated. 'I'd only just arrived.'

'I thought you said you'd been parked for a couple of minutes.'

Penny drove into an unoccupied parking space in Grosvenor Square, and switched off the engine. When she turned to look at Mark, her face was angry. 'Look, Mark, I don't know what you're getting at, but I don't like being cross-examined. What's the matter with you? Yesterday, you tried to suggest that I'd deliberately driven you into a trap at Kingsway Hall. No matter how things may have looked to you at the time, I didn't, and your accusation hurt! I don't know what's going on, with all these mysterious characters who keep arriving and departing, but they're nothing to do with me.' She paused for a moment and, when she spoke again, her voice was calmer. 'I thought I made my feelings for you pretty clear yesterday evening. I don't make a habit of inviting people to stay with me and, if you must know, it's pretty devastating to be turned down. Now, maybe that Inspector asked you to keep an eye on Miss America, and maybe he didn't. I only heard your side of the conversation, but you showed little concern for my feelings when you dashed out of my flat, doing your knight in shining armour bit! All right, I made a fool of myself, and it's my own stupid fault.' She took a deep breath. 'I drove to George Street this morning because the rehearsal was marvellous, and I wanted to tell you about it – perhaps persuade you to listen to the last part. If you must know, I was also prepared to eat bloody humble pie again, and apologise for being bad-tempered when you left, though God knows what I had to apologise for! I thought you were a friend. I want to help you sort out this whole shitty business with Berman, and catch the bastard who killed him.'

She looked away. 'If you want to know why I didn't come rushing up the stairs, full of the joys of spring, it was because when I got there, I was embarrassed. I wasn't quite sure what I was going to say, so I sat in the car for a minute, thinking about it. At that moment, you came running out of the building, looked at me as though I was some sort of monster, and threw yourself in the back of the car, shouting orders. Do this; do that! Don't watch her; don't speak to her! Wait for my next instruction; don't ask questions! And now, to cap it all, you start cross-examining me as though I'm guilty of something!' She was close to tears. 'If you don't like me, and you don't trust what I've got to say, I suggest you get out of the car and find yourself another driver. This one's had enough!' She faced the front again, her mouth set in a firm line.

Mark said nothing, and the car was very silent after her tirade. On the pavement in front of them, an elderly pair of Americans walked past – the woman in a floral dress, the man in a tropical suit of narrow blue and white stripes – heading in the direction of the American Embassy. Penny watched them, her chin held high.

'Penny, I'm sorry. I didn't mean it to sound that way.'

'Rubbish! There's no other way you could have meant it. I'm not a fool.'

'All right, but I was surprised to see you there, especially under the circumstances. It may not be your fault, but you've been showing up at the most unexpected moments, and I haven't known what to think. For God's sake, I'd just clambered down the side of a building! You were the last person I'd expected to meet. Vanzo was waiting outside the front door . . .'

'Who's Vanzo?'

He told her about opening the safe and finding the diary. As he spoke, Penny started the car and backed into the line of traffic, looking over her shoulder. Their eyes met for a moment, and she said: 'The best thing we can do is drive straight to the nearest police station.'

'No.'

'Why not, for God's sake?'

'Because we'll have to start again from scratch with a new bunch of policemen who'll want to write everything slowly out in triplicate. There isn't time. Bradshaw and company will have gone into the flat by now. We need to find a telephone and call the Inspector. If he's actually there for once, he could send a squad car over before they leave.' She was circling Grosvenor Square. 'Drive to the Westbury. It's just around the corner from here. We can call the Inspector from my room, and I can pick up some papers I need.'

Penny nodded silently, and accelerated. After a moment, she said: 'What do they want, Mark?'

'I don't know. I wish to God I did. They're convinced that I'm holding something that belongs to them, and they want it back badly enough to use guns or break their way in.'

'Why didn't you just ask them?'

'I should have. I'd hoped I could talk them into telling me.'

'That's police work.' Her voice was quiet. 'Sandor Berman's dead, Mark, and I think they're involved with killing him. For God's sake, let the police take over, instead of trying to be a hero.'

For a moment, Mark was angry. 'I'd be happy to, but when Vanzo and his friends tried to run us down yesterday, you didn't think it had anything to do with this.'

'I know. I'm sorry, I was wrong, but a lot has happened since then. Please, from now on, let the police handle it.'

'I will, but I've still got to persuade that bloody Inspector to take some action. When I talked to him yesterday, he was still convinced that the break-in at the flat was a coincidence.'

'Well, surely you've got proof that it wasn't.'

'I haven't got proof of anything, except a couple of names in a diary that proves Berman knew them. One thing seems to be clear. Up to now, we've been dealing with two different individuals, working independently of each other. When I spoke to him today, Bradshaw said he'd joined forces with Berman's French "partner" for the return of their property. Apparently, they were working separately until today, which at least explains how we left Bradshaw at the Westbury and found Vanzo at Kingsway Hall.'

They had reached the hotel, and Penny squeezed her car into a small space, under the watchful eye of the doorman. He saluted her. 'How long will you be, Miss?' She had become one of his 'regulars'.

Mark replied on her behalf. 'About ten minutes.'

The man saluted again. 'I'll look after it.'

When Mark collected his key, there was only a message from Geneva. Rudi reported nothing urgent, but could he call Mr Abe Sincoff in New York. In his room, Mark immediately dialled the Inspector's number. Penny sat on a chair by the door, watching him.

The policeman was in, for a change. 'Good afternoon, Mr Holland. I'm afraid there's nothing to add to what I told you yesterday afternoon.' He sounded vaguely irritated at being disturbed.

Mark ignored this. 'How soon could you get a car round to Berman's flat?'

The man was surprised. 'A few minutes, I suppose. Why?'

Mark reported what had happened, speaking as quickly and concisely as he could. The Inspector did not interrupt. When he had finished, the policeman said: 'Hang on a minute.' Mark could hear him issuing instructions, but the voice was suddenly cut off. Apparently, he had remembered to put a hand over the mouthpiece of the phone. Mark was still a member of 'the public'. A few moments later, he returned. 'Where are you calling from?'

'I'm at the Westbury.'

'Good. Will you be staying there?'

'No, I don't think so. It's the first place they'll try, if they're looking for me.'

'I can send a man round.'

'I'd rather not be tied down. I'll pick up a few things and go over to Miss Scott's flat.' He looked questioningly at Penny, and she nodded. 'I don't think they know where it is. You'll be able to reach me there until the concert this evening.' He gave the Inspector Penny's address.

There was a pause as the man wrote the details down. 'What about the American lady?'

'She should be all right. I made sure she wasn't followed, and I've arranged to meet her after the concert.' He remembered what Karen had told him. 'She thinks you didn't believe what she told you.' The Inspector was silent. 'Why?'

'It's not that I didn't believe her, sir. All I said was that it didn't seem to ring very true, in my opinion.' He seemed to be choosing his words carefully. 'That's not quite the same thing. Where are you meeting her?'

'After the concert, backstage at the Albert Hall.' Mark decided not to elaborate on the details. 'Anyway, Bradshaw said he wasn't interested in her. That's why he let her go.'

'Very well. Perhaps you'd like to call me when you see her. If this man Bradshaw is following you, he might decide that she could be a useful hostage. She may be an innocent bystander in all this, but she'll need to stay in touch with us, if only for her own safety. Where is she now?'

'Wandering round the town, keeping out of sight, I hope. They're not likely to run into her.'

'That may be so, but you should have told her to walk to a police station and ask for me. That would have been a better guarantee of safety.' His voice was more formal.

'Yes, I suppose you're right. We only had a few minutes to talk when Bradshaw arrived.' He did not mention the air ticket.

'Well, when you do find her again, please put us in touch. That's what we're supposed to be here for.'

'Yes. Have you run Bradshaw's name through Records?'

The Inspector hesitated. 'We've tried. I can't say we've found anything.'

'You might try the name Vanzo. He's the Frenchman who pulled a gun on me yesterday. That's "V-a-n-z-o".'

'How do you know that?'

'Bradshaw told me. They're working together. I think he's French, but with a name like that, he could be Italian.'

'Any first name?'

'I don't know it.'

'All right, we'll try him, and we'll put a couple of calls in to our colleagues on the Continent. Anything else?'

'Not that I can think of.' Penny was watching him carefully.

'Then I'll come back to you if anything shows up here. I hope you'll do the same.' He paused. 'At the risk of sounding like a cracked record, would you please leave this to us.'

'That's what I've done. I called you as soon as I could.'

'I suppose so. How did you get away from George Street when you gave them the slip?'

'By car. Miss Scott had just arrived outside as I was leaving.'

'Really? That young lady does get about, doesn't she?'

'Yes.' His eyes avoided Penny's.

'All right. We'll talk later.' He hung up.

Penny said: 'Why didn't you tell him about opening the safe and finding the diary?'

'It didn't come up. Besides, I want to check the diary myself against Berman's itineraries.'

Penny shook her head. 'There you go again! Why don't you just hand everything over to the police?'

'I will. I just want to satisfy myself first. I can check the names and dates quicker than they can. It's my kind of work.'

'Perhaps. There's something else I wanted to ask. Why did you ask me to drive you to my flat? If we hadn't stopped in Grosvenor Square, I would have gone straight there.'

'I don't know. It was partly panic, I suppose. Then I

remembered I would need my briefcase and the Berman file. I wasn't thinking very clearly.'

'It must be love!' She did not smile.

The phone rang, and Mark picked up the receiver. 'Hello?'

At the other end, there was silence. 'Hello? This is Mark Holland.' There was no reply. After a moment, the phone at the other end was disconnected.

Penny watched him as he replaced the receiver. 'What was that about?'

Mark was already moving about the room, collecting his briefcase and putting a change of clothes into it. 'I think it's time we were on our way.' He walked to Penny and took both her hands in his for a moment. 'I'm sorry about earlier. I shouldn't have questioned you like that, and I'm glad you showed up when you did.'

Her expression softened, and she responded with a quick squeeze of his hands. 'It doesn't matter.' She indicated the phone with a slight nod. 'Who called?'

'I don't know. He didn't say anything. My guess is that it was probably Bradshaw, checking to see if I had come back here.' Her eyes widened. 'So it's time we left.'

'You don't think they're downstairs? That could have been the house phone.'

'I doubt it. It's too soon. Besides, once they're in, they will probably have another look around the flat. If the Inspector moves fast, he might still find them there.' He released her hands. 'We'd better go.'

As they left the hotel, Mark paused to hand the doorman some money. The man looked briefly at the notes in his hand, and his smile broadened with a conspiratorial air.

'Thank you very much, sir. And don't you worry: I never saw the lady before!'

11

When they entered Penny's flat, Mark was frowning. Her mood had lightened, and she saw his expression and said: 'Is it as awful as that? I know I haven't cleaned it for days.'

'What? No, I just remembered something I should have mentioned to the Inspector.'

'Oh?'

'When Bradshaw phoned me at the flat to tell me he was on his way up, he warned me not to call the police, and cut the line immediately afterwards. I should have told the Inspector. Apparently, Bradshaw knew enough about the telephone system to be able to cut me off. It may not be important, but I'm not sure that most people would know how to do it. It might offer the police some sort of lead.'

'Do you want to call him back?'

'No, I'll do it later. There was something else, but I can't remember what it was.'

'What sort of something?'

'I don't know. I was going to ask Karen a question, but I can't think what it was about. Bradshaw's arrival put it out of my mind. It will come back.'

'Try not to think about it for a while. The more you concentrate, the harder it is to remember. What do you want to do now?'

Mark opened his briefcase and took out the clothes he had stuffed into it. 'I think I'd feel better if I took a few minutes to clean up. My mountaineering efforts down that wall have left me in a mess.'

Penny pointed. 'The bathroom's over there. Help yourself. I'll make us a sandwich.' She smiled. 'I'm always trying to persuade you to eat. It must be some sort of maternal instinct!'

'I'm glad. I'm hungry.'

'Good.' She walked into the kitchen and returned almost

immediately. 'The only problem is that I'm out of bread. Why don't you wash while I go round the corner and pick up a few things? There's a little shop near by.'

'Fine.' He walked into the bathroom.

'I'll be back in a few minutes. Do you like anything special? They have a good range of things.' She was cheerful.

'Anything will do.' He looked at himself in the mirror. His face was grimy, with streaks of sweat cutting their way through the brick dust that had accumulated on his sticky skin. 'My God, I look dreadful! You should have told me. What on earth did you think when I came running to the car?'

'Not a lot. I was too busy carrying out your instructions!' She giggled. 'On the other hand, I wonder what that doorman must have been thinking. The mind boggles! I'll be back soon.'

Mark filled the bath and lay back gratefully, soaking away the sweat and the grime of the morning. His body still ached. He wondered where Karen was, and pictured her sauntering along Oxford Street, looking in shop windows and moving with the crowds. She would appear to be a typical American tourist, visiting London, but oh, how much more beautiful! At least she was safely out of Bradshaw's reach, with enough money to buy the ticket home. He closed his eyes, remembering their love-making and her unexpected passion. It had matched his own. But there had been tenderness, too, and they had lain all night, half awake, hardly speaking, allowing their hands and their mouths and their bodies to express their feelings. They must have fallen asleep near dawn. He vaguely remembered hearing birds singing and had been about to tell her, but had hesitated at the sound of her even breathing. She had slept so quietly, nestled against him. When this was all over, he would keep his promise, and they would stay together. He would show her all his favourite countries and towns, sharing them with her. And after? They would decide that when the summer ended.

He heard Penny re-enter the flat, and finished washing. She called: 'There are clean towels in the airing cupboard behind your head. Are you nearly ready?'

'Just about.'

'There's no hurry. It won't get cold!'

When he had shaved and dressed, he reappeared in the living room. 'That's better. I'm feeling more civilised by the minute.'

'And infinitely more presentable.' She gave a mock bow. 'I put some things on the table for you to serve yourself. There's wine, or coffee in the machine in the kitchen, if you prefer.'

'It looks delicious. Do you have any scissors, by any chance? I broke a nail when I was doing my Tarzan act.'

She found some and, taking his hand, inspected the damage. 'That must have hurt.'

'Not at the time. I was trying not to come down three floors the quick way!'

She bent over his hand, repairing the damaged fingernail. Watching her, Mark thought: 'She's very attractive. If it wasn't for Karen . . .' But could she be trusted? At least the Inspector shared some of his suspicions. And yet, in the car, she had seemed genuinely upset. Or was it that attack was the best method of defence?

Penny looked up for a moment. Seeing his face, she said: 'Sorry. Did I hurt you?'

'No. I was irritated with myself for being so clumsy.'

They ate in silence. Penny had chosen several different cheeses and cold meats and some French bread, with bottles of red and white wine to wash them down. She had obviously gone to some effort to prepare the 'impromptu' meal. Mark discovered that he was hungry, and the food was excellent. When he had finished, she brought him a mug of freshly brewed coffee.

'I think I have a bottle of brandy somewhere, if you would like a glass.'

'No, thank you. It was all lovely. My God, if that's how you prepare a quick sandwich, I'll have to go into training for a proper meal!'

She looked pleased. 'What next?'

He took the diary out of his pocket and handed it to her. 'Look at the back pages first.'

She examined them. 'I see Bradshaw and Vanzo. Presumably the letters indicate countries. He's copied car plates.'

'You're quick off the mark. Do any of the other names ring a bell?'

She read them again and shook her head. 'I wonder why he didn't put telephone numbers or addresses.'

'He probably memorised them. Musicians like playing with numbers.' Mark told her about discovering the combination numbers of the safe.

Penny smiled admiringly. 'I would never have thought of that. Musicians live in a different world, don't they?'

'In many ways. It's a very enclosed world, despite the constant travel.'

'Which may explain why Sandor Berman had contacts all over Europe?' She returned the diary.

'I want to find out who those contacts were, and why. I have the feeling that it will answer all the questions, including why somebody wanted him dead.'

'Where do we start?' She joined him on the sofa.

Mark took out Berman's file from his briefcase. 'We may as well check a few of the dates against his diary. Let's start with Geneva, when he came to see me. Here we are: July the fifteenth. That was the Monday after his concert.'

Penny looked in the diary. 'What does "R des Marbriers" mean?'

'It's my office. He never seems to write down numbers.' Mark took out Berman's itinerary. 'His next engagement was in Lyon, on the eighteenth, playing the Beethoven Concerto. He probably drove straight there, after seeing me, or perhaps on the following day.' He looked in the diary. 'Here we are: "RH – Pl. Bellecour" written against the sixteenth. That must be the Royal Hotel in the Place Bellecour. I've stayed there.'

Penny smiled. 'Not bad! You make a very impressive detective. Where did he go from there?'

'It looks as though he swung north to Dijon. According to his itinerary, he played the Mendelssohn Concerto there on July the twenty-fourth. We need to count back a few days, to allow for the rehearsals.' He handed Penny the diary. 'Can you see anything?'

'Yes. He wrote "C – r Château" against the twenty-second.'

Mark said: 'I can't help you. It looks as though he stayed in the Rue Château, but "C" doesn't mean anything.'

Penny walked to the bookcase. 'I think I've got what we need.' She pulled out a thick red book. 'It's a Michelin Guide, listing all the hotels and restaurants. I'm afraid it's a few years old – the prices will make you laugh! – but it should help. Let me check Dijon.' A moment later, she gave a little cry of triumph. 'Got it! Hôtel Central, Rue Château 10.' She smiled at Mark. 'This is fun!'

He nodded. 'Between the diary and his itinerary, Sandor has provided us with a route map of his last tour. Let's keep going. His next engagement was a recital in Orléans, on the thirtieth. I wonder who his accompanist was.'

Penny nodded at the file. 'Are there any reviews?'

'No. He gave me this in Geneva. The concert was after that.'

'Of course. I wasn't thinking. I might have it at the office. He gave me a whole sheaf of reviews when he arrived. Wouldn't his accompanist have travelled with him?'

'Not necessarily. He could have found a local pianist, or his usual accompanist could have come in for the concert. I seem to remember him saying that he played recitals with an American pianist who lives in Paris. He could have come down to Orléans for the concert. It's not very far. Did Berman put an address in the diary?'

'Yes. He arrived in Orléans on the twenty-ninth.'

'In that case, he almost certainly met his regular pianist there. Otherwise, he didn't leave enough time to rehearse.'

'Elementary, my dear Holland!'

'Where did he stay?'

'Just a minute; I'm checking.' She read the diary, then quickly shuffled the pages of the Michelin. There was a look of satisfaction in her eyes. 'Mr Berman stayed at the Sainte Catherine in the Place Martroi.' She handed the diary and the Michelin to Mark for confirmation. 'He certainly didn't seem to stint himself on these little jaunts. The hotels in the Guide have all got two and three little pointy bits.'

'I was thinking the same thing. Going by the average fees in these places, he would have spent more on the accommodation, in most cases.'

'But why?'

'Who knows? Ego? Putting on some sort of display? It's hard to tell. It's as though he was accustomed to a certain life-style, irrespective of what he was earning as a violinist. But that seems pretty clear from everything we know about him.' He looked at Penny sombrely. 'It may also explain why he was involved with characters like Bradshaw and Vanzo.'

Penny watched him for a moment, and shivered. 'I feel as though somebody'd just walked over my grave!'

Mark nodded, and walked over to the window, staring out. He lit a cigarette. 'I'm afraid your words may be more appropriate than you think. If Bradshaw and Vanzo are anything to go by, he was involved in some very questionable partnerships.' Outside, the heat of the day was subsiding, and the shadows in the street were growing longer.

Penny said: 'If he was mixed up with characters like them, I'm surprised he let Karen go along for the ride with him.'

'How do you mean?'

She looked slightly embarrassed. 'Simply that, if he was involved in some sort of shady operation, I wouldn't have thought he would welcome witnesses.'

'It may not be as bad as that. We don't really know what he was up to. For all we know, he was simply buying and selling property, aided and abetted by the unctuous Eric Scutter.'

'I suppose so, but I never saw anyone try to obtain a bill of sale with a revolver.'

Mark shrugged. 'We may be letting our imaginations run wild. Bradshaw and Vanzo could be a couple of crazy characters, but it's hard to imagine Sandor as a gun-runner or a front man for the Mafia. As far as the trip from Monaco to London is concerned, I think it's probably as simple as Karen says it is. He was travelling home to London, and said she could come along for the ride. She asked him, if you remember. We know he came here ostensibly to make a record, so he offered her somewhere to stay for a few days – nothing more sinister than that.'

She nodded, avoiding his eyes. 'You're probably right.'

'You don't like her very much, do you?'

'Karen? I don't dislike her. I don't really know anything about her. She was rather odd, the only time I met her, but she had just learned about Sandor's death. I haven't seen her since then.' She looked steadily at Mark. When she spoke again, her voice was soft. 'I suppose I'm a bit jealous.' Mark said nothing, and returned to the sofa, picking up Berman's itinerary. 'I'm sorry. I shouldn't have said that.' Her voice brightened. 'Where did he go next?'

They continued to trace Berman's concert route all the way to Monte Carlo, with appearances in Tours and Limoges, and two concerts in Toulouse. In each city, Berman's notations, with the aid of the Michelin Guide, revealed where he had stayed. Penny seemed subdued after the initial excitement of their discoveries.

Mark was reading the itinerary. He paused for a moment, looking puzzled.

'What's wrong?'

'There's something slightly odd, which doesn't quite fit with all the rest. I've been picturing an imaginary map of France, tracing the progress of his tour. Now, we've just about reached the point where he met Karen at the Mirabeau in Monte Carlo. Look.' Penny read the itinerary, and Mark continued: 'He played the second concert in Toulouse on Sunday, August the eleventh, and we know from his diary that he arrived in Monaco on Wednesday the fourteenth. He met Karen on Friday the sixteenth, and left with her on the seventeenth.'

'Yes.'

'There seems to be a day missing. You'll notice that he nearly always left each town the day after the last concert. That makes sense.'

'Right.'

Mark returned to the itinerary again. 'Why did he take so long to get from Toulouse to Monte Carlo? It's only about a day's drive, but he seems to have taken three.'

Penny shrugged. 'Maybe he stayed on an extra day or two. If he left on the twelfth, he may have been quite late. I remember

Karen saying they didn't leave for Beaune until after twelve.'

'That's true, but even if he left late on Monday, he should have arrived by the Tuesday evening. He didn't get to Monte Carlo until Wednesday. That's an extra day.'

'He probably decided to take it slowly along the Riviera. Isn't Monte Carlo supposed to be very expensive? Maybe he thought it was cheaper to stay somewhere else *en route*.'

'Expenses don't seem to have bothered him all the way across France. It's probably nothing, but it caught my eye. Have another look in the diary.'

She read the pages again. 'There's nothing here, except that he played some Schumann.'

'How do you mean?'

'Well, against Tuesday the thirteenth, he wrote "Schumann".'

'Schumann?'

'Well, Robert Schumann, actually.'

'That's very odd.'

'Why?'

'He hasn't mentioned composers anywhere in the diary before. They're always listed in the itinerary. The diary entries have been the initials of hotels and the streets where they're located.'

'Yes, I suppose so.'

'There's more to it than that. There's not a great deal of music by Schumann for solo violin, and few violinists play his Concerto. Have you got the file?' She nodded. 'Just before the last page, there's a repertoire list, showing all the works he plays. Have a look at it.'

Penny checked the file. 'There's nothing by Schumann.'

'I didn't think there would be. Except for the chamber works there's very little for violinists. He was the great piano composer. Something else bothers me. A musician would never write "Robert Schumann", especially to himself in a diary. It would be like writing Ludwig van Beethoven or Wolfgang Amadeus Mozart. He might put "William Schuman", for the American composer, but he only has one "n".'

Penny read the diary again. 'I'm sorry. I misread that. The

Schuman in the diary only has one "n". But it is "Robert", not "William". What does it mean?'

'I'm not sure. All the other names in the diary are streets. Wait a minute; I've just remembered something! Does your Michelin have street maps of the larger cities?'

'Yes?'

'Something rings a bell. Look up Marseille. For the bigger towns, there should be a column called "*Répertoire des Rues*", listing all the main streets.'

Penny flicked rapidly through the pages, until she found it. Her finger ran down the page, and she looked up with a smile. 'Avenue Robert Schuman, with one "n"! He wasn't a composer after all.' She returned to the street map. 'I can't really see where it is, but it's somewhere just north of the Old Port. Sandor must have spent the missing night in Marseille, solving the mystery. You are clever!'

Mark was thoughtful. 'Why would Sandor spend a night in Marseille? He'd have to have made a special detour to go there.'

'Maybe he had friends there. After all, he didn't have to be in Monaco until Wednesday.'

'Yes, I suppose so.'

Penny lit a cigarette and stretched comfortably. 'Well, at least we know where he was. That's pretty good detective work.'

Mark nodded. 'Unfortunately, it still doesn't tell us anything more about him. I was hoping we would find a clue to why anyone wanted to kill him.' He took out a cigarette and reached in his pocket for his lighter. The message slip from the hotel fell out. 'Damn! I should have called New York.'

'Use my phone. I can claim it back from the office.'

'You're sure?'

'Sure.'

'I have a message to call Abe Sincoff. He's a kind of partner in America.' She looked puzzled. 'We share artists across the Atlantic. He looks after them for the United States and Canada, and I do the same for Europe. He's one of my oldest friends, and helped me tremendously when I first started my agency. Abe's always been my chief adviser. Without his help, I would never have managed.' He dialled the New York number and, within moments, was connected to Sincoff.

'Hey kid, you've been neglecting your godfather. What's the matter, pal: success gone to your head?'

'Hello, Abe. I'm sorry it took a while to get back to you.'

'Forget it. You people should learn a little Yankee know-how in your operation.' Abe was always extolling the virtues of New York's questionable professionalism. In Mark's experience, having suffered the endless delays of rude, unintelligible and apparently illiterate American switchboard operators, it seemed to him that Abe ran one of the few efficient offices he had encountered.

'How's Myra?'

'Great, but she's got me worn to a shadow of my former self.' A mental picture of Abe, bald and paunchy, with a roly-poly face, worn to a shadow by his solicitous wife, brought a smile to Mark's face. 'She's on a health class kick, complete with leotards and macrobiotic food, but I drew the line. At my age, the sight of all those female bodies wobbling in every direction could bring on a heart attack. So I told her I was developing a new line in men's wear: après-jog outfits, with built-in sweat stains in all the right places. If it takes off, I'll retire to Florida, and leave the music business to nice English fairies like you.'

'You'd never stand it, Abe. After ten days, you'd be climbing the walls.'

Abe's voice was stentorian. 'My boy, with the millions I'll make, I'll hire a *schwartzer* to climb the walls for me.'

Mark laughed. 'Abe, you're incorrigible! You're not supposed to use words like that in this day and age.'

'You're right, kid. I'll re-phrase it. I'll give employment to a *schwartzer*. Listen, I've got fantastic news. The beautiful Bianca has finally agreed to play London. Covent Garden made her the offer of a new production of *Butterfly*, and I'll be goddamned if she didn't accept, after everything she said.' Bianca Morini, an operatic superstar of legendary talent, beauty and sexual appetites, was probably the most important artist that they jointly represented.

'How on earth did they manage it? They'll never meet her fees.'

Abe chuckled. 'They didn't have to. Those guys are smart. They told her they'd hire that muscular Danish director for the production. Bianca's had the hots for him for the last six months, and the thought of all-night rehearsals for the big Act One love scene was more than she could resist. I tell you, kid, there are some things that money can't buy!'

'Is there anything I can do from here?'

'You could look into the movie possibilities. Some of those European television stations still work the art bit, and you might drop in on the Royal Opera House and make sure the red carpet goes to the cleaner's before she gets there. For Christ's sake make sure she has a dressing-room with a door that locks. Remember that night in San Francisco?'

'That door locked too, Abe. She just forgot.'

'Whatever. That was one command performance she hadn't planned to give before an audience! Why are you in London?'

'Recording sessions. I suppose you haven't heard the news yet. Sandor Berman.'

'He's bad news, Mark. I'd stay clear.'

'Why?'

'I met him after he gave a recital at the Little Carnegie a couple of years back. Not that he's a bad player. I liked him, but when we talked, he turned me off quicker than a rabbi at a Klan meeting. That's the most arrogant, cock-sure pain in the ass I ever met!'

Mark paused for a moment. 'He's dead, Abe. Somebody shot him during the recording session.'

'You're kidding! Je-sus! What happened?'

Mark briefly outlined the sequence of events in Kingsway Hall. Before he could continue, Abe interrupted.

'I knew I should have read my papers this morning, but I was running late.' Abe usually arrived in his office each day at eight o'clock, no matter how late the reception the night before had been.

'It may not be in the American press yet.'

'Who reads the American press? I get papers from London, Paris and Vienna delivered every day.'

'Really? I didn't know that.'

'Sure. Local news I get off the radio, but if you want to know what's happening around the world, read their newspapers. It's no use waiting for the information to filter through. That's terrible about Berman.'

'Yes. I suppose you don't know much about him.'

'Not really. He was one of Arnold's kids. I don't know where Arnie finds them all, but he's got a real ear for talent. If it hadn't been for his lousy personality, I might have done something for Berman. When did you sign him?'

'A few weeks ago. We didn't really sign – just a handshake. I was here partly to sort things out with him.'

'I guess he may have calmed down since I last saw him. That must have been at least two years ago. He said he had some old guy in Palm Springs sponsoring him at that time, but I forget the details. Shot? That's terrible!' For all his hard-edged patter, Abe was a kind man, dedicated to his musicians. 'Are you okay?'

'Yes, of course. I'm doing my usual job, picking up the pieces.'

'I know. Who was conducting?'

'Konstantin.'

'Steigel? Jesus, Heidi must have blown her top! How is he?'

'He took it very well. He even agreed to use the rest of the sessions to record a Beethoven symphony.'

'Hmm. Knowing that wily old buzzard, he probably organised the shooting! Is he really holding up okay? The last time I saw him, I was afraid to point an electric fan in his direction, in case I blew him over. He's looking awful frail.'

'He's tougher than you think, Abe. He'll probably outlast us all.'

'Yeah. With a broad like Heidi to look after him, you could be right.'

'He was in great form after the session yesterday, attacking everything in sight. He told me a nice story about a man who goes into a bar with a talking dog . . .'

'... and the dog says: "Maybe I should have said Stravinsky?" I heard it.' Abe always heard a story first. 'Speaking of which, did I tell you the one about Al Capone in the speakeasy? This is great!'

Mark's voice conveyed benign resignation. 'No, Abe, you didn't.'

'Wait a minute – you're going to like this! There was this speakeasy, see, with a five-piece band, and a big hood walks over to the leader and says: "Mr Capone is in da house."' Abe's imitation of a gangster was laughable. 'So the bandleader says: "Sure, Mister, sure. Is there anything we can do for him?" So the gorilla says: "Mr Capone will sing wid da band", and the guy says: "Right! Happy to oblige. What would he like to sing?" And the hood says: "Mr Capone is gonna sing *Life Is Just A Bowl Of Cherries*, in five-four time." Now, the bandleader says: "Hey, wait a minute! Nobody sings in five-four time. Songs are in four-four time." But the hood says: "Mr Capone sings it in five-four time!"' The menace in Abe's voice made Mark smile. 'Anyway, the bandleader says: "Okay, okay," the band plays the intro, and big Al waddles up to the microphone and sings: "Life is just a bowl of fuckin' cherries..."' Abe's laughter developed into a coughing fit, and Mark joined in. 'Great story, eh?'

'Lovely.' Mark made a mental note to bowdlerise it before passing it on to Steigel and Heidi. 'Abe, I've got to run.'

'Sure, kid. Listen, I really am sorry about Berman. Do they know who did it?'

'Not yet, but they're working on it.'

'I hope they catch the son of a bitch. Berman may not have had the personality, but he had talent. Call me again, will you?'

'I will, and give my love to Myra.' He replaced the receiver.

Penny was standing by the window. 'What was all the smiling about?'

'A new joke. Abe always has to be the first.'

'Is it repeatable?'

'Almost. I'll have to do a little mild censoring first.'

'I take it he didn't have much to say about Sandor?'

'No, although he did say there was a rich sponsor backing his career a couple of years ago. Abe heard him give a recital in New York, in one of the little debut halls. He's amazing! Nothing escapes his attention. As a matter of fact, he just gave me an idea.' Mark opened his briefcase, reaching for a leather-bound address book.

'What's that?'

'He said that if I really wanted to know what was happening around the world, I should always read the local papers. May I use the phone again?'

'Of course. Who are you going to call?'

Mark was already dialling. 'An old friend of mine, in Fleet Street. Hello? May I speak to Herbert Bailey in Records, please.'

Penny said: 'Who is he? I thought I knew a lot of Fleet Street people . . .'

'This is one of the back-room boys. They're often the most valuable.' He turned to the phone. 'Herb, is that you? This is Mark Holland.'

'Mark, you old sod! Where the hell have you been?' Bailey sounded genuinely pleased, and Mark remembered that he usually enjoyed a liquid lunch. It was better to ask a favour in the afternoon.

'I'm living overseas. I moved to Geneva.'

'Did you? I thought I'd missed you at the local lately. What are you doing amongst the Swiss, for God's sake? Don't you remember what Graham Greene said about cuckoo clocks?'

'I thought it turned out to be Orson Welles, but let it pass. I manage classical musicians.'

'Oh. Strange, but I always had you down as one of the cloak and dagger boys, with those mysterious trips you were taking.'

Mark laughed. 'You weren't a million miles from the truth, Herb, but that was a long time ago. I'm a reformed man since then.'

'Wish I could say the same. Am I going to see you?'

'I hope so, but I wondered if you could do me a favour.'

'Of course, as long as it doesn't involve folding money. It's been a hard month.'

'Nothing like that. Do you still look after all the foreign publications?'

'Most of them. We've cut back in the last few years, but we still keep a wide range. Where do you want?'

'What would you have from Marseille?'

'Marseille? That's child's play. I thought you were going to come up with somewhere like Bratislava or Tirana. Which one do you want?'

'I don't know. Is there a choice?'

'Hang on, while I check.' There was a momentary pause. 'Here we are. I can let you have *Le Provençal* – that's the main one – or *Le Meridional*, and I think they do their own edition of *Nice-Matin*. They always used to.'

'The first two should do nicely.' Mark looked at Berman's diary. 'Could you have a look at the editions for Tuesday, August the fourteenth, this year?'

Bailey sounded disappointed. 'Last Tuesday? I thought you were going to ask for something difficult. There's no challenge in that! Hold the line for a second, will you.' The telephone at the other end thumped as he dropped it on his desk.

Penny walked over to Mark and planted a chaste kiss on his forehead. 'That's for being a clever man.'

Mark smiled. 'Thanks to Abe. It may not tell us anything, but it's worth a try.'

Bailey had returned to the phone. 'Here we go. I've brought *Le Provençal* and *Le Meridional*. What do you want to know?'

'I'm not quite sure, Herb. I'm just generally interested in what was going on.'

'That's a fat lot of use!' Mark heard the papers rustling. 'The main headlines seem to be about Monsieur Le Pen of the *Front National*. He's a nasty bit of work, isn't he? We should put him in the ring with our Enoch – best of three falls. The trouble is they're both on the same side! What else is there? There's some Mitterand stuff and the usual old junk. It's a bit hard to know where to start, unless you want me to spend the afternoon reading to you in fractured French. How about giving me a clue?'

'I wish I could, Herb. A friend of mine was in Marseille last week in rather mysterious circumstances, and I wondered if there was anything going on that would explain his presence.'

Bailey grunted. 'I thought the official expression was "*Cherchez la femme*", but they don't usually bother to put it on the front page, unless he's very famous. Is he?' Back-room boy notwithstanding, his journalist's appetite was whetted.

'I'm afraid not.'

'In that case, you're looking for the proverbial needle. Why don't you come over and have a look for yourself? We can have a few jars, talk about the good old days, and you can read yourself stupid. I don't know what you're looking for.'

'Neither do I. That's the problem. You're probably right, but I can't come over at the moment. My friend arrived in Marseille last Tuesday, probably in the afternoon . . .'

'Then why do you want the Tuesday edition? I would have thought the Wednesday papers would have told you more.'

Mark snapped his fingers, startling Penny. 'Of course they would! How stupid of me! Look Herb, I know it's an imposition . . .'

'It's all right, I'm already on my way.' His voice was full of pretended long-suffering, and the receiver thumped on his desk again.

Mark turned to Penny, who was watching anxiously. 'I asked for the wrong day. If anything happened in Marseille when Sandor was there on Tuesday – if he was there at all – it would be reported in the Wednesday edition. There's probably a Robert Shuman Street or Avenue in half the cities of France. I seem to remember he was one of the bigwigs in the early days of the Common Market.' He smiled. 'And I was worrying about a seldom performed Violin Concerto! What was it I was saying about an enclosed world?'

Bailey had returned. 'Well, you picked yourself a more interesting day. Why is it the French love gory pictures, with blood and guts all over the pavement?'

'Why, what happened?'

'There was a lovely juicy murder on the night of the fourteenth. One of the local bad boys got picked off by an unknown assassin. I don't think much of the florid literary style. Listen to this: "Last night, as the city slept and a cold wind circulated in the narrow streets surrounding the Old Port, Jean Lucchini, a Corsican runner for the Marseille underworld, waited on a corner of the Rue de Mazenod for a rendezvous with an unknown assassin . . ." God, it goes on like that, line after line. My French is getting rusty, these days. Now, if you only wanted something out of *Pravda*, I could really give you a virtuoso performance. I get more practice with that.'

Mark felt a sudden tenseness. 'No, keep reading, will you.'

Penny, seeing his expression, walked over to the sofa, sitting at his side. She said: 'What is it?' in a low voice, but he shook his head, waving a hand for silence as he listened.

Bailey continued to read, translating quite rapidly. When he reached the end of the piece, he said: 'That's your main lead in both papers. They're both about the same. I always thought the French were supposed to be literary types. This lot make the *Sun* look like Sunday school required reading! Do you want me to scan through the other pages?' There was a pause as he searched. 'There doesn't seem to be anything much about musicians.'

Mark kept his voice impersonal. 'No, thanks. I think the best idea would be for me to come over and look for myself. Do you happen to have a local map of Marseille in your office?'

'Probably, although God knows where I'd find it at the moment. Why?'

'It's not important. I haven't been there for years. I was wondering where the Rue de Mazenod was.'

'Oh, if it's about the murder, *Le Meridional* printed a little street map, with a rather fanciful piece about the route the murderer might have driven. It reads like a load of bullshit to me.'

'Well, French journalism was always on the colourful side.'

'It makes a change from Russian! Let's have a look.' Bailey spoke almost as though to himself. 'It's a street running north to south by the old cathedral, just above the Old Port, between the Quai de la Joliette and the Avenue Robert Schuman.'

'Robert Schuman?' Penny looked up. 'I know where that is.'

Bailey's voice was curious. 'Are you interested in this murder, then?'

'No, Herb, but it makes a good story – better than all that National Front nonsense.'

'I suppose so, although Marseille is accustomed to that kind of thing. I always thought it was a bit of a dump. When am I going to see you?'

'How about tomorrow?'

'Fine. Come whenever you like, but you might as well wait until opening time.'

'I will, and thanks again. I'm sorry I couldn't be more explicit.' He replaced the receiver and sat, staring silently at Sandor Berman's diary.

At his side, Penny was waiting impatiently. 'What did he say?'

Mark looked at her. 'It may be nothing. The evidence we're going on is circumstantial, to put it mildly.'

'Tell me anyway!'

Mark hesitated before speaking. 'The main news item was that, on the night we think Sandor Berman was in Marseille, a local Corsican gangster was murdered on the Rue de Mazenod, which is a block away from the Avenue Robert Schuman. The police suspect that the murder was part of a hijack, which was carried out by an unknown assassin, who drove away in a Mercedes 450.'

'Oh.' Penny sat for a moment in silence, her eyes watching Mark's face. 'What did he take?'

'A large shipment of drugs.'

12

After a while, Penny said: 'It all fits together now, doesn't it?'

'I suppose so. We're still making certain assumptions. After all, we don't know whether Sandor actually was anywhere near Marseille last week and, even if he was, whether he was involved in all this.'

Penny was impatient. 'Oh come on, Mark! Look at the facts.

Sandor was obviously rich, living on an income he couldn't possibly have earned from playing the violin.'

'Yes, but there could have been . . .'

'Two men, claiming to be business partners of his, have been threatening you at gun point to return some valuable property which they say Berman has taken' – she paused for a moment, but Mark did not interrupt – 'and, the day before yesterday, without warning, Sandor was shot down in cold blood. The facts are staring you in the face!'

Mark nodded. 'We may as well add to the list that he drove Karen from Monte Carlo to Paris in a large Mercedes.'

She picked up the phone. 'What's the Inspector's number?' He handed her the policeman's card, and she dialled. As soon as she heard the ringing tone, she passed the receiver to Mark. 'For God's sake, tell him whatever you know.'

The Inspector was furious. 'Are you trying to tell me that you've been holding that diary for the past twenty-four hours, while you play at being Sherlock Holmes? I've a bloody good mind to do you for withholding evidence! I told you to stay out of this and leave it to us.'

'Before you get too hot under the collar, you might like to stop and think about how we stumbled on the facts . . .'

'Such as they are!'

'Whatever they are, would your people have done it any faster than we did? Would they have noticed an entry in a musician's diary saying "Robert Schuman" and spotted that something was wrong? And would they have the experience of the music world to check an itinerary against the entries in the diary, and work out the dates and places, leaving sufficient time for rehearsals and preparation? It's only because I happen to have been in Marseille that the "Schuman" entry even rang a bell. I'll bet you even money that I came up with the answers faster than any of you would have – and I called you the moment I did.'

'It doesn't excuse the fact that you deliberately neglected to tell us that you had opened the safe and taken the diary. Good God, man, I only talked to you a couple of hours ago!'

'You should be glad I found the combination to the safe.

Would you have guessed that he used composers' opus numbers?'

'We would have opened it just as fast.'

'Then why didn't you?'

For a moment, there was silence. When he spoke again, the Inspector was calmer. 'What else are you hiding?'

'Nothing.' It was too late and too complicated to explain about the money.

'You'd better be telling the truth, Holland. You're not outside the law any more, along with your death and glory boys in the Department!'

'Thank God for that! You might also remember that when I told you they had broken into Berman's flat because they were searching for something, you dismissed the idea and said it was a coincidence.'

The Inspector hesitated. 'I'm still not convinced that it wasn't. I want that diary.'

'Send a car round for it. You know where we are.'

'I intend to. If you'd handed it over immediately, we wouldn't have wasted twenty-four hours.'

'Always provided your experts would have spotted the discrepancies. Much as I admire our great English police and think they're just wonderful, my guess is that they'd still be scratching their heads over it.'

'Bullshit! You're not dealing with Dixon of Dock Green. This is the real thing.'

'All right, if it will get you going any faster, I can read you the list of names at the back of the diary, and the countries they belong to. You may want to start sending a few telexes.'

'That's bloody marvellous of you! Would you like to tell me how to do the rest of my job?' He sounded slightly mollified. 'You'd better give them to me anyway.' Mark read the names, spelling each one. 'Is that all he put?'

'Every last word. He used a kind of shorthand. He appears to have enjoyed making up cryptic lists.'

'There's not a lot to go on, but we'll contact the various authorities. I'll also be pulling in Mr Eric bloody Scutter for a few searching questions.'

'You won't get much change out of him. He's far too slippery to leave himself exposed. He spends his life one step ahead of half the tax collectors of Europe.'

'You could be right.' He sighed audibly. 'We'd better start from the beginning, since you seem to have worked out a scenario to fit everything together. You talk, and I'll listen.'

'It starts with the assumption that Sandor Berman, a young violinist starting to make his way in the concert world, found a very lucrative sideline, peddling drugs.'

'Based on what?'

'An income and a life-style far beyond his means.'

'You're joking! My God, if we assumed that every young man making more money than he should was trafficking in drugs, we'd have to pull in half the population of London!' His ill-temper seemed to have spent itself. 'Let it pass. Where does your story begin?'

'In Marseille. A local gangster was killed there last Tuesday night, and whoever did it stole a large shipment of heroin.'

'And you now think Berman did it. Why?'

'I know it may sound like a long shot,' – the Inspector grunted – 'but we think Berman was in Marseille that night. The man was killed one block from the Avenue Robert Schuman, and the notation Berman made in his diary could place him there.'

'Could!'

'That's right. I can't guarantee there aren't other Robert Schuman Avenues elsewhere in France. According to the press, the murderer was seen driving away in a Mercedes 450, and we also know that Berman was driving a large Mercedes.'

'Along with several other million people!'

'I know, but hear me out. We believe Berman took the drugs and continued on his way, via Monte Carlo, to London.'

'Did he bring them here?'

'No, I don't think so. Berman flew from Paris to London with the American girl, Karen Ackerman, and I don't think he risked bringing the stuff with him. Unless the Customs Department was out to lunch, he could never have whisked a large quantity past them.'

'Well, I'm glad to hear you think we do some things right!'

'I have better reasons for believing he didn't try. For the sake of argument, let's suppose that he did. Where did he hide it? It wasn't in the safe, and it wasn't in the flat. Whoever searched the place did a thorough job the first time. If they had found the drugs, they wouldn't have come back the same night for a second try.'

'Always provided that the break-in was linked to your drugs theory. Everything you've told me so far is pure speculation. Anyway, he could have got rid of the stuff before they broke in to his flat.'

'When? On the first evening, Sandor and the girl arrived in London, did a little shopping in the Edgware Road, and stayed in. The following morning, he stayed in the flat again, practising on the violin. Karen heard him, and said he didn't leave until he went off to a meeting at Magnum Records with Miss Scott. Don't forget, the American girl was an unexpected hitch-hiker. He'd hardly risk smuggling drugs in the presence of a comparative stranger.'

Penny whispered: 'I drove him back to the flat at six o'clock.'

Mark continued: 'Miss Scott drove him home from Magnum around six, and Karen came in shortly after that, to find him there. The next morning, he left the flat to go to the recording session at Kingsway Hall. You know what happened after that. So, unless Berman got up in the middle of the night, while the American girl was sleeping, he didn't have the time or the opportunity to deliver anything to anybody.'

The Inspector was silent for a while. 'All right, go on. So far, you've given me nothing but an imaginative story, based on the fact that Berman was richer than he should have been and *might* have been in Marseille on the night in question. Agatha Christie could do better than that!'

'The second part is more important, if you'll at least accept the hypothesis of the first. You may not like my story, but Berman's dead, nevertheless.'

'Keep going.'

'Enter Lewis Bradshaw, a sinister gentleman with a high-pitched voice and a menacing personality. He is connected with

Berman in some way, and his name is in the back of the diary. Let's assume, for the moment, that Bradshaw is Berman's London buyer. All that bullshit he gave me about business partnerships and property that belongs to him starts to become clear. Presumably, Bradshaw made some kind of down payment, which was why he talked to me about supplying the goods or returning his money. I think that Berman intended to deliver, but was killed before he could. He might have planned to double-cross Bradshaw, but I don't think so.'

'Why not?'

'First, because of the name in the back of the diary. Secondly, because he was taking a hell of a risk by not delivering. Thirdly, Bradshaw knew where he lived, and his telephone number. He called the flat on the morning that Berman was killed, and gave the American girl a hard time. If Berman had been planning to cut Bradshaw out of the deal, he wouldn't have made himself so easy to find.'

'I'll go along with that. Then who killed Berman?'

'Someone from Marseille – either Vanzo or one of his pals. After Jean Lucchini was killed and robbed, Vanzo and his friends must have set out after Berman. They either knew or guessed that he'd hijacked the shipment, or they could even have learned about it from London. Perhaps Berman didn't realise that Bradshaw had communications of his own with Marseille. Anyway, it wouldn't take long to find a musician if he's performing somewhere. I'm surprised they didn't catch up with him in Monte Carlo. I still can't make up my mind why they killed him before they recovered the goods. Maybe they thought he'd already sold them, or it could have been a vendetta, or a warning to other would-be hijackers, or simply a case of swift underworld justice. Whichever it was is no longer very important. They shot him.'

'You've got a lot of unanswered questions along the way, but I'm still listening.'

Mark paused for a moment. Penny had filled a wine glass and silently handed it to him. He took a brief sip before continuing. 'The missing link was found somewhere along the way between Bradshaw and Vanzo. I said earlier that Bradshaw may have had his own pipeline to Marseille, but between Berman's death and this morning, Bradshaw and Vanzo made contact with each other. I know that, because he told me so when he called. The drugs were still missing, so they joined forces and came after me, assuming that I knew where they were. Berman had told Bradshaw that I knew all about his business dealings, and had given him my telephone number in Switzerland. Perhaps he planned to tell me, and was killed before he could, or maybe he just pointed them at me as a diversion. Either way, the little bastard stuck me in the middle of it!'

There was a long pause. When he spoke, the Inspector's voice was grim. 'I hope, for your sake, that you're telling the truth.'

'I've no reason to lie. Besides, if I was part of it, why would I try to work it out for you?'

'I'll think about that. You haven't explained how the Frenchman found Berman.'

'If he told Bradshaw about me, he could have told Vanzo, in which case all Vanzo had to do was call my office in Geneva. Knowing how efficient my Swiss assistant is, he would have given them the exact times and locations of the recording sessions!'

The Inspector's voice was more friendly than it had been. 'Well, you've disposed of Berman and pinned the murder on the Frenchman. Where's the heroin?'

'I think it's still in France, and I have a pretty good idea where.' He heard Penny give a slight gasp.

There was an edge to the Inspector's voice. 'Are you going to let us in on your little secret?'

'It's in a lock-up garage, somewhere near the Gare du Nord. When Karen first told us she'd driven with Berman to Paris, I assumed he had a rented car. Later, when we were talking yesterday morning, I learned that he owned the Mercedes and kept it in a garage in Paris. She told me that they drove into the city, where he put the car away, and then took a taxi to the airport. I didn't really think about it at the time. So, if you want yet another guess, I think the heroin's sitting in the boot of that Mercedes, or somewhere similar, safely locked away in the garage. Karen mentioned that Berman told her he preferred to drive from one engagement to another, because he saved on the air fares. That surprised me, because most of the musicians I know haven't the time or the energy to drive from place to place. On the other hand, if Berman had set himself up as an international dealer, he'd chosen an ideal method of operation. Musicians spend most of their lives on the road and, in his case, he took it literally, driving from one concert to another – the fees were unimportant – and making his real income after hours with the little white packages hidden in the back of his car.'

'I see. That's a hell of a risk to take. His car could have been searched at any frontier.'

'But would it, especially if he was travelling during the summer months, along with millions of foreign tourists? Most European border officials have a healthy respect for classical musicians. The pop ones are a different matter. They're suspect wherever they go. I'm sure Sandor kept his precious violins on display and made a big production of being an international concert artist. I'm not suggesting that he left the drugs on the back seat, but they're easy enough to hide, especially if he travelled with reasonably small quantities on each trip and used the lock-up in Paris as a storage depot.'

'And the girl knows where this garage is?' For the first time, the Inspector was interested.

'I doubt it. When I asked her, Karen replied vaguely that Sandor kept the car somewhere near a big station on the north side of the city. Apparently, he drove her into the centre and along the Champs Elysées, so that she could at least say she'd seen the Arc de Triomphe. It was her first visit to Paris, and I don't think she knew the exact location of the garage. If we're lucky, she may recognise the place when she sees it. Otherwise, your French colleagues will have a very long search on their hands.'

There was a long silence. For a moment, Mark wondered whether the phone had been disconnected. He took another sip of wine, and lit a cigarette. Penny looked at him questioningly, but he shrugged his shoulders and waited. Finally, the Inspector said: 'Anything else?'

'What else do you want?'

'A great deal more than you've given me so far. It's all circumstantial evidence and speculation, without more than the occasional solid fact.'

'Except a dead violinist and a couple of very unfriendly characters with guns! Can you offer a better set of answers?'

The Inspector hesitated. 'No, not at the moment, but that doesn't mean I have to accept yours. There are too many "ifs" for my taste.'

'I'm not claiming to be a hundred per cent right, but I think I have the overall picture.'

'What are you going to do next?'

'Stay here, for the moment. I have to meet Karen after the concert and find her another place to stay until this is sorted out. She can't go back to Berman's flat.'

'The best move would be to bring her to us. We'll put her somewhere safe. Are you going back to the Westbury?'

'So that I can be a sitting target for Bradshaw and Vanzo? No thanks!'

'We can post men all over the hotel. They'd never reach you.'

'You can't guarantee that. You don't even know what they look like.'

'Miss Scott does.'

'She's only seen them very briefly: Vanzo for a few seconds outside Kingsway Hall, and Bradshaw for a moment in the rear-view mirror of her car.' Mark thought for a moment. 'I'll make you an offer.'

'What's that?'

'After I've found Karen tonight and made sure she's safe, I'll go back to the hotel – on two conditions.'

The Inspector's good humour seemed to be returning. 'I suspect there's going to be a catch!'

'Not really. I'll want a couple of your men, plain clothes, to help me. I should be able to describe Bradshaw and Vanzo to them.'

'No problem.'

'And I'll want a gun.' At his side, Penny said: 'No!', but the policeman was silent. 'I'm not going to be a decoy for you without being able to defend myself.'

The Inspector waited a little longer. 'You know I can't agree to that, although I wonder . . .' He lapsed into silence. 'How long is it since you left the Department?'

'Too long to count, and if you call them, I doubt whether they would think it was a good idea. I told you when we met that I didn't leave under the happiest of circumstances. You'll have to decide for yourself.'

'I'll think about it. That's all I can promise. When do you want to meet?'

'The concert will finish at about nine-thirty, and I've arranged to meet Karen backstage.'

'Very well, I'll see you there, and I'll give you my decision then. Unless I can think of something, the answer's going to be no.' He paused slightly. 'I would have thought some of your old contacts might have been able to help you out, for old time's sake.' The policeman chuckled. 'I didn't say that, of course!'

'There isn't enough time, and I don't have any old contacts. That was a lifetime ago.'

'If you say so.' His voice became official. 'A car should be round any time in the next half hour, to collect that diary.'

'We'll be here.'

'And, for Christ's sake, don't do anything else. To be honest, I don't know whether to believe your story or not. Either way, just sit tight, and we'll meet after the concert. If anything comes up, call me immediately. I'll arrange for you to be plugged through to me at any time.'

'Thanks.'

'Don't press your luck. I could still run you in on a dozen different charges, if I bothered to think about them. If you try anything else, I will!' He hung up.

Penny stood before Mark, hands on hips. 'What's all this nonsense about a gun?'

He smiled at her. 'Don't worry, they're not going to agree. I was trying him out. He wants me to go to the Westbury and wait for Bradshaw and Vanzo to come looking for me.'

'That's mad!'

'Of course it is. That's why I made a gun the condition. He'll never agree. Don't forget, he only has my word for half what's happened. Apart from Vanzo outside Kingsway, I could have made up the rest.'

'But why would you?'

'That's what he has to find out. Until he has something more concrete to work with, I could have arranged Berman's death myself, and made up the rest as a red herring.'

'What are you going to do?'

'Pick up Karen and drop out of sight. I can stay in touch by phone, but there's no point in waiting around London.'

'Where will you go?'

'I don't know. Somewhere just outside town, where they wouldn't think of looking. I'm sorry I told Karen to meet me after the concert, but it was the only thing I could think of at the time. I'll need to get my things out of the hotel.'

'But that's dangerous. They could be watching for you.'

'Yes, but I have an idea. We'll try it when they've collected Berman's diary.' He grinned. 'The Inspector was bloody angry, but in his heart of hearts he knows we probably unravelled Berman's codes faster than his own people would have.'

Penny walked over to the window, looking out. 'Did you say the Inspector was coming over here?'

'No, he's sending a car. I don't think he trusts me!'

'You can't blame him. Why won't you just leave things to the police? That's what they're there for.'

'Because it's sometimes possible to get more done without going through official channels.'

'He didn't seem to believe what you had to say.'

Mark shrugged. 'I can't prove anything.' He looked at his watch. 'It's getting late.'

'Not really. We're only a few minutes from the hall.'

'I know, but we have another call to make before the concert.'

'Where?'

'I'll tell you when the police have gone.'

She eyed him nervously. 'What are you up to?'

'Nothing serious.'

'Aren't you supposed to wait here until the concert?'

'Yes, but don't worry. We're not going to do anything illegal.'

Penny said nothing further, and busied herself with clearing the remains of the food into the kitchen. Her silence expressed her disapproval.

When the police car had left, Mark said: 'We ought to leave in a little while.' Penny was about to speak, but he continued: 'I told you, we have one more quick stop to make on our way to the concert.'

'In that case, I'd better change. How long have I got?'

'How long do you need?'

She smiled. 'I'll make it quick.'

'Do you mind if I make one more phone call?'

'Of course not.' She walked into the bedroom. 'I won't be long.'

Mark dialled the hotel and asked for the concierge. 'Hello, this is Mark Holland.'

'Yes, sir. What can I do for you?'

'Well, I wonder if I can ask a favour.'

'Of course, sir.'

'I'm tied up in a meeting at the moment, and I'm going to have to make a dash for London airport as soon as it ends.'

'Would you like me to order a minicab?'

'No, thank you. My problem is that I haven't checked out yet, and I'm going to be very pushed for time if I'm going to make my flight. Do you think one of the bellboys could go to my room and put my things into a bag for me?'

'Of course, Mr Holland – no problem.'

'Thank you very much. I won't have checked out, but I left an American Express voucher at the front desk. If they could make up my bill and give it to you, I can quickly sign it and be on my way.'

'Very good, sir, I'll look after it. I hope you haven't forgotten your violin case.'

'Good Lord, I almost had! Can you have that ready for me, too?'

'Yes, sir.' The concierge sounded pleased with himself. 'About what time should we expect you?'

Mark calculated. 'I'll make it as close to seven o'clock as I can. I have to check in at Heathrow by seven forty-five.'

'You should be all right, sir. It depends on the rush hour traffic, but the worst of it should have gone by then.'

'I'll try and make it a few minutes earlier if I can.'

'Don't you worry, sir. It will all be waiting for you.'

'That's very helpful of you. Thank you.'

Mark looked up to see Penny watching him from the doorway. She had changed into a wine-coloured cocktail dress, and was holding a hairbrush. 'What are you trying now, Mark? What's all this about Heathrow?'

'That's for the benefit of the hotel. When you tell them you have a plane to catch, they understand. I like your dress.'

She ignored the compliment. 'I thought the Inspector asked you to stay put.'

'That's what I'm doing. The only variation is that I'm going to check out of the hotel on my way to the concert.'

'But I thought you agreed . . .'

'I didn't agree to anything, Penny, and I have no intention of waiting around with Karen until Bradshaw and Vanzo find us.'

'What about your "deal", and the gun?'

'I won't be needing it.'

'I'm glad to hear it, but you can't risk going back to the hotel. They may be waiting for you. Why don't you let me go for you?'

'No. Vanzo has seen you a couple of times. He may recognise you.'

'But if they're waiting . . .'

'It's a chance I'll have to take. If they are, there are two possibilities. Either they'll be outside in the street, watching the entrance, or they'll be stationed in the foyer. I think they'll choose the street.'

'Why?'

'Because the foyer will be crowded at seven o'clock. They're not going to wave guns around in the middle of a hotel full of guests. As far as we know, they still want to talk, presumably to make some kind of deal for the return of the drugs. If they are there, they'll be somewhere near the forecourt, by the front entrance.'

'Then how will you get past them?'

'Easy.' He looked at his watch. 'Are you almost ready?'

'Another five minutes.'

'Good. We should be there by about seven o'clock, or perhaps a few minutes after. The later I am, the faster the concierge will be.'

As they circled Hyde Park Corner, Mark said: 'Will you go into Conduit Street from the Regent Street end?'

Penny nodded, tight-lipped. 'Why?'

'Because I hope you can find a parking place a few yards up the street, before you reach the front of the hotel. There's an entrance to the hotel through the coffee lounge, about twenty yards away. I'll go in that way. If Bradshaw and Vanzo are watching the front door, they may not have thought about it.' She nodded again. 'It shouldn't take me more than two minutes to go in, settle my bill, and collect my things.'

'Will you come back the same way?'

'No. Wait for exactly two minutes, then drive up to the front door. See if you can chat up that doorman, if he's on duty. I'll have my bags sent out, and follow directly behind. If we're lucky, we'll be out of the place before they've spotted us.' He watched her face. 'Don't worry so much! They may not even be there.'

She paused at a traffic light. 'I think you're starting to enjoy this. I'm just frightened!' Mark put his hand over hers, and she clasped it.

'There's nothing to be frightened of, and I couldn't ask for a better driver.' She relaxed enough to give a nervous smile.

As they approached the hotel, Penny said: 'There aren't any parking places.'

'Can you double park?'

'Yes.' Her voice was tense. 'Mark, be careful!'

He stepped out of the car slowly, watching the street ahead. There was no sign of Bradshaw or Vanzo. Moving swiftly, he covered the few yards to the side entrance of the hotel, entering the busy coffee lounge. A corridor at the rear of the room connected it with the foyer of the hotel, and Mark walked along this, quickening his pace as he approached the concierge's desk.

As he had anticipated, the foyer was busy. Most of the armchairs and sofas were occupied, and various groups of guests were standing in the open areas, preparing for the evening's entertainment. Mark's glance took in the room, passing rapidly from face to face, as he made his way to the desk. Seeing him approach, the concierge apologised to three young American women who were inspecting a London theatre guide, and produced the violin case and Mark's travelling bag.

One of the girls looked up. 'Hey! We were here first!'

The concierge treated her to a charming smile. 'I'm so sorry, madam, but this gentleman has a plane to catch.' Without waiting for her reply, he turned to Mark. 'Good evening, Mr Holland. You're going to have to hurry. It's nearly five past seven.' His voice was slightly reproving.

'My meeting lasted longer than I expected. Do you have my bill?'

The concierge produced the page and a prepared American Express slip. 'All ready, sir, as you asked.'

'That's excellent!' Mark took out a pen. 'Would you ask the bellboy to take the baggage out for me? There's a red Mini waiting by the front door.' He pretended to examine the account while the concierge snapped his fingers and gave instructions. A moment later, Mark signed the American Express slip.

One of the American girls said: 'Well, some people get service in this place! Men!'

The concierge turned to her with a beneficent smile. 'Yes, madam. May I recommend *No Sex Please, We're British*? I'm sure you'll find it most entertaining.'

Facing the front door, Mark could see Penny's car standing outside. The doorman was by her window, chatting happily, and the bellboy was stowing the baggage in the back of the car. Mark walked slowly to the glass door, waiting until the bellboy had finished. He already had a handsome tip ready.

As he entered the forecourt of the hotel, Mark moved fast, handing the money to the bellboy and entering the car as quickly as he could. Penny was about to leave, but the doorman walked in front of the car, holding up his hand.

Mark muttered: 'What the hell does he want?'

In an unhurried manner, the doorman preceded them out of the forecourt and walked into the street. He held up his right hand with all the authority of a traffic policeman, and grandly waved them into the road.

Mark strapped on his safety belt. 'So far, so good! Can you see them?' Penny shook her head silently. Her face was very pale.

Across the road, Mark saw two figures running towards a car facing in the opposite direction. 'There they are!' Penny was still edging forward, prevented from moving by the bulky figure of the doorman. Bradshaw and Vanzo had entered their car, which started with a roar. Vanzo, at the wheel, was pulling away from the kerb, preparing to make a U-turn. The doorman slowly moved to one side, satisfied that the way was clear, and greeted Penny with a crisp military salute. They had now entered the street, and the traffic light in front of them changed to green.

Almost involuntarily, Mark said: 'Go!', and the car leapt forward so suddenly that the doorman, with a surprised expression, had to jump to one side as they swept past. He recovered enough to regard Penny with a look of condescending contempt. Looking through the rear window, Mark could see Vanzo trying to edge his car into oncoming traffic. A London taxi refused it the space, and Vanzo waved a fist in his direction. By that time, Penny had raced into Bruton Street and, cutting past a sedate blue Volvo, was already heading into Berkeley Square. At the corner, she shot past an approaching lorry, which stopped short with squealing brakes and several loud blasts of its horn.

Mark clicked his tongue, watching with admiration as she steered in and out of the traffic around the square. 'Well, you know what they say about lady drivers!'

For the first time in the past hour, Penny suddenly laughed. 'Fuck 'em!'

He looked again through the window. There was no sign of the other car.

13

Penny parked her car in a street just behind the Albert Hall, edging it expertly into an impossibly small space. Mark watched her manoeuvre the Mini. 'I didn't think you'd fit it in. I would have needed a shoe horn!'

She shrugged happily. Reaction to the race from the Westbury had set in. 'There was plenty of room. I usually have to do it by ear.' Looking at the baggage on the back seat, she said: 'What about those damned violins? My insurance doesn't cover losses to a million and a half dollars!'

'We'll take them with us. They could be useful.'

At the Artists' Entrance, Mark collected their tickets and headed down the nearest staircase. At his side, Penny said: 'Aren't you going the wrong way?'

'No, we can look in on Konstantin. Besides, I don't want to sit through the concert with a violin case on my knees.'

'Can you leave it with the Steigels?'

'No, there's a better place.' He led the way, guiding her past various members of the orchestra who were now congregating in the lower corridor, awaiting the call to go on stage. Wives, children, girl-friends and hangers-on accompanied them, talking and sharing a last-minute cigarette. Several of the players nodded to Mark, ignoring the violin case.

He paused at the doorway of the men's dressing room. 'Don't you remember Edgar Allan Poe's "Purloined Letter"? This is the one place where nobody's going to notice an extra violin case.' Opening the door, he motioned to Penny. The changing room was littered with instrument cases of all shapes and sizes, and he laid Berman's, still closed, on a nearby chair. 'I'll pick it up after the concert.'

In the conductor's dressing room, Konstantin was wrestling with a collar stud, swearing under his breath. Behind him, Heidi was brushing his jacket. The conductor looked up with an exasperated smile.

'Good evening, my dears.' His fingers slipped on the stud, and he swore again. 'This stupid uniform that we wear! One of these days, I'm going to dress like Vova Ashkenazy, and to hell with tradition!' Ashkenazy had long since eschewed a white tie and tails in favour of a simple white rollneck. 'Heidi!'

'I'm here, Tino.' Her voice was cheerfully patient. 'Let me do it.' She moved in front of him and, as he let his arms fall to his side with a gesture of resignation, reached up and adjusted the offending stud. Her fingers moved like lightning and, a moment later, the white bow tie was knotted and fitted perfectly in place. She stood aside to allow Konstantin to examine his reflection with a satisfied grunt.

'Thank you, my dear.' Turning to Mark, he added: 'It has to be this or the rollneck. I know it is favoured, but I will not wear one of those dreadful white evening jackets. I'm a conductor, not a cabin steward!'

Mark watched in silence. As Heidi held the conductor's jacket for him, he asked: 'How is it going?'

Steigel threw up his hands in mock despair, and Heidi caught the jacket before it reached the floor. 'How does it ever go? Never enough rehearsals! They expect the impossible of me every time!'

'Well, at least you had more rehearsal time for the *Eroica*, courtesy of Magnum Records.'

Steigel snorted. 'One movement! What about the other three? Magnum Records are the only ones who benefit. *They* get the additional benefit out of my concert when we start recording tomorrow, and they won't even notice the difference!' He turned to scowl at Penny and, recognising her, his face broke into a smile. 'Good evening, my dear. You must forgive my bad temper. Did you enjoy the rehearsal this morning?'

'It was wonderful, maestro. Now I understand how one learns about music.'

'Oh *ja*.' His eyes became vacant with old memories. 'I

remember the way Bruno Walter used to prepare an orchestra, slowly reconstructing the music phrase by phrase.' He smiled. 'He was not always such a nice old man as legend would have you believe . . .'

Before Konstantin could continue, Heidi had placed herself between Penny and Mark and, taking an arm in each hand, gently but firmly steered them to the door. 'Don't let him start reminiscing for you now. He'll talk about the time Toscanini tore a score into shreds, and the concert will begin fifteen minutes late!'

Mark looked at his watch. It was almost seven thirty. 'We'd better go and find our seats.'

Konstantin was still peering in the mirror, readjusting his tie. 'I will see you after the concert. Don't bother during the interval. By the time I am changed, I will have to start again. The radio people do not permit delays, because it interferes with their news broadcasts! Heidi, where is my handkerchief?'

'In your pocket, Tino, where it always is!'

As they seated themselves in the hall, Mark said: 'Damn! I told Karen we'd be sitting on the other side of the promenade, next to the violins. Can you see her?'

'No, not yet.' The promenade was filled to capacity, and Penny looked across the mass of spectators, sitting or standing in the great central arena of the hall, her eyes moving from person to person. 'It's very full tonight.'

All the seats surrounding the arena were occupied, and Mark surveyed the huge building, with its rich red curtains decorating each box, and its solidly old-fashioned architecture. The acoustic 'clouds' that had been installed some years earlier seemed out of place amid the Victorian grandeur. All the way to the crow's nest of the top gallery, the great auditorium was a mass of faces, glowing in the reflection of the bright lights on the stage. The orchestra was adding the finishing touches to its tuning and, after a momentary silence, the leader came on to the platform, to be met by enthusiastic applause. Mark remembered previous seasons, when cheerful students and younger promenaders welcomed each leader with a carefully prepared chanted greeting. In a vast, undulating mass, those promenaders who had been seated now rose to their feet, gently pressing forward towards the stage. The house lights dimmed, and the audience waited expectantly. Mark searched through the faces, hoping to catch a glimpse of Karen, but could not find her. For a moment, his eyes picked out the head of a dark-haired girl with close cropped curls, but when she turned slightly, her face was not Karen's.

There was renewed applause as Konstantin entered, striding in from the staircase at the rear of the stage. He was a popular figure on the London concert scene. Waves of sound, with an occasional cheer, greeted him as he mounted the podium, and he bowed slowly, his body stiff and his eyes closed, acknowledging the greeting. As it slowly receded, he turned to the orchestra, bowing his head again until the silence was complete. He raised his arms, the baton scarcely moving, and the orchestra entered with a blaze of sound, playing Schoenberg's lush transcription of Bach's 'St Anne' Prelude and Fugue.

Penny seemed to be transfixed by the music, but Mark hardly heard it. His eyes were searching constantly among the faces in the audience, now lit only from the front. After a few minutes, he ceased to scan them with quite such concentration, and the music filtered into his consciousness, its noble melodies subtly enhanced by Schoenberg's tapestry of colours. Steigel caught the powerful forward pulse of the music, commanding attention and, despite himself, Mark found he was fascinated. The Prelude ended and, as the woodwinds introduced the stately Fugue, with its vague suggestion of the 'Old Hundredth' hymn, Mark's attention wandered again, and he searched through the darkened audience with renewed effort, desperately hoping for a glimpse of Karen. Where was she? He cursed himself inwardly for telling her to go to the violin side of the orchestra, diametrically opposite the seats where he and Penny were sitting. Had anything happened to prevent her from coming to the concert? A loud entry by the brass distracted him, and he sat back in his chair, resigned to wait until the house lights came up again. The work ended, to a wave of applause, and Steigel bowed and walked slowly to the exit, returning once to accept redoubled cheers. The hall was very warm, and Mark could see sweat glistening on the conductor's bald forehead.

As some members of the orchestra filed off the stage, leaving smaller forces to perform the Richard Strauss Oboe Concerto, Penny asked: 'Any luck?'

'Not yet. She doesn't seem to be here.'

'Do you think she had any trouble getting in?'

'I doubt it. I told her to join the queue around six o'clock.'

'Perhaps we'll find her in the interval. What will happen if we don't?'

'I don't know. She must be here, somewhere!'

'There's still plenty of time. I'll keep looking, too. Do you think she could have bought a seat upstairs?'

'It's possible, but I told her where to go. I don't think she would have changed plans.'

'Well, I'll keep looking upstairs as well.'

After a short wait, Steigel returned, preceded by a young oboe soloist, who received a warm welcome. After a moment's tuning, the oboist began to play, launching immediately into the decorative opening theme, accompanied by gentle string figurations. On any other occasion, Mark would have been totally engrossed. The concerto, a product of Strauss's final, mellow years, was one of his favourites, but he could not listen to it properly. With mounting apprehension, his eyes travelled across the promenade audience, already identifying the heads and faces that he had seen in earlier searches. Where the hell was she? And, if she wasn't there, what would he do after the concert? He could not go back to the Westbury, and she did not dare return to Berman's flat. How would they find each other again?

The oboist played superbly, his tone sweet, and Steigel's accompaniment was elegantly graceful, with touches of gentle humour. The music moved into the slow movement and, with growing frustration, Mark found that the atmosphere was becoming increasingly warm, making him drowsy. Lack of sleep over the past two days was taking its toll, and he leaned forward, ignoring the stickiness of his clothes and dividing his attention between the music and a constant watch over the audience. He was convinced that Karen was not there. Perhaps she was waiting to come in after the interval, preferring to sit in one of the bars, and join the crowds when they returned. Hadn't she said, that first day, that she wasn't 'into' this kind of music? But it was dangerous to sit alone in an empty bar. There was no guarantee that Bradshaw had not followed them to the concert. Suppose they were searching the hall too? What would they do with her if they found her? The soloist began the finale, the music dancing, and Mark looked impatiently at his watch. It was nearly ten past eight, and the interval would begin shortly. Where was Karen?

When the concerto ended, there was loud cheering. Steigel, with a broad smile, shook the soloist's hand, and they stood together, accepting prolonged applause. After three exits and entrances, including a solo bow for the oboist, who seemed slightly bewildered by the weight of the reception that greeted him, they did not return. The applause slowly died, and the house lights came up. The promenaders filed towards the exits under the arena, and Mark and Penny stood to allow people to squeeze past them in the general exodus.

'What shall we do?' Penny looked at him with a worried expression on her face. 'She may have gone out with the rest.'

'I don't think she was here. I spent the entire half watching that promenade. I'm sure I would have seen her.'

'Why don't we try the corridors outside? We might spot her there.'

'All right, but be careful. For all we know, our other two friends may be prowling around.'

Penny hesitated. 'I hadn't thought of that.'

'It's the most logical place for them to look.'

'Should we stay here, then? The Inspector will come in at the end of the concert.'

'No, I can't just sit and wait!'

'In that case, let's split up, and do a circuit of the main corridor. I'll go one way, and you go the other. We'll meet again at the far side. I'll take a quick look in the bars, in case she slipped into one of them.'

'Good. When you get to the other side, walk down into the hall as far as the promenade, in case she is over there. I don't think she is. I'm sure I would have spotted her by now.'

They parted company at the entrance, walking in opposite directions along the corridor that circled the main floor of the building. Mark shouldered his way past groups of people, his eyes scanning the corridor for any sign of the American girl. The refreshment bar was crowded, and he paused in the doorway, hoping that he might catch a glimpse of her, but she was nowhere to be found. When he had completed a half circuit, he met Penny, who gave a quick shake of her head.

'I'm sorry, Mark. I can't find her.'

'It's no good. She's not here.'

As they walked back to their seats, Penny said: 'Do you think she's waiting outside, with the intention of coming in afterwards? She could always slip in past the people milling around at the exits.'

'It's possible, but I don't understand why she would. You and I know our way around concert halls, but she's a stranger. I should never have told her to meet me here.'

The auditorium was filling, as people drifted back for the second half of the concert. In the corridors outside, the warning bells were sounding for the end of the interval. Mark continued to watch, looking at each new face as it appeared in the busy promenade arena.

At his side, Penny said: 'It's strange. I didn't expect to find myself feeling sorry for that girl, but I do. What a lousy business to get herself caught up in!' She looked at Mark. 'I'm sorry I've been rather bitchy about her.' Mark shook his head silently, unwilling to transfer his attention from the arena. Penny's voice was angry. 'It's disgusting to think of that little creep Berman, peddling his filth around Europe. What a shit he was! Knowing what we do, I'm glad they killed him!'

Mark nodded, still searching. Inside, he felt a steadily gathering panic. She had to be there! The house lights were dimming, and there was still no sign of her. Moments later, following quickly on the heels of the leader, Konstantin returned to the stage, receiving an enthusiastic welcome.

Over the applause, Penny said: 'I suppose you have to give the little bastard some credit for ingenuity. Who would ever suspect a concert artist of being a dirty little drug pedlar? I'm amazed that he got away with it. The car must have been an awful risk, even if he only carried small quantities. Trust him to brazen it out!'

Silence had descended upon the hall, as Steigel waited to begin the *Eroica* symphony. At that instant, an image from the recording session suddenly flashed through Mark's head, and he sat very straight in his chair. 'Of course!' He spoke aloud, without realising it. Penny glanced at him with a surprised expression, and a man in the row in front of them looked round with a gesture of irritation, his concentration interrupted. A moment later, Konstantin's hands moved, and the orchestra began to play. The opening chords, perfectly spaced, were crisp and commanding.

Mark stared into space, as one of the answers to a question that had been bothering him became clear. 'Of course! I should have thought of that before. Now I know why he behaved like that!' But where, in God's name, was Karen? What had happened to her?

Mark gazed across the promenade as the orchestra swelled to the opening theme, and a small movement caught his attention. A figure had entered from the staircase below, coming slowly into the promenade arena. He recognised the shape of the head first and, as she turned, her face was gently illuminated by the lights from the stage. It was Karen. She was standing directly opposite their seats, on the far side of the promenade, facing the violins, just as he had told her to. Touching Penny's hand, so that she looked up, Mark nodded in Karen's direction. He put his mouth very close to Penny's ear, and whispered: 'She's there – straight across, on the far side.' Penny scanned the audience, her eyes half closed, then nodded her head, smiling. Almost under her breath, she said: 'Thank God!' Karen had not moved from her position, but Mark could see her occasionally turn her head in the direction of the seats to her left. She was obviously looking for him, expecting to find him in the place he had described. Mark no longer heard the music. He concentrated his attention on Karen, willing her to look across the hall in his direction.

The first movement ended, to be greeted by the traditional London chorus of coughs and shuffling. In the short pause between the movements, Penny whispered: 'I've seen her. What made you start like that, just before she came in?'

He replied in a low voice: 'I'll tell you later; no time now. I think I have the proof the Inspector wants.' Penny's eyes widened, and the man in the row in front shifted in his seat, prepared to do battle. Mark was silent.

Steigel led the orchestra through a stately funeral march. Despite himself, Mark listened, seldom taking his eyes away from Karen's slender frame. She had ceased to look into the rows of seats to her left, and now stood, immobile, watching the orchestra. Mark wondered what was going through her mind.

It was clear to him that she had not come into the arena for the first half of the concert. Why? Had she arrived too late? Perhaps she had waited in one of the bars after all, until the end of the interval. With an inner smile, he reminded himself to tell her what agonising frustration she had caused, but he knew that he would not. He was too relieved to find her. Relaxing for a moment, he closed his eyes and settled back into his chair, listening to the music. Steigel's conducting was magnificent. It was Beethoven at his most noble, and the old conductor captured it at an Olympian level.

Another wave of tiredness flooded over him, and Mark opened his eyes, fearful that he might fall asleep. Karen had not moved, and he sat forward again, trying to concentrate his attention on the platform. As the movement drew to an end, Penny turned towards him, her eyes bright. She might have spoken, but Steigel launched quite suddenly and unexpectedly into the Scherzo, forbidding any relaxation of tension. The tempo was faster than Mark had anticipated, but the articulation and dynamics so well controlled that he was totally captivated by the performance. The strings seemed to whisper the introduction, and the full orchestra replied in a great roar of sound. It occurred to Mark that, in the hands of a great conductor, even the most unconventional approach suddenly became the only correct way to perform the piece. As the final three chords sounded, reverberating in the vast hall, Penny smiled and whispered in his ear: 'Well, at least she arrived in time for the best part!'

Mark nodded. When this was all over, there was so much to tell Karen about, so many pleasures in his life for her to share. And music? Would she enjoy it as he did? He was sure she would. She belonged to a generation which had rejected classical music as a symbol of its rebellion, but he could lead her back to it. Once she had listened, in the peace and intimacy of their own private world, she would understand. He smiled to himself. What a sentimental thought! Besides, there would be much more to their life than that. The music intruded on his thoughts again, and he turned towards the stage, following the sounds through the expressive gestures of Steigel's hands. He was not an extrovert conductor, given to dramatic musical exaggerations, and although he enjoyed verbal histrionics, one could not think of him as a sensitive, poetic soul. Yet, when he stood before the orchestra, hunched slightly forward and glaring over his spectacles, he achieved the subtlest and most delicate of orchestral colours, which he could then contrast with bold, forceful blocks of sound. The horns blazed their noble theme and Mark realised, with surprise, that the symphony was almost over. There would be the steady *decrescendo* in the woodwinds – Steigel would take them down to almost nothing! – and then the final triumph of the last pages.

In a short time, the police would take the Berman case over, and he would be free of it, now that he could convince them that he was right. Sooner or later, Bradshaw and Vanzo would be caught, and the case would be closed. Mark wondered whether the Inspector had already sent telexes across Europe, carrying the list of Berman's ugly 'contacts' to each country. It was no longer his problem. Nor Karen's. They would start their holiday and, this time, she would see Europe with him, share it through his eyes. Especially France. It was still his favourite country, with all its delights and diversities, and he would show it to her in a way that she would never have discovered alone.

And then, quite suddenly, he remembered the question that had been nagging at the back of his mind all afternoon. His glance returned to Karen, a distant, immobile shadow in the audience, and he began to piece together the other parts of the problem. It was all falling into place.

Looking towards the back of the auditorium, his eye was momentarily caught by a suggestion of movement towards the rear of the promenade section. There was a slight space at the back of the arena, created because the promenaders had crowded forward. On the edge of this area, a tall figure was moving. For a moment, the image did not register in Mark's mind, but there was something vaguely familiar about the man's stance. He turned towards a shorter companion, and a ray of light shone across his face. It was Lewis Bradshaw and, even from a distance, Mark could interpret his gesture as he signalled to Vanzo. Bradshaw had also seen Karen, and was now very slowly making his way towards her.

The orchestra burst magnificently into the finale of the symphony, horns and trumpets sounding their battle calls over the strings, and the tempo increased. The woodwinds played their last ascending scale, and the whole orchestra united for the final chords. There was a split second of silence, and then the audience erupted into sustained cheering. Steigel, his face streaming with sweat, shook the leader's hand and bowed, opening his arms wide to take in the orchestra which, at his command, rose to its feet. The promenaders roared happily and stamped their feet. Many of those who were seated in the many tiers and galleries of the auditorium now stood, clapping enthusiastically. The sound was thunderous.

As Penny turned to Mark, her smile froze. 'What is it?'

Mark kept his voice low, resisting the temptation to point. At this moment, such a gesture might attract attention. 'Bradshaw – and Vanzo. They're at the back of the promenade.' She followed his glance with a quick intake of breath. 'I think they've spotted Karen.'

Penny looked from the two men to where Karen was standing. 'They'll never reach her in that crush. She's too far away.'

Bradshaw had already moved forward, and was progressing steadily in Karen's direction, his tall frame edging past the applauding spectators. Karen, unaware, was still clapping her hands. It seemed to Mark that she had enjoyed the music.

'She's standing right next to an exit. For God's sake, why doesn't she go?' Bradshaw had drawn closer, gently pushing several promenaders aside. Mark could see one young man call something after him, but he was already farther on.

Penny's voice was tense. 'She doesn't realise he's there. Can we catch her attention?'

'She'll never see us, and she wouldn't hear me if I called to her in this din.' He gritted his teeth. 'Just go, girl! Get out of there!'

Bradshaw was now within fifteen paces of Karen and, as the applause was dying, she turned and walked down the exit stairway from the promenade. Within seconds, dozens of others surged forward, eager to escape before the crowd. To his relief, Mark could see that Bradshaw could no longer move forward and was hemmed in, forced to wait his turn as the good-natured audience jostled its way through the narrow exit.

Mark took Penny's arm. 'She's all right, as long as she finds her way backstage quickly. We'd better hurry.' Pushing past a number of slower-moving people, he strode up the stairway to the exit door. Penny, pulled along, almost stumbled, hanging on to his arm for support. At the top of the stairs, Mark glanced back. Bradshaw was still in the central arena, impatiently awaiting his turn to exit. Vanzo was somewhere behind him, lost in the crowd.

They half walked, half ran to the stairway down to the changing rooms, pushing through the glass door and ignoring the sign forbidding entrance to all but orchestral personnel. Mark thought he heard an attendant call out to them but, by that time, they were halfway down the staircase.

He left Penny by the narrow passage leading to the conductor's changing room. 'Wait for her here. I'll get the violins.' She nodded, wide-eyed. 'We could be out of here before they guess which way she went.'

The orchestra was still arriving from the stage. Some of the players, seeing Mark, were annoyed to find a civilian invading their domain, but reserved their irritation to a surly glance in his direction. A couple of others, recognising him, called greetings. Mark walked swiftly into the changing room, collected Berman's case, and headed back towards Penny. One of the orchestra players grinned at him and said: 'Hello, Mark.' He eyed the case. 'I didn't hear you playing tonight!'

Mark smiled. 'I'm looking after this for a friend.' The man nodded, and waved.

Penny was still waiting in the corridor. 'She's not here yet. Do you want to go up and find her?'

'No, it's better to let her find us. She knows where to come. We could miss each other if we move around.'

'I hope the Inspector shows up.'

'He'll be here.' Mark looked at his watch. 'The concert finished early. It was a shorter programme than I realised.'

At that moment, Karen turned the corner of the corridor. At the sight of Mark, she smiled and ran forward. 'Hi! I found my way easily, but I couldn't see you during the concert.' As she came forward, Mark had the impression that she was about to embrace him but, seeing Penny, she kept her hands to her sides. Instead, she turned towards Penny with a warm smile. 'Hello again! I didn't recognise you for a moment.'

Penny smiled nervously. 'We were trying to find you in the audience.'

'Oh.' Her face clouded for a moment. 'I didn't go in until the second half.'

'Why not?'

'I was going to, but while I was waiting in line for a ticket, I saw . . .' She hesitated, slightly embarrassed, looking at Mark.

Mark said: 'Penny knows what's happening. You can say what you like.'

Karen looked relieved. 'There were two men. I couldn't be positive, but they looked like the ones who were waiting outside the apartment this morning. I wasn't certain, but I was almost sure it was them.' She turned to Mark. 'How did you get away?'

'I'll tell you later, but you were right about the men. What did you do?'

'Well, I was almost at the box office, so I stayed close to the wall, and held my book up, as though I was reading it.' She tapped her shoulder bag. 'I don't think they saw me. They were down the end of the line.'

'What did you do after that?'

'After I bought my ticket, I watched where everyone was going, so I would know. Then I went to the john.' She laughed.

'I spent the first half sitting on the can, reading, until people started to come in at the intermission. Then I hung around, pretending to fix my make-up, until they were ringing those gongs for the second half. I waited until the last minute, and went into the auditorium. It was already getting dark by the time I got there. What's happening now?'

'You were right. It was Bradshaw and his French friend Vanzo. They spotted you in the hall, and were making their way towards you just before the concert ended.'

Karen looked frightened. 'Where are they now?'

'We don't know. Bradshaw was coming up behind you. We could see him from where we were sitting.' By way of explanation, he added: 'Our seats were on the opposite side of the hall. I had expected to be on your side. By the time you went through the exit, Bradshaw was still a few yards away. He was caught in the crowd, and couldn't reach you.'

'Will he come here?' She had moved closer, so that their bodies almost touched.

'Probably.' Mark turned to Penny. 'Will you go up to the Artists' Entrance, and wait for the Inspector?'

'Where will you be?'

'We'll lose ourselves in the hall.'

'Why not wait here?'

'It's the first place they'll look.' He walked to the staircase leading to the door with the printed 'No Entry' sign. It was crowded with orchestra players, carrying instruments, on their way home. Some remained in their stage clothes, while others had changed into civilian garb. Carrying the violin case, Mark looked like one of them. 'They'll probably try to come down the other staircase. With the sign on the door up there, they won't want to attract attention.' He looked at his watch. 'Stay with the Inspector, and we'll join you ten minutes from now.' Penny was about to speak, but he added: 'Hurry!' She nodded, and preceded them up the stairs.

'Hello! Mark Holland, isn't it?' One of the violinists from the orchestra placed a hand on his shoulder. He had thick dark hair, greying at the temples, and his skin was heavily sun-tanned. 'Don't you remember me? Terry Bellamy.'

'Yes, of course.' They had known each other for some years, and he shook the violinist's hand. Penny had already disappeared through the glass door at the top of the stairs, and he was anxious to follow.

Bellamy smiled. 'I haven't seen you for a long time. You're looking very well.'

'So are you.'

'Oh, I've just come back from a holiday.' He leaned forward confidentially, placing a restraining hand on Mark's arm. 'Don't tell the maestro, but I only managed this morning's rehearsal. He gets very upset when the orchestra changes personnel! I arrived home late last night.'

'Ah.' Mark took a step up the stairs, but Bellamy kept pace with him.

'Drove down to the South of France for a couple of weeks. The weather was fantastic!' He paused, blocking Mark's path. 'Terrible news about that young violinist Berman. I heard about it this morning. Does anyone know who did it?'

'No, not yet.' Mark started to move again.

'I heard him play, you know.'

'Really?' Mark paused.

'Yes. He was in a concert down there, and I went. Awful place, the Capitole. Dry as a bone!'

'I thought you were on holiday.'

'That's just what my wife said!' He winked. 'She gave me a right old time, saying it ought to be enough, playing fifty weeks a year, and going to a concert wasn't her idea of a holiday!' He shook his head good-naturedly. 'They don't understand! You'd think she would by now, after eighteen years of being married to a violinist. She was even more cross when I went backstage to have a word with him. He was good – a fine violinist.' Bellamy looked past Mark to Karen. 'Hello again to you!' She did not respond. 'I don't think you remember me from that night. It was a madhouse!'

Mark looked at his watch. 'We must be going.'

Bellamy nodded. 'Me too. I haven't unpacked yet. Why don't you give us a call?'

'I will.'

'Cheers!' He waved a hand, and went before them through the glass door.

As Mark followed him, he looked cautiously either way along the corridor. The passages were less busy but, to his left, there was still a small group of people: tail-enders in the crowd still anxious to gain admission downstairs and visit the conductor's dressing room. There was no sign of Bradshaw or Vanzo. Taking Karen's hand, he walked quickly in the opposite direction, almost pulling her along.

She quickened her pace to match his, her left hand holding the shoulder strap, which was in danger of slipping off. 'Where are we going?'

'Where they wouldn't think to look.' He continued along the corridor until they drew level with one of the many staircases leading to the upper floors of the hall. 'This way.'

Mark climbed the stairs as quickly as he could. At his side, Karen was breathing faster. A few stragglers, descending from the upper floors, passed them, but most of the audience had already left. A young man in an open-necked shirt, clutching a battered miniature score of the *Eroica*, eyed them curiously, but Mark ignored him, continuing to climb steadily. The backs of his legs were aching, and Karen's hand was pulling at his.

She was breathing heavily. 'Jesus, how high are we going?'

'High enough for them to miss us.'

'Can we slow down a little? I can't keep up with you.'

'I'm sorry. I didn't realise I was going so fast.' He relaxed his pace, but continued upward.

They had almost reached the top of the building and, moving cautiously, Mark led her from the corridor back into the hall. They were in one of the highest galleries. She followed him nervously as he made his way to the front row of seats, peering cautiously over the edge. They were about four storeys high, in the upper regions of the immense building. Above them, the great dome of the Albert Hall spread like an upturned bowl. Far below, the stage on which the orchestra had performed looked like a small scalene trapezium in a geometry book. Someone was turning off the main stage lights, and the platform was suddenly shadowed and grey. The empty promenade arena was a circle of red carpeting.

Karen peered down and leaned back quickly. 'Jesus! How can people sit up here? I get vertigo looking down!'

Mark followed her gaze, and felt himself flinch inwardly. 'It's a long way.'

She sat gingerly, deliberately looking away from the vast, empty space of the hall. 'Why did we come all the way up here?'

'Because it's the most unlikely place for Bradshaw and his friends to come looking.' His voice seemed to echo slightly, and he spoke quietly. 'The police will be here in a few minutes. We'll give them time to arrive, and go back down. Penny's waiting for them.'

'Good.' She took his hand. 'I've missed you! It's been a long day. What's been happening?'

'A hell of a lot. I think I know all the answers.'

'Oh Mark!' Her grip tightened. 'Why did they kill Sandy?'

Mark paused. 'Because he stole a shipment of heroin.'

'What?' She was wide-eyed with astonishment.

'He was a dealer, Karen. Maybe that's the wrong word. Trafficker might be more appropriate.' Mark's voice remained soft. 'That's where all his money came from. Playing the violin was a cover.'

'But how?'

'Easy. As a musician, he travelled all the time, driving from town to town, country to country. It was an ideal cover. We worked out all the details hours ago, and that list at the back of his diary gave the names of his contacts.'

'Oh God!'

'The only thing I couldn't work out was how he managed to smuggle the stuff from place to place. I needed to know that before I could persuade the police that all the circumstantial evidence fits together.'

'And you know?'

'I think so. It's a dangerous game, and the customs and police are on the lookout everywhere for anyone who tries.' She was silent. 'He had to have a place where no-one would ever think, or even dare, to look.'

'Where could that be?'

'I couldn't think, and then, during the concert this evening, I remembered a little scene during the recording session.' He picked up Berman's violin case and, unlatching the clips, opened it. The two violins, polished and shining, glowed softly in the dim overhead light. 'Sandor was listening to a playback of the concerto, and Penny went to look at his violins. He gave her a very hard time when she did, and warned her that they were worth a million and a half dollars.'

'Yes, you told me the same thing.'

'I know. Sandor was playing a del Gesù, lent to him by Arnold Silverman.' He pointed. 'This one. The other is a Stradivarius of his own, which he prefers to play in a concert hall. I only saw it for an instant the other day, when he was putting the del Gesù away. I remember thinking at the time that it had a strangely red mahogany colour for an instrument of its age. The other Strads that I've seen are more brown than red.'

'I still don't understand.'

Mark reached into a pocket. 'Do you remember when we were walking to the restaurant yesterday evening, and you asked me about Switzerland?'

'Yes.' She smiled. 'You told me not to forget Swiss banks!'

'I should have mentioned one other invaluable product.' He held it up. 'The original Swiss Army knife!'

She watched as Mark lifted Berman's Stradivarius from its velvet lining and turned it over, so that its polished back lay face up on his lap. With his fingers, he was feeling along the ribbed edge of the instrument.

'What are you doing, Mark? I thought you said that instrument was worth a fortune.'

'I did, but I was only repeating what Sandor had told all of us.' He inserted the blade of the penknife under the casing. 'If Sandor was telling the truth, it is worth a fortune. If it's what I think, it's not worth more than a few pounds.' He levered the penknife and, with little resistance, the back of the instrument suddenly came away. Inside, there was a black plastic bag, filling the entire space of the body of the instrument. The end of the bag, which fitted snugly, was bound with a piece of Scotch tape. Mark lifted the bag out, and pulled the tape loose. He unwound the plastic slowly until its lips parted. Inside was a white crystalline powder. His eyes met Karen's. 'Heroin, and worth a great deal more than this particular violin! What do you think it would fetch on the open market?' He closed the bag again, re-tying the tape around its neck.

Karen was staring at the bag, astonished. 'Good God!'

'It was a perfect means of transporting the stuff, wasn't it? What customs officer would dare to play around with a priceless Stradivarius violin, especially when its owner has just pointed out its immense value? And who would even question an international violinist, on his way to appear in the great concert halls of Europe? It's too bad that Sandor didn't tell you where he'd hidden it.'

Karen looked startled. 'What do you mean?'

Mark's voice remained calm. 'If you had known, you wouldn't have had to stay at the flat, fending off Bradshaw and trying to find where Sandor had hidden the shipment.'

Her face was pale. 'Mark, I don't understand . . .'

Mark shook his head in mock reproof. 'To think that you were the one who asked me to look after Sandor's violins! They've been sitting in the hotel safe all this time, ever since we met. If you had thought of looking at them, you wouldn't have had to fake that break-in at the flat, and cut up all those cushions and mattresses.'

She sat very still, watching him. 'What are you saying, Mark?' Her hands were trembling.

'You told me all of it yourself, Karen, this morning – just after we made love! The only trouble was that I was too besotted with you to take it all in. If only that bloody telephone hadn't rung!'

'Telephone?' She was eyeing him warily.

'Mr Lewis Bradshaw, the dealer's friend! Don't you remember, Karen? We were making all those plans for our happy holiday together! You gave a very convincing performance.'

'Mark, please!'

'You don't remember? You said you wanted to revisit all your favourite European cities with me. There was Rome and

Florence, and Monte Carlo and Beaune. And then, just before the phone rang, you got carried away: you wanted to walk through those little winding streets in Carcassonne and sit in the square with me! I was lying there, half asleep, listening to you, and that damned phone rang, to destroy our lyrical little scene. Bradshaw made me forget until hours later, this evening, during the concert. Carcassonne? Look at a map of France, Karen! Carcassonne lies between Toulouse and Marseille. Oh, you'd been there, all right, with Sandor Berman, on your way from Toulouse. It's only natural that he should have taken you to see it.'

'No, you didn't hear me right! I said I'd like to see Carcassonne with you!' She laughed nervously. 'I didn't say I'd seen it already. I guess I've seen pictures of it. Jesus, everyone knows about . . .'

Mark shook his head. 'I might have believed that too, Karen, if we hadn't run into Terry Bellamy just now. He knew you, Karen. He recognised you from the Berman concert. You're supposed to have met Berman in the bar of the Mirabeau in Monte Carlo.'

She was stumbling over her words. 'That's right. I did! He must have made a mistake. Wait a minute! Sandy was talking to a man in the bar the night I met him. I remember now! That must have been where he met me. I wasn't at any concert!'

'He met you at the Capitole, Karen.'

'No, it must have been the Mirabeau. He got the hotel names mixed up!'

'But the Capitole isn't a hotel. It's the name of the concert hall in Toulouse. You were with Berman in Toulouse, Karen, and probably a long time before that! He didn't pick you up in Monte Carlo. You were his partner.'

Karen had started to cry. She sniffed for a moment, fighting for breath, and reached into her shoulder bag. When she spoke again, her voice was more calm. 'No, Mark, towards the end, the situation changed. Sandy was *my* partner.'

Her hand had come out of the shoulder bag. It was holding a small chromium-plated revolver.

14

Karen moved one seat farther away from him. The gun in her hand was steady, and her eyes never left his face. For a moment, neither of them spoke.

At length, Mark said: 'That completes the picture. What do you hope to do now? The police will be here any minute.'

Her voice was soft. 'Get me out of here, Mark. You could find a way.' She nodded towards the plastic bag in his hand. 'There's enough for both of us. We could share it.' She paused. 'I like you, Mark. We go well together. I meant some of the things I said this morning. I could care for you. Help me?' Her voice was appealing.

'No, thank you.'

'Please! There's a lot more than you know about – enough for us to live on for the rest of our lives. I'll share it with you.'

Mark smiled. 'You mean the lock-up garage in Paris? I worked that out.'

'It's not in Paris.' Mark's eyebrows raised in question. 'Sandy owns a little house near Versailles. He bought it last year through that lawyer you went to see. I just said Paris at the time, because it was the first place I could think of when you asked me where he kept his car.' Her voice was pleading. 'See, I'm telling you everything! Help me now. When we sell out, we'll have millions! We can make a deal. The rest of the stuff's in the house, and I have the keys.'

Mark calculated. It was after nine-thirty. The Inspector should have met Penny by the Artists' Entrance. He needed to waste a few more minutes. 'You did fake that break-in, didn't you?' She nodded. 'Your story about the intruders standing in the dark was good. You had me going for a long time. How about the phone calls?'

She seemed almost pleased with herself. 'Not as many as I said, but Bradshaw did call. I pretended I didn't know who he was, and he didn't like it. I planned to tell Sandy to up the price. From then on, I was going to do the negotiating. I'm not hiding anything, Mark! Anyway, Sandy was weak.' Her voice was contemptuous.

'What about the second break-in?'

'Bradshaw must have sent somebody. He'd been to the apartment before, so he knew where the safe was.'

Mark nodded. 'And I'd told him that Berman was dead. Whoever broke in must have been shocked to find me there. No wonder you were so frightened!'

'I didn't think they'd try to break in while I was there. Come with me, Mark! You won't be sorry. I can make you happy!'

Mark hesitated, as though persuaded. 'As a matter of interest, where is the Chagall?'

'I hid it in the back of a closet, under some towels. I figured the police would never look anywhere that hadn't been disturbed. By the time the fingerprint men arrived, I'd tidied all the soft things back into the closets anyway. It's safe. We can take it with us when we go.'

'I see.' The minutes were passing. 'There's one thing I don't understand. When I gave you the money this morning, why didn't you just leave? You could have taken the first flight to Paris and disappeared. Why did you stay?'

She was silent for a moment. 'I need someone to help me, Mark. I can't do it all alone. You will help me, won't you?'

'Perhaps. You haven't told me why you didn't leave.'

'The police would have found me soon enough. When I go back to Paris, I want to be in the clear, travelling with you.' Her confidence was returning.

'You must have had a shock when we opened the safe, and found only the money and the diary. Didn't you expect to find the drugs there too?'

'Yes. I didn't know what to think. I knew Sandy hadn't passed them on – at least, I thought I knew. For a moment, I thought he had double-crossed me, but he would never have done that. He was too weak. I should have thought of his violins.'

Mark let her keep talking. The gun in her hand was starting

to waver. In a while, he would take it. 'That's the second time you've said he was weak, and you said he had become your partner. What do you mean by that?'

Her eyes left his face as she remembered. 'I met Sandy last year in Cleveland. He played some sort of recital there, I don't know where. We met up in a bar one evening, and had a few drinks together. I guess he was lonely. Anyway, one thing led to another, he came back to my apartment, and we spent some time together.' She sighed. 'I think he really cared for me.'

'What happened?'

'After that, he called me regularly, from wherever he was. He was always travelling! Then, last February, he suddenly showed up on my doorstep, without warning. I think he'd been playing in Minneapolis or Milwaukee, or some place like that. He stayed a couple of days and, when it was time for him to go, he asked me to go with him. At first, I said no. I mean, I liked him, but I wasn't crazy about him, or anything. I must have said something that triggered him off, because he told me about how he was a dealer, and how the concertising was a front. He said he wanted me to be his partner.'

'I see.' The Inspector must have reached the hall by now. In a few minutes, they would start searching. Mark kept his voice calm. 'Go on.'

She shrugged. 'There's not a lot more. We arranged to meet in Europe. Sandy said he had a big deal he was trying to set up. It was in Marseille. He said he wouldn't be able to move until later in the year, and would stay in touch. I didn't hear from him until the end of May. He called one morning, and told me everything would be set for August, so I arranged to wait and meet him closer to that date. He said we shouldn't be seen together too much, so I flew to Rome in late July. He told me that when he was ready, we would travel together. He was as excited as a kid!' She looked wistful for a moment. 'I guess he loved me.'

'Where did you meet again?' Mark noticed that the gun was now resting in her lap.

'In Limoges. What a dump of a place! I flew to Paris, and took a train there, and sat around in the Frantel hotel for two days. There was nothing to do there, except sit and stare at those lousy fountains in the square. Sandy was playing a solo recital with some pianist, so he didn't want me around. The next morning, he picked me up at the hotel, and we drove to Toulouse.' She shook her head at the memory. 'By the time he collected me, I was going stir crazy!'

'Why do you say he was weak?'

'He told me about the deal in Marseille. The man he'd contacted had stolen a big shipment of stuff from the local syndicate. He was desperate to get rid of it.'

'Was his name Jean Lucchini?'

'Yes.' She was surprised. 'How did you know?'

Mark decided not to elaborate. 'It was in the newspapers.'

'Oh. Anyway, this Jean Lucchini was working through Sandy. He was terrified the local boys were catching up with him, and wanted out. Sandy had offered him a rock-bottom price, and he accepted it without an argument.'

'And why was Sandy being weak?'

She stared at Mark for a moment. 'Don't you see? It was the perfect set-up. Lucchini was on the run from his own people. Everybody knew about it. There was a contract out on him.'

'Who was Lucchini?'

She hesitated for a moment. 'He worked for Vanzo. He'd stolen Vanzo's shipment.'

'What happened?'

'I talked to Sandy all the way down the road from Limoges to Toulouse. If Lucchini was a dead man already, why should Sandy pay out all the money for the stuff? He was doing the local syndicate a favour. Don't you understand?'

There was a sudden coldness in Mark's heart. 'In other words, you wanted Sandy to kill Lucchini?'

'Right!' There was a vague smile on her face, but it faded. 'Sandy was chicken. He just wanted to pay the man and go.'

'What did you say?'

'I kept talking to him, but he wouldn't listen at first. He was afraid of getting mixed up in a murder, but I told him he was being stupid. The police and the syndicate were looking for

Lucchini. If he was found dead, nobody would have been surprised.'

'What about the missing drugs?'

She shrugged. 'I thought they would assume he'd already sold them. Oh Mark, it was the chance of a lifetime!'

'What did you do?'

'When Sandy refused, we agreed to switch jobs. I was supposed to drive the car that night, while he made the trade. I told him to change places with me and drive. He needed to warn Lucchini, so he wouldn't be suspicious.' Her eyes shone. 'It was easy, Mark! He was waiting where we arranged, on the corner of a street. Sandy flashed the headlamps twice, the way we'd agreed, and he walked along the sidewalk in front of us, to the next street. I got out, and Sandy stayed at the wheel. Lucchini had his car parked there, and he opened the trunk and showed me the stuff.' She smiled. 'He was so relieved to see us! I went back to our car and opened our trunk, and he carried the stuff over and dropped it in. Then we both walked around to the front, and I leaned in the window to tell Sandy we'd made the transfer. He was so scared, he could only nod! Lucchini was standing next to me and . . .' She paused momentarily, looking down at the gun in her hand. '. . . I just pulled the trigger. For a moment, I thought I hadn't hit him, because he just stood and stared at me, kind of surprised. Then he fell on the sidewalk.'

Mark watched her face. It was devoid of expression.

She continued: 'I got back in the car, and told Sandy to drive, but he went haywire! He started to move, and hit one of the cars parked there. Then he stopped and froze at the wheel. He was terrified! Some people came running towards us, and he only came to his senses just in time. He could hardly steer the car. We drove out of Marseille and, as soon as we found a quiet country road, he stopped the car and burst into tears. He was hysterical!'

'What happened then?'

'I managed to calm him down after a while, and he lay in the back seat and slept. I stayed up front, waiting. I must have sat there for hours! Sometime around dawn, I started the car again, and drove back to the main highway. Sandy woke later, feeling a little better, but he was still scared. I drove while he rested, and we ate breakfast at a roadside café. After a while, he relaxed, and I kept talking to him. I just talked, all the time, telling him not to be frightened. Nobody knew it was us. Nobody need ever find out.' She seemed to have forgotten Mark was there, the gun resting in her lap. 'We bought the local papers. They had pictures of Lucchini, lying in the gutter, but Sandy read the reports and said they didn't know who had killed him. The only thing they knew was that somebody had seen a Mercedes driving away, but they didn't even take the number! Sandy wanted to sell the car, but I wouldn't let him. That would have aroused suspicion. Anyway, there are thousands of Mercedes in France. We stayed at the café for a while, and drank strong coffee, and I kept talking to Sandy, telling him that everything would work out. By the time we reached Monte Carlo, he was his old self again – a little shaky, but under control. Just for safety, we agreed to split up and stay in separate places. He dropped me off on the far side of town, and we arranged to meet again at the bar of his hotel. I was to make sure the bartender heard him offer me a ride to Paris.'

'So the rest of your story is more or less true?'

'Oh yes, Mark. I wouldn't lie to you any more, now that we're together.' She smiled. 'I really did sleep in the back of the car all the way to Beaune. I was still catching up! The next day, we garaged the car in Versailles, and took a cab into Paris. Then we found another cab, and went to the airport. Sandy thought it was better not to ride there direct from Versailles.' She heaved a sigh. 'I thought we'd made it!'

'Until Penny and I arrived at the flat, to tell you that Sandor was dead.'

She nodded. 'That's why I passed out. It was the shock, I guess. Someone from Marseille must have traced us all the way to London. I was so sure we'd fooled them! That's why you've got to help me, Mark, please! I'll do anything you want!'

Mark watched her face. It was beautiful – young and clean and fresh – and lifeless. Her eyes hardly seemed to focus on his. He spoke quietly. 'I can't, Karen. I'm sorry.'

She saw his expression, and brought the gun up again. 'Please, Mark!' He remained silent.

Karen stood, moving slightly farther away, and he saw her thumb slip the safety catch off. 'Then I guess I'll have to do it alone.' She looked down at the plastic package in Mark's hand. 'The bag, Mark. Slide it over, on to the next seat to you – slowly. Don't do anything silly – please! I really do care for you.'

'You won't get away, Karen. The police are already in the building. In a little while, they'll start searching for us.'

Her eyes seemed to become opaque. 'Don't say anything more, Mark. You're forcing me to . . .'

There was a sudden, sharp report, no louder than the pop of a champagne cork. It echoed across the dome of the hall. Karen's eyes grew wide with astonishment. She remained standing, her lips parted, and a thin dribble of blood escaped from the side of her mouth, running down her chin. For a moment, she seemed to be trying to speak. Then she took a step towards Mark and stumbled, falling at his feet. On her back, between her shoulders, a red stain was forming.

Mark looked beyond her, across the balcony. Vanzo was standing about forty feet away, his body half hidden behind the curve of the gallery. The silenced revolver was in his outstretched hands, and he was aiming down the barrel. Mark ducked quickly behind the front wall of the balcony, his face almost touching Karen's body. As he moved, he heard a second shot, and the bullet ripped through the backing of the seat in which he had been sitting. Transferring the plastic bag to his left hand, he reached out with his right for Karen's gun, lifting it from her lifeless fingers. Calculating that Vanzo, unable to see him, would be moving in for a closer shot, he waited for a few seconds. Then, using all his strength, he flung himself in the direction of the aisle leading up to the exit door. As he crashed to the ground, Vanzo fired again, and the bullet ricocheted off the plaster of the wall beyond him with a faint whine. Moving desperately quickly, before Vanzo could take aim again, Mark ran wildly up the few steps to the exit. From the corner of his eye, he could see the tall figure of Bradshaw closing on him from the other side. He tripped as he reached the arch of the entrance, plunging into the corridor, and another bullet, striking the plaster above his head, showered particles of paint and dust in the air. Mark pulled himself to his feet in the corridor. Behind him, he could hear Vanzo shouting to Bradshaw.

   He raced along the corridor to the nearest stairs. Footsteps warned him that they were close on his heels. Unwilling to drop either the plastic bag or Karen's revolver, he leapt into space at the head of the staircase. His feet touched one of the treads, and he threw himself forward again, allowing his body to go limp as he landed at the bottom of the the first flight. He fell and rolled, feeling a jabbing pain in his ribs, then jack-knifed his body so that it turned the corner of the staircase. He had gained a small lead on his pursuers. Rising painfully, he jumped the next flight, two and three stairs at a time, praying inwardly that his feet would not slip. Within seconds, he had reached the corridor below. Behind him, Bradshaw and Vanzo had caught up with each other, and he could hear their shoes clattering on the staircase above. Gasping for air, Mark ran along the corridor, hoping that the curve of the wall would offer additional cover. The footsteps behind him were closing again, and he turned in the direction of the next stairway. They must have had him in sight for a moment, firing another shot, and the bullet screamed as it bounced off the curved surface.

   Running down the next flight of stairs, Mark slipped and allowed his body to roll. He covered his head with his arms, and the hard edges of the stairs dug painfully into him, punishing his shoulders and ribs. At the foot of the stairs, he turned again and, without bothering to stand, let himself roll the length of the next flight. Vanzo and Bradshaw were not far behind, but he had the impression that he had again added a few yards' lead.

   In the next corridor, he ran again, trying to extend his lead. His right foot twisted agonisingly, and he limped along the darkened passageway, fighting against the pain and forcing his legs to move faster. For a moment, he stopped, leaning against the wall and struggling for breath, but the corridor echoed to the sound of the two men's feet, and he turned and staggered forward, ignoring the sudden, needle-like flashes of pain in his ankle. Another flight of stairs came into view, and he realised that it led to the ground floor. As he started down, his leg buckled under him, and he again rolled to the landing below. For a moment, he lay, unable to move, his head spinning. The footsteps were approaching and, with a supreme effort, he reached the corner of the staircase for the final downward flight. He could barely reach the edge of the stairs and, throwing the plastic bag ahead, pulled himself to the ledge with his left hand until he could roll his body downwards. He no longer felt the buffeting of his arms and body.

The pain subsided, and Mark lay at the foot of the staircase, waiting for his head to clear. Slowly, he turned until he was facing up the staircase. He leaned his right hand against the steps and, steadying his wrist with his left hand, aimed the revolver upwards.

Vanzo was the first to appear round the corner of the stair-well. He had run down the first flight of stairs at maximum speed, using the wall to break his momentun. For an instant, he stared wildly, searching for Mark, and then his eyes focused on the body at the foot of the staircase, and he raised his revolver in both hands, taking careful aim. At that moment, Mark squeezed the trigger. The little gun seemed to explode in his hands, thunderously loud.

Vanzo's gun fell, and the Frenchman, his eyes bulging, reached both hands to his throat. A stream of blood coursed between his fingers, colouring his hands red, and guttural, rasping noises came from his mouth as he fought for breath. Then his body curled over and, still clasping his throat, he fell headlong down the staircase.

A moment later, Bradshaw appeared round the corner, his gun held loosely at arm's length. Watching Vanzo fall, he stopped, staring down at Mark. Their eyes met for a moment, and with a gesture of resignation, he allowed his gun to fall from his hands, which he raised until they were at shoulder level. His eyes never left Mark's face. As he slowly walked down, he nodded in the direction of Vanzo's body and said: 'He shot Berman, too. I'm damned if I'll take the blame for his killings.'

Mark sat up, keeping the revolver trained on Bradshaw. He

saw the other man's eyes travel to the black plastic bag, lying on the floor a few feet away. There were distant footsteps. Someone was running in their direction. Watching Bradshaw, he grinned crookedly and nodded towards the bag. 'Why don't you make a try for it, Bradshaw? Go on! Make a grab for it and run! I'll give you a two-second start!' His voice was strained and harsh. The pain in his ribs increased as he drew a deeper breath.

At the sound of Mark's voice, Bradshaw started to lower his hands.

'Go on! Try it! I want you to try it!' Mark pointed the gun at Bradshaw's heart.

The man shook his head slowly, and raised his hands again. His eyes were wary. He was still breathing heavily, and his voice had an asthmatic burr. 'You're going to find it hard to pin anything on me, Holland. I'm in the clear. You saw Vanzo kill the little bitch.'

'Perhaps.' Mark rose slowly to his feet, pulling himself up against a banister. 'We can start by matching any of the bullets they find upstairs with your gun. Attempted murder will do for starters.' Bradshaw stiffened, biting his lower lip. 'And when the police start digging, who can tell what they'll find?' Bradshaw remained silent, his attention on the barrel of Mark's gun.

The Inspector was the first to arrive. He ran into view and, taking in the scene, stopped dead, stifling an exclamation. A moment later, Penny appeared behind him, with a man whom Mark did not recognise. Seeing the dead Vanzo on the floor, she shrank back, her eyes fearful. There was silence. Then the Inspector nodded to his assistant, who walked over to Bradshaw, standing close to him, while he strode over to Mark, extending his hand.

'I'll take that.' Mark handed him the gun. 'I thought I told you to stay out of this!'

'I had no choice.' Mark nodded towards the body on the floor. 'The dead one is Vanzo, and he's Bradshaw.' He looked towards the bag. 'They were after that package over there.' Almost as an afterthought, he added: "It's heroin.'

'I see.' He looked over to his assistant, who took Bradshaw's arm in a firm grip. 'Where does it come from?'

'It was inside one of Berman's violins. That's how he moved the drugs around. It's only a small delivery. The main supply is in a house in Versailles. You'll be able to get the address from Eric Scutter. He looked after the purchase for Berman.'

The Inspector nodded silently, as if lost in thought. In a corner, leaning against the wall for support, Penny was watching him. The Inspector turned to Mark again. 'Where are these violins now?'

'Upstairs, in one of the upper galleries.' He gave a weak smile. 'Don't try breaking the back off the other one. It's a genuine del Gesù. Berman told everyone the broken one was a Stradivarius. That's why nobody touched them.'

'Very ingenious.'

'You'll find Karen up there, too. That's her gun you're holding.' He paused. 'She's dead. Vanzo shot her.' He heard Penny gasp.

The Inspector looked at the gun in his hand, and turned towards Mark. His voice had a trace of sympathy. 'I'm sorry.'

'You don't have to be. She was Berman's partner.' He was very tired.

The Inspector frowned. 'What are you trying to say?'

'I told you: she was Berman's partner. They were in it together. It was she who killed the man in Marseille. We had enough time for a long talk before those two caught up with us. She was hoping to recruit me as a new member of her organisation!'

Penny said: 'Oh Mark!' She was crying.

Bradshaw cleared his throat, and the Inspector turned to face him. 'I would prefer to reserve any statement I make until my solicitor is present.'

'Yes?'

'I don't wish to say anything until I am legally represented. The only thing I'm prepared to say at the present time is that I was a bystander in this whole business. Holland here can testify that I had nothing to do with the girl's death. Vanzo shot her down in cold blood! He killed Berman, too. I had no part in it!'

The Inspector regarded him with contempt, but his voice was polite. 'I'll keep that in mind. Now, if you wouldn't mind accompanying my assistant, we'll see if your solicitor can be contacted.' He nodded to the other man, who led Bradshaw away.

Mark sat down on the stairs, resting his head in hands. He closed his eyes for a moment, but nausea and dizziness overtook him, making him lose his balance. Instead, he shook his head in an effort to clear it, and took out a cigarette.

The Inspector lit a match and held it for him. 'You silly bastard! Why the hell didn't you just wait for us?'

Mark stared at the end of the cigarette. 'I wanted to hear her tell the truth. I realised, halfway through the concert, that she'd been lying through her teeth, from the moment we met her.'

'How?'

'It doesn't matter. It was something she said this morning.' He drew on the cigarette, and his memory returned to the bedroom. He could still feel Karen's warm body nestling against his.

'Well, at least you came out of it alive – but only just. You look terrible! Are you up to talking about it now?'

'No.'

The Inspector gave him a hard look. 'I shouldn't really let you out of here. Considering your past record, God knows why I'm doing it!' Mark was silent. 'I'll have one of my men drive you home. I've already sent for a back-up force.' He glanced up the stairs. 'We have a long night ahead of us.'

'Yes.'

'Can you manage as far as the door?' Mark stood, and Penny ran forward to support him. The Inspector's manner became brisk. 'If you make your way to the Artists' Entrance, there will be someone to look after you. I'd better go and have a look upstairs.'

'It's about three flights up. You'll find her in the front row of the gallery. The violins are there, too.'

'All right.' The Inspector picked up the plastic bag, removing the tape and looking inside briefly. His face was expressionless. He turned to Mark. 'We'll talk in the morning, and you'd better bloody well be there!'

'I'll check back in to the Westbury.'

'Just as long as you're there!' The policeman started up the staircase. As he reached the first landing, he turned, smiling. 'And you were looking for a quiet life!'

Mark limped slowly along the corridor, leaning against Penny. He could feel his strength returning. He turned to look at her, but she avoided his eyes. 'I'm sorry.' She shook her head silently. 'I should have trusted you.' They walked a few steps. 'It was all lies – everything she said! She was worse than Berman. Killing Lucchini was her idea, and when he refused, she did it for him. She was proud of it!' Penny said nothing.

Konstantin and Heidi were standing at the Artists' Entrance. Seeing Mark approach, the conductor called out: 'Mark, where have you been? Heidi and I have been waiting for you downstairs.' His voice was testy. 'Really, my dear, we have been sitting around there for the past twenty minutes!' As Mark slowly came forward with Penny, he peered at them over his glasses. 'What's the matter with you?'

Mark smiled ruefully. 'Sorry I kept you, maestro. I had a slight accident.'

'Are you hurt?' His voice expressed concern.

'Not too badly.' He looked at Penny. 'I fell down some stairs.'

'Good God!'

Heidi bustled forward. 'Mark, my dear, are you all right? You should be more careful!'

'I'm fine. Nothing's broken.'

'We were worried when you didn't come to us.' She lowered her voice. 'You know how irritable Tino becomes when he has to wait.'

'Of course.'

Steigel was already standing by the door. 'Take a hot bath, Mark. It will draw any bruises out of your body.' He smiled. 'A good strong drink is also to be recommended. It may not cure you, but it does wonders for the system!' He frowned at the clock in the doorkeeper's office. 'You must forgive us, my dears, but I have a recording session tomorrow morning. Our car is waiting. Will I see you there?'

Mark smiled. 'I hope so. It was a good concert, this evening.'

'*Ja, ja*, it wasn't bad. It could always be better. Let's hope the recording engineers don't slice it to ribbons. Until tomorrow, then?'

'I'll try to be there.' He remembered the Inspector's warning. 'I can't promise.'

'No matter. Call me when you are feeling better. There are a number of important things I must discuss with you. I received a call from Berlin, and those damned Japanese have started sending me telexes again.'

'I'll look after it.'

'I know, my dear.' He smiled with genuine affection. 'You always do. Heidi!'

She almost ran to his side. 'Yes, Tino, I'm coming!'

Penny watched them depart. Despite herself, she smiled. 'He really lives in another world, doesn't he? If you told him he'd just won half a million on the pools, he'd still look grumpy, and ask you whether you could get him an extra rehearsal next Thursday!'

'More than likely. You're beginning to understand.'

'Yes, but I have the feeling you wouldn't want him any other way.'

A uniformed policeman approached them. 'Mr Holland?'

'Yes.'

'I understand you need a lift home.'

Penny said: 'Don't worry, I'll drive you. I always do!' Her smile was wan, and she turned to the policeman. 'We have our own transport.'

She drove him back to the Westbury. At the front door, Mark said: 'Will I see you again?'

Penny shrugged. 'I'll be here.'

'That's not quite what I mean.'

'I know.' She stared through the windscreen. 'Not this visit, Mark. I want to see you another time, but not yet. I watched your face when you told the Inspector about . . .', she hesitated, '. . . about what happened.'

'Yes.'

She turned to him. 'Will you call me?'

'Of course.'

'I'll look forward to it.'

He stepped out of the car, lifting his bag from the back seat. For a moment, their eyes met, and Penny gave a slight wave of her hand. Then she let in the clutch, and drove quickly away.

Mark checked into the hotel again. His room was still vacant. As he passed the front desk, the concierge, still on duty, called to him. 'Oh Mr Holland, there was a phone call for you, just after you left.' He searched among his pigeon-holes. 'I saved it, in case you missed that plane!'

'Thank you.'

He walked slowly across the empty foyer to the lifts, opening the note. It was from his Geneva office. The ever efficient Rudi had telephoned to say that there was nothing important to report.